Malevir
Dragons Return

Malevir
Dragons Return

WRITTEN AND ILLUSTRATED BY
SUSAN BASS MARCUS

MILL CITY PRESS
MINNEAPOLIS, MN

Copyright © 2015 by Susan Bass Marcus

Mill City Press, Inc.
322 First Avenue N, 5th floor
Minneapolis, MN 55401
612.455.2293
www.millcitypublishing.com

All rights reserved. No part of this publication may be reproduced, stored in a retrieval system, or transmitted, in any form or by any means, electronic, mechanical, photocopying, recording, or otherwise, without the prior written permission of the author.

ISBN-13: 978-1-63413-783-6
LCCN: 2015915704

Cover Design by Sophie Chi
Typeset by Emily Keenan

Printed in the United States of America

*To Stephen, Schwartz,
and Petunia*

The Veiled Valley and Beyond

Part I
Unexpected Detours

The Malevir as a Basilisk

Chapter 1

A TRAIL OF REEKING FUMES gagged the two sprites. Confused by the mountain tunnel's unfamiliar passages, they stumbled on shaky legs behind the monstrous basilisk that had cast a spell over their swelling, changing bodies.

Pausing in the gloom to catch his breath, Forestspice looked at his brother sprite and asked, "Bitterbud, do *we* smell that bad?"

As he picked at his straining breeches, Bitterbud groaned, "No, that's the beast. And look—my clothes don't fit anymore. Dirty, too."

"Your skin's turned green and bumpy."

"Yours, too. And my head feels stuffed with thorn rushes. What *are* we?"

Forestspice tapped yellow claws sprouting from his once-dainty fingers. "We don't look like Loblin anymore." Rubbing his temples, he leaned against a tunnel wall and slid to the floor. Bitterbud pulled him up and pushed him forward.

Ahead of them raced the basilisk that had bound them to his service with a goblin spell. They hurried to keep pace while dodging acid puddles the beast left in his path. The basilisk came to a stream that zigzagged down the middle of the tunnel and kicked up spray as he crossed it. Flying droplets seared the new goblins' skin, and they realized that any misstep along the damp cave passageway would cause burns and pain.

The basilisk screeched and broke the goblins' concentration. He stopped and raised one wing. With an elbow claw, he pointed to a niche hidden in the uneven rock wall. They backed away from him and huddled against the wall. The basilisk turned his body, looking like an enormous rooster with a lizard's neck and tail, and leaped away from them into another dim tunnel.

When his hulking silhouette disappeared, the transformed sprites looked at each other and shook their misshapen heads. In a dry spot within the niche, Forestspice faced his companion and groaned. Pulling at thick brown bristles that sprouted from his head, he whispered, "Bitterbud, may the Ways of the World protect us. I'm forgetting how to be a Lobli."

Bitterbud pointed to the ragged tip of his long ear. "Forestspice, wipe these bite marks. Maybe we can break the Malevir's spell."

The first goblin yanked a red cloth from his threadbare back pocket and scrubbed his brother's bitten ear. When the spell held fast, he found Bitterbud's rag inside his tattered shirt and tried again. Grieved to see that the wound still throbbed and Bitterbud was weaker than ever, Forestspice threw the rag to the stone floor. He closed his eyes and leaned against the rock wall. Bitterbud warily picked up the rag, shook it dry, and stuffed it into his sleeve.

Loud screams echoed along the tunnel. The goblins flinched and clutched each other. They could feel the floor bounce and rock as if shaken by an earthquake. As they looked in the direction the basilisk had gone, a blinding crimson flash forced both of them back against the wall, where they cowered.

"He attacked the dragons," moaned Bitterbud.

The beast did not return. They waited.

Long after the basilisk attacked their ancestral home cave, the surviving yewr of Orferan dragons rose from their night nests. They yawned and stretched, safely hidden in another cave a long way across the valley.

Claws lightly scratching the stone floor, two of them—dams—sniffed around a speckled object that sat barely visible in the gray light and shadows that enveloped it.

Hidden deep in a canyon wall, far from towns and settlements in the Veiled Valley, the Orferans' refuge brightened as growing sunlight filled the cave entrance. Cushioned by a mound of sand, a red and green spotted egg began to glow in the growing light. Abulafria, her sister dam Isabella, Aurykk the elder male, and young Draako huddled around the egg.

"Another full moon and no hatchling," blurted Draako, whose long-missing mother had watched him hatch many World-Turns earlier. "Is something wrong? Did our flight from the Sunriseside Mountains kill it?"

Aurykk looked at him with gleaming topaz eyes. "No, the egg rested safely in my cheek pouch, nephew, while I flew. Be patient. This hatchling soon will join our family."

Draako crept into a shadowy nook in the rock wall, where two curled-up brown weasels watched the action while grooming their fur. Abulafria lowered her great silver-blue head and gently warmed the stone floor of the cave near her egg. Sparks and smoky wisps from her silvery-blue snout soon warmed the sand and the stone floor glowed bright red.

"Look again, everyone," whispered Draako. "It's rocking!"

The egg wavered, then spun on its fat end. Tiny cracks opened between the spots on its mottled surface. A powdery cloud shot out from a large chip in the shell, followed by the small snout of the next dragon to become part of the family. Draako whooped and belched a few sparks, while Abulafria and Isabella brushed more sand over the hatching bed and began their song of welcome:

> "Come, little one, into the warm.
> Orferan love will keep you from harm.
> Open your sharp little newborn eyes,
> Come little hatchling, awake to your skies."

The dragon dams sang their rhyme until the powder cleared and two little eyes looked out at them from inside the collapsing eggshell. A small squeak followed the thrust of a baby dragon head and two stubby legs. His mother, Abulafria, gently pulled the remaining eggshell off his back and began to lick the egg whites that remained stuck to his tail. The weasels stopped grooming each other and sat up on their hind legs.

More squeaks echoed in the great cave as the hatchling nibbled on pieces of eggshell nearby. He found Abulafria's nose and began to chew on it.

"He's hungry, poor dear," sighed Isabella. The weasels ran circles around the little one until Isabella tugged them closer to her side. "Unless you have a treat to offer our hatchling, stand back while Abulafria weaves her parent bond." The furry female backed away and pulled the other weasel with her.

Draako jumped into the light with a small rat he had caught earlier that morning and he dropped it in front of Abulafria. "What will you call him?" he asked his aunt.

"I shall call him Drac'Argo, a *drac* name like yours, because you were the first to offer him food," Abulafria answered.

"Drac'Argo! I like that. 'Argo, 'Argo, my cousin 'Argo." Draako danced on his gangly legs while his tail banged the floor. The thumps bounced the hatchling, who fell back on his hind legs every time he tried to nibble the rat.

Aurykk shuffled over to Draako and pulled him under his leathery amber wings. "Calm yourself. Our Drac'Argo needs to eat and rest so he'll grow from hatchling to dragonet, like you. Entering this world is no easy task! Come to my corner and we'll talk about your flying practice."

While Draako followed the lumbering elder dragon to his nest woven with grasses and colorful rags, Abulafria wrapped her foreleg around Drac'Argo. She pulled him close to her chest as she lay at last on her own nest. One wing slowly fell over the hatchling, warm and fed, who fell asleep in that dark hollow. Abulafria rested her head on a nearby rock.

She licked her claws and cleaned her head, sniffed under her wing, then rested—with one eye open, alert to any sudden changes.

"In this shelter far from our pitiable ancestors, the beast known to all dragons as Malevir will not find us," she said.

Isabella's nest sat closest to the cave entrance. From there, she viewed the whole valley extending from the Sunsetside up to a range of mountains and foothills covered in fir trees. A constant rolling mist drifted across the valley and snagged on trees in ragged stretches. The thick mist settled into the valley, over gentle waves of meadows beyond, then high hills, before reaching scattered ruins near Anonom Trace. Past that, she could see as far as the meeting point of two mountain ranges. On a broad hilltop pushing above the central valley floor, she spotted smoke that rose slowly from cottage chimneys in the hamlet of Fossarelick.

"Foul air of Fossarelick, undeserving the gentle mists," she muttered. "Faithless villagers, for all the harm they have done us. Murderous Moktawls!" With a smoldering sigh, she curled her long spiky tail over her legs and turned her gaze from the valley.

The weasels, Gormley and Gúrmulo, snuggled into her flank. She lowered her copper-colored head to the edge of the nest. "Wise little friends of the Orferans, when the time is right, find our cousin, Anadraka. Draako misses his mother."

For the remainder of the day, she kept watch.

Chapter 2

A SPRING STORM PASSED OVER the mountains and surged toward the plain below. Rainwater cascaded down the cliff wall surrounding the dragons' lair and splashed the ledge beyond its entrance. Draako stretched his neck toward the brightening sky as he ambled outside.

"That last practice might truly have been the end of you," growled Aurykk as he followed Draako to the lip of the ledge. "You were lucky the winds carried you back here. Be careful this time. Let the currents flow under your wings and drop your legs a bit to get some lift."

Draako's front fangs scraped his lower lip as he dipped his head in respect. "I won't forget. Just watch me." He raised his head again, spread his wings, and jumped in the direction of the river valley that ran behind their mountain cave. Aurykk remained on the ledge, a grimace wrinkling his long jaw.

Overhead, clouds scudded toward the sunriseside. Draako felt the sun on his neck and back. His wings beat with the power of a dragon leaping into adolescence. Each flap thumped the air flowing around him: he reminded himself to work with the currents and not fight them. Soaring upward, he banked to the left and glided toward the river.

Draako began to feel uneasy as he dipped into the shadows of the river canyon. Muffled voices echoed from the rock walls on either side.

PART I: UNEXPECTED DETOURS   9

As he rode a downward current, he noticed small movements below and realized he'd found his weasel friends chasing each other on an island that sat midstream, splitting river rapids that churned around it. Draako could hear an argument. He hovered above them.

"Gúrmulo, you're wrong. It's time they knew."

"Nuts and wood rubbish, Gormley. Leave it be."

"It's time that who knew what, Gormley?"

Startled by Draako's deep voice, the two weasels screeched to a stop. They had not heard the young dragon land nearby. He ambled over to them and, with head held low to the ground, he looked deeply into Gormley's eyes. The little weasel's mouth fell open and she fell backwards.

Gúrmulo ran to her side and propped her up. "I suppose you're right. You tell him, sister."

Gormley blinked her eyes and took a deep breath. "Very well. It's bad news. During these past few World-Turns, while you and 'Argo grew in size and strength, so did that ugly beast that so long ago forced the Orferans from the Cave of the Ancestors. Soon he will attack the Veiled Valley, maybe the Cave of Refuge, too." She paused and scratched her whiskers.

Draako raised his head and looked up at the Cave of Refuge.

Gormley stood up on her hind legs. "In all directions, from Coldside to Warmside and from Sunriseside to Sunsetside, he has harmed the Valley folk. Gúrmulo and I have been among them and have seen the damage. The beast hates dragons but does not fear them. Only two creatures in the Valley make him tremble." The two weasels puffed their furry white chests.

"You? Stop boasting. You're telling tales again," Draako growled. "We are safe from him in the Cave of Refuge. And why should we care about the Valley folk? Let them rot. Isabella and Abulafria have told us about the Moktawls killing our kin. Besides, I like it here. I can fly and hunt and be with my family." He paused and blinked away an annoying itch in his eye. "Except for Mother . . ."

Gúrmulo shouted quickly, "The Moktawls are nothing next to

the Malevir. The beast flattened Anonom Village. Soon his claws will tear apart Fossarelick. Our one true friend in the hamlet, Seerlana, has disappeared, by the way, and so has the packet your mother left with her."

"Fossarelick, too? What does my uncle say?"

Gormley sat back. "To begin with, he gave me a task!" She raised her little chin. "He has agreed with Isabella. I am to look for your moth—for Anadraka. For some reason, he thinks she might be in the Cave of the Ancestors—alive!"

"Alive?"

"Yes. Gúrmulo and I have to prepare for our journey. We leave soon. Aurykk says that . . . well, he will tell you. Please carry us back to the cave."

Chapter 3

Nnylf had watched his mother, Seerlana, place the packet in the stone wall behind the firewood, but nothing filled the little hollow now. His younger sister, Azile, had also seen her, and they had all agreed to make it their secret.

Sitting on the bench where he usually slept, Nnylf tried to remember their hurried attempt to hide the packet. Through the small wood-framed window, he looked toward the mountains softly glowing in the late afternoon sun and remembered his mother in that moment: tall and strong, her black hair flowing behind her in the wind as she knelt by the wall to share her story. That was many Moon-Risings ago. One day she was weaving at her loom, but the next day she was gone. Only a trail of boot marks in the dirt yard showed that she had headed toward the Sunsetside Mountains.

After she left, their father, Eunan, soured. He lost his temper every time Nnylf or Azile was forgetful, or silly, or slept too long. How could she leave without saying anything to them? She had taken her hidden armor and her sharp-bladed durk.

Nnylf jumped up and ran out of his family's cottage. Dazzled by sunlight, he stumbled. Thudding into something hard, he fell back and lay sprawled on bare stones and dirt. He opened his eyes and saw Azile standing over him. Rubbing her forehead, she shouted, "That really hurt.

Didn't you see me?" The girl, nearly fifteen World-Turns old, extended a hand to her older brother. "Oh, never mind. I'll be fine. Here, let me help you up." Tugging on his arm, she asked, "What's the rush?"

"Sorry. Sun was in my eyes," Nnylf replied as he got to his feet and brushed the dust off his breeches. "And why are you in such a hurry, Azile?"

"I came looking for you to help me catch Bounder. He ran away from me down the hill toward the barley fields! Come on!" She pulled on Nnylf's arm.

"Ran away? I wonder . . ." Nnylf whispered, "Listen, something terrible . . . the packet is missing. Do you think Bounder sniffed it out and took it?"

"The packet is missing? But Mother said we had to keep it safe, for the dragons. Why would that silly dog take it, Nnylf? All he wants is food." Azile brushed her light brown hair from her eyes. She thumped onto a sagging wood bench near their doorway and looked down at her grimy feet. Drawing circles in the dirt with her big toe, she looked up again at Nnylf. Tears slid over her lower eyelids. "Why hasn't Mother come home? I hate when the other girls, like Alana, make fun of her ways."

"I don't know. Everything will be all right, I'm sure. Don't fuss." He paused and looked down at the fields. "Tell you what, we'll catch Bounder. Maybe he's playing with it, thinks it's a bone. Or it's still somewhere in the cottage. Show me, which way did that ugly dog run?"

"He is not ugly, just a little odd," said Azile, pulling a small red cloth out of her pocket and wiping her nose. "Come on. He went this way." As she nimbly raced down the hillside path, Nnylf hurried after her. At the bottom of the hill, they made their way into the barley fields. In the distance, two of the hamlet's oxen grazed among tall grasses. Passing row after row of the ripe grain, Nnylf and Azile saw no sign of their dog— but soon they heard snuffling among the barley stalks several rows over, then rough barking a bit farther on.

They crouched between rows. Nnylf's hand covered his lips for silence, and he signaled Azile to follow him toward a small clearing in the field. There, they saw a fat brown weasel running in circles. He was muttering to himself while turning around and around, his nose close to the ground.

"What's this?" Azile mouthed to her brother. Nnylf shrugged his shoulders and pulled off his tunic just as their dog Bounder leaped out from a row of grain and snatched the weasel by his tail. Surprised by the dog's attack, the weasel went limp. Nnylf and Azile ran into the clearing and grabbed Bounder. Azile pulled the dog up by the scruff of his neck and the weasel dropped to the ground. Nnylf caught it in his tunic.

"Bounder, sit!" Azile shouted, but the dog planted two strong front legs on the tunic and barked again loudly as the weasel poked his dark head out of its wrapping. "Nnylf," Azile said, "I think Bounder was chasing the thief who took our . . . our . . . you know." She glared at the weasel.

At those words, the weasel opened his black eyes slowly and squeaked, "Not me. I'm no thief." He hissed at the dog.

Bounder yelped and leaped back, the curly brown fur on his back spiking from fright.

The boy held onto the weasel even more tightly. "You're talking like me," said Nnylf. "That's impossible."

"No, it's possible. You and the girl know dragonspeech, so you can understand me, too, is all," he said and wiggled. "Let me go now; I mean no harm."

Wide-eyed, Nnylf and Azile stared down at the little creature still trapped in Nnylf's tunic.

"Matter of fact, I can help you. Gúrmulo is the name." The weasel closed his eyes halfway and gave a little nod.

"Help us?" Nnylf shook his head. "Gúr . . . mulo, what makes you think we know dragonspeech and need your help?" He pointed to the village up the hill. "This is the home of Moktawls. Dragons are not welcome."

"You're missing something, right? Looking for it? I could take you to it. Oh, and about that dragonspeech—I heard it from a dragon himself, about you knowing it, I mean. But this mutt here—"

Bounder began to growl.

"I mean . . . your fine dog here picked up my scent and followed me. He interrupted my important journey sunsetside. I must be on my way."

"Wait just one moment. What dragon? Why should we believe that you haven't stolen the packet?" Azile looked at Bounder sniffing the dirt and ambling toward the far mountains. "Bounder, come back here."

The dog returned to the clearing and settled down in the dirt at her feet. He tilted his head and kept an eye on the weasel.

Gúrmulo sighed and closed his eyes. "Do you see the packet anywhere in my fur? Look, if I don't leave now, she'll bite my tail off."

"What 'she' will bite your tail?" cried Nnylf.

"Hold that dog down," snarled the weasel. "Gormley, is who. She sent me to help Anadraka!" Gúrmulo struggled to free himself from the tunic. Pulling out a paw, he waved it in the direction of the peaks and said, "I must go to the Cave of Refuge; Gormley gave me a message for them."

"Them? Who is *them*?" exclaimed Azile. "And you speak of Anadraka? She sent you? How could she be living—and who is Gormley?"

Nnylf struggled with the weasel. "Azile means this: When she heard that the Moktawls had killed Anadraka, Mother made us promise to help keep the dam's packet hidden and safe. We don't know what to do now that it's gone missing."

Despite his tight grip on the tunic, Nnylf lost control of the squirming weasel. Gúrmulo sprang away into the rows of barley, shouting, "Then it's time you followed me!"

Stunned, the brother and sister sat and watched him disappear. The wind picked up. With a shiver, Nnylf slipped his tunic over his head and wriggled it down to his hips. Holding Bounder's neck with one hand, he turned to Azile and said, "Weather's changing. Well, then, shall we go after him?"

PART I: UNEXPECTED DETOURS   15

"Go after what 'him'?"

The brother and sister turned toward the voice of Eunan, their father. Looking from his dirt-crusted boots, past his grease-stained leggings, to his rough leather tunic, they gaped at his angry face and blushed. His bushy eyebrows hooded the stony glare he aimed at his two offspring.

"Why are you playing here with that useless hound? You've more than one chore to do. Can't you see a storm's coming, which means we need to hurry with the reaping?"

"We weren't playing, Father. Bounder ran away and we were worried that we would lose him. Others in the village might hurt him. You know how they mistrust us," Azile answered with a smile meant to charm him. Behind her back, she squeezed her hands together to calm her shaking arms.

More gently, Eunan turned to Azile. "You know that I need you to help us make a go of it. Times are hard. Some creature is roaming these parts and scorching our crops. The other Moktawls are looking strangely at us. And your mother's not here to help us." He glowered as his gaze turned toward the Sunsetside Mountains. "Besides, that dog always comes home whenever he has a mind to. And, look, something's wrong with his hind legs—his shins are covered with scaly patches." He slapped his hands on his thighs. "Enough nonsense," he sighed. "Azile, go to the cottage and tidy it up, then fix something to eat while I work on saving as much of our crop as I can. Nnylf, when you've done your chores, come back here to help me out. The other men have gone off somewhere."

Nodding obedience, Nnylf and Azile, trailed by Bounder, started up the hill toward their home. Their father, scythe in hand, trudged into the field. He glanced back at his children, then found the patch he'd been reaping and bent into his work once more.

Nnylf whispered, "Imagine, talking to a weasel! Did he really say Anadraka was alive, after all these years?"

"How? They say she fell after the Moktawls' fire arrows hit her, but no one found her body out there in the forest. Remember how the men screamed? They wanted her skin badly. All but Father."

Nnylf said nothing, but looked for a moment or two at the forest on the opposite side of the valley. He leaned toward her and whispered, "Azile, do you remember the enormous cave above the forest? Where we met the Orferans?"

"Not clearly. That was long ago and I was so little."

"Well, I remember. Only Mother and we knew it was up there. Why would the weasel . . . anyhow, do you suppose Anadraka survived and hid there?"

"I don't know. Nnylf, are you telling me you want to look for her there? We're not dragonriders, really. Anadraka might hurt us. How many times has Father said we can't wander in the forest anymore?"

"I know, I know. It's that old beast-in-the-forest story. I don't believe it. Too much like a fairy tale."

"The forest does hide something bad—but even if it were safe, Father needs our help. We shouldn't go there. This is our job right now." Azile pointed to their cottage, the oxen's hut, and the storage shed. She narrowed her eyes, and with a slight grin, she said, "Besides, if we could get away, we'd follow Gúrmulo to the mountain, wouldn't we? To find Mother?"

"I suppose you're right. I shouldn't be talking about leaving. Father does need our help." Nnylf thought for a few moments as they walked. "But what if Anadraka *were* still alive? Mother would want to know."

Nnylf paced in a small, tight circle. With one foot still raised, he punched the air and his face brightened. "Of course! Say, Azile, I know how to find Anadraka and help Father at the same time!" Nnylf felt like clapping and dancing a little jig.

Azile glanced first at him, then at their father down in the field. "Nnylf, forget the forest. They say strange things happen there." She picked up a twig broom and started to sweep the jumble of leaves and pebbles from the dirt in front of their cottage door.

"Oh, Azile, we know that forest like you know how to use your broom. We'll just be careful."

"I have to think about it. We could get in a lot of trouble. So go now. I'll cook something as soon as you fetch me wood for the oven. Some warmed-up bread and bean soup will cheer Father."

Nnylf chuckled to himself. Before picking up his ax, he threw a stick for Bounder. Walking to a pile of small logs nearby, he did not notice that the dog failed to bring it back.

Chapter 4

THE OPENING INTO THE CAVE led to a large gallery, hung with glowing stalactites. A clear stream burbled down the middle of the cavern floor. Along the walls, bones of snakes, mice, and birds lay in jumbled piles and a giant nest of bright rags hugged the wall farthest from the entrance.

Anadraka sat quietly in her nest and stared out toward the opening. Was this the day she would test her wing? A storm was brewing by Anonom Trace and she doubted her strength. Since the Moktawl attack she had not tried to fly. Dragon years are long, but dragon healing is slow. She lowered her silver-speckled blue head to lick her wing and felt the rough violet scar left by a fire arrow wound.

Stretching back her hind legs one at a time, she stood up. She raised her head to look at the ceiling high above her. One of its many calcite icicles, inching downward toward clumps of stalagmites growing up from the floor, grazed the scaly hide between her ears. Outside the cave, she saw a pale red glow behind the heavy dark clouds in the early evening sky. *How I would like to leave this lonely place*, she thought.

As she ambled toward the cavern entrance, one of her claws caught on something hard and sharp. Looking down at the floor, she could see the edge of a broken tablet by her foot. She lowered her head to sniff it and tried to read the dragon markings on its face. "Too dark in here." Anadraka nosed the fragment into the fading daylight and she read:

> "In nests of rainbow brightness
> Shall the wyrmlings come to light.
> Sheltered from the . . .
> The ruler of the night.
> One and only one will dare . . .
> And this will be the . . ."

The broken edge cut off most of the lines. Anadraka thought: *Here in the Cave of the Ancestors, one broken tablet was all that remained of the Prophecy of the Ancient Ones—that and the Mystic Scintilla. When dragons thrived in the Veiled Valley, all hatchlings had cracked through their shells and learned the Old Ways in this time-honored place . . . but no more.*

Leaving the carved slab that had fallen from high over the entrance, she lifted her gaze to the Sunsetside Mountains. "My dear family," she sighed, "hidden up there, far from the Valley and its dangers. If only I were with them now!" She inhaled the cool evening air, and as she shifted to revisit her nest, she heard the smallest of chattering squeaks. "Hmm, I wouldn't mind a warm, tasty bit to munch now." Sniffing, she searched for the promising prey that had stumbled into her hiding place.

At that moment, a weasel jumped forward and stood on its hind legs. "Ho, Anadraka, look at your old friend, Gormley!" she squeaked.

"Gormley?" She smiled. "Too bad. I was hoping for a snack."

"We'll talk about snacks soon enough. I came across the Valley with news of the family for you."

"News? Wonderful! But didn't the Moktawls see you climb up here?"

"In the dark and above that forbidding forest? Not likely. They know nothing of this place."

"Perhaps, but why did you say 'forbidding forest'? What's happening below?"

"The Moktawls think they have rid the Valley of dragons. Now they're hunting a new menace in the forest, a giant they call the Formorian."

"Formorian?" She shivered. "I only know the giant Rocánonom—

but share your news with me, please. I want to hear more about the family." She paused, noticing that the weasel was coughing quietly and her coat was dusty and bedraggled. "How rude of me! You need water." She nudged Gormley toward the flowing stream. "You must be thirsty after all that running and climbing. Here, refresh yourself."

Chattering happily, Gormley jumped into the icy stream. After a few sips, she leaped to the cavern floor and shook water droplets in all directions from her furry auburn coat. "The news, of course: All is well—if a bit dull—in the Cave of Refuge!" She paused and widened her forelegs in the air. "Your cousin Abulafria's hatchling, Drac'Argo, sired by your cousin Ruddykin—sealed in our memory—has grown so much that he longs to join his cousin Draako's flying practice."

As she listened to her little friend, Anadraka raised her head and considered the mountains. "The egg hatched? And Draako is flying?" she asked with a sigh.

"Draako is well and grows in strength. Aurykk hardly ever calls him 'wyrmling'!"

"Are they strong enough to return here?"

"Not in these troubled times, Anadraka. Even at night, the Valley folk would spot four large dragons together in the sky, and then there's young Drac'Argo."

"So I must journey to them—if my wing has healed."

Gormley trotted to Anadraka's side and examined the scar. "The wound has closed tightly and your muscles look strong."

"So you say. We will need to test my strength first." Anadraka's gaze swept across the ledge in front of the cavern. "But where is Gúrmulo? You two are always together."

Gormley had been rolling about in a ball of merriment, but her smile froze at Anadraka's words. She said, "On our way here, we stopped near Fossarelick and hoped to find Seerlana. I overheard her husband scolding his children. He ranted about Seerlana running away."

"Seerlana? Not there? But the packet . . ."

The weasel nodded and reassured her dragon friend. "Forgive me, but thinking you'd be ready, I sent Gúrmulo on to the Cave of Refuge to tell them you were coming—and that trouble has found Seerlana! I just hope he remembers the way and doesn't lose himself among the hill people."

"He will find his way . . . eventually. But what will happen when I return? The others know nothing of my escape."

"Knowing you'd return to us when you felt ready, I kept your secret, but the Orferans will show their pleasure when they see you again. So many years have passed and they still miss you." Gormley licked a paw and washed her ears and cheeks before continuing. "You haven't seen the scorched fields. Fires and famine have changed our valley."

"Scorched fields? Ah, of course, they blame the Formorian now."

"No, it's not that giant's work. I'll tell you more when we're on our way."

"On our way?"

"To the Cave of Refuge. A storm's coming. Rain will hide us if you fly above the clouds."

"Us?"

"Of course, you will carry me with you—with care, I warn you. I'm not going to run across the whole valley again!"

"Then we have to prepare."

Dragon and weasel set about cleaning the cavern floor. They swept scraps and bones outside, over the ledge, and into the wooded hillside below. With her long claws, Anadraka scraped gravel, stones, and dust to bury the broken tablet on the floor, then piled a few stone slabs on top. She tore apart her rag nest and pushed its pieces over the ledge, too, careful not to disturb certain herbs growing in turquoise-green clumps along its rim. Satisfied with her work, she returned inside to take a long drink from the stream.

"Shall we go?" asked Gormley. She had wrapped herself in a few rags she had put aside.

Anadraka tilted her head and looked at the weasel with some

amusement. "Gormley, you look like a dragon pellet."

Gormley shivered and whined, "Well, it's cold out there, and your claws are sharp."

"Good thinking," replied the dragon with a grin. "Or you could travel in my jaw pouch?"

Gormley shook her head brusquely. "Your claws will do."

They moved to the ledge outside the entrance. Above them, the sky was moonless and dark, filled with clouds. Anadraka stood at the rim of the ledge. She unfolded her wings and stretched her neck over the void below. Her spines and frill stood on end. In one leap, her legs and wings carried her into the open air. With a sharp turn, she came back to the ledge and landed with a skid. Winking, she whispered to the weasel, "You spoke truly. I am ready to fly, but I have to land more carefully."

Gathering Gormley in the claws of one front foot, Anadraka spread her wide wings across the ledge. She crouched, then sprang into the air again and flew quickly up through the clouds. She headed toward the great mountains.

Far below in Fossarelick, two young people were looking in the direction of the forest and thought they saw something fly into the cloudy evening sky. Their father had left to meet with the other Moktawls. They shook their heads and returned to planning for the next day, while at the edge of the forest, beyond the fields of Fossarelick, a small group of men sat around a large bonfire. Leaping flames and whirls of smoke blinded their view of the sky.

Some of the men, scrawny and shivering in their rough shirts and tunics, looked fearfully into the looming trees. Each of them clutched a wooden bowl and followed the antics of their short companion, the cook. Bald and portly, he hurried from man to man while carrying ladlesful of bean stew he had scooped from a large kettle on the fire. One other man, Atty, frowned above his long and drooping moustache. He stood and pointed toward the forest. The scales of his blue tunic gleamed in the firelight and a large silver amulet hung around his dirt-streaked neck.

PART I: UNEXPECTED DETOURS

"Tomorrow, we journey deeper into the forest. The Formorian will fall into our trap. We'll kill him and we will bring his body to our Elder, Cahal. So eat hearty, men. You'll need all your strength to capture that one. At least he isn't a fire-breather."

The men laughed uneasily and talked softly among themselves. One of them slowly rose and stood close by the fire. He turned to face the others. With a soft growl, he knotted his shaggy black brows and spat into the flames. "What are we doing, chasing after this goat-headed giant? We Moktawls have always hunted the flying beasts and put out fires they started every which way, all over the Veiled Valley. This Formorian business is not for the likes of us!"

"Eunan, you are mistaken," Atty spat. "We've killed every last dragon, but until this beast that burns our fields is gone, we cannot rest. Cahal knows the old and wise Ways. He told us to kill the Formorian and that's what we must do—or would you rather go back to Nnylf and Azile?"

"Old and wise Ways or no, these are hard times and I have barley fields to tend. I've no use for chasing after creatures brewed by our Elder in his nightmares. Tomorrow morn, Nnylf and I *will* be swinging our scythes, so I'll hear no more of this!" Eunan stomped his boots on the edge of the fire. Sparks shot high into the air above the men. Abruptly, he turned away and headed back to the village.

"Eunan, you'll miss the cakes I've brought! Atty, get him to come back," whined the little cook, who had turned with begging eyes to the group's leader.

"Eunan, stop," cried Atty, waving his crossbow. "You're letting us down, neighbor."

From the path leading up to the village, they heard Eunan shout back, "Ah, you're all just hurting your own selves and your families with this foolishness."

Only the hoots of owls in the trees beyond them answered Eunan. Atty threw a stick at his retreating neighbor, then turned to glower at his men. Silenced by their leader's barely hidden anger, the men leaned against trees bordering the clearing and soon fell asleep.

The next morning, Atty began his search for the Formorian. Strewn along a muddy path through paper birch and red alder trees, broad footprints led the company of Moktawls into a thicker part of the forest. Atty signaled his nervous men to follow him. Crouching, they spread out behind him and slogged up the slope. When the tracks ended, Atty whispered, "What happened? They've just disappeared."

Another Moktawl reached him and said, "How can that be? The trail was very clear." Atty looked at the man's scarred neck and lean face and remembered past hunts. He said, "The giant's cunning. Those footprints took us far from our traps into a rougher part of the woods. Mind you, Cahalson, if we don't find him first . . ."

A rain of falling branches hit their heads. Atty looked up and saw a two-legged creature twice his size leaping from one treetop to another. "There he is!" he shouted.

The giant glanced back at them and they caught a glimpse of his long goat face. With a shudder, Atty called out, "Follow him, men!"

The chase brought them up against a long stone wall, over which the giant had jumped with ease. Atty threw his rope to the top edge, but it slid back to the ground. "He's hiding in there. You"—he pointed to three of the men—"go along that side and look around this place for a gate or a gap. You and you"—he waved at two other men—"go that way and do the same. If there's an opening in the wall, breach it. Cahalson and I will scale the top somehow. We'll all meet inside this span of stones."

The scouting parties left. Atty and Cahalson heaved their heavy rope once more over the wall. The third time, its loop caught a tree branch and held. Finding footholds in the crevices between stones, each man in turn pulled himself up to the top of the wall, but no farther. They looked below with mouths wide open.

A vast, wild garden stretched below them, patched by dense shrubbery, brightly colored flowers, and rangy herbs scattered throughout. Beyond the untamed plantings and tall tufts of grasses and reeds, they saw fruit trees in meandering rows and the blue-green sliver of a lake or pond next to a clearing where stood a single, widely spread live oak. A dense tangle of dark woods lined the far edge of the clearing. A narrow path near the wall led through the garden. In the distance beyond all the growth, they saw a drifting column of smoke.

"I guess if there's smoke, there might be a chimney, and if there's a chimney, could there be a house?" Cahalson asked.

"Or it might be a trap." Atty frowned. "He's sly, that giant." He saw some of the other Moktawls making their way along the wall toward him and waved high in the air to them. "Jump down. We'll gather the men and look around this place."

Regrouped around him again, the Moktawls flinched at Atty's raspy command: "Move out. And quiet—not a word, understand?"

The men nodded. In a tight bunch, they advanced onto the path, always toward the rising smoke.

Chapter 5

AZILE AWOKE SLOWLY AS the dim morning light from the small window opposite her cot fell across her face. She looked in the direction of Nnylf's bench, but he was gone and had tidied his covers. Sitting up, she saw that his clothes—usually thrown in a pile—were missing, too. *He must be out already*, she thought, and she stood up on the hard dirt floor.

Pulling on a simple brown skirt over her chemise, Azile hurried to the fireplace to stir the hot embers and hang a pot of grain and water. She cut herself a slice of barley bread to quiet her hunger pangs. Barefoot, she hurried out the low doorway into the yard and down the path to the fields. The sky was overcast and heavy rain clouds hung on the distant mountain tops.

On their land, she could see her father tying sheaves of barley while, nearby, Nnylf was cutting stalk after stalk of the grain with more energy than she had ever seen him give to harvesting.

"Well, well, well!" she muttered to herself. Walking up to them, she said, "Good morning to you, Father . . . and Nnylf. I've come to help you. It looks like rain is coming."

"My girl, it's the washing you should be doing, and the porridge, too. I suppose the fireplace is cold now?" Eunan grumbled as he stooped to tie another bundle. "If your dream-struck mother hadn't run off—she and her notion that help would come from dragons!—we'd be eating better today, I tell you."

PART I: UNEXPECTED DETOURS   27

"The embers just needed a poke. Besides, I've already hung the porridge kettle." Azile braced her fists on her hips. "I see you had no trouble eating a bit of the bread I baked. As for the washing, the rain would soon soak it before even one pair of drawers could dry."

"Enough!" Eunan scowled. "Give us a hand, then. Nnylf here said he'll be taking the barley to market at Nosidam, and by the time he's back we'll have a new load for him."

"And I'll take the next load to the towns beyond, eh?" Nnylf looked up at his father with wide, innocent eyes. "But don't you think Azile should be with me to guard the barley while I find a buyer in the market?" He glanced at Azile, who smiled and walked to the next row and began to cut stalks. Eunan hardly looked up, but kept at his baling and merely grunted.

The little family continued working until they were ready to load grain on the back of their neighbor's donkey and into their own small handcart. After securing the grain and covering it with oiled tarps, they hauled the bundles up to the shed by their cottage. By then, large raindrops were dotting the tarps in big wet splotches. Soon a heavy rain followed. Eunan, Azile, and Nnylf ran into their cottage.

Shaking the rain from his shoulders, Eunan said, "Let's have that porridge!" He paused and watched his children intently.

After washing his hands in a basin, Nnylf dried them by running his fingers through his curly brown hair. Azile was lifting the heavy pot from the fire, her strong tanned arms and hands protected by a homespun towel. She watched her father scratch his beard as he said, "I've never seen you so eager to work in the fields, you two. With your help, who knows, we just might make it through this season."

Eunan scooped some cooked barley from the pot. "Now eat. You'll need your strength." Azile thanked her father as he placed before each of them a wooden bowl brimming with hot cereal drizzled with honey. He then filled another for himself. They sat together around their one rough wooden table near the small hearth and ate in silence.

After a while, the raindrops beat more slowly on the roof, and outside the small window, the sky brightened. "I'm done, Father. I'll be going back to the field now. Coming with me, Azile?" asked Nnylf.

"As soon as you help me clear the table and clean the dishes, I'll be down," she replied as she rolled up the sleeves of her chemise. She took her bowl and spoon to the basin and tilted a bucket to pour water over them.

Eunan looked from one child to the other and scratched his beard again. "No, Nnylf. We'll all go down to the field together."

Azile shivered as Eunan glowered at them from under his shaggy brows and said, "We have to wait for the stalks to dry after that rain. Tomorrow, you'll have a big load. Remember to stay on the road and don't stray into the forest."

As it led away from Fossarelick, the path to the market town of Nosidam ran close to the edge of the forest. On the open side of its rutted tracks, wildflowers buzzing with foraging bees covered the gently sloping meadows in shades of pink and purple. Nnylf grunted as he pulled the donkey back to the path. The donkey tugged back and dipped her head to nibble on the sweet flowers. Azile jerked the cart handles and wiped her damp brow with the back of her hand.

"I think I see it now, Nnylf, a way to enter the forest and climb the mountain. It's just behind that tangle of trees and bushes."

"Ooph, that's a good girl." He held a bunch of flowers in his free hand and was coaxing the donkey out of the meadow. "To the dragons' cave?"

"Yes, just beyond the forest."

"Good spotting! We'll stay on the path to Nosidam for now and sell the barley in the marketplace. After that, we'll have a chance to explore, just to see if Anadraka left any sign."

Azile pressed her lips together and nodded. "Then we will go home, give Father the coins, and—" She froze and looked past the path she had seen, then whispered, "What's that noise? Do you hear it?"

PART I: UNEXPECTED DETOURS

The donkey dropped her mouthful of flowers, began to bray, and pushed past Nnylf. She ran to the road, despite the heavy bundles of barley on her back.

"I need your help, Azile. This stubborn beast is running away. What scared her?" Nnylf grasped at the rope around the donkey's neck, but he could barely keep up with her as she trotted in the direction of Nosidam.

Azile looked behind them with a shiver. "A strange sound, Nnylf, like a baby crying, or maybe the whoosh of a wind gust—oh, I don't know. Wait, you're going too fast."

"I didn't hear anything. You're imagining it. There, she's quiet now. You take the rope and I'll push the cart. We'll make better time that way. And careful, I don't want her running off again."

They continued along the road, and soon they could see the red roofs of Nosidam in the hollow beyond the forest. Azile gripped the rope and nearly fell on her face as the donkey, eyes rolling, pulled her along at a brisk pace. By the side of the road, the bushes stirred. Hidden among their leaves, two large yellow eyes followed the siblings' steps.

When Nnylf and Azile reached the town, they found Nosidam's marketplace filled with farmers, cows, goats, and chickens. Small children ran among women and men intent on selling vegetables, animals, cheeses, or cloth. Nnylf and Azile elbowed their way through the crowd, coughing as dust raised by so many wheels and hooves floated around them. Under the canopy set up for sellers of grain, they found a small space and sat on the cart to wait for customers. From among the bales, Azile yanked out a small leather sack and offered her brother a drink of cool water from a brown and orange gourd.

"Thanks." He took a few gulps and handed the gourd back to Azile.

After hopping down from the cart, he waved to her and said, "I'm off to look for some buyers. You stay here and watch the cart and donkey— and give that poor beast some water."

"But Nnylf, you can't leave me here in the middle of strangers!" Azile looked at him with wide eyes. "What if a buyer comes to me? I can't watch the bales and talk to him at the same time."

He looked at the other sellers, who had no customers yet. They were sweeping the pavers in front of their stalls or gossiping with their neighbors. An older man was watching Nnylf. His gray hair and flowing moustache blew about in the breeze as he whittled a long piece of dark wood. Azile saw him wink at Nnylf then bend over his work again. *Do we know him?* she wondered.

She frowned as Nnylf said, "I don't think you have anything to worry about, Azile. Just sit tight. If a buyer comes along, have him wait. I'll be back right after taking a turn around this place."

As Nnylf's head and shoulders disappeared in the crowd, Azile turned to look around the marketplace. A dull pain was growing behind her eyes and her forehead felt hot. A few sips of water eased the discomfort and she realized with surprise that she was hungry. She reached in her pocket for a hunk of bread she'd tucked away that morning and began to nibble on it. The taste of food from home helped her relax.

She jumped as she felt a light touch on her shoulder and almost dropped her crusts.

"Sorry I scared you," said a young man, whose broad smile creased his handsome face. Dressed in clean breeches, a white shirt, and a dark green cape, he swept his feathered hat off his head and bowed. Through masses of deep black hair, he looked up at Azile and smiled again.

"I wasn't scared; I wasn't, sir. Just didn't see you," she said.

"Then I assume you always jump when you nibble on your crusts. Amusing, but let's do business, shall we? Ah, Aindle is my—sorry, no, please call me . . . call me Lustre—and I was looking for some—what do you have here? Ah, yes, some very good barley to take to the miller. May I look at your bales?"

"Yes, please," Azile answered in a soft voice while her eyes searched the marketplace for her brother. "We're selling it at a very good price and hope to leave right after."

The young man strolled to the donkey and patted her side. He said, "Your donkey needs water." He filled his hat with water from a large

PART I: UNEXPECTED DETOURS   31

flask and the donkey dipped her head to drink. The man bent his head to whisper in the animal's ear, but the donkey bolted and backed away.

Azile couldn't hear his words, but for a moment, she shook her head in disbelief—had he nearly bitten the donkey's ear? *No*, she thought, *he must be trying to calm her*. Indeed, the donkey stood very still while Lustre examined the barley. Pointing to the cart, he said, "This is very good and fresh grain. Name your price, and if it's fair, I'll take it all."

"Azile, I'll talk price with the gentleman." From the neighboring stall, Nnylf had been watching the stranger inspect the grain. He came back to the cart just as Azile was about to ask the stranger to wait for her brother's return.

She watched as the two young men talked, pointed to the grain, nodded, talked again, and finally shook hands. Azile felt her heart leap with pleasure as Lustre handed a small sack of coins to her brother.

"I have one small problem, my new friends," said Lustre. "Not expecting the availability of such fine goods today, I came without a horse and cart. I am visiting my uncle, who lives near here. For a fee, would you be willing to carry the grain to his hunting lodge? It's just inside the forest." He pointed to the path that the pair had taken to Nosidam.

Azile began, "We'd be happy—"

"Just inside the forest, you say? But, sir, no one lives there. How did you come to Nosidam without your own horse?"

Lustre replied, "My uncle and I rode into town on his horse, but he left me here in Nosidam while he went beyond to visit with a friend. I was going to enjoy the exercise of a long walk home."

"I understand," said Nnylf. He hesitated, but at last he agreed to help Lustre deliver the grain to the lodge for a few more coins, which the man paid him immediately. The cart rumbled along as the donkey led by Azile pulled and Nnylf pushed. The elegant man walked in silence beside them.

"How far is your lodge?" asked Nnylf, startled at the sound of his voice breaking the silence.

"It's not far, just beyond that turn in the road, where you can see a large fallen fir tree. My uncle will be delighted to meet you when he returns."

Both Nnylf and Azile looked in the direction the man had pointed, but they saw only vast stretches of tall trees climbing the slopes with no other path, signpost, or gatehouse.

"I don't see it." He paused. "And I know most of the people in Nosidam. Who is your uncle? Your clothing—excuse me, but it reminds me of the stories they told us about the days of dragonriders," said Nnylf. "Anyway, we won't be able to stay long."

With a chortle, the man winked at him and said, "Of course. And yes, I love those good stories about the old days. I'll tell you more about myself when we reach the lodge."

Just then, Azile pointed to a wide opening in the trees that they had not noticed as they walked toward Nosidam hours before. "There *is* a big fallen tree. I'm amazed we didn't see it." Shrugging her shoulders, she turned to pull the donkey along the main road, but the little animal was already trotting happily on the new path running deeper into the forest.

Azile thought, *This is near the path leading up to the dragons' cave.* Her heartbeat quickened. "Father said not to—"

"It's all right, young lady," said Lustre. "We're quite close."

They continued through the shady woods. Intent on catching up with the donkey, Azile failed to notice a jutting tree root on the path, and she tripped over it. Stumbling on for a few steps, she found her balance and brushed her hair from her eyes. As her fingers passed her ear, she cried out, "My little gold earring is gone! I must have lost it when I tripped. Please, let me look for it." The others had reached a bend in the path and were hurrying ahead.

Azile searched all around the root and the grasses nearby but found nothing. "Wait, wait! I've lost my earring," she called after them; but they already were at a stone wall extending far on either side of a tall iron gate at the end of the path.

"Hurry up, young lady. The afternoon sun won't last much longer, anyway," Lustre called back to her.

With a wave of his hand, Lustre unlocked the entrance and said, "Please, after you. I hope you will eat and drink with me before you return to your village."

"Thank you, but we'll just unload the bales and be on our way; we must go back to Fossarelick while we still have daylight."

"Ah, but Nnylf, your poor sister has eaten nothing but two crusts of bread today."

"How did you know my name, sir?"

Lustre laughed. "Why, you told me your names when you sold me the barley."

Nnylf looked at Azile to ask her if she had mentioned their names, but Azile shook her head and looked at the ground. She smiled at her brother when he said, "Very well, Lustre, thank you for your kindness. We are a bit hungry and thirsty. Just a quick bite and we'll be on our way—please?"

They followed the young man into a stone house and tower surrounded by wildflowers, shrubs, and fruit trees. The donkey rushed into the garden and nibbled on an unexpected banquet of flowers and fruited shrubs. "Let her eat," said Lustre. "My servant will take care of her. Please, come in, come in."

Chapter 6

DRAAKO CREPT ON THE TIPS of his claws from Aurykk's nest, past snoring Isabella, and out to the broad ledge extending over the cliffs below. He had tried to sleep, but dreams of past battles with the Ancestors haunted him: visions of their first terrifying attack followed by another, when Seerlana and her children had urged flight and rescued him. He hardly knew the subtleties of flight then, but the children had ridden his neck hump and escaped with him to the Anonom plain where Aurykk led them to safety. Then the boy and girl had run off, and after that, he never saw them again.

His mother was a faint memory. She separated from Seerlana after that escape and Draako had not seen her since. He looked back into the warm depths of his safe cave. He felt grateful for the older dragons' care.

Dawn breezes gently scattered leaves and small bones lying about the ledge. Draako felt a sudden gust beating him back and he tucked his head under one wing. Peeking out as the wind eased, he was astonished to see his weasel friend standing in front of his nose, and just beyond her, a very large dragon. He knew the weasel well. He sniffed at the Silver-Blue.

"I've brought her," announced the weasel as she peered into the cave entrance. She turned to ask, "Where's Gúrmulo? Hasn't he told you the news?" But when Draako said nothing, Gormley frowned. "He's not here?"

PART I: UNEXPECTED DETOURS   35

Anadraka, her claws clicking on the gravel, turned to face Draako. "Please excuse my sudden landing. I came to be with family. Gormley told me about the dragonet, my son."

Draako looked from the dragon to the weasel and back again. Little tendrils of smoke drifted from his dry throat. His jaws hung open in wonder. "Hello, Gormley," he managed to say then looked closely at the Silver-Blue. "Not to be rude, but . . . but your scales shine and you are very solid, so you're not a ghost, are you?"

Anadraka hummed and was about to answer him, when Isabella emerged from the cave, her eyes burning red. Flames curled around her dagger-sharp teeth. Draako felt panic as his aunt poised to attack, but the newcomer shouted, "Cousin!" and Isabella stumbled to a halt.

Anadraka stretched her neck to touch noses with the other dragon. The copper dam pulled back, lowered her jaws, and studied Anadraka with half-shut eyes.

"*Cousin*, you say? Impossible. The only family I have lives in this cave."

Gormley, perched on Isabella's shoulder, muttered in her ear, "She *is* family. I see Gúrmulo did not get here in time. I warned him that my message was of the greatest importance. Oh! I never can count on him!" She jumped to the ground and darted here and there. "Gúrmulo, where are you?" she whimpered.

Isabella's head reared up. "Family? And Gúrmulo, you say? He hasn't visited us for days—paid his respects and left when you did." She looked closely at Gormley. "What have you two little ones been up to?"

Gormley groaned. "Gúrmulo, what happened to you? I knew this wouldn't work."

Draako chased her and demanded, "Knew *what* wouldn't work?"

Gormley answered, "That Anadraka lives! Can't you see?"

The other dragons came out of the cave to see the cause of the ruckus and Draako's head swiveled as a squeaky voice from the cliff's edge interrupted Gormley's cries: "Nothing happened to me. I was just delayed, is all. Sorry for the fuss."

Draako felt bubbles of dragon laughter rise in his throat as he watched Gúrmulo climb paw over paw onto the ledge, shake dust from his fur, and trot to Gormley's side. A light brown dog, many times the weasel's size, followed close behind, but at the sight of the dragons, he stepped back and cowered near the edge.

"There you are, you good-for-nothing weasel." Gormley darted at him. "Wouldn't you know she would arrive before you!" Gúrmulo backed up slowly, but Gormley started to chase him around the ledge and into the cave, right between Aurykk's legs. The dog ran after them and disappeared into the dark.

Three pairs of dragon eyes blinked as they recognized the new arrival and whispered, "Anadraka."

The Silver-Blue bowed her head and returned their gaze with a gentle rumble. "My family," she said. "I longed to be with you for many lost seasons."

Abulafria hurried to her and curls of sweet-smelling smoke wreathed their heads as they rubbed noses. "Dear cousin, here is your son."

Draako's big heart skipped a few beats as he regarded Anadraka with wide eyes. He drew nearer to her side. She lowered her head and studied him carefully. "Your name?" she asked.

"I . . . I am called Draako," he responded.

The dam raised her head and exhaled a great cloud of smoke. "Draako, alive and so big, so strong!" Her eyes had turned a golden yellow and her scales began to glow like opals. "Are you really my Draako?" She raised her scarred wing and folded the young dragon within its web of sinews.

"*Your* Draako? Oh, yes!" Draako sighed and belched a small cloud of his own.

Isabella extended her long neck, sniffed at Anadraka's smoky exhalations, and relaxed back on her haunches. "Cousin, you've returned! Come meet 'Argo, my nephew."

Draako relaxed with his family and burped little puffs of smoke, while Aurykk offered Anadraka the remaining dormice and roasted mushrooms. She nibbled until Isabella nuzzled her. With a shake of her head, the Copper motioned to a fresh nest she had prepared for her cousin. "I imagine you'd like to rest now," she said. "You are safe with us again."

"Mother," whispered Draako, once they had curled themselves into the cozy twist of rags and twigs, "why did you not send me a message? Did the Moktawls' arrow hurt you?"

"It did. I was helping Aurykk search for my mate. The Moktawls' fire arrow hurt my wing badly. They meant to hunt us all to the death. I did not want them to find your hiding place here. I escaped them. Although I know the healing Ways, I was weak and would have died. Our weasel friends found me in the Cave of the Ancestors, where I'd been hiding. Gormley gathered the herbs I needed to ease my pain and Gúrmulo brought me food and water."

"They didn't tell me about your hiding place."

"No, only they and Aurykk knew I was alive. I see no one here expected me."

"We did not." Isabella spoke up. "Did the Ancestors attack you in the Orferan cave?"

"No, and I saw no sign of them, not even the shadow of a bone."

At the mention of the Ancestors, Bounder howled and jumped into Aurykk's nest. His shaking eased as Gormley patted him and said, "They won't find you here."

Draako remembered his galloping fear when the roaring Ancestors had chased him with their fire. The two children had warned him as soon as they saw the red eyes of the dragon spirits lowered in menace. The girl had urged Draako to fly away, but panic gripped him. The boy had taken hold of Draako's neck fringe, scrambled onto his back, and pulled the girl up beside him. Their warmth and weight alarmed him at first, but the girl calmed him with brave words. Propelled by their commands, he raised his wings and leaped from the ledge just as the ghostly Red dam, Tinta, had pounced.

"Mother, the children," he yawned. "I can't remember their names. They"—another yawn—"saved me," he muttered dreamily. Then he fell asleep, snug under Anadraka's wing.

Chapter 7

BEYOND THE MOUNTAINS RINGING the Veiled Valley and deep into the Coldside, there lies a desert pocked by plungeholes—once entrances to basilisk colonies and their network of tunnels. A Fossarelick cottage could fit easily into any of the holes, sink into an open tunnel beneath it, and wedge against the platform of a broad nesting chamber. Each tunnel's twin descended from an opposite plungehole, and the nesting chamber spanned the distance between them.

Far below, basilisk females used to dig out larger chambers connected by the same tunnels, which provided the perfect temperature and security to hatch their offspring. When the hatchlings grew and reached their full height, as tall as a small fir tree, they resembled enormous roosters with long, thick reptilian tails, deadly venom in their claws and spittle, and hypnotic eyes that could paralyze any target caught in their gaze.

Other creatures, giant lizards with no gift of speech or fire breath, shared the desert with the basilisks. They laid their eggs in flimsy nests scattered across the desert floor. The basilisks, beaks plowing through gravel and sand, stalked them for meat and sport. They gobbled lizard eggs whenever they stumbled upon a nest.

One season, a lizard egg failed to hatch and lay glowing and undetected behind a rocky pillar. Over time, its light and heat transformed surviving lizard hatchlings into dragons gifted with added strength, a hefty amount of wisdom, and extraordinary powers. From then on, the basilisks faced their equals.

As if to match the dragons' transformation, three peculiar basilisks emerged from widely separate plungeholes. Each of them had two heads sprouting from a split neck, wings capable of flight (unlike the basilisks' stunted wings), and one other ability: shape-changing.

Before this new breed of basilisk emerged, dragon families had formed clans and established lairs where natural caves tunneled through mountains surrounding the Veiled Valley. Led by dragons with silver scales and a hypnotic power that could overwhelm any other creature, the clans defended themselves against these new, two-headed beasts. They called them aiglonaxes.

Hunger and persistent rage drove the aiglonaxes to swoop upon the few basilisks out scouring the desert floor. They devoured them and the remaining dozen hiding in their chambers until only the strange new creatures remained. Solitary, the aiglonaxes tracked each other to the death until just one survived, the largest and strongest, who called himself Aindle.

Aware that dragons would hunt and try to overpower him, this survivor retreated to a mountain aerie far from dragon lairs and hunted small prey while he spied on the dragon clans. He watched in disgust as the Orferan clan befriended humans settling in the Veiled Valley. The dragons helped them build a lodge deep within the Sunriseside Forest.

Aindle ached to live in the valley, too; it was so much more hospitable and plentiful than the desert. To do so, he decided to disguise himself whenever the need arose—as a human, a powerful hork, or even a dragonrider named Lustre—while never losing his aiglonax powers. He plotted and waited for the time when he would be once more the strongest, fiercest, and smartest creature the valley had ever known—for the day when all its riches would be his and the dragons would lose their powers. They would fear him again and call him the Malevir.

Only one thought spoiled Aindle's dream: the little brown weasels that lived with the Orferans. He'd seen them carry messages across the

PART I: UNEXPECTED DETOURS   41

valley for the dragons. Aindle's heart raced when he thought of them: so small, so deadly. He knew how a basilisk had died while trying to eat one.

Nnylf sat with Azile and Lustre at a table near the hearth of the young man's lodge. He ate quick bites of the food placed in front of them. Sweet, spicy bread, creamy butter and yellow cheese, pears and apples, and nuts and dried berries filled their plates. Lustre poured cool milk into shiny white cups from a clay pitcher that Nnylf had not noticed before. He wondered at the ceiling, higher than four men one above the next, that spanned over his head. Held up by massive wooden beams, its planks must have been darkened by years of smoke from the wide fireplace centered in one of the long walls.

Relaxing in a heavy carved chair opposite them, Lustre lifted a pretty green cloth to reveal a honey-coated cake and he cut them each a piece. "I can't thank you enough for your kindness. I hope this small meal will satisfy." He cut himself a slice of cake, too, but left it untouched as he murmured with a sweet smile, "How do you feel, my young friends?" He watched Nnylf and Azile gobble the sweet. The past seasons had been hungry ones for Eunan's little family.

With new energy, Nnylf and Azile now chewed, swallowed, and licked their lips. After eating every crumb on their plates, they smiled.

"This was a feast, Lustre. Very kind of you. Even so," Nnylf said, turning to his sister, "Azile, come. Father expects us home tonight." As Nnylf expressed his thanks, he rose from the table, but he was surprised to feel his legs as heavy as logs. His head nodded and he struggled to find his way to the door. Azile, too, felt her eyes itching with sleepiness, and she stretched with a big yawn.

"I mustn't put you on the road to home now. You are so tired," said the man. "Why don't you sit for a moment here? Rest a little."

Nnylf and Azile nodded slowly and let him lead them to a long bench, where they sat for a moment on billowy, soft cushions. Soon, Azile slumped to one side, yawned, and curled into a cushion. Nnylf closed his eyes and began to snore loudly.

The man who called himself Lustre walked to the hearth and crouched while humming a low and dark tune. An acrid green mist enveloped him until the humming ended and the mist fell away. A hork stood in the young man's place. He knocked on a silver disk attached to a wall lining the hearth. A knob popped out. He pulled it with a sharp tug and stepped back. A grinding noise tore the air as a door to one side of the hearth opened and a hunched, shadowy creature emerged.

"Kralbong, happy to be in the light again?"

The creature grunted and glared at him.

"I have a job for you."

The hork pointed to the visitors. His brutish helper glowered at them while the hork made certain of Azile's steady breathing and Nnylf's soft snores. With little effort, the goblin and his master lifted them onto their shoulders and carried them up a winding stairway on one side of the great hall. Their heavy footsteps faded as they climbed the tower.

Chapter 8

ATTY AND HIS MEN WERE NO closer to the smoke rising in the distance than they had been after climbing over the wall. They gathered in a clearing hedged by thorny bushes and brambles and looked back into the forest, gloomy now in the fading light of evening.

Kolvak, the plump little cook, wiped sweat from his brow with the red rag he always carried in his back pocket. "Atty, the men are tired and hungry."

The other men grunted and nodded.

"Shall we stop and rest for a bit, maybe eat a little something?"

Atty shrugged and slipped the strap of his haversack off his shoulder, letting it fall with a thud to the ground. He pulled out a homespun woolen shirt with a high collar and sleeves patched in moss green at the elbows. Yanking it over his head and down to his hips, he glowered around the circle of eight men.

"Hungry? You say you're hungry? And what about the paunch on that Formorian? Maybe it has a taste for a stew of Kolvak?"

Kolvak shifted his feet and backed up to stand next to Cahalson. "I was just thinking—"

"Don't . . . think," Atty growled. "That's my job." He sat on the end of a fallen log near the forest path and began to massage his forehead. "Men, see what you can find to eat nearby. I still have some bread from this morning. Does anyone else have something to share?"

A few of the men dug into their own sacks. They handed Kolvak some spotted apples, a handful of dried peas, and an onion. Others searched in the brush for nuts and berries or, hoping to flush out a rabbit or squirrel, they cut through brambles. Atty ordered Kolvak to start a fire. After piling up branches and slim logs, the cook coaxed a flame from embers he kept alive in a small metal case.

Atty turned to Cahalson. "We'll take turns watching while the other men eat and rest. With the first light, we'll start the hunt again, right?"

Cahalson frowned. "I don't see that we're getting anywhere. These woods are magical, I tell you. We keep walking, and we are nowhere nearer that smoke."

Atty jumped up. "What are we—sniveling sheep or Moktawls, the slayers of dragons? Cahal, your father, warned us about our fate if we do not destroy the Formorian." He slumped back to his seat and held his head in his hands. "We must kill it or we are lost."

Cahalson pushed his face closer to Atty's. "You may wear a tunic of dragon hide, but most of us don't. We're only chasers of dragons, not slayers. We haven't seen one since your arrow wounded that silver-blue dragon—which, I remind you, no one has ever found."

"You shame your father when you talk like that. We Moktawls *will* slay the creature—together." He heaved a sigh and patted the younger man's shoulder. "Let us end our quarrel, neighbor. We need to rest. Come sit."

Cahalson stepped back and muttered, "I respect my father, but, like Eunan, I know that a meager harvest lies in our fields now. If we abandon them, we'll be hungry this winter." He sat on the other end of the log and tore at a chunk of cold, dried sausage he'd kept for himself.

A faint smile eased Atty's frown when he saw his men return with pigeons, acorns, cattail heads, and fiddleneck ferns. Kolvak, humming a charming melody, had filled his stewpot over the fire with water and was cutting up the birds. He dropped pieces into the bubbling broth.

As the men waited for their supper to cook, Cahalson's brother, Kirrill, muttered, "My wife, Sherca, also knows how to cook us a bird for supper, if I can catch one, but it takes her hours to clean and cook it up." He lifted his cap and scratched his head. "Kolvak has his water boiling in a few blinks, his pigeons plucked and cut up, a tasty smell in the air . . ."

No one else commented. Atty had no appetite and Cahalson stared into the fire, lost in his thoughts.

A shrill cry echoed in the woods. The startled cook dropped his wooden paddle. The other men jumped up to search the forest shadows. Atty called in a hoarse whisper, "Kolvak—cover the stew pot, wrap that branch with your rag, and make a torch for us. Kirrill, Manch, and you others—ready your daggers and follow me. Cahalson—stay here by the fire with Kolvak and the other men."

Kolvak stamped a foot and pouted. "Don't leave us! Whatever that was will come here and eat both us and our nice supper." But, seeing Atty's angry face, he turned away and busied himself. Atty did not see him hide his red rag in a pocket. Kolvak cut a stout branch from a shrub and wrapped a kerchief around one end. He smeared it with some seed oil he'd saved and stuck it in the fire.

Taking the smoldering torch and holding it in front of him, Atty said, "We'll go this way, men. It came from there."

As Atty and his four men left the clearing, he heard Cahalson's laughter. He looked back to see those remaining by the campfire throw down their weapons and gather around Kolvak. Cahalson said, "Let's eat. Who knows when they'll be back." Atty scowled as the young man held out his bowl for a portion of stew, but he shrugged his shoulders and led his men deeper into the woods.

As the little band searched through trees and shrubs, Atty—with Kirrill close behind him—listened for the strange call. Again and again, that sad cry filled the air. It sounded close at times, faint and far off at others. The men abandoned the path as the sound drew them forward. They peered into the gloom and gripped the hilts of their durks.

"Remember this, men," Atty said in a low voice. "Stay low and keep quiet as a feather dropping from a hen. This time we'll surprise the beast." He lowered the torch and stamped out the flame, but he stepped back when Kirrill pulled at his sleeve and jutted his chin toward a far tangle of bushes.

Atty cupped his ear with his hand. A new noise, like a donkey braying, sounded as though it came from somewhere near the smoke. Kirrill pointed that way. Atty nodded and urged his men to follow the braying.

Chapter 9

ALTHOUGH SMALL STONES AND LOOSENED tree roots scraped her cheek and fell to the valley below, Seerlana slowly pulled herself up to the edge of the jagged rock above her. One hand reached for the tree root knot hanging over the side, and she raised a foot to push herself onto the dead wood of a broken stump. Grateful for the cloud that covered the mountaintop and hid her, she crept on knees and elbows toward the cave and slid down to rest against a heap of stones on one side of its entrance. She caught her breath and listened. Within the cave, she heard angry, squeaking chatter. In a few moments, it stopped.

All was quiet. After what felt like half the night, Seerlana thought she heard little footsteps shuffling toward her and the cave entrance. She held her breath.

A small shadow leaned out of the cave. "Now you'll be telling us you've lost your way, Seerlana, and will appreciate a little bite to eat and a place to sleep for the night?"

Seerlana released her breath in one slow hiss. "Gormley, you are indeed here! I thank the Ways of the World for this."

"Old Aurykk will be none too pleased to see that you have left your children behind."

"The journey would have been hard on them. The trouble I had finding you nearly destroyed me."

"But why have you come here now?"

Seerlana paused, then leaned toward the dark shape and whispered, "I have the packet." She extended her arm toward the weasel's voice. In her sun-browned hand was a small square object, wrapped in red rags and tied with silver twine. "The Moktawls are hunting again. I feared for Anadraka and thought I should bring it to you."

Gormley did not answer. Her silhouette vanished. Seerlana sat shivering in the thickening mist. She could barely see the other mountain peaks; the valley below disappeared in the fog.

When the weasel returned, she jumped into Seerlana's lap and licked her cheek. "Here, eat these mushrooms and berries. There is a cascade of fresh water on the other side of the ledge. You should rest now. The others will be ready to welcome you in the morning, and this will keep you warm until then." With her teeth, Gormley dragged a reed mat into Seerlana's arms and dashed into the cave.

As she chewed on handfuls of food, Seerlana looked out into swirls of mist and thought about Eunan and their children. *How could the wife of a Moktawl even think of meeting with the dragons*, he had shouted at her. *A foolish idea; all the dragons were long gone*, he'd said. But Seerlana knew that only dragons could help them fight the evil within the forest, the wickedness that threatened to force them all—farmers and Moktawls alike—into servitude.

Years before, Seerlana had met with Anadraka on the open and windy plain bordering their hilltop village, Fossarelick. Hidden from sight by the dark of a moonless night, Seerlana and the dragon dam spoke with soft, swift sounds. After escaping a battle with ghostly Ancestors, Anadraka had been on her way to her clan's sunsetside refuge, but first she had a favor to ask of Seerlana. She'd passed her a small packet. "No one but you and the children must know about this. If I perish, you will bring it to Aurykk in the Cave of Refuge. He will tell you the next step to take."

"The children and I will keep it safe. Thank you for trusting me—"

At that moment, a fiery arrow had struck the ground several lengths behind Seerlana. Anadraka had leaped into the sky, and Seerlana crouched low as she ran back to the village. She heard men shouting, and she turned to see her husband and other Moktawls using their crossbows to shoot at Anadraka. Hiding in the shrubbery near a pathway up the hill, she shuddered at the shrill cry of a wounded dragon.

Anadraka had tried to stay in the air, but her burning wing forced her down as she drifted over the Sunriseside Forest. The men ran after her and their voices faded in the distance. Seerlana clutched the packet to her chest as she ran up the hill to the family cottage.

Nnylf and little Azile should have been asleep, but the dragon's cries of distress had brought them both to the cottage door. Seerlana hugged each one, took them by the hand, and led them to the firewood stack. "I have met with Anadraka and she gave me this packet. We must hide it, especially from your father. The survival of our dragons depends on it." She'd pulled a few large, loose stones from the base of the wall behind the logs and told them, "This will be its hiding place. Never touch it, unless I am gone. It is our secret."

A few warm tears dripped into Seerlana's ears now as she lay back, wrapped in the mat on the rough ground outside the cave. *The arrow must have killed Anadraka. I had to come here . . . but how will my family ever forgive me for leaving them?*

Her eyes grew heavy, her breathing slowed, and she fell asleep.

Chapter 10

AINDLE, THE AIGLONAX, COULD borrow different bodies whenever he needed them—sometimes like Lustre's, but more often a stomping, bullying hork's. He had his own style: tall and thin, sheathed in rough, pale blue-green skin, with sepia and purple thatches of hair sprouting from his bumpy scalp. He liked his hork body. Its humanish face, arms, and legs made him more agile, but he was a basilisk at heart, and he had a beastly appetite.

After locking the sleeping Nnylf and Azile in a tower room, Aindle raced down the spiral staircase. His goblin servant Kralbong trotted behind him and reached for scraps of cake left on the table. Aindle pushed him back into the doorway. "Don't touch that!" he snarled. "I've no use for a snoring sluggard. It's magicked with sleeping powder, you fool."

Kralbong slunk away and crouched by the fireplace, cheerless now except for a few glowing logs. He wiped his green lips and four long, bladelike teeth with the back of his paw and glared at his master. Ignoring Kralbong's grimaces, Aindle buttered the four round loaves of bread remaining on the table. He tossed one to Kralbong, who caught it with one claw. Stuffing chunks of bread into his big purple mouth, Aindle grabbed the cheese, nuts, and berries scattered on the tabletop and gulped them, too. Patting his long belly, he stood, belched, and strode out into the garden.

PART I: UNEXPECTED DETOURS   51

"Kralbong! Come out here. I thought I told you to take care of that donkey."

Hearing his shouts, the little donkey looked up from the coneflowers she was munching. As Kralbong stepped out the door, she brayed and ran off.

"Go get her, you clod, and cut her up for my supper. Bring the pieces to Four-Arms and tell her to make me a good roasted donkey heart with apples and honey sauce. Then stewed donkey shoulder, and stuffed donkey stomach, and . . . clod, what's keeping you? Move!"

Kralbong lowered his two long arms to the ground and loped after the fleeing donkey.

Aindle picked up the sheaves of barley he had bought from his young visitors and smashed them between his powerful fists. Soon barley seeds streamed from his hands into a large-mouthed clay jar at his feet. He picked up the filled jar and carried it into a low wooden hut behind a clump of trees at the edge of the garden, where he barked at a short and sturdy woman with four arms standing by a long worktable. He pushed the jar into two of her hands and said, "Grind these seeds into flour. I want at least forty loaves of bread by suppertime."

Aindle waited for her answer, but the little woman said nothing. She carried the jar to a large, flat block of stone and poured some grain onto its surface. She picked up another broad stone, laid it over the grain, and started to grind the barley between them. Aindle regarded her for a few minutes and, feeling satisfied, he returned to his house.

The woman raised her head to watch him leave, but he took no notice.

Kralbong bounded through rows of fruit trees as he pursued the escaping donkey. On the way, he plucked an apple and, opening his wide mouth, stabbed it with one of his fangs. Snatching at another piece of ripe fruit, he tossed it down his throat, while the first apple hung from his fang. As he bent close to the ground to follow the donkey's hoof prints, he heard footsteps nearby. The apple slipped off his fang and rolled away from his feet. Without a sound, Kralbong lay flat in the dirt and eyed the rolling apple. He swiveled one ear in the direction of the braying.

He could hear someone calling, "Bless the Ways of the World, it's my donkey, the one I lent to Eunan. Come here, you rascally beast." He saw a brawny man scuffling through the rotting leaves. Other men were with him.

The goblin scratched his ear and fingered his still-aching scar. The hork had bitten him there to make him, once a Lobli sprite, his slave. He raised his head and saw five men, dressed in dark, stained clothing, circling the donkey. One gray-haired man dived for her rope lead, but she dashed away. Her panicked brays faded into the shrubbery beyond. The men ran after her, shouting and waving their hats. The one in a shirt with patched sleeves stayed behind. He kicked at the dirt and mud and tore at his hair.

Kralbong's apple rolled by his boot and stopped in front of him. The man peered into the dense bushes and muttered, "An apple? And what in the Ways of the World smells so rotten?"

Kralbong crouched and with his claws flicked at clumps of soil and twigs on his belly. Muttering, "Clod," he came up behind the man.

Ready to swipe at the man's throat, an ear-piercing cry surprised him, and he ducked. Too late. The goat-headed giant jumped on both of them.

Kralbong screamed as the giant pushed the man aside and tore at him with his huge fingers and jagged, yellow nails. Kralbong lunged with his sharp fangs but staggered backwards as the giant's horns dealt a powerful blow to his chest. He narrowed his yellow eyes and prepared to dash back when in one stride the giant landed on Kralbong's back. The goblin fell on his face. Breathless, one thought filled his head: escape. He rolled on the ground and shook off the giant. Aching all over his body, Kralbong staggered to the lodge.

The man was Atty. He felt a strong jerk on his arm and saw the ground fall away below him. The giant had leaped up into the trees and

PART I: UNEXPECTED DETOURS 53

was carrying him away. Atty wanted to scream, but he could only whisper "help" and squeeze his eyes shut.

When he managed to open them again, he was relieved to see his men struggling with the donkey in a clearing just ahead of them. Before he could call attention to himself, he realized he was falling away from the giant—and directly into a large prickly hedge. This time, he screamed loudly as clusters of thorns pierced his breeches and scraped at his arms and neck. When he looked up, the Formorian giant had disappeared again.

Kirrill left his donkey in the care of the other men and ran to pull Atty from the hedge. But when he was free, instead of thanking him, Atty's face turned purple as he shouted, "I *told* you, I *begged* you to be quiet. All it took was one donkey and you were yelling and running like a bunch of boys. No wonder the Formorian found me first—but thanks to you, we've lost him again." Atty sat in the grass and grimaced each time he pulled out another thorn.

Kirrill said, "Odd. My donkey shouldn't be here. Eunan's boy, Nnylf, loaded her with grain for the market in Nosidam. Why or how did she get over that wall?"

"Ouf! Ouch!" Atty yanked out the last few thorns. "Nnylf? Why would he be here? Haven't we told our children to stay out of the forest? Full of hidden dangers."

"Hidden? You mean, besides the giant?"

"Yes, Kirrill." Atty glared at his fellow Moktawl, whose shoulders shivered under the thin weave of his woolen tunic. "When you ran after that donkey, another creature—a goblin, I'm sure of it—attacked me. I hardly had time to look, but dark, dirty hair covered its body and long fangs were sticking out of the top and bottom of its mouth. If the giant hadn't snatched me . . ." He stopped, then looked around at his men. "The giant did me no harm, not one scratch," he said in a daze.

"Looks like he rescued you, instead." Manch grinned and poked a straw in the gap between his front teeth.

"That he did," mumbled Atty as he stared into the treetops.

Kirrill urged him to call the Moktawls together. "If the donkey is here, then so is Nnylf. We can't leave Eunan's boy to the mercy of these creatures. We must find him."

The leader looked again at his men. "I suppose you're right." He rubbed the back of his neck and looked into the treetops again.

"Back to the camp, then?"

Atty nodded, "Yes, but Kirrill, do something about that donkey. Let's go!"

Three of the men tied the donkey's legs together, then carried her between them on a long branch as they hurried back to their campsite to reunite with Cahalson and the others.

When they returned to the clearing, Atty saw Cahalson, Kolvak, and the others sleeping soundly around the campfire. Manch, a big, muscular Moktawl, spat out his straw and strode over to the soup kettle. He banged furiously on it with the hilt of his durk. His dozing comrades sat up quickly, jumped to their feet, and flashed their own durks in all directions. Recognizing Manch, they lowered their weapons and their heads.

"So this is how you guard our camp?" shouted Atty. "While you were asleep, we five fought off a creature or two who might have enjoyed biting a chunk out of you, nice and peaceful as you were, if they had come upon you."

"Creatures?" a chorus of thin voices rose from the hunters' throats.

Atty said, "Cahalson, you'd better listen to this: a stinking, fanged goblin was lurking in the orchard and nearly killed me. The Formorian was hiding there, too. That goblin was about to have me for supper, I'm thinking, but the goat-headed giant fought him off and rescued me."

Another Moktawl scratched his gray beard and added, "It's true, men. We all saw it. The giant hurt not a hair on Atty's head, and I'd say that the goblin and the Formorian are not the best of friends."

"Right! The wall we jumped keeps those creatures in and the rest of the world away from this nasty place," said Atty. "Why is that goblin here?

Cahal wanted us to hunt the Formorian, but I think we have something much worse to worry about."

Cahalson looked around the circle at Manch, Kirrill, Atty, and the others. Grimacing, he shook his head and slapped his hand blade, a short but sharp durk, against his palm. In one swift motion, he flipped his blade and it hit the dirt next to Atty's boot.

"I've got good aim, right, Atty? So I should have been there to help you," Cahalson smiled. "Sorry for doubting you." He began to stuff his gear into his haversack.

Chapter 11

Kralbong rubbed the bruises on his belly and lurched up the winding staircase. Aindle heard him groaning with each step as he lugged a small, marble table. At the door of the tower chamber, Kralbong set it on the gritty stone floor and waited for his master. Panting, Aindle joined him and coughed out a spell.

A heavy bar slid back from the door and into the wall. Kralbong pushed the door open with his leg. Entering the round and gloomy room, he placed the table near its one barred window, removed the cloth covering bowls of watery soup, and licked his fangs. The hork bent over Azile, who was deep in sleep. He paused for some moments, then lightly stuck a pin into her toe. After a few moments, he did the same to Nnylf, while Azile watched him with heavy eyes.

"Ouch!" shouted Nnylf as he sprang up from the bed. His eyes widened when he saw the two beasts and he shrank back into his covers. Azile pulled her blanket over her head and started to sob.

Aindle leaned forward and thrust his gaunt blue face close to Nnylf's nose. "You weren't afraid of me when you ate at my table, young man. Delicious cake, wasn't it? Sorry that it made you so sleepy." He smirked. "And you," he said, pointing a long, bony finger at Azile, "you were happy to gobble my butter, cheese, and sweet bread that you piled on your plate."

Nnylf raised his hand to cover his nose. Kralbong had edged closer

PART I: UNEXPECTED DETOURS 57

to the two youngsters. Azile lowered the cover and, between hiccups, whispered, "*Your* food? Lustre fed us. Who are you?"

The hork's shoulders shook as he laughed and pushed Kralbong back. "Stay away, clod. You know humans can't stand a goblin's smell." He watched them for a few moments, then straightened to his full height and shouted, "I *am* Lustre. Today you see me in my hork body. Lovely, aren't I?" He twirled around and grinned. "I have waited a very long time to find you and bring you here."

He noticed Nnylf and Azile exchange a quick look. "You can't be Lustre." The young man paused and looked at Azile with a furrowed brow. "He wouldn't have brought us here just to trap us like this."

Aindle cackled, then frowned at Nnylf. "You have something I need."

"What? We're poor. No one will pay a ransom for us. We sold our barley fairly to that young man, who was even kind to our donkey. The donkey—what happened to her? She belongs to our neighbor, Kirrill!"

Kralbong crept forward again, licking his fangs. Aindle raised a club in the air to strike him. Azile, standing with her hands on her hips, shouted, "We can't help you. Let us go. Give us the donkey and our cart."

Aindle lowered the club. Holding out his weapon, he pointed to the dragon heads that decorated its length. Poking it into Azile's stomach, he said, "I make the rules here, and you are staying put." He pushed his club harder. "Tell me where the dragons have hidden their treasure or you will be my supper tomorrow and Kralbong here will eat my leftovers."

Nnylf gulped and lowered his eyes, but Azile stuck out her lower lip and said, "What treasure? Why do you think we know anything about dragons? Everyone says that the Moktawls have killed them all."

"Liar!" The remains of bread curdled in Aindle's stomach. "You know very well that some still live. You two escaped my attack on your Orferan friends. Their treasure holds the key to dragon power!" He pushed her back and turned to look again at Nnylf.

A crooked smile spread over his long, thin face again when Nnylf gasped. "*Your* attack?"

Aindle smirked again. "Yes, and you were there."

With a wave of his hairy blue hand, he ordered Kralbong to take Nnylf and collect bread from the hut. The goblin dragged Nnylf, screaming and twisting in his grasp, all the way down the staircase.

Azile rushed toward the door, but Aindle shoved her back and shouted, "I told you to stay here. Sit!"

Azile stumbled to a low stool near the cot. She looked up at the hork, her lips pressed together in a scowl. "I don't know about any treasure. We're from a family of farmers and nothing more. You would know that, since you've been spying on us. I heard you crying in the forest as we passed."

Aindle said, "Me? I never cry. That was the goat-faced giant." At those words, they heard Kralbong moan at the base of the stairs.

"How can you say you are Lustre? You're nothing like him."

Aindle puffed out his chest and paced around the small tower room. "Before you met me in the marketplace, I took on the body and garb of a dragonrider, like the one who lived here long ago. I have to say, I never liked his looks—so weak and fussy—but sometimes the disguise is useful." He twisted a tuft of hair. "I'm a good enchanter, too. That cake you ate contained a sleep spice I cooked up just for you and your brother." When he reached the door, he said, "I'll be back soon and you'll tell me everything—or you'll wish you had."

With a snort, he walked out and slammed the door shut. Azile heard him slide the bar in place to lock it.

Ignoring the soup, Azile took a quick look around the room. No hidden doors or other openings offered an escape to the outside. She pressed up against the window. Standing on her toes to look beyond the tower, Azile noticed tiny bits of rock and dust at the base of one bar. She wiggled it, but the iron rod would not loosen.

As she reached toward the next bar, she again heard the cry that had startled her on their journey to Nosidam. This time it was soft and very close, like a goat's bleat. She jumped back and flinched as a huge hand grasped the stone windowsill. It wrapped around both bars and ripped them out. The window collapsed and a man-sized hole opened to reveal a giant with a goat's head. He quickly moved his finger in front of his mouth and nose. "Shhh," he whistled, and patted the edge of the opening. His waving hand invited her to come closer.

Caught between scary creatures, Azile felt her heart thumping against her chest. As she warily drew closer, the giant reached through the hole, picked her up gently, and pulled her out of the tower, placing her on his back. Azile gripped the wool on his neck with one hand and clung to his shirt with the other as he climbed down the side of the tower, then leaped up and swung from tree to tree, away from the lodge.

Once the shadows of the woods hid them, the giant lifted Azile from his back and settled her on a thick branch, while he leaned back and watched her.

Now what? she thought. *Nnylf is with that filthy goblin. If the hork finds me missing, who knows what they will do?* Tears filled her eyes.

She felt a gentle pat on her knee. Looking up at the giant, she saw him point to the lodge in the distance. He pointed to himself, then to the lodge, and to himself again.

"You're going back to the lodge?"

Bleating softly, the giant shook his head. He pointed again toward the lodge and reached his arms out as if he were hugging it. He looked at her again as he shook his fist in the direction of the lodge.

"You're going to crush the lodge?"

The Formorian lowered his eyes and slowly shook his head. Looking up again, he pointed in the direction of the lodge. His finger then pointed to his heart, which he patted with his huge palm.

"Are you saying that the lodge is your home?"

The giant bleated loudly and slapped the branch, and Azile nearly fell off. Clapping his hands, he scrambled down the trunk of the tree and signaled for her to jump into his arms.

Trusting that the giant meant her no harm, Azile breathed in deeply and leaped from the branch. After he caught her with ease and set her on the ground, he turned and went deeper into the woods, and Azile ran close behind him as they worked their way through the forest tangle.

Nnylf was standing next to a colossal basket. As he watched the goblin and a four-armed woman heft loaves of bread into it, he heard the hork puffing on his way to the cook's hut.

Aindle stomped through the doorway and bellowed, "Faster, faster! My stomach is growling and I want my bread *now!*" He caught Nnylf staring at the woman's arms and laughed. "Our fine cook here was once a lady with two arms who worked this lodge and its farm with her husband. My spell transformed her into a littler woman with four arms, so she could make my meals with more power and speed but take up less room."

"We never knew anyone lived in the forest!" exclaimed Nnylf. He turned to stare at the cook, who wiped her four hands nervously on her flour-dusted apron, while Kralbong growled at him. Nnylf shuddered as Aindle laughed, "All this is *my* home now!"

He pointed a blue-veined finger at his chest. "I tell you, I am that Lustre you liked so much. When I took this place from her"—he pointed to the little cook—"I changed her husband into a bleating giant. Now he spends all his time frightening the villagers and farmers in the Veiled Valley. They call him the Formorian and they say he's caused all their troubles." Aindle roared in laughter again. Then, glowering at Kralbong, he shouted, "You clod, keep working. I'll be at the table before the sun sets and I'll want my supper—including roasted donkey parts—when I get there." He stomped out of the hut and back to the lodge.

Nnylf ran to the door to follow Aindle, but Kralbong seized his arm and pulled him back. The old woman placed four more loaves in the basket, but she froze as a long, sad cry, like the sound of a wounded goat, pierced the air. Kralbong shrank against the wall, moaned, then slunk out the door. The woman followed him. After a few moments, she returned.

"Kralbong has gone to the orchard," she squeaked to Nnylf. "Follow me. Come this way. No time to waste." She moved a few planks in the floor, and Nnylf saw that below the opening was a ladder. "Go, go," she urged him, and he hurried into the hole.

The woman replaced the planks and darkness surrounded Nnylf. His feet slipped on the damp rungs. When he felt the last rung, he jumped off the ladder and landed in a puddle of muck. He felt foul water soak through his leggings. As he tapped along the dank wall in the dark, he steadied his legs and splashed toward a dim light in the distance. Over the sound of trickling water, he thought he heard loud thumps, like heavy hoof beats. The faint light ahead blinked out.

Nnylf gulped. He could still catch the comforting smell of freshly baked bread that barely masked the stinking water flowing around his ankles. He pressed up against the wall but pulled away from it when he felt slime smear and soak his sleeve. He crept forward, but, stumbling over a rock, he fell to the floor. Drenched from head to toe, he sat up and listened again. Softer than his uneven breath was the sound of water falling from the roof of the tunnel. The thumps had faded away.

Nnylf knew he could not stay there, wet and cold as he was. The woman had offered him a way to free himself from Kralbong, to find help for Azile. Four-Arms must have known this tunnel led away from the lodge, but to what? Nnylf moved on, following the wall. He grimaced as rough stones caught threads of his tunic. His hands ached from cuts and bruises.

As his fear and worry grew, his eyes, now used to the gloom, noticed the distant light again. He struggled toward it.

Chapter 12

ATTY LED HIS MEN OUT OF the clearing, but not by the enchanted paths that had misled them before. Following the line of trees the giant had used to elude them, he brought the Moktawls to the edge of an orchard. As they entered a grove of apple trees, the donkey bolted away from Kirrill and began bucking over a mound of earth. Kirrill ran after her.

Atty called out, "What are you doing now, girl? What a bother she is." Kirrill pulled her away from the mound.

Atty looked carefully at the spot she had attacked. "Well, look here. A wooden door in the ground."

The donkey strained against Kirrill to kick it again and he turned to the other men, saying, "I think she wants us to do something with it."

Cahalson snorted, "Not likely. She kicked it."

Kirrill sniffed, "Can't be all bad. I smell food, something like baking bread under it." The donkey stomped her front hooves and shook her head, as if she thought the men were dim-witted.

"Could be that she smells danger, not bread, and it frightens her," said Cahalson. "The goblin might be down there. She's not too fond of him!"

Atty spoke up. "Oh, him. He doesn't scare me. I'm going in. Who wants to follow me?"

PART I: UNEXPECTED DETOURS   63

"Then my durk and I had better go, too," added Cahalson. No one else volunteered. Cahalson added, "But look you, Kolvak, calm that donkey before she wakes up any other wicked beasts that might be prowling around here."

Kirrill and Kolvak gathered some overripe apples scattered at the base of a row of trees. They piled some fruit around the donkey and tethered her with several strong ropes to a thick tree trunk.

"Kolvak, stay here with that poor animal. Eating ought to keep her quiet for a while," said Atty. "And you, too, for that matter."

Kolvak leaned against the tree and crunched into the bright red skin of an apple. Squinting one eye, he looked around at the men and grumbled, "Right, but don't be long—and for the Ways' sake, be careful. This place has too many surprises."

He slid down the trunk and pulled his cap over his eyes, hugged himself tightly, and sighed. Soon, he was snoring. The donkey stretched her neck to chomp at the half-eaten fruit that rolled out of his hand.

"Wake up, you lazy fool," shouted Atty as he nudged the cook's leg with his boot. Kolvak sat up, pulled off his cap, and looked around with bulging eyes. "Oh, back already?" he asked.

Atty shook Kolvak's shoulders with both hands and yanked him up to stand by the donkey. "Don't you budge from this spot until we return, understand? And watch out for creatures! Here, hold this torch."

Kolvak stepped over the fruit scattered around the donkey. He hugged her around the neck. She licked his face and brayed softly. "That's a good girl. It won't be long now, you'll see." Kolvak wiped his face with his red rag. The donkey bit it and tugged, but Kolvak yanked the rag away from her. "Patience, girl," he whispered. He waved the smoking torch back and forth. "I'll keep a sharp lookout, Atty."

"Right you will, Kolvak. Cahalson, give me a hand with this trap door."

Cahalson and Atty raised the heavy door up and away from the opening it hid. Manch and the other Moktawls kicked the dirt away with their boots and stared at the opening with hollow eyes. "We'll not be following you into that place, Atty. That goblin could be waiting for us below."

"*I* am going with you, Atty. It can't be worse than waiting out here," Cahalson said, lowering his foot to the first rung.

Before Cahalson could take another step, a fetid smell descended on them like mist over a waste pit. Atty felt his arms being slashed through his tunic and whirled around to face Kralbong again. His arm burned as he struggled to free himself from the goblin's grip, and panic clouded his vision as the beast tossed him to the ground.

Eunan paced the gravel outside his cottage door. Nnylf and Azile were days late. The road between his village and Nosidam was direct and easy. "They should have been home by now," he grumbled. The barley was only half harvested, and so much more work lay ahead of them. He looked down the road again, but he saw only some village women washing clothes at the spring that ran along the base of the hill.

Eunan raised his arms over his head, then slapped his sides. He growled, "I'll just have to waste more of my time now to find them in Nosidam." Inside the cottage, he packed some coins, a water gourd, and a few cold meat biscuits in a leather pouch. Tucked into his pouch strap, his durk's case pressed against his ribs. After hefting a bale of barley on his shoulder in case he might make a sale, he set off down the path to the road that skirted the forest.

The afternoon sun passed its highest point and tall trees along the roadside cast long shadows. Halfway to Nosidam, Eunan needed a rest. He stopped to lay his load down in the dense leaf litter under a beech tree. His shoulder ached from carrying the bale of grain, and sweat trickled down his neck. Leaning against the tree trunk, he gulped from his water gourd and gazed into the deepening gloom of the forest. To his surprise, Eunan saw an unfamiliar path that led uphill and ended at a long, gated brick wall just visible through the dense forest growth.

Near a large tree root that stretched across the path, Eunan spotted something that sparkled in the dappled light. Replacing the gourd in his

PART I: UNEXPECTED DETOURS 65

pouch, he left his belongings by the tree and picked up the object. He wiped off sand grains and leaf dust, turned it over in his palm, and recognized his daughter's earring—the very one he had given her when she was a tot. As he looked up and down the path, he now saw three different sets of footprints and donkey hoof tracks, too, all leading to a gated wall.

They were here, he thought to himself. *I told them never to enter the forest.*

One track looked like marks made by a man's boots, much bigger than his children's footprints. His thoughts awhirl with worry, Eunan dashed back to the beech trees and hid the bale of barley in some nearby shrubbery. The earring slid easily over his little finger. He tightened his pouch strap and gripped his durk.

Nnylf and Azile are beyond that wall and I'm going to find out why.

Eunan pulled and pushed at the gate, but it would not open. As he looked for a way to scale the wall, he saw trees with thick long limbs nearby. He climbed one until he hung over the wall and looked into a vast, overgrown garden. In the distance, he could see smoke rising out of a chimney.

With an eye to the ground thick with old, intertwining tree roots, Eunan wondered what dangers hid in that wooded tangle. He grabbed an overhanging branch and clambered up to crawl from tree to tree toward the column of smoke. Rough bark, thorns, and twigs scratched at his arms and face as he moved closer. Once in a while, he would lie across a broad, thick branch to rest and rub his wounds, then close his eyes for a few moments.

As he hid among the branches of an ancient oak, Eunan caught sight of someone moving through the trees below—a hulking, massive creature. As it passed, it turned to look back. Eunan saw that it was a giant with a goat's face.

It really does exist!

The creature, like him, was moving toward the column of smoke, and someone much smaller was chasing him. A beam of sunlight caught the shorter person's face.

Azile!

She was chasing the brute, and not the other way around. But where was Nnylf? In a daze, Eunan slid to the ground and, at a distance, followed them unsteadily into a grove of fruit trees. Looking back, he realized the sun was reddening the top edge of the brick wall far behind him and night would soon be upon them.

Eunan trailed the giant and Azile into a clearing. In the dim light of early evening, he saw that the giant had carried his daughter to the top of a lofty live oak whose massive branches could support twenty times their number. The beast waved his arms toward the lodge beyond the grove and Azile nodded. She lay along one branch as the giant leaped to the ground. Before long, she was asleep.

Less worried now about his daughter's safety and more curious about the giant, Eunan sought a branch of his own in the live oak. From there, he watched Azile and scanned the gardens and woods around them.

Chapter 13

THE ORFERANS GATHERED AROUND Seerlana. Inside the immense cave, she felt small and definitely not up to the task at hand. Gormley sat behind her and gently rubbed against the back of her leg. "Go on. Tell them about it."

Seerlana turned a quizzical look to the weasel. "You mean about the forest?"

"Of course I mean the forest! And tell them about the Moktawls, while you're at it."

Seerlana's hand shook as she showed them the packet. "Anadraka," she said, "please tell the young ones about this."

Anadraka looked at Draako and Drac'Argo with soft amber eyes, then said, "I shall. This packet holds just a stone covered with writing, but the Veiled Valley's fate depends on it. Before we look at it more closely, we need to know what Seerlana has seen in the valley."

Seerlana cleared her throat and, encouraged by the dragons' kind expressions, she began her tale: "The Veiled Valley needs the help of its dragons again. A nightmare's beast has taken the heart of the forest between our village and the town of Nosidam. Fossarelick animals have wandered into the forest and disappeared. Days later, by the side of the road, we find their heads and little more. On many nights we hear heavy footsteps on our roofs. The day before I started my journey to this cave,

Manch found his oxen lying on their sides, blood oozing from their torn throats. Our farmers have gone to harvest their fields only to discover half the grain flattened or burned."

"Burned, you say?" asked Aurykk.

"Then the Moktawls think we're attacking again," Isabella growled.

Gúrmulo ran around the circle of dragons and hopped onto Isabella's shoulder. "No—they think you all have died. It's the Formorian they fear, a strange creature, a giant with the head of a goat."

Seerlana ran her fingers through hair matted with sweat. She said, "Nothing like that has ever been seen in the Veiled Valley. Cahal, our Elder, has ordered the Moktawls to find and kill it."

"Killing, always killing," muttered Isabella.

Draako looked at his mother. "What about that stone? How could it help?"

Anadraka sighed and licked the silvery scales between Draako's ears. "My dear one, on that stone our Ancestors carved a prophecy. Whoever is able to read it has the Sight. He or she is the Rightful Reader. It might be you."

"The Rightful Reader in our old stories, the one born to lead the Orferans?"

No one answered him, so Draako turned to Seerlana. "What do you know about this prophecy? Why me? How could *I* save the valley? I hardly know it except for you and the boy and girl—"

"Who are my children," said Seerlana. She took a deep breath. "They rescued you from those fierce dragon spirits, some of whom were murdered by Moktawls. The Rightful Reader could help them and so many other Valley folk now."

Draako coughed a puff of smoke as he muttered, "The boy and girl are also children of a Moktawl."

Seerlana's heart fluttered as she remembered the danger Nnylf and Azile faced long ago on that day they visited the cave. "They are your friends. Many years ago, they came with Anadraka and me to the home cave. The spirits of the Ancestors surprised us there and attacked you."

"Mother, why did they attack?" asked 'Argo.

Abulafria answered, "The Malevir maddened them, had them believe that Moktawls would find the Cave of the Ancestors and their treasure. Seerlana, do you think we can banish the beast and give the Ancestors peace—if the Rightful Reader is found?"

Seerlana answered, "Anadraka told me the beast had attacked again and swept away her mate, Lugent, who had been the Rightful Reader. The Ancestors retreated—perhaps far beyond the Coldside—and this Malevir, as you dragons call him, transformed the forest into a terrifying place. If he frightens everyone away, he will be free to find the treasure. Yes, whoever reads this stone will help stop him."

Drac'Argo hopped to his cousin's side, rubbed his young head against Draako's wing, and shouted: "Draako, Draako, try to read it!"

Anadraka and Abulafria let out slow streams of smoke. Aurykk rose slowly, stretched his long neck, and dipped his head to face Anadraka. "The time has come, brave dams. No one has had the Sight since . . . since Lugent was carried off. The people of the valley and the dragons of the mountains need hope. If Draako has the Sight, the Veiled Valley will listen to him."

"Me? But I can't even fly that well!" said the young dragon.

Gormley snorted and squeaked at all of them, "Ridiculous! Draako leaped into the air on the day of the attack with two children riding on his back, and he was much younger then. Of course he would fly better now, if he practiced."

Seerlana knew the young dragon needed some prodding. "Draako, test yourself before you try to read the stone. Now that morning has come, you can practice without being seen by humans if you fly away from the Valley."

Isabella trudged out into the light and peered over the ledge. Aurykk, the Golden, said, "A river valley lies behind this mountain, and if Draako flies there, he will have a large area to practice."

Seerlana joined them at the edge to follow the old dragon's gaze. As she turned to face him, ready to agree, she saw Fossarelick in the distance. Not one person was out and about in her village. Looking beyond it, she saw billows of smoke rising in the middle of the forest. "My friends, we have little time to waste. Look at Fossarelick and the forest."

*   *   *

Erif erif ot em enola
Only to me is given the Fire
Erif erif ot em enola
When men alone cannot prevail,

Draako read the stone to himself. "What does this mean, Mother?" he asked as he looked up into Anadraka's eyes.

'Argo pushed forward and said, "Let me see, let me see." After looking at the stone and turning it around several times, he blurted, "Nothing! I see nothing but scratches here."

Abulafria pulled 'Argo to her side and said, "Cousin Draako, whoever reads this incantation is worthy to lead the Orferans against our enemies. You see the words?"

"Yes."

"How many lines do you see?"

"Four. Two in ancient dragon speech and two in the words we use every day."

Aurykk shuffled to Draako's side and spoke in a hush. "Careful now. Do you truly see those lines?"

Draako nodded and read them aloud.

Soft yellow smoke drifted out of the other dragons' nostrils. They looked at each other and nodded. Aurykk spoke first. "Draako, you have the Sight." He sighed and paused for a few moments. "You might tremble as I tell you this, but the Sight demands that you become an Orferan leader. You must start by flying with Isabella, Abulafria, and Anadraka to the Valley people. You will renew our bond with them. We

PART I: UNEXPECTED DETOURS 71

will face the enemy together."

The great golden dragon trudged back to his nest and turned around a few times before settling into its soft materials. "Old and weary as I am, I will remain here with 'Argo and await your news."

Draako stood up, trembling. "Dear Uncle, you are hardly old—only a few hundred years. And even if I have this . . . this *Sight*, I would not know where to start. I'm not ready to lead anyone."

Gormley spoke up. "Practice flying; memorize the prophecy. Here, take the . . . where is it, where's the stone?" All heads turned to search the cave floor. The stone had vanished. Then Gormley glimpsed Bounder dashing out of the cave, the stone in his jaws. "Catch him! The Ancestors will not answer Draako's call unless he recites the lines from memory."

Draako muttered, "Not so hard. I learned it in one glance."

Gormley and Gúrmulo scurried to the ledge, where they saw Bounder's tail disappear as he leaped over the boulders and headed down the slope. "Bounder, you mindless mutt! Stop!" They waved at the dragons as Gúrmulo said, "Don't worry. We'll find him and the stone," and they hurried after the dog.

"Why would Bounder steal the stone?" asked Isabella. "I thought he was your faithful dog."

Seerlana returned her stare. "He might not be all that he seems." She turned to Draako. "Go now. Keep out of sight. Practice."

"Yes, though I would talk more with you, you must go now," said Anadraka. "You have a better chance of finding that dog than those two little weasels!"

Draako entered the bright light bathing the cave's ledge. He stretched his wings and lifted his head. Toward the Sunriseside, he could see smoke billowing out of the forest. To the Sunsetside, large, dark clouds were approaching the plain. His legs barely supported him as he nervously made his way to the edge of the platform. Beating the air, he felt wonder and surprise as he rose up.

Draako soared past the mountains that hid their refuge. Below him, the two weasels were scrambling down a rocky slope beneath the ledge. He felt a rush of air beating at his eyelids and ruffling his scales as he flew over the peaks. Higher still, he cut through wispy, low clouds and dipped into another broad valley sitting within a ring of high plateaus covered in spiny gorse bushes, their yellow flowers opening in the morning dew. A braided river dotted with islands ran along the valley's lowest point.

He dipped toward the largest island, barren and rock-strewn, except for a crooked tree with branches that extended over the swiftly moving current. The weasels were there and urging an otter to dive under an overhanging branch that dragged in the river's flow. Several times the sleek swimmer tried to pull another furry animal out of the water and onto the island's shore.

As Draako folded his wings to alight on the island, his claws scraped the pebbles and stones underfoot. Each step he took stung, and he could see that his rough landing had torn a few scales from his heels. *Not well done this time. Better work on it.*

When Draako looked for the otter again, he saw instead a soggy, furry thing by the tree's twisted trunk. The otter slid into the current.

Gúrmulo ran to Draako. His damp fur dripped, and when he reached the dragon, he was panting. "He's nearly drowned and won't let go of the stone. Quick! Help me." The weasel ran back to his sister, who was standing on her hind legs near the rescued creature. Draako followed him, waddling gingerly on his raw claws and toes.

"Please, Draako, pick him up and dangle him upside down. That way the water will drain out of him," pleaded Gormley.

Draako looked more closely at the motionless figure. "So, it's Bounder!" he snorted, and puffs of smoke circled around the weasels' heads.

"Kerchoo, kerchoo!" they sneezed as they pushed the dog closer to Draako. "Of course he's Bounder! Please, do it. In his state it can't hurt."

Draako gently hoisted Bounder into the air by his hind legs. When his head swung close to Draako's eye, the dog hummed a low, annoyed growl. After Bounder's eyes narrowed into slits and the growl grew louder, Draako lowered him between his claws.

"That stone is mine, Bounder. I don't know why you took it. Return it to me."

As Bounder struggled between Draako's legs, a shrieking wind rocked the tree. Uprooted, it nearly toppled into the current. Frightened, the weasels ran under Draako's legs while the otter watched, shivering, from the opposite riverbank. The water churned and heavy waves rolled over the river bank. Draako could see the otter disappear into nearby shrubs.

Then, between gusts, Draako heard someone howl, "Release my servant!"

He scanned the island, but no one was there. A heavy rain began to fall from the storm clouds rolling in. Turning his head into the wind, Draako saw a flash of red scales and glinting scarlet eyes.

The ear-piercing voice bellowed again, "Release my servant and meet your doom, you pilfering pipsqueak!"

Still gripping Bounder with his claws, Draako trembled and uttered the first line of the incantation: "*Erif erif ot em enola!* Whoever you are, I am no thief!"

"What boldness that you speak the words of the Ancestors!" The wind dropped and in its place stood the outline of a dragon. His misty form towered over the young dragon. Draako could see the hills beyond through his wavering shape. This ghost was twice the size of his mother, who was a big dragon, taller than the great fir trees that grew along the mountainside.

"I am Draako, son of Anadraka and Rightful Reader of the Erif Stone."

The dragon ghost bent closer to him and Draako could feel a deep chill enter his bones. "If you are the Rightful Reader, recite the whole message. Bounder, set free the stone. Wyrmling, read!"

The dog dropped the stone. Draako pressed his forelegs against Bounder's squirming body, in case the spirit meant to trick him. "Who are you to command me?"

"Never mind. Read."

"Very well," Draako said, his curiosity growing.

> *"Erif erif ot em enola*
> *Only to me is given the Fire*
> *Erif erif ot em enola*
> *When men alone cannot prevail,"*

The ghost rose up and, lifting his head to the sky, he roared, "The Rightful Reader is among us again. He has the Sight! He will lead us and we will follow, against the men and all that is theirs!"

Draako coughed.

"What troubles you, Draako son of Anadraka?"

"It's not that simple . . ." Draako paused and stared through the rain and wind at the dragon ghost. The creature's eyes had faded from red to gold and he leaned closer to Draako again. His hazy form glowed as red as autumn maple leaves.

"Of course it is a simple task. The other Ancestors and I have waited so long to avenge the Moktawls' wrongs," snorted the Red.

Draako put his claws over the stone and cast Bounder loose. The dog crawled away and shivered in the cold. "Great changes have come to the Veiled Valley. I see you don't know about them. Moktawls no longer hunt dragons. Our real enemy aims to make slaves of dragons and men. It enchanted you and will destroy all that is good. This I know from Seerlana, friend to dragons and mother of Nnylf and Azile."

"Nnylf and Azile? Moktawl snollygosters who helped traitor dragons escape. I, Ruddykin, was the one who attacked them, but they disappeared near the Trace."

"You? Don't call *them* traitors! If the Ancestors had only allowed, we would have ended the Moktawl attacks. Listen, we have friends in Fossarelick, and the Orferans will help them save the Veiled Valley from

PART I: UNEXPECTED DETOURS

the beast. I do not fear the Moktawls." Draako paused. "Are you the same Ruddykin who was once mate to my aunt Abulafria?"

"Abulafria?"

The spirit faded, and Draako feared that the ghost had left him. He shouted into the rising wind, "Yes, I am nephew to Abulafria. She is well and hatched your son, after . . . after you left us. We call him Drac'Argo."

"Abulafria is alive!" the spirit's voice rose above the storm. "And with our son! Oh the Ways, the wonderful Ways of the World!"

Draako answered, "Yes, the dams Abulafria, Anadraka, and Isabella are ready to fly with me to renew our bond with the Valley's people. We shall find the enemy and the true Protectors of the forest."

As the wind buffeted Draako, he heard, "True Protectors of the forest—but that would be the Ancestors."

"No, I mean all living dragons who want to live in peace and the men and women pledged to their service. You spirits have lost your love for humankind. You care only for pearls and gems. If the Malevir overruns our valley, *he* will seize the cave and *he* will steal the dragons' treasure, not the Moktawls."

"Young dragon, you mistake us. Buried under those pearls and gems is the Mystic Scintilla, which gives us the breath of fire. We shall need all the power of the Ancestors to defend it."

Draako called the dragon spirit to reappear. "Your power alone is not enough. We need the strength of many to fight this evil one." Draako's courage grew stronger as he spoke, and his legs no longer trembled. "You say you will follow my lead against our enemies. Do you intend to honor your word?"

"The essence of a dragon is honor. The Ancestors and I will fly by your side when the time is right and you have gathered your forces."

He looked down at the dog that had covered his head with both forepaws.

"Bounder, the stone is his. Follow him now and help us with all your strength. The time of your courage and power approaches—soon all will change." With those words, the spirit of the red dragon disappeared. The powerful rainstorm lashed at Bounder, the weasels, and Draako.

Draako nuzzled the dog. "Come, you mischief maker. I'll carry you back to the cave. Weasels, I know you can climb up there on your own." With slow steps, Bounder slouched back to Draako. The dragon knelt and licked him gently. "Don't be afraid. I am going to warm you with my fire breath." While sheltering the dog with one outstretched wing, Draako circled him with a gentle flame. "Feel warmer now? Hold onto the stone and don't lose it. Off we go!"

Draako, dangling Bounder in his claws like a limp puppy, leaped into the air with a great push of his wings and left the little island behind. The weasels ran after them.

Chapter 14

Kralbong the Goblin©

N<small>NYLF EDGED ALONG THE DAMP</small> wall and worked his way toward the light. His heart fluttered as he caught the noise of a scuffle outside and the rough shouts of men. The stench that always signaled Kralbong's arrival filled the air as Nnylf climbed the steps out of the tunnel. He peered into the waning light of late afternoon.

In a cloud of dust and flying fruit, Nnylf saw a Moktawl struggling to free himself from Kralbong's fangs, while Kolvak the cook launched apples at the monster. The other Moktawls ran to rescue Atty, but with inhuman strength, Kralbong batted them away.

As Nnylf slowly rose from the hole, he heard Kralbong growl and push a battered Atty into the bushes. The men lunged at the goblin and sliced at him with their durks, but Kralbong swatted them like flies. Then he turned and lunged at Nnylf, who looked around for an escape. Blinded by fear, Nnylf ran out of the grove to the shore of a large pond overgrown with reeds. Kralbong soon came after him and chased Nnylf along the pond's shore. His legs pumping with goblin strength, Kralbong nearly caught up with the boy—but a loud noise startled him and he veered to look at its source.

The goat-headed giant had dashed out of the woods with a crash and jumped between Nnylf and the goblin. With a roar, he rushed at the startled goblin.

Kralbong screamed and turned to flee, but his gaze remained fixed on the giant as he ran. He stumbled into the murky pond water. The goblin's arms thrashed as he tried to push himself out of the pond. Looking down, he howled in horror as steam began to rise around his legs. The giant lumbered toward him and, wild-eyed, Kralbong wallowed deeper into the water. Clumps of black fur on his thighs shriveled and popped as he floundered back.

The Formorian picked up a boulder and raised it over his head as the goblin cried out with every step. The boulder smashed into the Kralbong's chest and knocked him down into the swirling currents. Nnylf, Atty, and the other villagers stared with open mouths as Kralbong's body began to boil.

In less time than it takes to swallow, his arms, legs, and belly swelled up until they exploded. Kralbong's head shot up into the air and sailed over the treetops. Only a cloud of foul vapors drifted above the water to remind the onlookers of the goblin's menace.

The giant turned to glare at all the men, then nodded at Nnylf. Without a sound, he ran into the woods. No one dared follow him.

"No wonder that goblin smelled so bad. He's never taken a bath, I tell you, and you can see why! One foot in the pond and he started to cook, thank the Ways," Kirrill shouted out.

Nnylf's legs buckled under him. Lying back on the grass, he saw Kolvak wrapping a bandage around Atty's wounds. Atty and the other men circled around him. "What in the Ways of the World are you doing here? And where is your sister?"

Nnylf shook his head and replied weakly, "I could say the same of you all. I thought you were hunting the Formorian." He shivered in the chill of a breeze that signaled the approach of evening. Once more, the Formorian's sad bleats filled the air. The men looked around them and Atty held his hand out to Nnylf. "Up you go. We're not so sure what we're hunting anymore. We've learned that Formorian fellow means us no harm."

Nnylf replied, "Something more frightening than the giant or the goblin lurks here. Azile and I learned that we can't always trust our eyes to tell us the whole story."

"What are you talking about?"

Nnylf cleared his throat. "Sometimes what we think we know is not so." He paused and chewed his lower lip, looking back toward the lodge. "I hope Azile is safe. She is trapped in the tower of that lodge over there." He pointed in the direction of Aindle's home. The chimney smoke was much thicker than he remembered it. "We didn't mean to come this far. A hork tricked Azile and me into the lodge. He was going to eat Kirrill's donkey. He looked like a young gentleman when he bought our barley in the marketplace, but when he brought us to the lodge, he cast a spell on us, I guess, and he changed himself into a hork. Then he made us his prisoners."

"Why would he do that—I mean, go out of his way to trap you and Azile? You're from a family of farmers."

"I don't know; he said something about the dragons' treasure—that's it!"

Cahalson strode forward and elbowed Atty aside. Pushing his angry face close to Nnylf's, he said, "That's what comes from your ma being chummy with dragons. I knew it would bring us trouble."

Atty grabbed Cahalson by his broad shoulders and led him away from the boy. "Leave him be, now. That was years ago, and since we killed that dam over the forest, we've never seen another dragon."

"There still might be dragons," mumbled Nnylf. "The young Draako escaped, and his family—"

"What's this? What else do you know about the dragons?" Atty scowled as he shook out his dragon-skin tunic.

"I . . . I'm not sure what happened. As you said, it was so long ago."

"Humph! No more talk about dragons. If we don't want a hork attacking us, what with his goblin missing, we'd better find a place to hide for the night, back in the woods and out of sight."

Cahalson added, "The woods it is, for I'll not go nearer that smoking chimney until daybreak. Who knows how many horks and goblins we'll find there." He shook his head. "Could be those beasties are the ones killing our animals and burning our fields."

"And it's not the Formorian, either," said Kirrill. "He's hunting the same prey we're after: first the goblin, and now maybe that hork." He pulled on the donkey's rope with one brawny hand and Kolvak's collar with the other.

Nnylf and the men picked up their gear and left the orchard. They followed a path that ended in a clearing bordered on the far side by an enormous tree, with massive limbs stretching in every direction.

"This will do," whispered Atty. "Hide in the growth just past the tree—and be quiet now, not a word. We'll take turns on the watch and just use hand signals until dawn. That's when we'll move against whatever rules over this place."

Eunan watched as his neighbors and friends gathered below. The sight of Nnylf nearly shook him from his hiding place, but he gripped the branch tightly and waited until everyone but Cahalson was asleep. Azile was snoring softly on a stout branch high above him. Meanwhile, the cook Kolvak had taken Kirrill's donkey to a grassy hummock behind the clearing, where she grazed and he munched on apples until both of them sank into slumber under a bush.

Eunan found a coin in his sack and threw it at Cahalson. It hit the Moktawl's shoulder and bounced in the gravel around his feet.

"What was that?" Cahalson whispered to himself and looked down. He noticed the coin and picked it up. With a frown at the winged dragon pressed into one side of the coin, he recognized old Veiled Valley money.

"Shhh!" A strong hand covered his mouth. Cahalson jerked up to see

PART I: UNEXPECTED DETOURS 81

Eunan wrapping him with one arm and signaling him to stay quiet with his other hand.

Remembering Atty's orders to remain silent, Cahalson raised both palms to ask Eunan why he was there. Eunan pointed to Nnylf, sleeping under Atty's dragon-skin tunic draped over his curled body. Eunan raised the side of his hand to his brow as if he were searching, then pointed again at Nnylf. Cahalson nodded. Eunan raised his eyes into the dense branches of the live oak and pointed above them. Then, turning to Cahalson, he mouthed his daughter's name; the Moktawl's eyes widened in surprise. Eunan nodded vigorously and pantomimed the shape and gait of the giant while pointing again at Azile, hidden among the leaves.

The two men squatted next to Nnylf's sleeping form, and Eunan explained in barely a whisper all that he had done and seen since he had left the Moktawls.

At dawn, Cahalson and Eunan were still talking quietly as they sat near the base of the tree. Some of the men stirred and rolled over before rising from their hiding places; others straddled tree limbs, rubbed their eyes, and looked around, bewildered.

Atty ran his fingers through his thin hair and wiped his moustache. His eyes widened with surprise and he shouted, "Eunan of Fossarelick, what in the Ways of the World are you doing here? You said you'd have nothing to do with this hunt." He stood up, straightened his leggings and shirt, and joined Cahalson and Eunan by the tree.

Kolvak had started a small fire and was already by their side with mugs of strong, dark herb tea. Sipping the hot brew with care, Eunan repeated the story of his adventures and the search for his children. His son's appearance interrupted the story.

Eunan greeted Nnylf with a hearty hug. Then, frowning, he said, "I should be spitting angry with you, but Cahalson told me about the beast's trickery. If you had listened to me we'd all be safe at home." The other men nodded and suddenly everyone was speaking at once.

Eunan heard Nnylf's voice above the others: "I never meant to harm anyone. That big hork tricked us. He locked Azile in his tower room. Come on, we can save her!"

Before Eunan could tell him that Azile was closer than he thought, a bellowing voice thundered across the clearing and chilled his blood. He quickly pushed his son behind him and faced the hork.

Aindle walked across the clearing. His arms cradled Kralbong's torn and putrid head. "Where is the rest of my dear old goblin? I am indeed one big hork, but you'll never reach Azile." When no one spoke, he narrowed his eyes and said, "Speak up! You are on my land, and you will pay for the loss of my servant." Still terrified, the men scarcely breathed.

"You're scrawny, but fattened up you'll make a good meal for goblins." He looked from one to the next, licked his blue lips, and said, "Except you, Nnylf. I have other plans for you." Eunan fell backwards as Aindle pushed him aside. Helpless to stop him, he watched Nnylf raise his fist and run toward the hork.

Aindle pinched his nose between a thumb and forefinger and blew out a mist of green snot that wrapped around the boy, then rose and enveloped all the Moktawls. Eunan's legs refused to move. Without a word, not even a breath, he felt as though time were standing still. A high-pitched hum filled his ears and he could hardly hear Aindle shout, "That will keep these Moktawls and you quiet while I wring the secret of the treasure out of that girl."

Aindle raised his head and sniffed the air in all directions. "What smells scorched and ashy? I asked the cook for bread, but that's more like burnt wood." He glanced toward the orchards and the garden, then suddenly heaved Kralbong's head into some bushes at the edge of the glade. "My palace! My palace!" he screamed and bolted in the direction of the lodge.

Eunan felt his eyes itching to weep, but not a drop welled up. All his thoughts were on his children: Azile trapped on a tree limb above him and Nnylf trapped in the hork's spell. He couldn't feel his fingers and

PART I: UNEXPECTED DETOURS   83

all the world was a blur. How much time had passed since the hork had left them?

"Ouch!" He felt a pinprick in his finger. He could move his eyes! Blinded by the tears that rushed up to fill them, he could barely see the slender person standing in front of him.

A familiar voice reassured him, "Sorry, Father. A little wound is the only way to break the hork's spells." Azile wiped away his tears with the corner of her sleeve.

"You! How?" Words failed him, but Azile had left him and was circling the Moktawls. First Nnylf, then the others began to move, shaking their heads to clear away a tangle of thoughts left by the spell.

Eunan clasped Azile's hand and led her back to Nnylf. "My children," he said and pulled them both into his arms. "How did you break the hork's spell, Azile?"

"When the hork woke us this morning, I saw him end Nnylf's sleeping spell with a pinprick. After he left you and ran to the lodge, I climbed down from this tree. The hork's poison didn't reach me up there. I knew I needed something sharp to free you, and I noticed something on Father's finger that gleamed in a sunbeam. It was the earring I'd lost in the forest. I slipped it off and used the point to awaken each one of you. Now my ears match again." Azile patted her earlobes.

Atty thumped Eunan on the back and said, "Happy family reunion, neighbor—but now we must think quickly before the hork returns. What worried him enough to leave us here?"

Kirrill was hopping from one foot to the other when a sight in the distance caught his eye. "Look over there! More than chimney smoke worried the hork."

Chapter 15

DRAC'ARGO HOPPED ABOUT AS he flapped his wings, smaller than those of his cousin. "Take me, too. I can fight like Draako." Aurykk chased him from the cave entrance, and with a nibble or two on 'Argo's tail, he nudged the dragonet toward his nest. Isabella and the other dams had taken long drinks from the waterfall near the ledge and were grooming each other's scales with their ridged forked tongues.

Draako had returned Bounder to the cave and invited the weasels to dry his fur and warm him. Gormley draped a large nest rag over Bounder's shivering flank and tapped the dog's dry nose. "You cheating scamp!" she scolded. "You've been spying for the Ancestors. Where's your loyalty to Nnylf and Azile? Aren't dogs supposed to be faithful friends?"

Bounder sneezed and lowered his head. Whimpering, he covered his ears and eyes with his paws.

Gúrmulo nudged away one paw and spoke into Bounder's ear. "Stop whining! The Ancestors might help us now and so must you. Why did the red dragon call you his servant?"

Gormley pushed Gúrmulo aside and leaned closer to the dog's mouth to hear him whisper short barks. Bounder sneezed again loudly. She patted him and said, "He wants to answer us. Treat him more gently."

Gúrmulo laid his head near Bounder's jaws. "He says that Ruddykin forced him to spy on Eunan's family, because of Seerlana and her children."

PART I: UNEXPECTED DETOURS   85

Seerlana stepped out of the shadows by Aurykk's nest. A woven red cap hid her long dark hair. Dressed in dark green leather armor that covered her arms, chest, and upper legs, she had the look of a dragonrider. "Anadraka trusted me with the stone. The ghost dragons must have been watching us when she gave it to me for safekeeping."

Gormley spoke for Bounder. He wanted his listeners to know that after the Moktawls wounded Anadraka, the red dragon appeared to the dog and warned him that he would burn the family's farm if Bounder did not bring the stone to him. The dog had only wanted to keep the family safe.

Bounder looked up at all of them and began to whimper. Gúrmulo added, "The mutt must have run away to find the stone. Seerlana had already left Fossarelick for the Cave of Refuge and Bounder feared the dragon's fire breath." More yips filled their ears. "That's his story. Now the Rightful Reader's time has come."

"Yes," agreed Gormley. "Draako, you flew through that storm. You're ready to lead. The Valley needs you. Time to bring its people together."

"Why now? It won't be easy." Hearing Bounder's whimpering, Draako turned to calm him. "Little friend, don't be afraid. The red dragon will not harm Seerlana's farm or her family."

Bounder closed his eyes and lay quietly on his side, but his flank rose and fell with rapid and labored breathing.

Gúrmulo studied the dog carefully. "Something's wrong with this mutt. Maybe he took a chill after the otter pulled him from the cold water."

Aurykk rose from his bed of rags, leaves, and odds and ends. He lumbered over to the shivering dog, listened carefully to his wheezing, and called both weasels to his side. "You and Gormley must remember that Bounder is no mutt. He's more than he appears to be. Help him now. Run down to the white willows by the stream. Tear off a young live branch and bring it here. Seerlana will use it to brew him some tea for his fever."

Gormley ran out of the cave. Seerlana crouched next to Bounder and stroked his fur. "Poor puppy, poor puppy. We never knew." She wrapped her old brown skirt around him and laid her palm against his nose. "It's quite dry. He must be very sick."

'Argo sidled up to her, stretched his wings, and covered the dog's flank.

The dams were dozing in the sunlight that bathed the ledge. Abulafria's eyelids fluttered as she rose from her nap and gazed inside at the sick dog. "I feel the beast's powers growing while we hide here. We dams should leave Bounder in your good care, Aurykk and—"

Seerlana interrupted, "Here comes Gormley with the willow bark. Help me brew the tea, please." Gormley bit the white willow branch into small pieces that Seerlana steeped in a water-filled pot, heated by Isabella and Anadraka.

A short time later, Seerlana covered her hands with thick rags from Aurykk's nest and poured the brew into a hollowed stone. She carried the makeshift bowl to Bounder. Gormley and Gúrmulo rolled him onto his belly and lifted his head.

The dog opened his drooping eyes as he sniffed the tea's strange, bitter smell. Gormley coaxed him to lap at the tea until he emptied the bowl. Then she took turns with Gúrmulo, licking Bounder's ears. Soothed, the dog sighed and settled into an easier sleep.

The three dams were standing near the cave opening. Anadraka whispered to Draako, "We can't delay. Bounder will heal. Will you fly with us now into the Veiled Valley? Seerlana, you must come with me."

Hearing her name, Seerlana stood up. She tugged at her armor and slipped her durk into a hidden pocket.

The weasels stopped licking Bounder's head. Satisfied that he was cooler and his nose was moist, they stepped forward. "We'll stay with Bounder and Aurykk, and—yes, 'Argo, you, too. Once we know that this puppy is better, we can help in other ways."

Seerlana needed to convince Fossarelick that the dragons would help fight their common enemy. Astride Anadraka's hump, she gripped the

PART I: UNEXPECTED DETOURS 87

dam's frill tightly. Leaning forward, she shouted into her ear, "There's the village, but I don't see anyone moving about."

"Seerlana, your villagers might be hiding somewhere close by. We'll set down far enough from Fossarelick to keep from frightening them. When you reach the village, you might be able to ferret out someone." Seerlana thought she heard Anadraka chuckle.

The other dams and Draako landed near them, watching as Seerlana ran through scorched barley fields to the hilltop village of Fossarelick. She sped up the path to her cottage. The door swung in the wind, and within the single dark room, the hearth was cold. With cautious footsteps, she entered the circle of cottages where her neighbors lived. At Kirrill's door, she knocked a few times, then warily pushed it open. No fire warmed their hearth, and the drab and shadowy cottage nooks were empty. She climbed the ladder to their sleeping loft. When she stepped onto creaking floorboards strewn with dried reeds, she heard a slight cough from a gloomy corner.

Seerlana stood quite still, then cleared her tight throat and called out, "Don't be afraid. I'm Seerlana, your neighbor, here to help you. Come out, I won't hurt you." She tiptoed toward the corner.

The top of a head peered over a pile of coverlets. Kirrill's young son, Kurnan, looked at her with wide eyes and raised his hand to wave weakly. "I'm hungry," was all he could whisper, a little whimper catching in his throat.

"Hungry? Where is your mother? And Alana, your sister?"

"They left me here, told me to hide, said they were going to find some food."

Seerlana reached into the pouch she had slung over her armor, then realized that her strange clothing was scaring the boy. "Kurnan, I really am Seerlana, but perhaps this clothing makes me look odd to you. Here, eat these dried berries and parched grain, and never mind my funny garb."

Kurnan reached toward her and, grabbing the morsels, gulped them down and began to cough again. Seerlana held her drinking gourd to his mouth and urged him to sip some water. Wiping his wet lips with the back of his hand, Kurnan leaned back, exhausted, and said, "We thought the Moktawls had lost their way in the forest—they've been gone so long. Maybe the Formorian attacked them. Eunan was the last to leave us. He went to look for Nnylf and Azile."

"Nnylf and Azile? But why aren't they here with their father?"

"They took a cart full of barley to sell in the Nosidam market. When they didn't come back, Eunan went after them. Now he's missing, too." Kurnan's lower lip quivered and tears spilled over his cheeks. "Something has killed most of our goats and burned our fields."

"Nnylf and Azile, missing as well . . . could they have gone to the Cave of the Ancestors instead of the town?" she mused. Then Seerlana smiled softly at the boy. "Kurnan, are you brave?"

"I try to be."

"Are you as brave as Nnylf and Azile?"

The boy sat up and lifted his chin. "How brave are they?"

Seerlana bent closer to him. "I will tell you a secret you must promise to keep from anyone else, at least until I give you permission to share."

Kurnan's eyes widened and he said, "I am big enough to keep a secret. How brave have Nnylf and Azile been?"

"Listen carefully. They are friends with one of the Veiled Valley's strongest Protectors."

"Do Moktawls live elsewhere in the Valley?"

"Not Moktawls, Kurnan. These Protectors use not only their strength, but also good magic."

"As in wizards?"

"No." Seerlana paused and looked into his eyes for a few moments. "No, not wizards. Dragons."

"Dragons eat people."

"Our dragons don't."

Kurnan ruffled his tousle of dark brown hair and bit his lip. "Nnylf and Azile—they're friends with a dragon?"

Seerlana nodded.

The boy asked, "You say I could be . . . um, brave like them?"

Seerlana dried his tearstained freckles with her sleeve and said, "Yes. They became friends with Draako, a young dragon. Many World-Turns before that, Draako's mother made me her one human friend. Would you like to meet a dragon and learn to be its friend?"

Kurnan's squeezed his eyes shut and shrank back under the coverlets.

"Don't believe the old stories. Moktawls have thrown curses at dragons for a long time, but they have forgotten a dragon's true nature—at least, all but the red ones. Dragons wanted to be our protectors, until we turned against them. My friend Anadraka is kind and gentle. When I met her, she was warming her egg in the great Cave of the Ancestors."

"Where's that? What egg?" Kurnan asked.

"The Cave of the Ancestors lies at the very top of the forested mountain overlooking Nosidam. There, the dragons knew that a great evil was coming to the Veiled Valley. They looked for friends to help fight it. The silver-blue dragon, Draako, who hatched from Anadraka's egg, has grown powerful enough to lead us against this evil. At this very moment, Draako and three dragon dams wait for me beyond the barley fields. They will feed the people of Fossarelick if you and I help them."

"Why would fierce dragons do that?"

"The dragons used to like the people of the Valley, and they want to live in peace again. Moktawls hunt dragons, but their true enemy now hides in the forest."

"The Formorian? Cahal sent men to find and kill him."

"No, something much worse."

"Worse than the giant?" Kurnan threw off the coverlets and stood up shakily. "Show me your dragons, please, and I shall keep your secret. I want to help. I want to see them—but just not too close."

"Do you have something to offer them? Dragons love a gift, especially a shiny one."

Kurnan scratched his head and rubbed his nose. With a quick smile, he said, "I know! Alana has a little metal mirror. It's in that box." He emerged from his hiding place and picked his way through baskets of dried dung, wool clippings, and candle stubs to a chest that came up to his knees. He opened the lid, and from deep inside he pulled out a palm-sized object wrapped in cloth. Turning to Seerlana, he said, "This should please a dragon. My sister likes it. She looks at it all the time, mostly when she talks about Boag's boy, Carliel."

The corners of Seerlana's eyes crinkled as she smiled and asked, "Won't she miss it?"

"I don't think so. She always laughs at Carliel."

Seerlana led Kurnan down the ladder and outside. Moving quickly, they crossed the barley fields.

Part II
Leaving What Is Known

Forestspice the Lobli Sprite©

Chapter 1

A FIRE WAS RAGING THROUGH ALL the hork's outbuildings. The woman with four arms hid in tangled underbrush near the hut and watched the hork. She could hear his screeches as flames spread from the bakehouse and followed the path up to the lodge. Although it moved slowly, the fire would soon burn Aindle's roost unless he could find a way to put it out, but his spells were having no effect on the fire. The woman worried as she saw the hork prepare another spell. With a grimace, he crouched low to the ground, then leaped high into the air. The charm he screamed suspended him over the end of the lodge closest to the burning trees. He chanted a second stream of words and rose in the air, hidden by a wide black cloud that covered the remaining trees and the lodge.

Fat drops of rain fell from the cloud, drifting from one blazing point to another. The cloud thundered, but the woman noticed new fires flare up wherever his raindrops were not falling.

She heard Aindle growl, "That thieving Alluxana; she used her arms—my gift!—to set fires. When I find her, I'll roast her over these burning logs."

He uttered another spell and the cloud became a sickly blue-green mist; he floated to the ground. Grabbing a big shovel from the smoking toolshed, he began to dig a firebreak in the path of oncoming flames.

PART II: LEAVING WHAT IS KNOWN 93

Hidden in billowing smoke, the woman ran for the tunnel opening as soon as the bakehouse fire subsided. She tapped along mold-covered walls until she came to a passage that would lead out into the orchard. The cool damp surface soothed the palms of her hands that stung from the heat of the glowing coals she had pushed away from the tunnel opening.

At the far end of the tunnel, Alluxana saw a ladder standing by an open trapdoor. She reached the top rung and sniffed the air for Kralbong's telltale stink. Nothing. Weaving her way through the grove of fruit trees, she came to the pond she remembered so well and stumbled over a sharp object, one of the goblin's claws. It reeked. Soon, she caught another whiff of his stench and, following her nose, she came to a clearing.

Passing behind its bordering shrubs, Alluxana found the monster's torn and shrunken head underneath trailing branches of a large bush—but before she could look more closely, the nearby sound of hoarse whispers made her pause. After jumping behind another clump of bushes to hide, she raised her head and saw a tall, familiar figure in the center of a group of people.

With hand signals, the goat-headed giant had the attention of the hork's boy captive and a group of men. They looked from the giant to a tall girl, who labored to explain his meaning. She raised her chin and spoke out to them all. "His real name is Fulgid. He and his wife Alluxana are Forest Protectors. Before the hork enchanted them and took the lodge and these lands, they helped protect the dragons' cave from all intruders."

Fulgid looked at them all with sad, yellow eyes swollen with tears. He turned to the girl and pointed to one of her earrings, then extended his finger toward her.

"No, I can't break the spell you're under," explained the girl. "You'll need more powerful magic to do that. Besides, your strength will help us if the hork attacks us again."

A man in a dragon-skin tunic coughed and said, "Your lodge is burning, Fulgid, and the hork ran to save it for himself. He gives no thought to us. Now is the time to attack him."

"Yes, Atty, and I, for one, am ready to repay the beast for all the damage he has done to our valley," said another man, patting his durk.

Atty nodded. When he asked if the giant could lead them to the lodge, Fulgid nodded his goat head and punched the air. The boy and girl warned them that the hork would be more dangerous than ever. The fire had set back his scheme to take the dragons' treasure and he did not expect any new distractions. The beast would use his sorcery if he knew they were near.

Alluxana thought: *Their tunics tell me that they are Moktawls from Fossarelick.*

Atty's boot scraped the ground. With his eyes locked on the giant, he said, "Our new friend knows the hork better than any of us. We have to cross this line. In the past, we defended *only* our village. Starting today, we will defend our valley. We have no choice but to follow Fulgid to the lodge."

The boy and girl exchanged worried glances, but they agreed with Atty. His men wearily stood up to follow the giant, muttering among themselves.

As the group left the clearing, Alluxana crawled from under her hiding place. Darting from tree to tree, she noiselessly trailed them.

Low streamers of smoke greeted them as they approached the orchard. Hiding behind an old, thick tree trunk, the giant squatted and signaled to the girl. On her knees close to his side, she watched his movements and explained his meaning to her companions.

"The giant will cross the orchard to have a closer look. We are to stay hidden here until he finds the hork and returns for us."

Atty and the others nodded and gave Fulgid their thumbs-up. He rose and climbed into the nearest apple tree. "Looks like he'll be using a treetop approach, Kirrill," the boy whispered with a chuckle to a brawny man walking with him.

Kirrill nodded. "He's used to moving that way, Nnylf."

PART II: LEAVING WHAT IS KNOWN   95

"And to surprising his enemies," Atty reminded them all, and finding a tree with a stout low branch, he pulled himself up and sat above the gathering smoke. "Each of you, do the same. Get yourselves off the ground and out of sight."

The girl pulled Nnylf back to the side of Fulgid's tree. One man followed them as they climbed up. He and Nnylf shared the end of a thick branch. The girl climbed to the topmost branches and disappeared into the foliage while the rest of the Moktawls found shelter in other trees.

Alluxana waited until they all were resting quietly in their hiding places, then crept around to another row in the smoke-filled orchard and ran lightly after the giant.

A donkey's bray broke the silence. Alluxana saw a round little man running through the clearing after a donkey. One Moktawl jumped down to the ground, and with a voice nearly strangled by anger, he croaked, "Have you lost your senses, Kolvak? You were supposed to stay back in the woods with her!"

"Eunan, I tied her rope to a tree but she chewed right through it, the rope, that is. She followed Kirrill. Look at me—I'm all sweaty from running after her." Kolvak plopped onto a broad tree root and wiped his head with his faded red rag. The donkey brayed again. Eunan pounced on her, both his hands around her jaws. "Shush, now. Kolvak, look for some fallen apples in the orchard. Bring them here. That should keep her quiet for a while."

"I . . . I . . . go there? But she's not my donkey. Kirrill should be going, not I." He looked over his shoulder and saw that Kirrill was already at his side.

"Get up, you lazy lardnup, and come with me. We will gather so much fruit that my little donkey will fall asleep and not bother a soul." Kirrill and Kolvak ran low toward the orchard and disappeared into its smoky lanes.

Eunan walked the donkey over to a patch of tall grass and urged her to eat. The donkey rolled her lips back from her gums to show her teeth, but catching Eunan's baleful stare, she shook her head and began to graze. Just as she started to look around for something more interesting to eat, Kolvak returned with an armful of apples.

"Where's Kirrill?" Eunan asked.

Kolvak shrugged and said, "He went down one row. I followed another. Lost sight of him. He'll be along soon." The cook dumped fruit in front of the donkey, who knelt on her forelegs to chomp her treat.

"That's not good." Alluxana watched Eunan race over to Atty and tell him about Kirrill's disappearance. Turning back to Kolvak, Eunan said, "You stay here. Not one word, mind you, and keep that donkey quiet or we'll all be in trouble. I'll watch for Kirrill from up in that tree." Eunan returned to the branch he shared with Nnylf. "If Kirrill doesn't return soon, we'll come down from the trees and look for him. What do you think?"

Before the boy and girl could answer, a fierce cry startled them. It came from the lodge.

Chapter 2

SMOKE MIXED WITH GROUND FOG stopped Kirrill in his tracks. Which way did Kolvak go? He bumped into a mist-shrouded apple tree and dropped his durk. Sighing, he bent to pat the ground and his groping fingers sank into a rotten apple. He wiped the muck on his legging. After a few more pats he found his durk and two firm apples, which he stuffed into his pack. *I had better head back*, he thought. *This is useless—can't see a thing.*

Turning one way, then the other, he listened intently. Soon, he heard his donkey's bray. He moved in the direction of that familiar sound while feeling his way from tree to tree, then stopped in a panic as he realized the mist and smoke were thickening. He sensed that something dreadful was close.

As he leaned panting against one of the trees, he noticed his legs quivering. An awful smell hung in the mist, a smell that reminded him of his struggle with Kralbong in this very orchard not so long ago. But, no, the monster was dead. He had seen him explode out there on the pond. Kirrill took a deep breath and pushed away from the tree. Best to go on; the mist would hide him from whatever was out there. With unsteady steps, he continued through the orchard and hoped he was far from the hork.

Aindle sat in the smoldering ruins of his house and considered his spellbound captives in the clearing. He wiped a thin layer of soot from his eyelids and stared at the broad stone fireplace—all that remained of the stately hall. The tower also stood, but its wooden staircase had burned away. He needed to force secrets from that boy and his sister. With the spiral staircase gone, he could not reach Azile. As he leaned against the hearth, a skink scuttled across the floor.

That's it, he thought. *I could climb the walls as a lizard.* Muttering a string of incantations, he stretched out his arms. In the glare of a brief thunderbolt, his limbs shrank inward. An oversized gecko flexed legs once belonging to a hork.

Scrambling up the rough stone wall, Aindle reached the open gap that once was the doorway to the tower's cell. The girl was missing, and a large hole took the space once filled by a barred window.

Aindle wanted to roar his rage, but only a tiny bark came out of his mouth. Blinded by his anger, he missed his footing at the doorframe and slid wildly down the tower wall. The jagged stones tore at his thin lizard skin. When he thumped onto the floor below, he regained his hork form and rubbed his cuts and bruises. Without the girl and boy, he was no closer to the dragon treasure. He had to find them again. He just needed helpers.

Pulling his scraggy body up to its full glowering height, he placed his fingers on the hearth wall, knocked several times on the silver disk with his nose, and stepped back. With a loud crack, a door handle popped forward. He pulled on it and, as it opened, some of the stones fell away, revealing a tunnel reeking with the smell of unwashed goblin.

Before entering the passageway, he stooped to pick up a large slab of charred meat that had slid off a broken spit. He sprinkled it generously with red powder, tucked it into his belt, and crawled through the doorway. Once inside, he stretched out his long, livid arms to reach the walls on either side of him and lumbered through the dark.

This tunnel led to burrows where Aindle had imprisoned goblins like Kralbong, and he groped his way in the dark to find just the right place to trap one. A horde of goblins would be his best weapon against the Moktawls. This time Azile and Nnylf would not escape.

PART II: LEAVING WHAT IS KNOWN

From a wall on one side of the tunnel, a broad ledge jutted above his head. He dropped the meat on the tunnel floor just below the ledge. With an easy leap, he landed on the ledge, crouched, and waited. Soon he heard grunts and the sound of scratching claws. Aindle remembered how easily he had subdued Kralbong when he had enchanted the Loblin sprites. This time, he would force a single goblin to head an army of its kind and defend him when he seized the dragons' treasure.

Aindle peered over the ledge and saw a goblin below who had stopped and dropped to his knees. The creature sank his fangs into the meat and wrapped his green tongue around the edges as he licked crusts of charred flesh. But, after swallowing a few bites without chewing, he sank back against the wall. His eyelids drooped and he slid to the floor. Chunks of meat fell out of his drooling mouth.

As the goblin lay snoring, Aindle thudded to the floor beside him. "I know this one! Bitterbud! How did he escape me?" He savagely bit the goblin's nose, waking the creature, who screamed with pain. When he saw the hork, he shrank back against the wall.

"Bitterbud, you are still my thrall. Do you hear me?"

The goblin groaned and nodded.

"Bring your brothers here. Promise them a feast of human flesh. They'll find it by the live oak in the clearing, a banquet just for them." The goblin licked his dripping fangs. "But . . . if they do not come, I will lock them in this tunnel forever."

The goblin pulled down the tip of his nose and began licking his wound. Aindle glared at him until he stopped. "Go, you stinking clod!" Aindle screamed, and the goblin scurried back into the dark, down to the goblins' burrows.

Lost in a maze of smoldering branches and smoky vapors, Kirrill stumbled from one tree trunk to another, hoping to find his companions again before the hork found him. A sudden cool touch on his arms made him jump. He pulled out his durk.

"Put that away, you fool!" scolded a chirpy voice. "You need my help. Follow me—this way." Kirrill felt two hands grip his arm and pull him down an open row between the trees until they stood just outside the grove. The smoky mist was lifting, and in the clearing he could just make out a few branches of the great live oak.

When he looked again at his companion, he gaped at her four muscled arms and nearly lost his balance. "Who are you? Where did you come from?" Kirrill tried to pry twenty small fingers from his arms, but the woman held fast.

"Don't—I'm too strong for you, but I mean you and your people no harm. Try to understand: What you see is not who I am."

He looked at her. Hardly bigger than his boy, Kurnan, she had large green eyes ringed with long black lashes, and her cheeks on an otherwise aging face were flushed pink. "Like Fulgid, the one we call the Formorian?"

"Good, you understand. I am Alluxana, wife of Forest Protector Fulgid. Yes, yes, an ordinary woman bewitched by the hork into this strange being." She looked at her hands as she loosened her grip. "Still, these four arms give me a strength I have not felt in years, and for now my need to stop the hork is stronger than my fear of him."

"Why did you hold my arm?"

"To keep you hidden. The beast opened the door to the goblins' burrows."

"And out came that awful smell!"

"Yes, indeed; goblins never bathe, so they reek. You saw what water did to Kralbong?"

"Kralbong?"

"That nasty goblin you saw explode when he fell into the pond. The hork surely will use an army of goblin slaves to attack you all. We must warn your men to defend themselves with water."

Alluxana stood on her tiptoes to explain further, and Kirrill lowered his ear to hear her more clearly. With each word his eyes widened in fear.

PART II: LEAVING WHAT IS KNOWN   101

He followed the woman's tiny, quick steps, and they hurried back to the orchard. She had Kirrill call his companions and explain her strategy against the goblins.

Everyone dropped out of the trees as Kirrill and Alluxana passed beneath them. The little woman hardly noticed their stares as Kirrill explained her presence, his missteps in the orchard, and his encounter with Alluxana.

Quickly the group understood that they needed a change of strategy; they gathered around Kirrill and Alluxana to hear her plan. She was about to speak when her eye caught a slight commotion on a hummock near the clearing. A contented little donkey was standing on the slope and had buried her head in a pile of ripe apples. A short and roly-poly man sat leaning against the donkey's side. He stopped chewing on his own piece of fruit in mid-bite and gawked at the little woman, his usually sleepy eyes wide with surprise.

"Who is that?" Alluxana nodded toward the hummock.

Kirrill cleared his throat. "That's my little donkey, nearly eaten by that monster, it seems."

"No, I mean that little man."

"Oh, that's our camp cook, Kolvak. I've asked him to watch her until we go back to Fossarelick."

"Kolvak? Are you sure?"

Kirrill nodded vigorously.

"Kolvak," she mused. "I can't help noticing that he doesn't look much like the rest of you Moktawls."

"He's from the Coldside. Came to Fossarelick about five or six seasons ago. Said he was poor Flacher's cousin from Anonom Trace. Not too smart, that one, but he knows how to cook a fine stew from almost nothing."

"Flacher?"

"Oh, Flacher, yes, one of our bravest men. Died before Kolvak arrived. Had no family left in Fossarelick."

Alluxana nodded and walked toward the hummock. Kolvak rolled onto his knees and struggled to stand. He whistled soundlessly and strolled behind the donkey, who gave him a little kick with one of her hind legs. Kolvak stumbled, then squatted on the grass.

Kirrill saw him pick up something that had fallen out of his pocket—a threadbare red rag—and noticed Alluxana's eyes narrow as she watched Kolvak amble out of sight down the far side of the hummock. "I'd watch that one," she said with a slight smile. "He has a few secrets he doesn't want to share with you just yet."

The men laughed.

"He's a coward—he'll jump if you sneeze," snickered Cahalson. "All he thinks about is his next meal."

Kirrill called to the cook, "You, Kolvak, take that donkey back into the forest and hide her while we rid ourselves of the hork. We'll call you when it's safe to come back."

Kolvak kept his eyes on the ground as he gathered an armful of apples and led the donkey down the hummock and into the trees. He looked back only to mouth a good-bye before hurrying away.

Alluxana left Kirrill and pushed her way through a mass of tangled weeds. Calling the villagers to her side, she uncovered a large sack with more than a dozen glazed clay pots stored inside. "Each of you, take one and fill it with pond water. Return to the live oak and climb to where you can sit and see the ground below, but where no one sees you. When the goblins come, watch me down here. I will shout, "Now," and that will be a signal to aim for the closest goblin head and toss water on him."

Some of the men raised their voices to object, but Alluxana silenced them with a frown and stern words. "You saw the way Kralbong died. The other goblins will meet the same end. Just do as I say."

Each villager nodded. They chose their pots, which they filled with pond water. Hiding high in the huge tree, they sat quietly and waited. Already, a faint but disagreeable odor of unwashed goblin was drifting into the clearing.

Chapter 3

KURNAN HAD NEVER SEEN a dragon. The men of Fossarelick bragged about killing all of them long before he was born. But Seerlana had led him to a glen far beyond Fossarelick's fields. Now, right there in front of him was a beautiful blue silver-streaked dragon as big as Kurnan's cottage, sparkling in the sunlight.

When the creature lowered his head, his blue eyes shone like the sky on a clear summer day, and little curls of smoke wound around his nose. Seerlana tugged Kurnan's hand to bring him closer. She moved her lips, but Kurnan heard nothing. The dragon answered her with something like a hummed song.

Seerlana smiled at the mysterious sounds. "Draako agrees to meet you. If you allow it, he will sniff you and listen to your thoughts."

Close to the dragon's great head, Kurnan smelled something wonderful, like toasted bread covered with honey. He licked his lips and gazed into Draako's shining eyes. *How amazing it would be*, he thought, *to be friends with a dragon, to learn about the world outside the Valley*. Trembling, Kurnan held out his gift.

Draako lowered his snout to sniff Kurnan from his feet to his matted hair. His humming was deep and soothing. Seerlana smiled again and said, "I think Draako likes you. He will find us food and water."

The dragon turned away without taking Kurnan's gift and leaped into the air. Kurnan saw him circle in the sky. He watched the dragon's wide wings beat steadily as they carried him over the fields and past distant hills. He turned to ask Seerlana how she knew dragon speech, but he saw that she, too, gazed in silence toward the horizon, and he decided to hold his question. They waited while their shadows grew longer.

By the end of the afternoon, four dragons appeared in the distance. Kurnan realized that although Draako was the smallest, he flew faster than the other three, who were much bigger and fiercer-looking.

Kurnan hid behind Seerlana and squeezed his eyes shut. Clenching his fists, he realized his sister's mirror was still in his right hand. He felt the thud of each dragon's landing and slowly opened his eyes.

At first, their brilliance dazzled him. Two silvery-blue dragons dipped their heads and ambled toward him and Seerlana. One of them stood next to Draako and draped a scarred wing over his back. Behind them, another smaller dragon distanced herself from the others. She dropped to her knees as she rested in the weeds. Her eyes had narrowed; tendrils of smoke wreathed her copper head and neck. Her long, dark, spiny tail switched back and forth like that of an angry cat.

Kurnan's breath eased as the largest dragon dam began to croon sounds that reminded him of his mother's barley stew. He closed his eyes again, this time without squeezing, and lay back in the weeds himself. He saw his father and mother smiling at him as they held out their arms to him and his sister. As he dozed, other visions of family peace and love wrapped him in deep contentment.

A loud, rude shriek woke him from his reverie: the copper dragon was poised to jump, spewing flames into the air with every scream. Although Kurnan's legs threatened to pick him up and carry him away, he yearned to see her more closely. Alana's mirror tickled his palm. He unwrapped it, then faced the Copper and held the mirror in front of him. With slow, soft steps, he walked toward her.

The mirror glinted in the sunlight and a beam bounced off it into

Isabella's eye. She stiffened and ceased her shrieking. Her dark tongue darted out between her fangs and Kurnan jumped back.

Seerlana laughed. "She was after that large red scorpion. From the way Isabella is licking her lips, I think she enjoyed it."

The great silver-blue dam moved to Isabella's side and lowered her head to look into the copper dragon's eyes. Kurnan could feel the heat surrounding them and he looked back at Seerlana. She nodded and waved with the back of her hand. Kurnan offered the mirror gift again.

"Isabella is a dragon whose anger has deepened over the years—but Fossarelick needs all the dragons' help. And the dragons need the Valley folks' friendship. Try to win her over and you can make a beginning."

Isabella crouched and studied him. He placed the mirror on the grass in front of her, closer to the gleaming scales of her snout, and he stepped back. She tilted her head and looked at her reflection in the metal.

"She is wondrously beautiful," Kurnan said.

"She likes the mirror," whispered Seerlana, "but sometimes copper dragons prefer gifts of art. Here, draw a picture for her." Seerlana put a piece of charcoal in his hand and provided a section of papery tree bark.

"But what should I draw?"

"What do you think Isabella would like?"

Kurnan knelt next to the bark and looked at the dam's head. Without thinking, he began to sketch. Surrounded by umber scales with hints of violet streaks, her broad eye hardly blinked. The iris gleamed greenish-gold and her pupil opened to the sides, like a cat's eye. Lacking the means to copy her colors, Kurnan sighed and drew Isabella's eye as well as he could with the dark charcoal twig.

While Kurnan sketched, Isabella's head lay a few feet from his feet. The tendrils of smoke had stopped drifting from her snout. She gazed at the picture and rumbled. Her big eyes stared, and Kurnan thought he heard her say something.

The sound of distant bells filled his ears when she spoke to some part of his head. "*I did say something,*" she murmured. "*You have kind thoughts, like Seerlana, and that is why I allow you to understand my speech. Come closer.*"

The silver-blue dragons bobbed their great heads. Seerlana laughed lightly as Kurnan's mouth hung open in surprise: "I hear her."

Draako asked, "*Will you help us win back the friendship we once had with the people of our Veiled Valley? If they see that you trust us, they might join us to fight the Malevir.*"

"Mala-what?"

"*Malevir—the beast that took the Sunriseside Forest and attacked your fields, all to steal the dragons' treasure.*"

"Our Elder calls it the Formorian. It's a giant, he said, and the men who fought . . ." Kurnan paused, embarrassed. ". . . who hunted dragons have gone to kill the giant."

Isabella gazed deeply into Kurnan's eyes and he heard her say, "*Your Elder is wrong, Kurnan. We dragons are your friends, and the Formorian is not the Malevir. A different, more powerful creature has spoiled the forest and blighted the Valley.*"

"But Cahal's wisdom has guided Fossarelick all my life."

"All your life?" asked Seerlana.

He grinned. "I guess that's not so very long, is it?"

Seerlana frowned, "Long enough, but Cahal does not understand our danger. We shall talk to him. When my friends of Fossarelick hear that the Moktawls are in terrible danger in the forest, they will listen."

"What shall we say?"

"That the Moktawls should return to Fossarelick and fight the Malevir—with our dragon friends."

Draako lifted his wings, revealing a wheelbarrow filled with baskets of fruit, root vegetables, breads, icy butter, and herbs. "*Take these to the village. Feed your families and tell them—when they are ready to hear it—that they are enjoying a gift from the dragons, their friends.*"

Seerlana added, "The food and medicinal herbs will help change their minds. Even Cahal will give his blessing."

"I don't know that he will accept gifts from dragons," said Kurnan.

"He must," answered Seerlana.

Beneath the wings of the dragon dams sat more baskets of provisions sorely missed in the village. Seerlana pulled an abandoned cart into their circle, and Kurnan and she loaded it high with the remaining baskets.

Turning to the dragons, she said, "When the villagers agree to help, I will prepare them to meet you. What will you do while you wait for my message?"

Draako spoke for all the dragons. *"Whatever we can to keep the Malevir away from the treasure."* He turned his head to question the dams, but Abulafria and Isabella had flown off.

Anadraka waited for Draako. When he was satisfied that Kurnan and Seerlana were well on their way, they sprang into the sky and soared beside the others. Anadraka and Draako dipped their heads and wished Seerlana and Kurnan good fortune.

Chapter 4

AINDLE WAITED BY THE HEARTH. Sticky drops of ichorous sweat clotted on his knotted forehead. He wiped the black glop from his face with the hem of his shirt, which sizzled as acid burned through it. He turned to survey his ruined outbuildings, cursing that he had no time to repair the fire's ravages.

We'll go now to the dragon ancestors' cave with that Nnylf, he thought. He ran inside the tunnel to greet his goblins. The distant pounding of heavy, flat feet reached his twitching ears. Once more, he leaped up to the ledge from which he'd ambushed Bitterbud and gaped as a rushing mass of goblins stampeded past him toward the door without heeding his calls. *My spell should have stopped them,* he thought.

His bewilderment turned into rage as they thundered on, not toward the orchard and the clearing beyond, where he had left the boy, but to the remains of the bakehouse. The mob raised a cloud of dust and ashes as each goblin fought for any remaining bit of parched grain, loaves, and scorched fruit in the bakehouse. Aindle looked for his goblin slave, but the swarm of struggling beasts hid him. The mob's howls and grunts began to fade as, one by one, they tumbled into a hole in the bakehouse floor.

Strings of froth dripped over his fangs as Aindle screeched and howled in anger. Remembering Nnylf, he looked away from the charred shed through the orchard and toward the clearing where he had left the villagers. Failing to hear the screams of struggling men and the shrieks of feasting goblins, he frowned. Not a grunt or growl reached his ears.

Most of the goblins had disappeared into the hole that led to a tunnel branching in several directions. The wild and chattering rabble single-mindedly pursued a shaft that veered away from the orchards and sloped uphill.

One last goblin slid past Aindle into the hole. The hork screamed, "Come back here, Bitterbud!" and his claws caught the creature's ragged collar before the goblin could escape. Bitterbud howled as the hork's cold and powerful hand tightened around his neck. Aindle thought he heard the goblin whisper something to himself as he whined and twisted in his grasp.

"That's right, remind yourself that you are mine." The hork yanked him up by his long arm and pushed him toward the orchard. "We're going this way."

Loping between two rows of apple trees, Aindle and his captive reached grassy hummocks that bordered the clearing. Only the buzzing of insects in the warm sunlight disturbed the deep silence of the open space.

The rough bark of the tree branch sheltering him from the brutes below chaffed Nnylf's knees as he wrapped his legs tightly around it. Reaching the far side of the meadow, the hork shouted at his cowering goblin and shook his blue-tinged fist in the creature's face. Nnylf's glance at the rushes revealed a fleeting view of Alluxana's watchful eyes and her raised finger that warned the party to remain silent and motionless. He could not see Azile above him, and when he looked for his father and the other men, every one of them had blended into the greenery. He gripped a small pot of water and scarcely dared to breathe.

Soon Nnylf stopped breathing altogether as the hork and goblin trudged toward his tree.

Aindle was saying, "You stay here and watch for the scum you call your brothers. When they turn up, you all must follow me to the mountain cave. Together we will attack it and lay siege to the treasure. Guard this place while I look around."

At the hork's sharp tones, the goblin hunched his shaggy shoulders and, leaning against the live oak's trunk, he sank to the ground. The goblin licked his fangs and glared at Aindle, but when the hork raised his fist, he lowered his head and nodded. Aindle leaned closer to his trembling snout: "I warn you, the goblins will serve as my army or I will drown all of you. I'm going to search the grounds." He turned on one sharp heel and loped back through the orchard and around the garden.

Meanwhile, the goblin slowly pushed up against the tree trunk until he was standing again. He raised both arms into the air and danced a little jig. Looking around the clearing, he scratched the bristles on his chin and snorted loudly as he bobbed his head around the base of the tree.

Nnylf had been squeezing the little jar so tightly that his arm had fallen asleep. Horrified, he watched the pot slip out of his hand. It tumbled over itself and broke against the goblin's head.

Shrieking, the goblin frantically swiped at the water burning its hair, face, and neck. Looking up, it screamed at Nnylf. Attracted by the ruckus, the hork returned and the goblin pointed a smoking finger at the boy in the tree.

Aindle's wicked smile returned as he aimed his knobby finger at Nnylf. "Please accept my invitation to join me down here, young man."

A sickly green cloud wrapped around the boy. Queasy, Nnylf felt his body unable to move. The cloud lifted him off the tree limb and plunked him, stock-still, at the beast's feet. With a wave of his hand, the hork blew away the remaining droplets cooking the goblin's head and shouted, "Follow me! March and make it fast!"

Nnylf's legs moved forward at the hork's command, but his head refused to turn and his arms remained stiffly at his sides. *What has happened to my father and the others?* he worried. The goblin's stench nearly choked him.

PART II: LEAVING WHAT IS KNOWN   111

Groaning softly, the goblin pushed Nnylf forward, and they followed the hork back through the orchard toward the fire-wracked lodge.

Alluxana pushed her head and shoulders out from her hiding place in the bushes and watched them until they disappeared beyond the garden. She splashed pond water on the ground where Nnylf had fallen under the hork's spell, then signaled the men and Azile that it was safe—but, shocked at the scene below, they stayed in the trees.

Picking up the edges of her wet skirt, she squeezed out the water weighing it down and tied the hems in a knot above her knees. Without a glance behind her, Alluxana stepped carefully around the edge of the clearing and slid behind a row of fruit trees.

Chapter 5

DEEP BELOW THE CLEARING, the noisy rabble of goblins pushed on, driven by a great need. Along a length of snaking tunnels that sloped uphill, they ran and ran until they entered one last narrow passage that connected to a broad underground hall. Dozens of goblins shuffled into it until, as one, they hesitated—then gasped.

An oil lamp flickered at the center of the towering space. Without a sound, every goblin dropped to his knees and stretched his arms toward a dark figure chained next to the lamp. One of the goblins approached the figure with care. His claws tore away thick rags that had bound the creature's eyes and gagged his mouth.

The goblin nodded to his companions and melted back into the crowd. Out of the glacial stillness, they began to chant:

"Rocánonom, Rocánonom."

In the trembling lamp light, they saw the quavering creature lift his head and reveal his worn gray face, weighted by a long and knotted white beard that dragged at his feet. His teeth were yellow and broken. His withered arms, bound together by chains, hung wasted in his hollow lap, covered only by a worn and dusty fleece.

"Who speaks to me?" he croaked. "Forestspice? Are you free of his spell?"

His yellowed eyes opened wider as he looked from one goblin face to another. He searched among the goblins; turning to his left, he wavered.

PART II: LEAVING WHAT IS KNOWN   113

With a grimace, he lifted his heavy arms and pointed at one of them.

"There you are, Forestspice. Come forward."

The bold goblin who had freed Rocánonom's eyes and mouth pushed his way to the front of the crowd. He fell to his knees and plucked at the thick brown bristles that covered his head and back. One hand fingered old scars on his left ear that now pulsed painfully. He bobbed his head and crawled toward the sad creature.

"Unchain me, my good fellow, and help me to stand again."

Forestspice and other goblins sprang forward to bite and pull at the chains binding Rocánonom to the cave floor. When they shattered, Rocánonom shook off the remains of his shackles. Despite his aching joints and weak legs, he stood and looked across the wide space at his rescuers.

With a soft sigh, he spoke to them all. "You sensed my pain and sorrow from far away, and here you are now! You have freed me, and so I shall free you." As his gaze swept across the crowd, he saw all their eyes watching him, their faces twisted in grimaces and roughened with warts, cysts, and oozing wounds. "The beast's curse is about to end. Let us begin."

As Rocánonom uttered the last word, every goblin pulled a red rag from a hidden pocket or fold in ragged clothing and waved it above his head. The old man straightened himself and bowed his head deeply when Forestspice offered him his own rag.

"Thank you," he said in low tones. Rocánonom then lifted his gaze to the crowd around him and held the rag above Forestspice's shaggy head. The goblin tore at the tattered garments covering his body until they dropped in a heap at his feet. The other goblins followed his example.

"Do as I do, dear fellows." The creature shook out the rag to its full size and lowered it to Forestspice's head. The others imitated him and, like Rocánonom, wiped each other's heads, necks, shoulders, and the rest of their bodies, right down to the crusty spaces between their toes. Having finished their scrubbing, the goblins gently sank to the cavern floor, piled atop each other, and fell asleep. Snores and whistles echoed from the cave walls as Rocánonom applied the rag to his own body, then rolled it into a ball and tucked it into Forestspice's fist.

The great figure thrust his arms in front of his face and whispered a set of spells. Soft bubbles floated out of the sleeping goblins' gurgling mouths. Rocánonom lifted his chin and began to sing. With every verse of his chant, his voice grew louder until the tune filled the cavern. The words called upon spirits of earth, air, fire, and water. The walls of the vast underground chamber shook, and as the tremors died away, the creatures awoke with a jump or shudder.

Forestspice opened one eye, then the other. He gawked at the giant towering over his companions. Hair like burnished copper strands wreathed Rocánonom's now youthful face. A broad smile crinkled the corners of his bright green eyes. His powerful arms opened widely to greet his followers.

While the creatures regarded each other and their leader, their gasps of wonder and pleasure became a crescendo of cheers and laughter. Each goblin's body had shrunk to that of a little sprite whose skin was pale green and dotted with emerald green patches. Every sprite wore brown leggings and a matching shirt tied in twine at the waist, from which hung a tool sack. On their feet, copper slippers gleamed as the softly glowing cave walls grew brighter.

Each sprite had distinct features: pale green freckles, a trim and pointed beard, a plum-shaped nose, or ears curved like rose petals. Some sprites' pates were hairless, while tufts of unruly auburn hair sprouted from other heads.

Turning and twisting, the sprites begged their neighbors to tell them how they looked. They shook hands and patted one another's shoulders as they recognized old friends. After hugging each other, they grinned broadly and joined hands to circle-dance in twos and fours.

When the dancing became raucous, Rocánonom cleared his throat. The crowd grew still and attentive to the giant before them. "My friends,

PART II: LEAVING WHAT IS KNOWN

your joy warms my heart. Because you rescued me from the beast's painful chains, you gave me the heart to restore us all to the form for which we had been destined. As chosen friends of the Ancestors and their wyrmlings, we are bound with the Forest Protectors to defend the Veiled Valley and the dragons' cave. We must help them reclaim the Veiled Valley from the Malevir."

Forestspice stepped forward, still fingering his freshly healed ear. "Master—"

"Not your master, Forestspice; I will not be that. If you will allow me, however, I shall be your leader."

The crowd cheered and everyone clapped small green-speckled hands. A chorus of cries and songs rose in the dusty air. "Hurrah for Rocánonom!"

Forestspice spoke again. "We bring news. The Malevir goes to the Cave of the Ancestors—now, as we speak. He has ensorcelled the Forest Protectors: Fulgid a goat-headed giant and Alluxana a four-armed woman."

Rocánonom nodded and looked through the crowd. "As such, Alluxana and Fulgid might have more strength than the Malevir imagined. Now, where is Fernfallow? Is he among you?"

The sprites looked around at each other, then shook their heads and shrugged their shoulders.

"If not with you, dear Loblin, then he is still among the villagers of Fossarelick. He will find a way to help them." A wave of murmuring swept the group, but Rocánonom gained their attention once more as he shared his plans. "Prepare yourselves to follow me out of this place. Walk two by two, side by side. Cease all talk, and those of you at the rear, listen carefully for footsteps following us. We must reach the great cave before the beast does."

The newly restored Loblin formed their lines. Each sprite held onto the shirt hem of the fellow in front of him as they followed Rocánonom out of the huge underground hall. The giant held his little lamp in front of him and led them into a broad and low-ceilinged tunnel. He stooped as his long legs plunged down the passageway and the sprites trotted silently behind him, with Forestspice at the end of the procession.

Nnylf kept his eye on the hork. The beast had reached the ruined lodge hearth ahead of him, and the goblin who struggled to keep pace moaned as he rubbed his scalded green skin. Stiffly turning his enchanted body to look back at it, Nnylf saw the shivering creature wiping salt from his eyes with a little red rag and felt sorry for him. "There, there, now, old fellow. I am as scared as you are," he whispered. "Do you have a name?"

The goblin nodded and waved his three fingers ahead to remind Nnylf they must not stop. Nnylf thought he heard the goblin say "Budderbud," and he repeated the name.

"No," the goblin sniffed, "Bitterbud it is. Move ahead to stay alive." After a few more steps, he added, "I'm sworn to serve this evil one, but I'm not really a goblin. Remember that."

They reached the hearth. The hork shoved them both into the burrow tunnel ahead of him and ordered them to speed up. "I am easing my spell so you can move freely, but don't you try to escape. I'm watching you and so is my servant." He glared at Bitterbud.

"I can't see anything!" Nnylf shouted. "How do you expect me to find my way?" He patted the wall by his side and quickly pulled back his hand, now streaked with slime.

Aindle laughed and threw a fireball ahead of them. It floated along the tunnel's ceiling and lit up damp clefts and crannies in the walls. Nnylf and Bitterbud stumbled over rocks that littered the passage as Aindle pushed them along. With Bitterbud close by, every breath Nnylf took nearly choked him—but now Nnylf felt pity for the brute, who was just as much the beast's prisoner as he was.

Aindle forced them to halt as he paused to consider two new tunnels ahead of them. Stretching out his hand, he reached toward his fireball, which swelled until its glow filled the tunnel on his left. Long creamy walls radiated countless crystals that glittered and winked in the light

PART II: LEAVING WHAT IS KNOWN   117

of the burning sphere. When he shifted the fireball to the other tunnel, they could see deep crevasses scarring the floor and sharp stalactites hanging from the ceiling. Eyes wide with wonder, Nnylf and Bitterbud followed the hork and strained to stay apace with him as he hurried into the glittering passageway to the left.

As he jogged along, Nnylf noticed that the path no longer followed the hill's slope, but had turned downhill. He thought, *This isn't the way to the Cave of the Ancestors.*

Between sparkling walls, the passageway widened and the air surrounding them smelled sweet, like burnt sugar. Bitterbud poked Nnylf's shoulder. He pointed to a shallow marble shelf just inside the opening of another passage to their right. A round platter of honey-coated biscuits and plump berries was sitting on the shelf. As Bitterbud reached for a sweet, Aindle bellowed, "Don't touch that! It's poisonous!" He stood in front of them and slapped the goblin's hand with such force that the cowering beast fell back and bumped his head on the stone floor.

"Stand up, stand up, you dolt." Aindle dragged him to his feet. "The dragons built this path to fool the ignorant and careless, but I know their tricks. Turn around. We're going back."

Aindle grabbed an arm of each captive and yanked them back to their starting point. He continued, "I remember now—across the end of this tunnel sits a shallow pool. It turns into a sucking whirlpool. It traps the unwary, pulls them down, and drowns them." Nnylf shivered, while Bitterbud moaned and rubbed his bruised head. "I know a way to get around it," smirked the hork. "Move!"

As they followed him into the entrance of the rock-strewn passage with its jagged walls and uneven footing, the hork threw another fireball before them. Orange flares danced over the craggy surfaces and cast eerie shadows. Distracted by the show of light and shadow, Nnylf nearly tumbled into a deep gap in the floor. He grasped at Bitterbud's shirt, and the goblin pulled him to the side.

Nnylf's legs felt heavy and his feet dragged as they picked their way along the path. The higher they climbed, the louder grew sounds of rushing water. Bitterbud began to tremble, so strong was the memory of the water that had once seared his face.

"Soon we will cross into the dragons' cave," Aindle growled, then turned to glare at Nnylf with his burning yellow eyes. "And you, little man, will help me find their treasure."

Chapter 6

HE WOULD HAVE JUMPED ON the beast's back and torn off his head, but four small yet powerful hands yanked the hem of his shirt and Fulgid fell backwards. He clung to a nearby tree trunk. Finding his balance, he looked around and saw the little bakehouse cook at his side. "Dear wife, why did you pull me back? I was ready to break the hork's neck!"

Alluxana put her finger to her lips. "Be quiet; let him go for now. Besides, his basilisk ichor would have burned you to the bone. The time for his reckoning will come soon," she whispered, "for I think the dragons are coming back to the Valley."

"The dragons? But how can that be? Don't the Moktawls want to slaughter them all?"

"Sit, my love, and listen carefully. The Moktawls are those very villagers, the new friends you met in the forest. Azile is the daughter of one of them—Eunan—and I think they're ready to work *with* dragons now, not against them."

Fulgid shook his massive goat head. His muscled legs quivered and, nearly collapsing, he squatted on a large charred stone before the hearth. "The longer the beast's spell works on me, the less clearly I think. Help me, Luxie. Why are those men in this cursed place? And Azile . . . she understands me. She's so kind, so, so . . . she knows what I am thinking, like you. How?"

Alluxana placed her four hands on the giant's shoulders. "When Azile and Nnylf went to market in Nosidam, the hork in his dragonrider guise tricked them. He looked like you when you were young. The boy and girl followed him here to our lodge."

"That beast took it all: the animals, our orchard, our . . ." Fulgid looked around before he sighed with a shudder. "Our home. Why does he hunt those two young people?"

"He knows that the last living Valley dragons, the Orferans, accepted them as friends—like their mother, Seerlana."

"The dragons banished the Malevir long ago—or so they thought. I wish they had succeeded." He sighed and patted the hearth stone. "Luxie, I need rest. Come sit with me by"—he groaned—"what used to be our great chimney piece."

Alluxana folded her hands in her lap as she sat by her husband and rested her head on his arm.

Fulgid went on. "So, this hork thinks the dragons have shared secrets with the boy and girl?"

"Oh, yes, indeed, he thinks they know how to find the dragon's treasure—and, worse, he cares not a berry for the treasure itself."

"What could be worth more than the dragons' immense treasure? With it, he would own the entire valley."

Alluxana's gaze traced the treetops leading up to the peak above them. "He aims to destroy the dragons' power. That gone, all of the Veiled Valley—and the lands beyond—would be his."

"The dragons have ancient powers that a hork could never overcome."

"If he takes the Mystic Scintilla buried underneath their treasure, he destroys the source of the dragons' fire breath, intelligence, and will to live."

Fulgid blinked, and a string of bleats escaped from his goat mouth. "We can't let that happen. Forest Protectors are pledged to defend their cave from all intruders."

"Yes, and to help protect the Mystic Scintilla. If we fail to help the dragons, the Valley will fall into his hands."

PART II: LEAVING WHAT IS KNOWN   121

Fulgid lowered his massive head onto his knees and moaned. "How, I ask you? Look at us, Alluxana—two Protectors, now like babies in the nursery. Homeless. Useless."

Alluxana rose and pulled Fulgid to his feet. "Not babies, no, not at all. These strange bodies of ours have given us new strength, and we'll put it to use."

Fulgid looked into her eyes. "To outwit the beast?"

"Come with me, dear husband. There are ways to help the villagers and dragons stop the beast before he reaches the treasure."

The two Forest Protectors, trapped in their odd bodies, trotted through the orchard toward the clearing.

The Moktawls were waiting in the clearing for Alluxana's return. Slouching against or squatting near the massive low branches of the live oak, they stared at the ground and no one dared to speak. Kirrill suddenly sprang to his feet after spotting movement in the woods. In a hoarse whisper, he urged his companions to hide again, but before they could scramble into the upper branches, two figures emerged from the surrounding bushes.

"It's the baker and the giant!" shouted Atty.

Azile ran to Fulgid and hugged his thick arm. "We were so worried about you," she cried. "Have you found my brother? Did you see what happened to him? My father and I fear the worst."

Alluxana stepped forward. "The hork and his goblin have taken Nnylf into the burrows. He has one idea in his ugly head: steal the dragons' treasure, with Nnylf's help."

Azile began, "Nnylf doesn't know any—"

But Cahalson pushed her aside and snorted, "Well, let the hork have the treasure. Maybe then he'll leave us alone."

Atty faced him and barked, "If he takes the treasure, what will happen to us? The beast will make us his prisoners, too. I say—"

Eunan shouted, "Enough squabbling! Did you forget my son? You're arguing while the hork threatens him and everyone in the Valley. So tell me—if the beast wants the dragons' treasure, why attack us? No dragons are around to defend it."

"Wrong!" Alluxana shook her head. Frowning, she walked slowly toward the little band from Fossarelick. She looked up, paused, and said, "The dragons are still with us, and the beast must never take their treasure."

"Impossible! There can be no more dragons!" Cahalson bellowed and faced the Moktawl leader. "Atty, you know we mortally wounded that dam, and no other creatures have flown over the Valley since."

Atty nodded. "We thought our arrows hurt her badly, but I'm not so sure we killed her. If we had, then that hork—"

Alluxana interrupted, "If all the dragons were dead, the hork wouldn't need to find the treasure. They *must* be alive, because he wants their Mystic Scintilla, buried deep in the treasure."

Listening to their arguments, Azile realized that the hork might have unimaginable ways to hurt her dragon friends. She tapped the woman on one of her four shoulders. "What's the . . . Scintilla?"

"The Mystic Scintilla gives dragons their power. I don't know why, but the beast thinks you and Nnylf know its hiding place. Perhaps, because of your mother's friendship with . . . oh, my." Alluxana looked down and licked her lips.

Eunan whispered, "Her friendship with . . . with whom?"

Alluxana looked around the circle gathering around her and Fulgid. The men were scowling, and Azile shook her head and lowered her eyes. Alluxana coughed. "Oh, she has known so many people across the Valley. The hork must assume that she has heard something and shared it with the children."

Azile looked up, then took two of Alluxana's hands and spoke to everyone around her, "Alluxana, please stop. I can't keep Mother's secret any longer."

"What have you and Nnylf been hiding from me, Azile?" Eunan asked.

"Father, the Moktawls wounded that dragon dam many seasons ago. She was Anadraka, a Silver-Blue—and my mother's friend."

Eunan's eyebrows knotted as he said in a low voice, "Tell us more."

Chapter 7

Kurnan had hardly noticed the fields and forests they passed through as they raced back to Fossarelick. Now, he paused with Seerlana at the foot of the path leading up to their village. Frowning, he watched a figure pacing at the top of the hill. Cahal stood there, one spotted and thick-veined hand on his hip, the other waving a durk in the air above his head. Kurnan could see him shouting and stamping his feet.

"Cahal doesn't know us. Maybe your dragonriding armor scares him."

"Cahal ought to know you, his grandson. And he blessed Eunan and me on the day we were married. He held our children in his arms soon after they were born. Of course he knows us."

Seerlana took a few steps up the path, but she froze when Cahal called out, "Halt, you demons. Not another step! You can't bedazzle Cahal of Fossarelick. Be gone or suffer my wrath and my curse."

Seerlana cupped her hands to her lips and called up, "Cahal, you see Seerlana, mother of Nnylf and Azile, and wife of the Moktawl warrior, Eunan. And don't you know your grandson?"

Kurnan could see the old man squint as he stared at them. His white hair like a ragged cloud flew around his face in the wild gusts of wind blowing across the Valley.

"You are demons in the guise of Seerlana and Kurnan." A few of the women and children gathered behind their Elder. Every one of them had some improvised weapon in hand: a pitchfork or threshing flail, a kitchen knife or sturdy pot-stirrer. "You'll not step one foot in our village. Be gone, I said."

Kurnan ran toward him and called out, "Grandfather, I truly am your Kurnan. Test me and my answers will help you see."

Seerlana came to stand beside him and added, "Test us both. We are kinfolk, and you know our stories."

Cahal argued with the people standing closest to him. Seerlana watched him step forward, turn away, then face her again. She suspected he was planning to attack and she felt for her own durk tucked in her boot. She told the boy to stand behind her. The crowd of villagers hesitated, but Cahal screamed, "For the Ways of the World!" and charged down the path.

"Stop! Stop! I beg you, Father. He looks like our Kurnan—he might not be a demon at all." Kurnan's mother, Sherca, pulled at Cahal's sleeve. He stumbled and fell forward on the path, his nose in the dirt.

Another younger woman reached under the old man's arms to lift him. Nose to nose with her leader, she said, "Listen to me, Cahal. She is the very likeness of my cousin, Seerlana, except for that strange garb. You must test them, you must."

Cahal looked at the faces around him—worried, anxious faces—and he spat in the dust. "I shall test them for you, Shaklana. So, Kurnan, your sister has lost something dear to her. What is it?"

Kurnan and Seerlana looked quickly at each other and Seerlana nodded. Kurnan answered his Elder, "My sister Alana is missing a beautiful carved mirror, given to her by her friend, Carliel."

Sherca wailed, "You see, you see? You would have killed him!" She started toward her son, but Cahal pulled her back roughly, saying, "I haven't finished yet. Now I will test the woman."

Taking a few more steps down the hill, Cahal shouted, "Ten World-Turns ago, a terrible battle took place in the field behind you. What happened then that changed our lives?"

Seerlana shifted uncomfortably from one foot to the other. "I can tell you that the Moktawl warriors fought a dragon that had flown close to Fossarelick. They say they killed her and that the dragons will never return, but—"

The Elder shrieked, "They *say*? *But*? Nonsense! Our warriors did indeed banish the dragons, and since then we have lived peacefully in our valley—until now. These days have seen cruel changes: a giant, the Formorian, is destroying our crops, and our men have not returned from their hunt after him." He paused and looked at them both with suspicion. "You're the giant's demons in disguise, aren't you?" he said, waving his blade in their faces.

Seerlana brushed away her angry tears and stepped close enough to Cahal to look into his eyes. "We are neither monsters nor demons. We are who we seem to be, and we have come to ask your help to fight the worst monster of all."

Kurnan's mother pushed past the village headman and ran to embrace her son. Kurnan hugged her as she kissed his warm forehead and brushed back his hair. "See here—the scar from his fall when he was just learning to walk."

Seerlana's cousin, Shaklana, ran to them and asked Seerlana to roll up her right sleeve. "There it is, the burn mark. No demon would have that ugly pink patch. Seerlana tipped a pot of hot oil when she first learned to cook and the accident should have made her weep, but I remember she bit her lip and hid her face against the wall as the Wise Mother tended to her wound. We knew then that she was among the bravest of us." The woman playfully pushed Seerlana's shoulder. "You should have been a Moktawl," she laughed.

Seerlana shook her head. "Not I," she murmured. She pointed to the provisions Kurnan and she had pushed across the countryside. "In the wheelbarrow and cart, you'll find fruit and root vegetables, loaves of bread and crocks of sweet butter, and—most needed—medicinal herbs."

"From our men? Or did Nnylf and Azile buy all this in the Nosidam market?" asked Kurnan's mother. "Where are they? I thought they'd be with you."

Seerlana frowned. "I don't know. They might be in Nosidam. Kurnan says that my husband Eunan is not among you."

Shaklana spoke up. "No, he's searching for Nnylf and Azile."

Seerlana gasped. *Nnylf and Azile, my sweet children—they're not here! What have I done?* She covered her mouth with her hand as she felt her lips tremble. "The men might still be in the forest. Perhaps they have all found each other." She pushed the wheelbarrow toward Shaklana. "Please, take this food and the bundles of herbs that Kurnan and I brought from the land up coldside."

Cahal tucked his durk into his waistband. With a slight bow, he said, "Seerlana, you have been away so long. You must understand my confusion. Now I believe you are one of us; but why is Kurnan with you? And why were you up coldside?"

Seerlana rubbed her nose and answered, "I traveled to the Trace for something particular that I needed while my family worked on the barley harvest. When I returned, the village was deserted. I looked around and found only Kurnan, hiding in a loft."

"We were hungry and frightened," said Shaklana. "While you were gone, many of our fields were burned; we had nothing to eat. Those of us who were able went into the forests hoping to find something. We returned with berries, thin roots, and acorns. Sherca looked for Kurnan, but he had disappeared."

Sherca interrupted, "I screamed, sure that the Formorian had come back and taken my boy. Thank the Ways of the World he was with you."

"Kurnan told me that you had gone to gather food. He looked so hungry. I fed him from my pack and invited him to come with me to . . ." Seerlana paused, not ready to tell them about her dragon friends.

Looking at his feet, Kurnan finished her sentence: "To the Coldside, where the village near Anonom Trace might help us. I took the mirror in case we needed it—you know, for signaling."

Alana stepped forward. "Where is my mirror? Carliel gave it to me. You had no right to take it." She glowered at Kurnan and looked ready to shake him upside down.

PART II: LEAVING WHAT IS KNOWN   127

Cahal interrupted, "You went to Anonom Trace to find help—now I understand why you and Kurnan left Fossarelick. May all blessings of the Ways be with them. Thank you," he said. "Come with me. We shall take this bounty to the great hall. Alana, we'll talk about the mirror later; you two boys help her bring those supplies up the hill."

His arm around Kurnan, the village Elder led his people up the path to his hall, a long and low building attached to a two-story house shaped like a barn. Its heavy wood-paneled doors, carved with figures of dying dragons bristling with arrows, made Seerlana shiver.

Sherca wrapped her brindled shawl around Seerlana's shoulders. "You're shaking with cold and hunger. That strange garb can't be enough to keep you warm. Sit here by the hearth. Kurnan, you and the other boys build a fire. That and a good bowl of pottage will warm you."

Shaklana and Sherca plucked spiral-rooted sotopats, turnips, green parsepouches, and bunches of savory herbs from the pile of vegetables and set to cleaning and chopping them. Alana and her friends ran to fetch water with wooden buckets.

After steam began to rise from bubbling cauldrons, Sherca poured in the cut tubers, roots, and herbs. From a hidden larder she pulled down a pottery crock, and into one cauldron she emptied chicken bits preserved in their own fat. The comforting smell of warm cooking spread through the lodge. Shaklana placed trenchers of buttered dark bread along the length of the main wooden table and carried a wobbling stack of bowls and cups to be filled with soup.

Kurnan sat with his mother and sister while they dipped the grainy bread into their bowls and slurped their supper. He held his bowl in both hands and tilted it to drain the last drops. Wiping his mouth with the back of his hand, he excused himself and ambled over to the hearth before Alana could pester him again about the mirror.

As the evening darkened into night, fire crackled in the wide hearth. Shadows danced in corners of the long room as drafts pushed through cracks in the upper story and gently rocked lanterns hanging from brackets overhead. Warmed by soothing soup, the sleepy villagers carried their coverlets and mats into the hall and fell asleep on the floor with quiet snuffles and snorts.

Cahal sat slumped and snoring in a large oaken chair near the hearth. Sherca had covered him with a quilt. It bore shaped patches of dragon skin that marked his standing as a master Moktawl. They glinted in the firelight. Seerlana studied them and tightened her lips.

Kurnan found a low stool at the other end of the open hearth and poked a long stick into a pile of embers. Seerlana walked away from Cahal and stood next to the boy. She cleared her throat and whispered, "The food and herbs were good."

Kurnan nodded. "Mother brewed a sweet tea. Now, everyone has relaxed and sleeps soundly." He giggled. "Grandfather snores and snorts in his sleep."

"That's good. We can thank Draako for that. Imagine if we had brought nothing but ourselves." Seerlana paused, then clasped her hands until her knuckles turned white. "Kurnan, I must tell the villagers about the Malevir and all that has happened to the Veiled Valley."

"But when? I'm scared. What will Grandfather do when he hears about the you-know-whats?"

Cahal snorted and shifted in his chair.

"Hard to tell, Kurnan." Seerlana shook her head. "But we shouldn't have mentioned Anonom Trace. Now we'll have a harder time explaining."

A loud cough startled them. "Explaining what—and who or what is Draako?"

They turned to meet the stern glare of Cahal's eyes as he threw off the quilt. "Kurnan—you think my snoring is funny? Tell me now, before the others awaken, what really happened to you. Speak up. I don't hear so well, but I still have my wits."

Kurnan asked the old man to sit again, then he and Seerlana knelt by his side. Seerlana spoke first. "You heard all our whisperings, so now I must ask you—what do you know of a dragon named Aurykk?" Seerlana asked.

"Aurykk was a golden dragon and cousin to Lugent, the fiercest silver dragon ever known to this valley. I would have been proud to have his silver scales decorate my quilt and my tunic, but no one has seen Lugent in any part of the Veiled Valley since my youth. As for Aurykk, Kirrill tried to bring him down long ago, but the dragon escaped. The wounds probably killed him, anyway."

"Lugent is gone, but Aurykk and a few other dragons live still."

Seerlana held her breath as she waited for Cahal's next word.

Chapter 8

Nnylf had no idea how much time had passed when he and his captors finally wriggled out of one last dark tunnel into dazzling light that streamed through the broad entrance of the cavern. Aindle shoved him onto a flat-topped boulder and screamed, "*Where* is that treasure?"

Nnylf shrugged, wincing as the hork's claws dug in.

"Tell me now. I will have it!"

Nnylf glanced at his own dusty, bruised feet, then across the gallery.

Aindle followed his gaze and smirked. "Your memory betrays you. Soon enough I will know everything."

The hork spun away from him and launched a fireball. The glowing orb wove around sparkling stalactites that hung from the highest point of the ceiling. Directly beneath the hanging rock formations, a brook flowed out of a wide, dark break in the far wall. Aindle directed his fireball into the gloom and, calling the goblin to follow him, dashed after it.

Bitterbud, terrified of water, widened his eyes and avoided the stream by slinking along the passage walls. He barely kept up with Aindle, who disappeared deeper into the gloom.

Nnylf released a long sigh and looked around. The cave looked familiar—but it was too tidy for a dragon lair.

Azile was right. The dragons left this place long ago and Anadraka didn't come back.

He gazed upward and saw a slab of rock hanging crookedly from the

PART II: LEAVING WHAT IS KNOWN 131

arch of the cave's entrance. With bright daylight to help him, he could see it had deep peculiar markings that ran right up to its broken edge.

Dragon glyphs, he thought. Then he shook his head. *How did I know that?*

He stared as, bit by bit, the strange marks danced on the surface until they formed words that began to make sense. Although the transformation mystified him, clearly he was reading dragonspeech!

> . . . *Malevir*
> . . . *to banish pain and fear*
> . . . *the Draako, heir of Lugent, blessed with Sight.*

The Draako! Nnylf's mouth dropped open. *My dragon friend, Draako?* He blinked and caught Aindle watching him with a scowl as he stood by his side.

"What are you gawking at out there? Don't think you can bolt through that entrance into the sunlight!" Aindle screamed. "I brought you here for one purpose. If you cheat me, I will leave you here to die. Stop squirming." Aindle uttered another charm. "Bitterbud, you watch the boy while I look around. These irons will hold him fast." A heavy chain appeared and clamped tightly around Nnylf's ankle. The hork fastened it firmly to a stake rooted deep in the boulder where Nnylf sat.

Aindle walked in circles and kicked at the dust on the cavern floor. "No dragon has been here in quite some time. Not a footprint, rag, or bone in sight." He scratched at the warts on his chin. "Maybe they took it with them!"

Nnylf returned his glare. "Took what?"

"Don't play the dolt with me." Aindle bent over Nnylf, who pulled back from the hork's sour breath as the beast said, "We have come here for dragon treasure. You know where they have hidden it."

Nnylf glanced again at another pitch-dark opening in the wall behind the hork. Aindle followed his gaze. "Ha, thought you could trick me?" He turned, and with his fireball leading him, Aindle left them to search deeper in the cavern.

As Bitterbud squatted next to Nnylf, he lazily traced one circle and then another in the dirt floor. Sniffing and coughing as dust rose in puffs around his bony finger, the goblin drew the image of a dancing Lobli, dressed in a little suit, smiling and waving. Bitterbud pointed to the picture and then at his own chest. "Me," he whispered.

He would have said more, but the hork bellowed, "You clod of a goblin, come here!" Bitterbud swept away the drawing with one hand and hobbled into the shadows to answer Aindle's bidding.

When he turned to gaze again at the broken slab over the entrance, Nnylf remembered the dragon screams, fire, and smoke that had filled the cave ten World-Turns ago. Azile and he were so young, yet every word thought by the blue dragonet had entered his head. *"I am Draako. We must flee from the Ancestors!"* he had said.

Aindle and the goblin disappeared into one of the tunnels off the main gallery. Silence surrounded Nnylf, deep in thought. His eyes swept over the arch and each side of the entrance. Along the threshold, he noticed several flat stones, half buried in dirt and covered by twigs and dried leaves. Intent on reaching them, he jumped up, but the chain tightened around his leg and he fell forward. His nose struck the rock. A sharp pain hammered his face from forehead to chin. When Nnylf touched his nose, he saw bloody splotches on his fingertips. He wiped them on the back of his breeches.

Nnylf pulled on his chain, but every tug made it tighten. He groaned, then asked himself, *What did they mean, those words up there?*

"The Draako, heir of Lugent, blessed with Sight," he whispered, and he felt a strange quivering between his shoulders.

The hork's shadow loomed large against the tunnel's walls as his fireball led the beast and goblin deeper into the shaft. Once the supernatural light had dimmed, Nnylf stood and grabbed his stone seat on two sides. Preparing to rock it back and forth with all his strength, he bent to grasp it and tumbled backward, the boulder still between his hands. It felt lighter than a loaf of bread. Cradling it, Nnylf inched toward the pile of stone slabs and winced as the chain dug into his leg.

Nnylf reached the stones and lightly rested his boulder next to them. He brushed away dust and debris from the pile of slabs and pushed the smooth top slab aside to look at the one just underneath. Something about the slab's shape reminded him of the fragment over the arch. As he brushed away dirt sticking to its surface, Nnylf felt grooves and gouges. More markings—curlicues and odd shapes like those he had seen in the fragment overhead!

He brought his face closer to the slab; more symbols lifted and rearranged themselves. He mouthed the words he could decipher:

> *"In nests of rainbow brightness*
> *Shall the wyrmlings come to light.*
> *Sheltered from the . . .*
> *The ruler of the night.*
> *One and only one will dare . . .*
> *And this will be the . . ."*

He looked up at the marks on the slab above the entrance and down again at the stone he had just cleaned. Putting the two pieces together, the lines made more sense:

> *In nests of rainbow brightness*
> *Shall the wyrmlings come to light,*
> *Sheltered from the Malevir,*
> *The ruler of the night.*
> *One and only one will dare to banish pain and fear*
> *And this will be the Draako, heir of Lugent, blessed with Sight.*

Before hurrying back to the spot where Aindle had left him, Nnylf replaced the stones and piled debris on them, brushed his tracks, and scattered some twigs and leaves over his path. Sitting once more on the rock and wondering at his newfound strength, he pretended to stare at his feet.

Aindle followed his fireball and searched all sides of the tunnel for a clue. He saw no vault in the smooth stone walls. No hiding place befitting dragon treasure revealed itself. He looked everywhere for some sloppy mistake, but found nothing.

He roared with rage. His bellowing echoed up and down the tunnel and he turned to strike out at the cowering Bitterbud by his side. The goblin twisted to dodge his master and yelped with pain as Aindle beat at his head.

"Worthless clod, don't stray from me again. I am going back to the other passage. I might have missed something." The hork rubbed his elbows and muttered a new incantation. In barely two breaths, he turned into a large black bat and flew quickly into the first tunnel. His squeaks bounced off the rock walls.

Bitterbud ducked and ran to a shallow cleft along the wall. Out of Aindle's sight, he pulled a red rag from his sleeve, wiped his head, and pushed the rag into the deepest shadow of the cleft. He rejoined Aindle, whose bat wings flitted from one end of the rocky ceiling to the next, high above. The trembling goblin shrank from water flowing into a wide pool farther back in the passage. A waterfall, glowing scarlet in the light of the fireball, ruffled the pool's surface with ripples and eddies.

Ignoring the goblin's low moans, Aindle flew around the cascade and scanned his surroundings. He saw not one mark on the rosy marble walls, not a single crack in the cavernous ceiling overhead.

With squeaks and grunts, Aindle alighted by the pool and returned to his old blue and warty self. Looking around one last time, he sniffed and spat a sticky, green glob that exploded the water around it as it sank and disappeared. "Clod of worthless filth—we've left that stubborn, lying boy alone for too long. He knew the dragons hid no treasure here.

PART II: LEAVING WHAT IS KNOWN   135

Come, it must be elsewhere."

Aindle hurried after the fireball as he returned to the cavern's main gallery. Bitterbud frantically jogged after him, and his shoulder brushed along one wall while he kept his feet away from the stream's edge. Hiccupping with fear, he screamed, "Wait, wait, sir, I can't see!"

Nnylf heard the goblin's frantic call and slumped against the rock just as Aindle bounded into the expanse of the gallery. He sniffed and spat another gob of ichor that hissed as it struck the limestone floor. His glance leaped from wall to wall and along the floor before settling on the boy.

Nnylf looked up and scowled. "I told you. I don't know anything about dragon treasure."

"Snollygoster! You lied to me again! For that, you will suffer." Aindle's next charm conjured wriggling iron chains that snaked around the boy's arms and legs until he could barely wiggle his fingers. "You will rot here, for all I care. Your sister and the rest of those dolts from Fossarelick will be heading to Nosidam for help, and I will be waiting for them."

Nnylf twisted but the chains squeezed his limbs. "Stop!" he cried as the sharp links dug into his wrists. "Help!"

With a flick of his bony finger, Aindle wrapped a coarse cloth around Nnylf's head and gagged his mouth. "Ha! Even if you *could* cry for help, no one would hear you. These chains will hold you until your life drains away. We leave you to the worms."

Aindle gripped Bitterbud's thin arm and pulled. "Come, you meal for maggots, make ready for Nosidam."

The goblin, mouth sagging at the corners and eyes reddening, nodded to Nnylf before they marched out of the cavern. The hork's gnarly feet kicked at the dirt and twigs, yet missed the pile of slabs by a handbreadth.

Chapter 9

THE LATE AFTERNOON SUN WAS fading as a band of unlikely companions made their way toward the Nosidam road. Arriving at the wall the Moktawls had crossed when they first entered the forest, Alluxana turned to face everyone; with a finger across her lips she signaled silence.

Fulgid prepared to hoist each person over the wall, but he halted as immense shadows blocked the sunlight of midday. Cahalson and the other men turned to look through the trees and up at the sky; their mouths hung open and their eyes widened.

Overhead soared a clutch of flying creatures: the smallest dragon with brilliant blue scales, another larger one with a slim copper body, and two more great dragons sheathed in shimmering silver-blue.

Cahalson rubbed his eyes and stared again at the dragons as they filled the air with whistles and trills. "Down, men. Don't let them see you."

Fulgid bleated and Alluxana reminded them, "The dragons will not attack. Up there, see—it's Seerlana's dam, Anadraka. Indeed, you did not kill her."

Cahalson stood tall again and admitted to Azile that he had scarcely believed her dragon stories—until now.

Azile did not answer him. She swayed and whispered to herself. Eunan put his arm around her shoulders, but she shrugged and stepped away from him. All her attention focused on the dragons' song. She muttered softly, "They are calling to us! I'm trying to understand . . ." Her arms shot up over her head as she waved. "Oh, I hear them. The dragons ask me if I am the same girl who joined in the battle at the Cave of the Ancestors!" Stretching her arms toward the sky, she shouted, "Yes, yes, I am Azile, daughter of Seerlana, your trusted friend."

Eunan stared at his daughter and gasped at her words; when he looked up again, the smaller blue dragon lowered his long neck in Azile's direction. The air shimmered around them as the creature dipped and soared high above. While he sang out a cascade of trills, Azile turned to the Moktawls and her new friends to say, "That dragon is Draako, the one that Nnylf and I rode years ago when we escaped from the battle. He has grown so strong and beautiful."

Eunan grasped her hand. "What battle? Why have these dragons come here? Do they mean us harm?"

Alluxana cried out, "No! I told you . . ."

Azile shook her head as if to clear her mind. "It's so strange. Every note they sing I hear as words." Looking up at Eunan, she whispered, "They say that they have come out of hiding to help us and the Valley people. Mother is well and has returned to Fossarelick. They say that Fossarelick and Nosidam . . ." Here, Azile chewed on her lower lip before she continued: ". . . must join the dragons and face the Malevir together, or the beast will kill us all. "

Atty, who'd overheard her, said, "The dragons ask us to make a stand against the beast who has been burning our fields and stealing our livestock. Brothers of Fossarelick—now we're talking! On to Nosidam, then!"

"No, Atty, not just us," Azile whispered.

Cahalson spoke up. "Right—we can't face the Malevir without help. We have no weapons to fight a hork. Even with dragons at our side, you know he could turn us all into field mice and eat us for lunch by calling on just one charm!"

Azile looked up again at the dragons flying above in figure eights. "How will we know where to find you?" The men could barely hear the dragons' whistles and trills. Azile listened to more dragon song, then answered Cahalson. "Our dragons are wise, and their magic is stronger than the hork's. Draako says that we have much work to do, but they will find us when the need is greatest." As Azile finished speaking, the dragons whirled away toward Coldside.

Eunan came around Cahalson to Azile's side. "I ask you again about that battle at the Cave of the Ancestors."

"Oh, Father, we have so little time!"

"I must know, Azile. You *will* help me understand why your mother left us."

"You won't like this." She paused, looked into her father's eyes, and said, "Mother had to help her friends, the Orferan dragon clan. She comes from a family of dragonriders who lived in hiding near Anonom Trace. They sent her away from the Trace when the Malevir's mischief started to hurt people."

Azile heard a sharp intake of breath, and Eunan staggered back and rested against the wall for support. "How could this have happened? A dragonrider? Seerlana? I thought that she was a village girl from those parts, sent to Fossarelick to marry me. Did she lie?" Eunan's lips tightened as he shook his head.

"No! Mother wouldn't do that—but how do you tell your Moktawl husband that your dearest friend is a dragon named Anadraka? The very dragon later wounded by Moktawl arrows?"

Another round of gasps from several throats filled the air.

"Anadraka had warned her that the Malevir had begun his attacks on the Cave of the Ancestors, the mother lair of the Orferans. He murdered the Reds and other dragons, then enchanted their ghosts. They say he killed the great dragon leader, Lugent. Without him to oppose them, the enchanted Reds and other dragon ghosts were gathering to attack the cave where Draako, Anadraka, and the other dragons were still living,"

Eunan leaned forward. His face close to that of his daughter, he whispered hoarsely, "Did your mother take you to that cave?"

PART II: LEAVING WHAT IS KNOWN 139

Azile bowed her head, then nodded. "Anadraka came one night. We followed Mother to meet the dam in the meadow beyond our fields. Draako was with her. We had met them before—they were our friends. The dragons taught Nnylf and me the ways of dragonriding on nights when you slept soundly. One moonless night, the Moktawls were away on a hunt, so we flew to the cave.

"After we landed, dragon spirits attacked. Nnylf and I were hanging onto Draako's frill while Mother rode Anadraka and distracted the ghosts. Isabella and Abulafria came out from hiding and together we escaped, thanks to Draako's powers. We flew coldside toward Anonom.

"As we approached the mountains, a huge golden dragon flew alongside us. He was Aurykk, Draako's uncle. We all landed in a meadow; then we riders climbed onto the Golden's back. Draako and the others went on to the Sunsetside Mountains while Aurykk carried us to safety and left us in the fields near Fossarelick. Mother never saw Anadraka again until the night the dam was wounded."

Atty stepped forward. With a tight smile, he spoke to all the people gathered around Azile. "Our purpose has changed, brothers. Azile's story has made that clear. We Moktawls could just shrug our shoulders and go home to our families, wait for this cursed hork to make slaves of us all—or we could rekindle our friendship with dragons and do as they ask."

Eunan rubbed his cheeks streaked with tears. "You've forgotten Nnylf; what has become of him? Shouldn't I track the hork and rescue him?"

Kirrill patted Eunan's shoulder, cleared his throat, and said, "I'll go with you; we have been through a lot together."

Azile pleaded, "Kirrill, Father, Nnylf's dragon will find him. Draako promises to do so. He asks that you and Cahalson return home and change Fossarelick hearts. Fulgid, where will you go?"

Alluxana answered for him. "Back to the lodge. He says he needs his hat."

"A hat?" She shrugged. "You know best. Well, then, Alluxana and I will go to the forest outlook over Nosidam. We'll spy on the beast. Atty and you other men will wait for us, under cover of the forest and hedges, until we rejoin you and Fossarelick on the road. The dragons will be watching for—"

Before Azile's last words, one of the Moktawls raised his durk in the air. "We'll do it, Azile. As Atty said, his first thought's for the welfare of Fossarelick and our children. If he tells us to follow the dragons, then—"

"I didn't hear Atty say that," Cahalson interrupted. "He was giving us a choice, and I say all of us should go home to our families. Yes, the dragons exist, but who knows if they have left their evil ways?"

Azile fumed. "What evil ways?" she cried. "It was the hork who burned our fields and stole our animals, not the dragons. They're fierce but kind creatures. Dragons fought us with fire only after the Moktawls vowed to kill every one of them with their arrows! The Malevir fooled us all by making us fear dragons. Don't you understand his purpose? He would take our valley and beyond as his slave kingdom! Draako said that Nosidam will be his next victim." Shaking with the force of her words, Azile sank to her knees and tears dropped unheeded down her cheeks. Fulgid hoisted her up to the top of the wall.

Eunan turned to the giant and said, "Enough! Fulgid, help me get up there. I will return to Fossarelick and do as the dragons say. We have wronged those who would be our friends. Are you coming with me, Kirrill and Cahalson?"

A grim-faced Kirrill nodded.

The giant first lifted Eunan, Kirrill, and Alluxana onto the wall, then he extended his massive hand to Cahalson.

Cahalson hesitated. He rubbed the bridge of his nose, then looked at the two men waiting for him above. "Yes, yes, I'm coming, but we only have Azile's word and that one sighting. I'm just telling you." He grunted as Fulgid pulled him up and over the wall.

Seerlana was shivering in the gloom of an empty grain silo with Kurnan, whose head rested on his knees as he crouched against the stone wall at his back.

PART II: LEAVING WHAT IS KNOWN   141

The dragonrider knelt at his side and lifted his chin with her finger. "Cahal frightened me, too. At least your mother and the others were strong enough to keep him from poking us with his durk."

Kurnan looked up and cried out, "But he didn't believe us, and I can't blame him. Who would?"

"Your mother, for one, and the others, too; yet he is Fossarelick's Elder. No one dares disobey him." She crouched in front of him and patted her leg. "Look. I have a small enchanted blade hidden in my boot. Anadraka gave it to me at the Cave of Refuge. It can cut through anything."

"Like that door?" Kurnan pointed to heavy wood panels that sealed the entry to the granary against a stone threshold. He pulled at her sleeve. "Seerlana, if we escape, we'll never convince the villagers to join us."

Seerlana nodded. "But if we stay, we risk dying. Cahal will convince many of them that we are with the enemy. They could come for us at any time. How can we make them believe us? If we don't, everyone in Fossarelick will die."

Kurnan stood and crossed to the doorway. He ran his hands along the bottom of the panels. "I thought so . . . here is a spot weakened by the gnawing of mice."

Seerlana knelt beside him. She felt the jagged edges of the rotted wood. Gingerly, she poked the panel's end with her durk and chips crumbled at the touch of her blade. "Kurnan, listen carefully. I will stay here. You will crawl out and leave tonight. No moonlight will betray you. Run quickly to the road and head toward the forest. Think hard of Isabella and call to her once you are far enough from Fossarelick. She will come, I know she will."

"I can't leave you, Seerlana. They will punish you for my escape—and what can Isabella and I do to help, anyway? They still believe dragons are the enemy."

"Leave your cloak and cap and do not worry about me. When you find Isabella, she will know what to do." Seerlana ran the point of her small knife over two sides of the panel until she had framed a little hinged door. Using both hands, she pulled it inward until it opened. "You will just fit through here."

Kurnan froze. "I can't."

Seerlana's gruff whisper made him jump. "Kurnan, go! We have no time to dally."

Drawing a deep breath, Kurnan knelt and, forehead scraping the ground, he crawled through the opening. Then he turned back and muttered, "I have never been so scared in my life."

"The brave always feel afraid when they face danger. It's natural," she assured him. "Now, go. May the blessed Ways of the World be with you."

She closed the opening.

Kurnan slid along the granary wall until he reached the side facing away from the village. Pushing off into the night, he stumbled onto a dusty dirt path that followed the slope downward. In the dark, every step he took threatened a fall. He picked his way around stones and clumps of dried grasses until he reached the road. Looking back, he saw that the village was quiet and dark except for one glowing window in his grandfather's hall.

Isabella, he thought, *I'm coming. Where are you?*

The afternoon light had faded. Eunan and Kirrill wheezed as they hurried along the road. They struggled in the dark to keep up with Cahalson, who was eager to reach Fossarelick.

Eunan watched with envy as the young Moktawl jogged easily toward the village with hardly a stop for water or bread. Now, Cahalson turned to encourage his companions but tripped over his own feet when he saw something darker than the night sky over his head. "Quick! To the trees. A monster—above us—flying!" He pulled the men off the road before they could stop him.

Eunan looked up and watched a creature fly across the sky and away from them without a glance in their direction. "No, Cahalson, it has no

PART II: LEAVING WHAT IS KNOWN 143

interest in us. It's one of Azile's dragons, that copper dam we saw before over the forest."

Kirrill puffed: "Could she be headed to Fossarelick? Ways of the World, the village will be in danger!" Dashing to the road again, he began to run but stopped to catch his breath and steady his trembling knees.

"Kirrill, wait!" Eunan shouted. "If all that my Azile says is true, the dragon will not harm our families. Something else is drawing her that way. We'll follow it." Eunan could see that Kirrill limped now and then. "Kirrill, you too tired to go on?"

The big man shook his head and joined his companions on the road home.

Hours went by, and clouds hid the stars while they struggled to stay away from the gloomy forest and fields bordering their path in the dark. They followed another sharp curve in the road, and they were startled to see that same dragon, this time on the ground not too far ahead of them and close to someone small. Cahalson shouted and, brandishing his durk, he raced ahead. Eunan jogged to keep up, but Kirrill, huffing and puffing, fell behind.

When Cahalson approached them, the dragon squealed and backed off. The small figure—he could see it was a boy—waved and jumped as if calling for help. Before Cahalson could attack, the dragon leaped into the air and flew high above them. She circled and her cries tore the air.

Eunan and Kirrill caught up with Cahalson and Kirrill called out, "That's my boy! My son! It's Kurnan! We're here, boy. Hold on. We'll save you."

Kurnan held up one had to stop his father while the dam flew in loops above them. "Put away your blades," he shouted. "Isabella is my friend." He looked at the men's astonished faces. "Hello, Father." He smiled. "Yes, I was talking to a dragon."

Kirrill frowned at Kurnan. "Are you under some kind of spell, son? Our family is no friend to dragons."

Kurnan said, "No spell, Father, but this is all new to me—having a dragon friend, I mean."

Eunan added, "Like Seerlana."

"Oh, I just left Seerlana in Fossarelick. Grandfather locked us in the granary but she helped me escape," blurted Kurnan. "Grandfather thinks she is a demon sent to bewitch the village."

"Could be . . ." mused Cahalson.

"No, no," shouted Kurnan. "Not at all. Seerlana came back to warn the villagers about the Malevir. Let me tell you about it," he said eagerly.

"We know about the Malevir, son," said Kirrill as he hugged the boy.

"Seerlana really did come home?" Eunan whooped. "Bless the Ways of the World! And we *do* know about the Malevir and his plans." Frowning, he added, "He has taken Nnylf prisoner."

Kirrill embraced his son again and stepped back to look up the road toward Fossarelick. "We need to make our own plans now—how to rescue your son Nnylf and how to free Seerlana. What does your dragon say, Kurnan?"

The boy looked up at the circling dam, whose musical calls alternated with his silence and furrowed brow. "She says that you must go to the village. Seerlana . . . Seerlana's not in the granary now. She's . . . she's . . . I can't hear her." His frown deepened. "Oh, well, you'll see when you get to Fossarelick. After Grandfather hears your news, he'll change his mind. Now, Isabella and I have a job to do."

The copper dragon alighted once more, but not too close to the Moktawls. Kurnan approached her, and the men watched them in awe as Isabella bent her head to bump Kurnan's shoulder gently and tousle his hair with her tongue.

Kirrill cleared his throat. "Ahem—up to the village then, eh?" He jostled Cahalson and Eunan, who followed him toward Fossarelick after a few more glances at the boy and dragon wrapped in leaves swirling around them in the late night winds.

Cahal stormed into the granary that imprisoned Seerlana. Anger contorted his pale face and he raised his blade in her direction. As the

PART II: LEAVING WHAT IS KNOWN   145

dawn sky brightened sunriseside, Seerlana could see his eyes darting from Kurnan's jumbled cap and cloak to her face.

"Wicked demon, horrid witch, you have stolen the boy and sent his spirit to the wraiths, haven't you?" he screamed. "You will not harm any more good people of Fossarelick. I . . . I . . . ahhhh!" The village Elder's eyes rolled back and he collapsed onto the hard granary floor.

Seerlana ran to lift his head and smooth the wisps of white hair that had fallen over his eyes. She pressed her cheek near his sagging mouth and felt a faint breath.

Just then, Shaklana dashed into the granary with two of the older boys. Her eyes widened as she saw the old man stretched out on the floor, his head cradled in Seerlana's lap. The boys slipped their arms under his body and carried him to the lodge hall.

Shaklana lowered her eyes and muttered, "I am so ashamed, Seerlana. Cahal thought he was protecting us but . . . but . . ."

"But he could not accept the truth. The dragons will help, not hurt us. Let me come with you to the lodge so that I might tend to him. Where are those medicinal herbs?"

The two cousins joined their neighbors in the hall, where Cahal was lying on a blanket spread across one long table. A pot of hot water was boiling and Sherca had arranged various herbs on broad leaves scattered over the table close to the old man's still form. Seerlana was relieved to feel his breath against her damp palm, and she ran her fingers through a few small piles of seeds, dried leaves, and roots nearby.

"Here, Shaklana," she whispered and pointed to some of the plants. "Take a pinch each of the lyvrwort, the milk thistle, this yellow herb, and the minced dandelion root to brew a strong tea. I'll make a paste from these wild yams and those dried herbs I had in my sack, and you will massage it into the back of his neck and head until he awakes. That's when you give him the tea. Now, hurry, please."

Those villagers not heating water or mixing medicines stood around the table bearing Cahal. One rubbed his hands and feet while another fanned his head with a clean cloth, all intent on their leader's every twitch—except Alana. She scuffed across the wood plank floor to the open doorway and, leaning against the doorframe, stared into the distance, down the path leading away from the village.

Thoughts of Carliel and her lost mirror brought tears to Alana's eyes. Wiping her damp cheeks with the back of her hand, she squinted as three shadows appeared on the road. They grew in the dim light as they approached Fossarelick. Backing away from the door, she shouted, "The wraiths are coming—they're coming for Grandfather! I see them down on the road. Look for yourselves!" She ran to the corner near the huge hearth and, shivering, squatted close to the fire.

Sherca handed the teacup she'd been holding for Cahal to her neighbor before hurrying to the door to see for herself. Outside the lodge, she ambled to the top of the path that led to the road and broke into a broad smile. "Those are no wraiths! Not at all!" she laughed. "Alana, it's Kirrill, your father come home, and two others are with him. Kirrill, Kirrill!" Before anyone could hold her back, Sherca ran down the path to greet the travelers.

Seerlana ignored the tumult at the door and called Alana back to the table. "Here, girl, your Grandfather's eyes have started to flutter. While I hold up his head, massage the rest of this paste into the muscles on the back of his neck. Slaney," she said to the woman holding the cup of tea, "be ready to wet his lips with the brew, once I tell you to start."

Alana's shaking hands could hardly keep the mixture on her fingertips and her eyes squeezed shut. Another village woman took the paste and pushed her away. "Go to your mother, girl. She's shouting something; who in the Ways of the World knows what." She began to rub the paste along Cahal's spine below his skull.

Alana ran to the door in time to see Sherca just a few steps away from the approaching threesome. As the biggest one wrapped her mother in his arms, Alana felt her head whirl; her next sensation was a sharp pain as her forehead hit the dirt.

PART II: LEAVING WHAT IS KNOWN

*　　*　　*

A heavy rain began to soak Fossarelick as Kirrill, Eunan, and Cahalson ran directly into the hall, Sherca leading them. When the men entered, most of the villagers stepped away from the table and looked at each other, speechless. Sherca walked beside her husband Kirrill, who carried a dazed Alana in his arms. Cahalson hastened to the table and frowned as he realized his father lay there scarcely breathing. Eunan, stunned at the sight of Seerlana working to revive Cahal, backed away from them all and leaned against a wall.

Chapter 10

DRAAKO BENT HIS HEAD INTO the strong wind as he flew among the storm clouds gathering over Fossarelick. Satisfied that the villagers had freed Seerlana, he soared up, urging his strong wings to carry him directly to the Sunsetside Mountains. *Aurykk will help,* he thought. *He will know the next step.*

With a glance at the lightning and rain pelting the village behind him in the Valley, Draako banked his body to the left and descended toward the stone ledge outside the Cave of Refuge. Thrusting his hind legs in front of him, he landed in front of the entrance. Dust and grit swirled around him as his wings fluttered and he stretched his neck to peer into the cave.

A volley of barks and growls greeted him. Bounder dashed out of the cave entrance and bared his teeth, but the dog's threats ended at once when he recognized Draako. With a soft whine, he backed into the cave and bumped into the two weasels, who peered out sleepily, then rolled and tumbled out of the cave. They skittered up Draako's leg and sat on his shoulders.

"What happened to the others?"

"Where have you been?"

"Why have you returned?"

"Has the Malevir destroyed the World and its Ways?"

PART II: LEAVING WHAT IS KNOWN 149

Draako's head swiveled from side to side as their torrent of questions fell on his ears. He nuzzled his little friends and set them gently on the ground in front of him. Bounder, after taking a few hesitating steps away from the safety of the cave, sniffed the air a few times and sat behind the weasels.

Draako's eyes softened into a gentle green as he chided Bounder, "Come closer, puppy. You are safe with me." He answered the weasels. "The dams wait for me sunriseside. I bring good news: we have new allies—Moktawl warriors—and I've found Azile, Seerlana's daughter. But I also bring bad news: the Malevir has made Nnylf, son of Seerlana, his prisoner, to help him find the Mystic Scintilla."

"How d'you know?" the two weasels asked at the same time.

"As we were flying over the forest, Azile's thoughts reached me. She heard my call and told me about Nnylf. She was at the hork's wall, with the Moktawls and two other strange creatures I have never seen before."

"Can you tell us what you saw?"

Draako stood tall and spread his wings as he described the Moktawls, the goat-headed giant, and the tiny woman with four arms. Lowering his head, he murmured, "Azile has grown so tall! You should see how well she commands the rest of them, especially the giant!"

Gormley licked her paws, cleaned her whiskers, and turned to groom her brother. "Here comes Aurykk."

Draako looked up as the Golden's head emerged from the cave. An ashy haze swirled around the old dragon's snout. His eyes blinked and focused on the new arrival.

"Back so soon?" Aurykk muttered. "Well, come in. Don't dawdle." His gaze fastened on Draako's wings. "Looks like your flying skills have improved, anyway," he said, and a smoky chortle bubbled out of his jaws.

The weasels and Bounder sidled over to the far edge of the rock-strewn platform. Draako hardly noticed their chattering. He followed his uncle inside and sniffed the appetizing scent of freshly chopped bats and berries filling his nostrils.

"Thought you might like to share in this small feast I've prepared: lots of seared fresh bat, and you're just the dragon to help us finish it off."

Draako had never heard Aurykk call him a dragon. He had become used to "wyrmling."

"So kind of you, Uncle. I can't remember my last meal." As he spoke, he spotted a round-bellied creature trotting over to them from Aurykk's nest. His four sturdy legs carried him quickly to Draako's side.

"Why, 'Argo, you look nearly big enough to fly!" Draako blurted. Little curls of smoke darting from his nostrils betrayed his surprise. His cousin's scales formed a pattern of red and bronze stripes across his young back.

'Argo sniffed Draako's snout. "Been practicing."

The dragons huddled around the meat, nut, and berry mixture spread daintily across a bed of chinquapin leaves. After the younger dragons gulped nearly every last morsel, they set to chomping on the greens. The weasels picked at stray chunks of meat and Aurykk belched in satisfaction while patting his belly.

Draako used a claw to pick at a nutshell lodged behind one of his back grinders. "Only a dragon who has lived your sort of life would know how to prepare bats that well, Uncle. Which reminds me—"

"My sort of life," Aurykk snorted. "What does that mean?"

"Um, I mean, you've learned a lot and had many adventures, haven't you, over hundreds of years in this valley and beyond?"

The old dragon licked his forefoot and groomed around his jaw. "Adventures? Not the kind I'd hoped for. In *this* sort of life that I've led, when I wasn't preparing delicious bites to eat, cleaning my nest, running after young dragons, or sleeping, I was protecting our lair, hiding from the Moktawls, defending the last of the Orferans from the Malevir, and searching for . . . for Lugent."

"Lugent? My father?"

Aurykk looked directly into Draako's eyes. "A great warrior dragon.

PART II: LEAVING WHAT IS KNOWN

A Silver who stayed with Anadraka until his death—or disappearance." A spiral of amber smoke curled into the air above Aurykk's head and he looked toward the mountains.

Draako stood to look outside as well. Bounder and the weasels were sitting on their haunches just inside the entrance, staring at him. "I hardly knew my father. I was so young when we came here." He paused. With a smile, he looked at the dog and said, "I am happy to see that Bounder is well."

The dog lowered his head and, grunting, rested it on his front paws. His ears, however, perked up with every word Draako spoke.

Draako continued, "I know that my father fought the Malevir, but I cannot believe the beast could kill a Silver. On my flight sunriseside, I learned that Fossarelick has its own Malevir stories. Our friend Azile— you remember her, Seerlana's daughter? I told you she spoke with me as the dams and I flew over them. The Malevir tried to force her and her brother to show him our hidden treasure. She told me the beast has taken him. I also know now that the Moktawls feel ashamed to have hunted us. They no longer blame us dragons for their damaged crops and maimed animals."

"Yes, yes," said Aurykk impatiently and he scratched one of his spikes with a rear claw. "I sensed all that when you arrived. What else, then?"

"You wanted us to find the Malevir so that together with the villagers and their new friends, we could defeat him . . . somehow."

"That's not much of a plan," grumbled Gormley.

Draako turned to face her. "That's why I am here. I thought that Uncle Aurykk might teach me about the Malevir, so I could plan our attack."

Aurykk shook his head and waved at them all. "Come over here to my nest. It will comfort you as I tell you about the beast."

The dragons and their furry companions settled into the soft rags that cushioned Aurykk's nest and looked up as he began to speak:

There was a time, before the battles between men and dragons, when the Veiled Valley was green and covered with trees, berry bushes, and wildflowers. Birdsong filled the air from early morning until sunset. Sunriseside, a mountain poked its peak above a vast, dark forest. At the base of its tree-covered slopes, far below our ancestors' cave, a lodge housed a large family of Valley folk.

The youngest among them, unlike their great elders, thought it was just a tale that a dragon lair lay hidden within the craggy summit looming over them. The family, including grandparents, aunts and uncles, and mothers and fathers, worked in their fruit tree orchard while their children tended egg-laying chickens and a few goats that supplied them with wool, milk, and cheese.

The family grew so large that some of the uncles and aunts took their children and moved away to make their own homes in what is now the town of Nosidam. They cut away at the forest to build their houses. They learned to make tools and furniture, which they traded for clay pots, clothing, and other items their cousins knew how to make.

Food was hard to find in the town, and so they traded with their family still living in the forest. Nosidam became a market town because, over time, more people built more villages. They needed a place to meet, trade their goods, and exchange news. Nosidam served the purpose.

PART II: LEAVING WHAT IS KNOWN

Some of those villagers moved to the central valley and turned their tree-dotted meadows into fields of golden barley that waved in the breezes. They harvested the grain and brought it to market in Nosidam. And so life in the Veiled Valley continued in this way: planting and harvesting, growing and cutting, trading and traveling. Only one man, his wife, and their children remained in the lodge. They tended their orchard and cared for their animals. Even though their children begged them to move to the town, they refused to leave, and for a very good reason. I had come to ask them to stay.

You see, the Malevir had returned to the Valley. He began to attack us and the settlements. Many dragons died. After one brutal raid, I placed all the surviving Orferans under a spell and left them asleep in our ancestral cave. I needed the man and woman at the lodge, loyal to their tradition of serving us as Forest Protectors. They agreed to help. With every change of season, the woman went to the cave in secret to care for the sleeping Orferans.

Every time his wife made that journey, the man—Fulgid—would sit and snooze in the evening by the great hearth, under a large silver disk embedded in the heavy stone surround. His children thought he enjoyed dozing near the warmth of the dying cook-fire, and they left him there undisturbed. As soon as he heard the contented snores of his family echoing from the rooms upstairs, he stood and pressed his ear against the stone wall.

One night changed everything. Sooner than he expected, he heard a set of faint knocks behind the silver disk—his wife, Alluxana's signal. Immediately he pressed with all his weight on the silver disk, which flipped up on invisible hinges, and a knob popped out. Pulling on the knob, Fulgid strained and sweated until he had opened a doorway in the wall. From the dark passageway behind her, Alluxana stumbled out into the dim light of the great hall.

"They are stirring," she whispered. "Soon, we must awaken them and keep our promise to the golden warrior."

I learned later that as my sleep spell weakened, all my dragon family had begun to awaken. Alluxana had made two discoveries—a speckled egg that lay half-buried in a pile of sand and the faint remains—the outlines—of Tinta and Ruddykin, our red dragon cousins on the cave floor.

Aurykk's story abruptly stopped as Gormley squeaked, "What happened to Lugent?"

Gúrmulo clamped his paw over Gormley's snout and said, "Patience! Aurykk will tell you soon enough!"

Gormley pushed away her brother's paw and, staring at the great dragon elder, she insisted: "You are hundreds of years older than any of them—Anadraka and the rest. Why were they asleep? Where were you?"

Aurykk grimaced. "I was away."

Gormley thumped her tail on the cave floor and shook her head. "Everything you say only confuses me more."

Aurykk stepped away from his nest and raised his golden head until it nearly grazed the rocky dome overhead. "All of you, follow me this way and

PART II: LEAVING WHAT IS KNOWN   155

you'll hear the rest of the story. Leave Drac'Argo to his dreams for now."

Pressed into his cousin's side, 'Argo had fallen asleep and was snoring loudly. Draako slid the dragonet's curled body into the far side of the nest, cushioned by soft, clean leaves and moss.

Aurykk heard Draako whisper to himself, "Where are we going?" as they went through an unfamiliar door and into a vaulted passageway. "I didn't know there was more to the Cave of Refuge."

As Aurykk guided his little group through the passageway, he noticed Bounder's drooping ears. "Don't drag your tail, Bounder. Ruddykin's not there, and I can assure you he won't harm you."

"I'm not worried about him," growled the dog. "It's just the itchy scales on my aching hind legs. Can't you make them feel better?"

Gormley skittered to a halt. "Bounder, did you just say something?"

Aurykk whispered to her, "Don't fret about Bounder," and nudged the dog to move on.

Bounder answered with a bark, "Never mind me. Just look carefully at everything we pass. The paintings, the sculptures—remember them all."

Gormley jumped onto Draako's neck and clung to his silver-streaked frill. "Draako, what is happening to Bounder? He's acting strangely." But Draako had no answer for her.

Bounder turned back to look at them, then lowered his head and padded on.

No torch fire, no openings to the outside world lit the passageway, yet the walls glowed with a soft light. Tapestries and paintings of dragons battling misshapen birdlike monsters covered the walls. At the end of the passageway stood a silver sculpture. Like a sentinel, it guarded the entrance into a vast hall, furnished with long marble tables covered by bowls and baskets of red gems, amber, and pearls.

Heeding Bounder's advice, Draako studied the sculpture: the figure of a dragon much taller than himself loomed overhead. Its wings looked like they were about to unfurl and its front claws extended toward the enemy underfoot. The dragon's victim looked like one of the monsters in the paintings.

Aurykk took a moment to lick some giant black pearls filling an alabaster bowl. A few whiffs of his warm breath polished them. He called to Draako: "You might think it a statue of Lugent, your sire, but you are looking at your mighty grandfather and my uncle, Argenfort, one of our greatest silver dragons. We see him here at the moment he is killing a basilisk. What do you think?"

Speechless, Draako gazed at the fierce dragon statue and its smooth scales that gleamed and sparkled. "But how could a Silver be my grandfather? I am a Blue."

"Blue like your mother now, but your silver stripes and speckles are spreading, and I have no doubt that you will be a Silver before you live two hundred summers—just like Lugent, your father. Your cousin 'Argo shares a different heritage, as you might know. Now, all of you, come over here." Aurykk pointed to another hall beyond this one, a room that ended in an immense window piercing the mountain wall. Through its amber panes the afternoon sunlight passed and highlighted Aurykk's brilliant scales as the small group stopped a few steps away from it.

"I lived with the other dragons in the Cave of the Ancestors from the time of my hatching; you know that I have seen many generations of dragons join our family. From the cave's terrace, we watched over the Veiled Valley and its people. Except for a few riders, our friends the weasels, the giant Rocánonom, and the Loblin, no one ever saw us because we flew at night and slept in our lair all day. We were happy to live there undisturbed, guarding our treasure and the Mystic Scintilla. We thought we'd seen the end of the Malevir."

"Did Fulgid and Alluxana know about you?" asked Draako.

Aurykk's eye color deepened to an angry rust. "After the Malevir came to the Veiled Valley."

"The beast?"

"An aiglonax. He hatched from the egg of a basilisk, but looks and acts worse than a hork or a basilisk. As large as any great dragon and winged like us, he has two heads. When he chooses, he changes his

PART II: LEAVING WHAT IS KNOWN 157

shape. His paralyzing gaze and the acid ichor that seeps from his scales can harm all but a Silver or a griffin. Only a true Silver has magic strong enough to fight the Malevir's many spells.

Draako felt his head spinning among the dust motes caught in the streaming sunlight. "You said Lugent was a Silver. Why didn't he—"

Aurykk's eyes turned red. "Before he could defend his family, the Malevir attacked him and spirited him away!"

Through wisps of smoke, Aurykk moved closer to the window and gazed at the Valley beyond. He continued his story:

> Now you will hear about Lugent and me. The day the terror began—the warmest day of the year— all the dragons ached for a nap. Isabella and Abulafria covered the egg and followed Anadraka away from the main chamber, with Draako not far behind. They went along a passage that led to a deep pool. They dived in and the pool whirled them down to Anadraka's hidden chamber—and our treasure hoard.
>
> On guard against attacks from the Malevir, Lugent had stretched himself across the threshold while Tinta and Ruddykin snoozed in the shadows of the marble passageway. Thinking that everyone looked peaceful and contented, I hopped over Lugent to reach the terrace outside for one more view of the Valley before enjoying my own rest inside.
>
> I must have dozed in the warm sunlight, because I awoke suddenly to the sound of shrieks and roaring. I saw Tinta and Ruddykin's heads thrashing in wild circles, and their screams of pain told me they had been blinded. Lugent had

suffered the same wound; I saw that his eyes had lost their power to overcome the beast, yet he still battled the two-headed, green-scaled aiglonax with useless spells.

The Malevir had wings wider than yours, Draako. I recognized its screeches as poisonous incantations. It bellowed, "This valley should be mine. I'll rid it of every loathsome lizard." In the next moment, that hideous aiglonax transformed himself into a whirlwind that carried Lugent away. When I turned to help Tinta and Ruddykin, I saw that their great bodies had crashed to the floor. They twitched and writhed for a few moments more, and then all was quiet.

Hoping to heal them, I cleaned their wounds and cast a sleeping spell. Meanwhile, the three dams and Draako had slept through all the fighting and uproar. My next spell brought them sleepwalking up into the main chamber. They lay enchanted next to the Reds, and I must say they did snore a bit.

Satisfied that I had secured my family, I intended to leave the cave, but I noticed that half of our great stone prophecy had fallen to the floor. I quickly covered as much of it as I could with some rocks and debris.

A vile odor from another tunnel hit my nostrils; I moved with care and looked into the dark passageway. Within, I saw two goblins cowering against the wall dressed in torn shirts and leggings. They gasped and their crooked black teeth

PART II: LEAVING WHAT IS KNOWN 159

chattered. One looked up at me and coughed, "Please spare us, O Great Dragon King. I am Bitterbud, and no harm do I wish you."

I saw a red rag on the floor between him and the other goblin. "Bitterbud, you say? And you there, who are you?" I noticed that the other goblin also clutched a red rag and his eyes bulged out of their sockets.

"Forestspice, gre—gre—great dragon lord! Would you have a little cake or fruit? Beetles and worms have we eaten. I'm still hungry."

"Those red rags tell me more about you than you might have imagined. You once followed Rocánonom?" They nodded. "But this Malevir has you in his thrall now?" They nodded again. "I shall spare your lives, but you must promise to help us."

"Oh, yes!" blurted Bitterbud. "Happy I will be to do so."

"Where is the good giant?"

"The Malevir ensorcelled him deep within this mountain. The beast wants your treasure."

I said to them, "I know." My plum cakes fell into their hands. "When you eat these, the beast's mastery spell will lift—though your goblin bodies will remain—and you will lead your brothers to Rocánonom. You will free him." They swallowed the cakes in two bites.

I told them, "The Malevir will not find our treasure. He thinks he has killed us all, and in a few World-Turns he will call you to him from the depths of this tunnel. Follow him and do his bidding. Never let him know I have released you from his spell. You will be our spies. Sleep now."

The goblins slumped down to the floor and their throaty snores echoed in the dark. I knew that the Malevir would not return to the cave itself for many Sun-Risings, and that for now they would rest.

I left the Cave of the Ancestors in search of Lugent, but the whirlwind and my cousin had disappeared toward Coldside. The sleeping Orferan survivors needed protectors while I searched for Lugent, so I decided to shift into human form and pay a visit to the lodge.

That night, I descended to the lodge. Dressed in light leather armor and looking like a young rider, I knocked on their heavy wood door and waited for their footsteps. Fulgid opened his home to me, and without question he invited me to warm myself beside the broad hearth.

As I sipped the rich broth he offered me, I told him that I journeyed in search of the Malevir. I explained that the beast was attacking the Valley to destroy its dragons, take its lands and goods, and enslave its inhabitants. Fulgid called Alluxana, who, in her night bonnet and robe, came to sit with us near the fire's warmth.

"Your clothing is out of place," she said in soft tones. "This valley has no riders, only farmers and townspeople."

PART II: LEAVING WHAT IS KNOWN   161

"So, you've heard the stories of those who rode dragons so many World-Turns ago?" I asked.

Fulgid cleared his throat and said, "Before our ancestors farmed the land, they rode with the dragons. They came to this valley because the dragons found it for them and taught them how to coax the goodness from the soil. Alluxana and I, we would have felt honored to ride a dragon!" Fulgid slapped his knee with a heavy hand and his broad shoulders shook with laughter. "But I cannot see Alluxana nor myself on their broad backs now!"

Alluxana covered her smiles with one hand and said, "Quiet yourself, Fulgid, or you will wake the others."

"Where do you suppose the dragons have been all these years past?" I continued.

Fulgid lifted his brown pointed cap and scratched his head. "With farms, villages, and towns filling the Valley, the dragons decided to leave us for other lands—don't you think so, Luxie, dear?"

His wife took a deep breath and looked up. "No, my heart, I don't think so. I often have seen dragons in the night sky when I look for signs of weather around the moon. They have not left us—yet."

I gulped, astonished that Alluxana had seen us. "Yes, some dragons remain, but now that the Malevir intends to destroy them, I have come to you for help—for the dragons."

"We, help the dragons? Ha, that is a good joke!" Fulgid slapped his knee again and guffawed. But when Alluxana cleared her throat, Fulgid turned to look at her with questioning eyes. "It's not a joke?" Alluxana shook her head slowly. "I see. Well, then, dear sir, please tell us more. Who or what is this beast?"

My tale of the Malevir's origins and his threats made the two listeners tremble and groan. "Fulgid, the cap you wear belonged to a rider whom I—that is, whom the dragons knew many spans of time past."

"This old patched thing? Why, I found it in the attic under a pile of tattered . . ." He paused a moment. "Under a pile of tattered leather armor!" He turned the hat over several times and gazed at it as if he had never seen it before.

"You come from dragonrider families, both of you. Your ancestors used to guard the forest and the lands beyond. Whenever they saw creatures intent on attacking the Veiled Valley, they would warn their dragons, who would restore peace to the land. The Orferan clan lived in a great lair at the top of the forested mountain here, above your lodge. A long passageway connects your hearth to the dragon retreat. They still live there, but . . ."

Alluxana gasped. "But—but—what? These are the very words of our elders, but we thought them mere tales. What of these dragons? Did the Malevir carry out his threats?"

PART III: OLD FRIENDSHIPS RENEWED   163

I answered her by describing his attacks, our wounded, and the sleeping spell I had cast. I also shared the plan I had for the two goblin spies I'd found in a nearby passage. I asked Fulgid and Alluxana to follow the passageway through the mountain to the dragons' lair with every change of season. Renewing their Forest Protector duties, they would look after my sleeping family in my absence.

Before I left in search of Lugent, I told Fulgid how they could find me if they needed my help. "Do you see those red threads loosely sewn along the inner edge of your cap? Pull one out, then put the cap back on your head and I will hear your thoughts. Remember, the hat has only a few red threads, so choose carefully your moment to summon me."

As I rose to leave, creaking stairs leading to the children's rooms startled Alluxana. Smiling, she squeezed my hand in both of hers and dashed up the stairs to block her curious family.

Fulgid had one last question. "Your name, sir?"

"Aurykk. Aurykk, your friend for life."

Draako spoke up before the Golden could continue: "Azile told me that when the Malevir trapped Nnylf and her in the lodge, they met Fulgid and Alluxana, but they had changed."

"The Malevir's attack came after their children had grown and moved to Nosidam. But that is another story. Fulgid has pulled a thread from his hat. We must leave here and find him."

Part III
Old Friendships Renewed

Gúrmulo and Gormley the Brown Weasels©

Chapter 1

As HER BROAD, POWERFUL WINGS carried Anadraka high above gathering storm clouds, she banked sunriseside towards Nosidam. She and Abulafria were flying to the Cave of the Ancestors. Anadraka heard Abulafria call to her. *"Fog hides the great cave. I long to see it again, but first we need to find Fulgid and Alluxana."*

"You're right, of course." Anadraka dipped her long neck and followed her cousin toward the forested slopes below the cave. Heavy rain pelted the pond and lands surrounding the lodge's scorched skeleton. The dams landed in a clearing and spread their wings over their heads.

After the storm passed, Abulafria sniffed and jerked her head back in disgust. She hissed, "What is that foul mess in the tall grass?" She poked at the suspect object with a small tree branch. "A goblin head. A nasty one. Its ear has Malevir bite marks."

"The beast has been here," Anadraka said with a shiver. "The fog's lifting. I can see the Protectors' house. Burned!" She was in the air and swooping over the orchard toward the ruined lodge. After landing near a crumbled wall, the two dams snorted and sniffed at scorched wood, stone, and pottery.

What started the fire? Anadraka wondered. *I do smell something else odd here. Basilisk acid has eaten away at the hearth. A trail of it points to that doorway.*

The crack of a twig underfoot startled them both. They jumped away from the hearth and heard a loud *ooph* as Abulafria stumbled into a

PART III: OLD FRIENDSHIPS RENEWED   167

goat-headed giant. The creature quickly leaped aside and waved one arm. "Don't hurt me! I'm Fulgid, Alluxana's husband. Don't you remember seeing me with her and Azile a few Sun-Risings ago, when you flew over the forest with Draako?"

He held his other trembling hand toward them and said, "This is my dragonrider hat, the one with the red threads. The rider Aurykk told me to pull a thread if I needed his help; but look, you've come instead . . ." He paused, puzzled, then looked up at the dragon dams again. "Anyway, I thought the Malevir had taken my hat, but no—it has been safe all these years, locked in a stone vault beside the bakehouse."

Faint wisps of smoke curled around Anadraka and Abulafria's heads as they listened to the giant's little speech. Anadraka thought, *Fulgid? But Alluxana said he was a man.*

"Yes, yes, I am a man!" shouted Fulgid. "Ignore this wretched body under the Malevir's spell. I'm really old Fulgid."

He hears us! Sad Fulgid, what did the beast do to you and Alluxana?

Fulgid crouched and sat on a charred log. "My ladies, I'm so happy you understand my bleats. Luxie and the young rider Azile expect me to meet them soon near the lodge gate, so I'll keep my story short. Before you fled to the Sunsetside, Alluxana returned from your cave earlier than was her habit. She pounded on this hearth door loudly. I let her in. Luxie ran into my arms and pleaded with me to find a hiding place. She said that your dragon family was fighting a terrible battle in the Cave of the Ancestors."

Anadraka scratched the scales of her left wing, but her mind was on the memory of that day. "I must tell you that after our sleeping spell wore off, we settled into our old habits and watched Draako grow. Alluxana visited us often and shared all she knew about dragonriders—and about you, of course. She became Draako's tutor in dragon ways. We were hoping that in those sad but quiet times, Draako might learn the skills his father would have taught him had Lugent survived. He would need them to become our Silver if ever our Aurykk should fatten or lose his strength, or"—she sighed and looked quickly at her cousin—"if Lugent failed to return. Draako would be ready to accept riders if the Malevir forced the Ancestors to attack us. Aurykk visited the cave, too, between his quests for Lugent. He, too, shared knowledge of dragonflight with Draako."

Fulgid's goat eyes widened. "Aurykk? But I told you that Aurykk was the name of the rider who visited us the night we became your caretakers!"

Abulafria looked at him with gentle golden eyes. "Not caretakers, but friends. Aurykk, our elder and a golden dragon, takes human form when he must."

Anadraka continued their story: "After Aurykk's spell weakened and we learned to love and trust Alluxana, we tried to heal Tinta and Ruddykin, but neither tincture nor remedy could restore their eyes or close their wounds.

"As time went by, they began to weaken and fade. Their bodies turned to vapor. We could hardly see them where they lay. One day, they were gone. Only a rough shadow remained on the cave floor in their stead, a shadow smelling faintly of the Malevir's ichor. We mourned Tinta and Ruddykin, who became something worse than dead."

"Worse? What could be worse than losing your family?" Fulgid bleated, fingering the red thread he had pulled. He placed the hat on his head and twisted it to fit over his folded ears.

Anadraka and Abulafria looked at each other and little curls of smoke escaped from their nostrils. Abulafria's eyes began to redden as she remembered that day. She looked to Anadraka. "Where were we—Isabella, Draako, you, and I—when the storm and the second attack began?"

Anadraka's fangs gleamed in the growing shadows of evening. "The pain of that time makes me want to bite and slash—don't cringe, Fulgid, I can control my rage. I remember: we were sharing the beauty of our emeralds and topazes in my chamber when we heard crashing thumps above us."

PART III: OLD FRIENDSHIPS RENEWED

Abulafria continued, "We flew up into the main chamber. Fierce blasts of cold wind whirled us against the walls and sharp stones that hang from the ceiling. A storm followed. It boomed and streaked the air with lightening. No rain fell. From roiling clouds above our mountain, a host of shadows poured onto the ledge, each spirit dark as a pit."

"And their huge red eyes all staring at us . . ." Anadraka shivered. "'You have failed us,' said the towering shade closest to us. 'Your Golden has left you, and all hope for dragons has left as well. We will conquer the Valley and destroy everything in it.' We screamed back at them that it was our duty to protect, not destroy, the Veiled Valley. The leader came so close that we felt our scales crackle. He said utter destruction was the only way to save the Valley. We could feel anger flaming into our throats. How could they threaten the Valley that all dragons were meant to protect?"

Fulgid paced around the hearth and walked in and out of the tunnel leading to the goblins' burrows. He faced the dragon dams and bleated, "*Ba-a-a-ah!* Many pardons—that wretched wailing sound comes out of my mouth when I am distressed. How did you survive those demons?"

"No, they weren't demons," said Abulafria, "but spirits of our ancestors who had been growing in strength. The Malevir had infected them with his cruel enchantments. They intended to surround us with their vapors and force us to join them. As the spirits of the ancestors closed in on us, Ruddykin's voice came out of that poisonous mist, and I remembered his faint and stinking shadow on the floor of the cave. Ruddykin, my own mate! Flaming with wrath and a desire for revenge, with his honeyed words flowing over me, he almost had me joining their dark forces."

"But our Draako broke the spell," said Anadraka. "As if possessed by a powerful spirit, he spoke to the shades in a strange and deep, rumbling voice. He said, 'No harm will come to this valley as long as I, Draako, am here.' He stood on his young dragon legs and pointed his long claw at the spirits. His wings spread full behind him and he said, 'Be gone, all of you, or the wrath of Lugent will fall upon you and blow you as cinders to the edge of the world!'

"Through the looming shadows, we could see the faint glowing face of the moon. The mists quivered and all those angry ancestor spirits left. Draako stood in a daze. He remembered only the attack; we were alone again and all was calm. But not for long," she snapped. "The Ancestors attacked again a few sunsets later, after I had brought my rider and her children to the Cave of the Ancestors to meet Draako. He'd grown quickly into his large feet and wings."

"You mean Azile and Nnylf?"

"Yes. The attack began and the Ancestors' spirits surrounded Draako. As I tried to come between them and my son, Nnylf jumped onto Draako's neck. His sister clambered up behind him. Grabbing Draako's still-tender frill, they flew out of the cave. Seerlana flung herself over my neck and we escaped toward the Coldside. Aurykk appeared suddenly, as if he had dropped from the sky. He told Abulafria to place her egg in his jaw pouch and guided us toward the Cave of Refuge."

"Did the Malevir try to find you?"

"No," answered Anadraka, "an unbreakable guardian spell has protected my family there. I would have joined them if not for my need to find Seerlana and search for my dear Lugent. In a field near Fossarelick, I gave Seerlana the Rightful Reader's stone for safekeeping—for Draako—in case I died. Moktawls discovered me as I stood talking with her. Their arrows injured one of my wings as I flew away and I returned to the abandoned Cave of the Ancestors, sure that the Malevir was working his evil elsewhere."

"How did you survive the attack?"

"A weasel cared for me—look." She pointed to her violet scar. 'I still have the mark of the Moktawl fire arrow."

Fulgid sighed. "I don't understand. What weasel?"

Anadraka felt impatience as she replied, "Gormley, one of a pair of weasels Rocánonom of Anonom Trace sent to help us. Now, you know

PART III: OLD FRIENDSHIPS RENEWED

that we have little time for stories of the past when present dangers menace our future."

"True. You ought to find Azile and Alluxana. They're not far from here. I hope Aurykk will be here soon, so I'll wait for him."

Anadraka sighed. "It is good to find old friends again."

Fulgid nodded and pointed toward the road. "Fly that way. You'll pass the Moktawl band. Azile and Luxie should be coming along to join them."

Chapter 2

WITH THE SPRITES FORESTSPICE and Mallowseed ahead of him and others quietly filing behind him, Rocánonom squeezed past rock formations that narrowed another leg of the tunnel. Where the ceiling rose high above his head, the giant stood and stretched. Using hand signals, he cautioned his band to remain quiet, and soon he heard scratching and muffled shouts in the cavern's main gallery. Puzzled, he mouthed to Forestspice: *Peek around the rocks. You are small enough to find the source of those sounds without being seen.*

Forestspice patted his trembling brother Mallowseed on his back and waggled his head in the direction of the gallery. Mallowseed sighed, shrugged his shoulders, and followed his friend. Dashing from behind one stalagmite to another, they managed to cross half the cave floor before bumping into each other. Forestspice whistled like a frantic sparrow, and Rocánonom and the band of sprites joined them in the gallery. No monster lurked there to ambush them. Instead, a tall boy lay chained to a rock. Filthy cloths gagged his mouth and covered his eyes.

They clustered around the boy, now thrashing against the rock he was bound to. Rocánonom's thunderous voice soon stilled him. "Do not move. We are here to help you." He untied the cloths wrapped around the boy's head. "There, now you can breathe easily. Soon my companions will break these chains and you will be free to swallow soothing water."

PART III: OLD FRIENDSHIPS RENEWED

Rocánonom heard the boy gasp for clean air. Speechless, the boy blinked again and again, as if struggling to understand the cheerful little creatures encircling him and the giant who was wiping his face with a cooling cloth. A minty scent rose from the youngster's skin.

Several sprites pulled out ironworking tools from their sacks and hacked at the chains while Rocánonom hummed a tune almost too faint to hear. Shackles around the boy's ankles shattered. Then the chains fell away, sizzled, and became a cloud of beetles. The shiny green insects massed into the shape of an arrow and shot out of the cave entrance toward the sky. The giant called to his little sprite captains: "Forestspice and Mallowseed, follow the beetles. They will lead you to the Malevir. Soon, we'll meet again in our Nosidam refuge."

The two Loblin left just as the boy tried to stand on his reddened and scraped legs. His knees shook. He called out, "Bitterbud was here!" and crumpled to the cave floor.

Several sprites hurried to pull him up. Rocánonom asked them to stand back, and he carried the boy to a low stone ledge padded with his cape. Sweetnettle, a round and smiling sprite, offered a fistful of rags, but the giant shook his head and pulled a bright scarlet coverlet from his hip pouch.

Rocánonom gently covered the boy, whose eyes closed as warmth surrounded him. The giant hoped that the sweet berry and peppery spice smell would help the boy breathe deeply and slide into a soft and easy sleep.

Rocánonom felt a tug on his tunic hem. "Master . . ." began a small voice.

The giant clicked his tongue in disapproval. "I am no one's master here."

Sweetnettle began again. "Ah-hem, well, then, Rocánonom, sir— who is this boy? Why is he here?"

Earlier, the giant had looked around the cavern's vast gallery. He had seen hork tracks near one of the tunnels. Turning to the sprite, he said,

"Sweetnettle, you will find answers to your questions there." Rocánonom paused and pointed to a tunnel. "I heard the boy call for Bitterbud. Please search that marble-lined passage. Look for anything that might belong to that Lobli."

The eager sprite tugged a green knit cap over his carrot-colored curls and marched toward the tunnel. Pausing under its arched opening, he heard Rocánonom and the others singing an old tune that reminded him of bright moonbeams. With his first step into the tunnel, he nearly choked in surprise as the walls pulsed with light that came from everywhere at once. He patted his tool sack, pulled up his brown leggings, and walked ahead.

On either side of him, narrower tunnels glistened with green and yellow gems embedded in their walls, but Sweetnettle's little copper slippers never changed course. Past the trickling waterfall and the black pool of water beneath it, around blocks of marble gleaming white in the unnatural light of Rocánonom's incantation, the sprite pressed on— until, near a dark cleft in the wall, his nose twitched. Taking two fist-sized stones from his tool sack, he smacked them together until a small flame danced between them.

In the light of the flame, the sprite could see something tucked into a deep cut in the wall. He used a pair of silver tongs to pluck the object from its hiding place, stuffed it into his sack, and dashed back through the tunnel to the main gallery.

Rocánonom was rocking the boy in his arms when Sweetnettle ran up to him. The sprite thrust the rag he had found toward Rocánonom. The giant bent his head to sniff it and smiled at Sweetnettle. "Thank you, good fellow. Bitterbud has left us a clue. Your find tells me much—but right now, let's help this boy. We must learn more about him."

Aindle lingered outside the entrance to another mountain tunnel that climbed away from the Cave of the Ancestors. He had sent Bitterbud

PART III: OLD FRIENDSHIPS RENEWED 175

into it to find his fellow goblins. "Bring them to me by the sun's setting tomorrow." He had lowered his long blue face until his piercing yellow eyes looked into those of the goblin. "You will find them, clod, because the pain you will feel if you do not will be worse than water burning your worm-eaten flesh. Now, go!" At those words Bitterbud fled into the tunnel.

To rest and renew his strength, Aindle eased himself under an outcropping of rock and began to transform himself from a hork into a basilisk. Stunted wings folded over his feathered flanks. Scales covered his long scabrous beak. Acid venom oozed from his talons and seared whatever it touched. His long, reptilian tail switched back and forth.

In his basilisk body, Aindle regained the powers he needed to disguise himself as Lustre again. As such he would charm the people of Nosidam, then he and his army of goblins would force everyone to obey his commands. He could taste the pleasure of watching a future battle between the Valley's towns: they'd slaughter each other, he would take their land and goods, and he would find the dragons' treasure—and the Mystic Scintilla. Aindle snorted angrily in his sleep and a fetid vapor coated the overhanging rock, hissing as droplets of acid pitted its surface.

Bitterbud waited for the monster to slide into snuffling snores, then he slunk out of the tunnel entrance. Without a sound, he crept down the mountainside toward the Veiled Valley and the forest road leading to the Sunsetside.

The basilisk awoke when the sun rose high above the roofs of Nosidam. Midday heat had no chance to wither the plants close to his feet; the grassy patch and dainty wildflowers on which he had rested had quickly shriveled and died, except for a cluster of rue.

Eager to pursue his plans, Aindle rolled away from the rocky overhang. He shook his leathery wings, stretched his colossal bird legs, and stood. A stride or two brought him to the edge of a cliff, and he looked down the mountainside toward the town below.

Behind him, a buzzing sound grew into a high, loud whine. Frowning, he turned and saw a strange object moving toward him—a huge arrow. It grew larger, darker, and more pointed, until it reached him and began to pierce his skin. Each wound forced his acid plasma to ooze upon the tiny biting attackers; around his feet, dozens of scorched emerald beetles littered the ground and writhed as their legs and wings shriveled.

Aindle staggered, then kicked the beetle carcasses aside. His eyes blinked. *Where did these creatures come from? Well, they're dead now.* His beak snapped and he straightened to his full height. His body began to spin like a top in a cloud of gravel and dust. A deep incantation vibrated inside the cloud. Two strong arms thrust out of it, and as the dust settled, a young man emerged: the very one Nnylf and Azile had met in the Nosidam marketplace.

Stepping daintily away from the piles of crushed and smoldering beetles around his boots, Aindle brushed his white shirt and luxurious velvet trousers with an elegant hand gloved in buttery green leather. After adjusting his feathered hat so that the wide brim shaded his eyes, he shouldered a thick, heavy pouch and began his slow and easy descent into Nosidam.

Forestspice and Mallowseed halted their chase after beetles. They smelled goblin and spotted a little one scooting down the mountainside. They wanted to follow him, but to keep Aindle in sight, they needed to track Rocánonom's arrow. After looking back at the goblin's trail, they glanced uphill and then at each other. With a wink or two, they nodded and shook hands. Forestspice hurried downhill to follow Bitterbud while the other sprite pursued the beetles' lead.

Unaware of nearby sprites, Bitterbud hurried away from Aindle as fast as his crooked legs could carry him. *I must warn the Protectors,* he thought. Hurtling down the mountain trail, spurred by the urgency of his mission, he dodged low-lying thorny branches and rocky outcroppings until he reached the lower slopes. He came to the stretch of forest bordering the walls around the lodge.

PART III: OLD FRIENDSHIPS RENEWED

Bounding over the wall, he reached the edge of the clearing and crouched atop a rock shaded by a huge, heavy-branched tree. He caught his breath and rested there for a few moments until, horrified, he realized this was the same oak that had hidden the Moktawls until the hork had discovered Nnylf and locked him in his spell!

He looked around the clearing but saw no one. He backed away from the giant tree, its long, thick limbs bending down as if to snatch him, and soon he realized he had crossed the clearing and entered a grove of fruit trees. An apple fell as he stood within the grove.

"Grick!" he yelped as he felt another apple hit him, and then several more. Looking up, he saw a little man sitting astride a stout branch just overhead.

"Phew, Bitterbud, you stink. Here, take this and wash away that awful smell." The man sucked in his ample stomach to reach something in his pocket. With a flourish, he tossed a fluffy red rag into Bitterbud's claws.

The goblin looked up at him in wonder. "A Loblin rag?" He scratched his ear with a jagged claw. "You know my name?"

"You don't recognize your brother Fernfallow? The Valley folk call me Kolvak," the little cook laughed. "You surely need a friend right now." Fernfallow chomped on the apple he held in one hand while the other hung onto the branch before he dropped lightly to the ground.

Surprised and bewildered, Bitterbud stood fixed to the spot where the rain of apples had pummeled him.

Fernfallow said, "Go on, brother, use the cloth to wipe your snout, your hairy ears, and that dirty neck while I sing the spell away." Fernfallow began a melody much like the one that Rocánonom had sung just days before when he lulled the goblins to sleep. Soon his chant calmed Bitterbud, now curled like a fern head on the orchard path and snoring deeply.

"Hmm, a bit too sweet," Fernfallow chuckled as he tugged the rag from Bitterbud's claws and wiped him clean from head to toe. Soft bubbles and gurgles punctuated the goblin's snorts, while a cloud of honey-tinted mist surrounded him and remained like a blanket until some time had passed.

When the cloud lifted, Fernfallow stepped closer and smiled to see that Bitterbud had taken on the look of his fellow sprites. Gone were the goblin's sharp snout and protruding yellow fangs, the oily fur that grew between scales and claws, and the ripping breeches and tunic that had barely covered him.

Bitterbud blinked and yawned as the spell weakened, and he awoke to see that his hands and arms were a pretty pale green with smooth emerald patches. He patted his face; it had a small upturned nose. His hair was soft and curly. Better yet, his wounded ear was small again and unscarred. He smiled at his long, walnut-brown shirt, matching leggings, and boots of supple copper cloth. He wriggled his toes. Around his waist, he felt the tug of a thick twine belt from which hung a small tool sack.

Fernfallow gripped him by his shoulders and smiled broadly. "Now, Bitterbud, we've broken the Malevir's hold on you."

The reunited sprites jumped when a voice shouted from somewhere in the tree branches above them.

"Are you a Lobli thanks to Kolvak—or should I say *brother Fernfallow*?"

Fearful that the hork might have found them again, they cowered behind the nearest apple tree. Fernfallow called out, "Who goes there that knows us so well?"

Forestspice jumped down to the ground, thumping as he landed. Bitterbud and Fernfallow started again and turned with raised fists and hammers to face their attacker, but their tools clattered to the ground as they recognized a brother sprite. Smiling mischievously, Fernfallow lowered his head and butted Forestspice in his little round paunch, and Rocánonom's captain found himself sitting squarely in the dirt with his legs splayed out in front of him. He began to laugh until his whole body shook.

Within moments, however, he sighed. "I, Forestspice, am so happy

PART III: OLD FRIENDSHIPS RENEWED   179

to see old Bitterbud again. Fernfallow, you know me from the Trace. We have missed you among our kind. Like Bitterbud, I and other Loblin were prisoners of the Malevir. The beast enslaved us in a prison burrow within the mountain, you know. He enchanted Rocánonom and left him to die in chains deep in the mountain. His withered body had no power to free itself."

"Where have you been?" asked Bitterbud.

"With the Moktawls," Fernfallow answered.

"Why didn't I see you in the clearing with them?"

Grumbling while chomping on the core and stem of his apple, Fernfallow answered with a shiver, "Kirrill's donkey and I hid when the hork came into the clearing. He's a beast from the First Turns of the World—a poisonous basilisk and shape-shifter. He changes his look to harm," Kolvak whispered, "not like Aurykk, the golden dragon who can change his shape to help others. But what news of the other Loblin?"

Bitterbud sighed and wiped his nose with a leaf. "That golden dragon freed our spirits—Forestspice's and mine—from the Malevir's magic, but not our bodies. Not then. We promised to watch the Malevir for him and pretend to be under his spell. Many Moon-Risings later, Aindle commanded me to bring all the Loblin goblins to him."

Forestspice said, "But I led my brothers away from the Malevir through the tunnels to Rocánonom."

"Yet the hork caught me again before I could follow you. He took me up into the mountain."

Forestspice said, "*That's* where you were. We were so worried. But, Fernfallow, why do you have this oddly human form and name? You were the merriest of Rocánonom's Loblin before our struggle with the Malevir."

Still looking very much the Moktawl cook, Fernfallow replied, "The giant knew that the friendship between dragons and Valley folk had nearly died. He hoped to find a way to renew that friendship. He needed a watcher to live among them. So he sent me to Fossarelick, and they let me stay. I lived there as Kolvak, the village cook."

"What story did you tell them?"

"That I was an orphan, that I came to find family in Fossarelick, that I was Flacher's cousin from Anonom Trace. It was easy. The Fossarelick folk think I'm a fool who only dreams of food. They do like my cooking, though."

"Easy for a Lobli to make a feast out of scraps. With the right tune, plums and cakes fall into your hands," said Bitterbud.

Forestspice added, "The people of Fossarelick do not know the face of their true enemy. The Malevir grows stronger every day. We freed Rocánonom from the Malevir's curse, and he freed the Loblin from serving the beast as goblin slaves. We followed him to the cave of the dragons' ancestors. There we found a Fossarelick boy chained to a rock. He is free now; Loblin are caring for him."

Bitterbud jumped up and yelped, "You freed Nnylf? Thank the Ways of the World! The hork wished him a slow and woeful death. Where is he now?"

"Asleep, guarded by Rocánonom in that cave. But no sleep for me. I have to go back up the trail to follow the Malevir. Mallowseed is tracking him. I must catch up to him."

"Wait," said Fernfallow. He faced a grassy hummock on the edge of the orchard and pursed his lips in a bird call. A little donkey peered over the top of the hummock, then sauntered down its slope towards the sprites.

"Lovely animal," whistled Bitterbud. The donkey bowed her head and a giggling sound slipped through her large teeth.

"You think so? Where's my red rag?" *Just wait till you see this,* Fernfallow thought. He took his crumpled red rag from Bitterbud's hand, then squeezed the juice of several apples over it. Starting with the donkey's ears, he scrubbed her entire body down to her hooves. As he hummed, a thick, rosy mist wrapped around Fernfallow and his four-footed companion. Forestspice caught glimpses of emerald sparks and ribbons

PART III: OLD FRIENDSHIPS RENEWED 181

of orange and violet dancing in the cloud.

When the mist cleared, the sprites blinked their eyes in disbelief. Milkthistle stood before them—the happiest, rosiest Lobli they had ever known.

Fernfallow explained that Milkthistle had journeyed to Fossarelick with him after Rocánonom disguised her as a donkey. Fernfallow had offered her as a gift to their Elder, who loaned her to his son, Kirrill.

Milkthistle leaned into Forestspice's arm and gave it a squeeze. "I've really missed my brothers. Fernfallow and I have seen and heard about the Malevir's terrible deeds. The beast trapped me and would have eaten me, but Creepervine—I mean, Kralbong—could not catch me." She smiled.

"Creepervine? That rascally fellow?"

Fernfallow grimaced. "Our mischief-making brother died as a cruel and angry goblin. Aindle starved him and forced terrible tasks on him. Creepervine would have eaten ensorcelled Moktawls had he not burned in that pond." Forestspice and Bitterbud looked at each other and shook their heads. Fernfallow added, "Milkthistle and I hid in the forest when you and the Malevir entered the clearing and captured poor Nnylf."

"A short while ago, I escaped from the Malevir, asleep on a cliff high above us," blurted Bitterbud. "Before he lay down, he talked about going to Nosidam to charm the townsfolk and have them start a battle."

In one voice, the other sprites shouted, "A battle?"

Bitterbud twisted a curl around one of his pudgy fingers. "A battle between Veiled Valley towns, to weaken the dragons and their Fossarelick friends—or worse." He shook his head several times.

Fernfallow squatted by the pile of squeezed apples and buried them under layers of dirt clods and dried leaves. After picking up the bundles Milkthistle no longer carried on her back, he handed one sack to her and flung the other over his shoulder.

"Come, my fellow Loblin. Let's move on. We need to find the Orferans. Perhaps up coldside."

Fernfallow, Bitterbud, and Milkthistle began to walk toward the wall surrounding the lodge and its grounds.

Forestspice hesitated. "I cannot go with you. Mallowseed went on alone to track the Malevir. He might be in danger. May the Ways of the World protect you and bring you safely back to Rocánonom." He waved and raced away, pebbles flying under his boots.

The trail was steep, and Mallowseed's copper slippers slid in the dust and gravel that covered the path. The sprite could see Aindle's jaunty figure far ahead—gliding along, sometimes skipping, other times dancing a little jig.

Disguised again as a dragonrider, Aindle had covered his white shirt with a light vest of bronzed leather armor. Blue and gold feathers bounced above his wide hat brim with every step, and his bulky pouch bumped against his slender hip. Soon he would arrive in Nosidam.

Mallowseed hoped to keep him in sight. From time to time, he leaped over small craters that Aindle's acid drops had burned into the trail. The sprite nearly squealed as he felt a tap on his shoulder. Whipping around to face his attacker, he sighed with relief as he recognized Forestspice.

"You here?" he whispered. "I thought you were trailing that goblin."

"That goblin turned out to be our dear Bitterbud. I found him talking with long-lost Fernfallow. I surprised them—but Milkthistle surprised me more."

"Our sister Milkthistle! Where has she been?"

"Like Fernfallow, living in Fossarelick. Milkthistle disguised as a donkey—can you imagine? Rocánonom sent them to watch the villagers."

The two sprites hugged and continued after Aindle.

Chapter 3

*N*OTHING *WILL STAND IN MY WAY NOW.*

Aindle approached the arched gateway leading into Nosidam. With a tug on his hat brim, he lifted his sharply sculpted chin and squinted in the bright sunlight.

Good! I see it's market day again. Just the place to find a few helpful fools.

Aindle strolled through the crowded streets, past one- and two-story wooden houses and into the main square, where farmers and artisans had set up their stalls. He stopped at a stand where a young man and woman were hurrying to arrange their apples in a pyramid of bright reds, yellows, and greens. Nearby on a battered stool sat a gray-haired man whose shaggy moustache hid his mouth. He hummed as he whittled a chunk of soft wood. Looking up from his work, he stared at the stranger.

"Hello, my good man," Aindle greeted him. "What are you making there—a toy, perhaps?"

"I'm my own good man, not yours," he grunted and turned back to his whittling after studying Aindle's boots.

"My apologies," Aindle replied. "I see you've made a head and two strong shoulders."

"Uh-hum."

"Looks like one of those scheming Fossarelick Moktawls to me," Aindle went on.

The marketplace hubbub died. All eyes were on the two men. The woodcarver scratched his chin with the tip of his durk and slowly gazed up at Aindle. The apple farmers in the next stall forgot how to breathe when he answered, "You've been here before and you bought good Fossarelick grain from two young people, but I'll wager you've never been among the fine folk of Fossarelick. You don't look like you even know what it means to lift a pitchfork or build a barn."

Aindle removed a glove and picked at imaginary lint on his sleeve. Looking directly at the whittler's ear, he whispered, "I know plenty. The wizard Malevir has enchanted those 'fine folk,' as you call them. They plan to attack Nosidam soon. I heard it from . . ." He paused and leaned closer to the man's face. "I heard it from one of their own, their Elder."

Joined by a few other marketplace vendors, the young farmer and his wife approached Aindle and the whittler. "Say that again, sir. We all heard you whisper something about an attack on Nosidam."

Aindle straightened up, and in a deep voice, he said, "Yes, I heard directly from the one man who knows the village better than anyone else. I've just come from there. Hmm, nice apples—mind if I try one?" He stretched his arm to grab a rosy piece, then flipped a gold coin into the young man's palm.

"What? Tell us what you heard!" shouted a plump lady as she pushed the farmer aside, hugging one of her honking geese around its straining neck.

Buyers and sellers in the marketplace began to crowd Aindle. He stood even taller and declared, "The Formorian, a hideous goat-headed giant, has destroyed the fields and cottages of Fossarelick. Its villagers have joined with a wizard, called in some parts the Malevir, to fight the monster. They think the Formorian serves all of you, and now they plan to lead an attack on Nosidam. I have come here to warn you all." He paused. Then, satisfied that these people believed his lies, he said, "And to help you, but now I am weary. I need to meet with the Nosidam council, then rest."

PART III: OLD FRIENDSHIPS RENEWED   185

A man, stooped and balding, stepped out of the crowd. Dressed in a green suit that glimmered in the sunlight, a shirt as white as milk, and boots that reached his knees, he loosened his chiffon tie and said, "Good sir, my name is Fergus. I lead the Nosidam Council. How can we serve you?"

Aindle bowed and introduced himself. "My name is Lustre, and I am pleased to meet you, Councilor Fergus. Would you grant me two favors?"

"Willingly, Lustre."

"Gather your council to meet with me, and find me some decent lodgings and a bountiful supper for the evening. I can pay you well."

Fergus reached to take Aindle's arm, but the hork danced easily away from him as if distracted by the abundance of fine goods in the market. "Such healthy, fat geese you have, good woman . . . and look at these fine and plump cucumbers, those tasty berries, and the sumptuous cloth you have woven. Pity if Fossarelick destroys it all."

As the panicked townspeople and vendors milled around the marketplace, they punched and shoved each other to find a place near Aindle. Fergus cowered from their raised fists and glowering faces; but Aindle felt a rush of pleasure as his power over them grew. He heard several shout out:

"Take him to the council now, Fergus! Why do you not hasten?"

"Fergus, don't dither. We have no time to waste!"

"Oh, oh, oh! What shall we do? Where shall we go?"

Amid their screams and wailing, Fergus looked confused. He began to hiccup. "Good sir, the people must be calmed." He twisted his neck cloth and dabbed it across his sweating forehead.

Aindle jumped onto the planks of a fruit stall and—with little regard for the plums he had squashed—he shouted to the throng, "People of Nosidam, unjustly blamed by Fossarelick for the Formorian, do not worry. Rest easy. We have time to plan our defense. Now that I am here to speak with your council, your homes and families will be safe. Soon the threat of Fossarelick will be nothing but a laughable memory."

He smiled at the hopeful faces looking up at him. He assured them that they could return to their work or homes because he would take care of everything at the Council Hall. Their shouts and cries faded. Aindle was pleased to see people patting each other on the back and shaking hands.

The woodcarver was sitting on his worn stool as he watched the newcomer's progress down the street. "The Malevir? Couldn't be," he muttered. "But that liar is no rider."

Forestspice and Mallowseed followed the beast into the heart of Nosidam. Although Aindle's transformation had ended in a total disguise, barely visible footsteps with seared edges had marked his trail up to the edge of town. Now that poisonous puddles were no longer a threat, the sprites quickened their pace and reached Nosidam just as Aindle was soothing the marketplace crowd. With a quick leap, Forestspice hid inside the canopy of a well and Mallowseed jumped into a basket of onions and turnips. Because of their small size and forest-colored clothes, no one had noticed their movements. They held their breath and listened to the beast's speech.

Aindle was leaning toward Councilor Fergus, whose hands were clasped in front of his forehead as he whimpered about the coming attack. Without anyone noticing, Aindle caught the little man's ear in his teeth and nipped it. The councilor clapped one hand to his ear, but he quickly lowered it, nodded slowly, and waited for Aindle's next move. They left the square and headed toward the Council Hall.

Forestspice had dropped to the ground and was jogging from the shelter of one shadow to another as he followed Aindle and his new captive. Mallowseed, turnip greens clinging to his legs, crawled out of the basket and looked for his brother, then stifled a cry when he saw an old man stand in Forestspice's way. He gulped and gripped his tool sack. "I'll skewer him if he touches one hair," he murmured, planning his next move.

PART III: OLD FRIENDSHIPS RENEWED

After colliding with a boot leg, Forestspice thought of using a charm to escape, but quickly the face belonging to the body attached to the leg lowered to his own and said, "Hello, Lobli. Please stay. I am a Protector. Call your brother here."

Mallowseed was leaping across the square to jab the man's ankle with his durk, but after reading his brother's face, quivering in a mass of signals, he pocketed his weapon.

"Now look at you two! Eyes like two frightened cats!" The old man scooped the stunned sprites up in his arms and gently dropped them into his deep sack.

Forestspice coughed and complained as tools and chunks of wood bumped and scraped against his legs. "What are you doing to us? We have to follow the—"

"Quiet, manikin! I'm helping you."

Hugging the writhing bundle of Loblin to his chest, the man spoke through the sack: "Soon we'll be at the Council Hall and you will be free to track that gossip- and trouble-monger."

Forestspice stopped complaining and whispered, "Then tell us your name and purpose."

The man had stopped walking, and he rested his bundle on the ground. Opening the sack's mouth, he reached in to help the two sprites crawl out. "I am Luchaer, the only Protector left in this town." He coughed. "At least, the only one who remembers he is such."

Forestspice brushed wood shavings from his leggings and tunic. "That so-called Lustre—who is a wicked beast disguised as a dragonrider—made slaves of the Loblin until we freed our leader, Rocánonom, from the beast's enchantment."

"Enslaved you? Why?" Luchaer whispered as they huddled in a corner behind the Council Hall. "And Rocánonom . . . familiar name, but I can't remember exactly—"

"A good, kind giant, and once Protector of Anonom Trace."

Luchaer looked bemused. "Ah, yes, I remember stories of him told in the Trace when we were young." He smiled and pulled out a red kerchief. Wiping the sweat from his brow, he pointed to a small open window. "That's your way into the chamber, but—"

"Then it's true!" Mallowseed burst out, staring at Luchaer's kerchief. He frowned. "Or . . . did you steal that rag from one of our own?"

Luchaer scowled. "Suspicious little pine knot, aren't you! But no, my mother gave this to me before she left the Trace to come here—made me swear by the Ways of the World to keep it with me always." Pocketing his kerchief, he said, "Don't leave yet. I have so many questions. Most importantly, who is that Lustre who claims to be a rider?"

Forestspice looked directly into Luchaer's eyes. "He is the Malevir himself. A hork or a basilisk, too, if he chooses. Now, sir, we thank you for your help."

"Of course—the Malevir." The old man leaned his hand against the stone wall and took a deep breath. He looked back toward the square to see if they had been followed, but the crowd had dispersed. No one was in the street. "I feared as much. We must find a way to stop him! The beast soon will have all the councilors in his service." But when he looked down, he gasped, and his shoulders slumped.

The two little creatures were gone.

Chapter 4

BOUNDER REFUSED THE INVITATION. His fur stood on end as he growled, "The Red will find me and chew me up if I go with you. Why not leave me here to guard the Cave of Refuge, Aurykk? 'Argo needs me."

The dog stiffened his legs and held his ground until the elder dragon gathered him in one of his huge forepaws and dangled him high above the cave floor. "The dragonet is ready to fly. Ruddykin has trusted us to care for you," he said, his smoking snout close to the dog's panting tongue, "so you might as well travel with us. Don't you agree, Draako?"

Bounder sneezed. "But . . . to hang from your claws like a cat's favorite toy while you fly above the clouds? I'll faint and fall. I'll tumble through the air, head over paws, like a dried leaf in winter, like a sparrow in the storm, like—"

"Yes, yes, I agree," Draako interrupted him. "We can't let that happen to a friend, so you will travel in my pouch, safe and warm."

Bounder's ears lifted as he looked up and down both dragons, searching for a hidden pouch.

Draako chuckled, then opened his jaws wide as Aurykk explained, "No, not outside our bodies. Our jaws are wide and quite flexible. See? In one corner behind the last grinder tooth, each of us has a hidden pocket, which we can fill with air and, just so, we can carry our prey long distances while keeping it alive. Tastes better that way once we reach our lair."

"Prey! Inside your jaw? Oh no, not that! I'm afraid you will swallow me—accidentally, of course." Bounder shrank back into the cave's shadows toward the passage leading to Aurykk's lair, but 'Argo pushed him back, toward his dragon elders. "Stop pushing. You'd never have to worry about the cave because I would be the best guard ev—"

Bounder's raised front paw froze in midair at the Golden's first hummed note. A melody sparkled and flashed in the air, and the curly-coated dog sank to his knees and sighed. Moments later, he was asleep.

Draako faced the cave entrance and blasted a huge sooty breath. His next intake of air puffed out the scaly folds surrounding one of his jaw hinges. Spreading his jaws wide, Draako opened the pocket with his tongue and a claw, picked up Bounder, and placed the dog in his new sleeping quarters. With a deep breath and another flick of his tongue, Draako closed the ballooning pocket.

The Golden smiled. "Well done, nephew. The weasels will run ahead to Nosidam. We will meet them again later, I assure you. Now Bounder's time has come."

Draako, with a heavy lump sagging in the corner of his jaw, looked sunriseside. "Ard do dalk now. Uncle, vah do ee go, dis tine?"

"You shouldn't talk with a full mouth." Aurykk winked. "We go to the Protectors' lodge to meet Fulgid. He has called me by pulling the thread of his rider's cap. 'Argo, are you ready?"

The young dragon nodded, even as the knees of his forelegs wobbled. He looked to his cousin. "I'll be fine as long as you two are by my side."

Draako stretched his wings, then folded them close to his silver-streaked flanks. Scratching an ear with one claw, he squinted toward sunriseside and sent out his thoughts: *"You're no longer a hatchling, brave 'Argo, and I think you'd like to see Abulafria again. Uncle, do you suppose the dams have reached the Cave of the Ancestors?"*

"Their first stop was going to be the Protectors' lodge," Aurykk muttered, then blew a short flame. "Ways of the World—of course! Fulgid called me because the dams have found him. How long will Bounder stay asleep?"

PART III: OLD FRIENDSHIPS RENEWED   191

"Until we reach the lodge," Draako replied. With one leap off the ledge, he soared into the air and looped back to join his uncle. 'Argo whooped and belched sulfurous bubbles as he flapped up and away from the ledge. The three dragons flew sunriseside toward the mountain and their ancestral home.

Waking in fits and starts, Bounder blinked his eyes but saw nothing. His dream of flying and swooping down on a herd of horses vanished as he felt the tug of Draako's wings. The dog realized that these dragons intended to carry him along despite his fears, and he was surprised to find himself so comfortable, dry, and warm. His only complaint was a nagging itch that had started between his toes and continued up his legs and along his spine.

In the absolute dark that surrounded him, he reached for his tail to scratch it and wondered at the way it had wrapped around his body. When did it grow so long? He stretched out his back paw to grasp his tail's end and gulped. He felt three long toes at the tip of his paw and a fourth toe behind them, each ending in a long, sharp claw. Like a dragon's foot! But he was no dragon. The muscles in his back began to twitch. Perhaps he was still dreaming.

Quite rapidly, Draako's jaw pouch was shrinking and Bounder thought he was going to burst through the membrane. His breath grew short and labored as he felt Draako's neck turning and twisting in flight. That was it! Draako was going to eat him at the end of the flight! He lowered his head and howled as he felt his back gripped in spasms.

Draako must have heard his cries; Bounder felt the pull of the ground as the dragon began a sharp dive. He stretched his forelegs in front of him and braced against the pouch for a rough landing. Instead, he felt only a gentle bump before the dragon opened his jaws and pulled Bounder out of his travel berth and into the light of day.

Draako and the Golden were resting against the crumbled wall of a large burned-out house. 'Argo was sniffing at the entrance to a dark tunnel leading into the hillside behind the ruins of a great hearth. Shivering, Bounder shook his head and began to speak, but his mouth felt odd, as if it were hard and narrow. He rolled his tongue and discovered his teeth were gone.

The dragons were laughing and hiccupping little puffs of white smoke. Bounder felt Draako's wing gently push him to the edge of a long puddle of black water. "Look at your reflection, Bounder. What a secret you've kept from me! See how big you've become? No wonder my jaw pouch aches."

Bounder opened his mouth to growl, but, unsteady on only two legs, he fell into the puddle with a squawk. Embarrassed and miserably wet, he shook his head and wriggled his body to dry off. His muscles twitched and shivered as his skin adjusted to his growing body.

Then, as the puddle's surface stilled, Bounder lowered his gaze. No dog looked back at him. The creature in the water at his feet had an eagle's wings and talons, a beaked head flanked by two feathered horse ears, a lion's body, and a dragon's hind legs and tail. He stomped on the creature, then realized it was his own body mirrored in the rippling water below him. Another long, pitiful squawk came out of his beak. "What have I become?" he howled.

Abulafria landed next to him. "Bounder, you're a griffin again!"

Bounder shook his head and found his voice. It was husky and low. "I need to rest. I don't understand." He stumbled backward and squatted on the edge of a broken wall.

A shadow fell over him, and when he looked up, he recognized Anadraka circling overhead as she aimed for a landing. The other dragons had reassured her that nothing was wrong, so she glided to the ground, folded her wings, and approached Bounder with cautious steps. "So many changes in so little time! Now Bounder takes his turn."

The newly formed griffin shook off his dog ways with difficulty. He meant to scratch his flank with his hind leg but instead ruffled the thick feathers of one wing. Losing his balance, he fell back on his lion's

PART III: OLD FRIENDSHIPS RENEWED 193

haunches and felt the sting of spikes protruding from his hind legs. A high yelp and a series of whistles came out of his beak as he struggled to stand.

Draako's head was wreathed in white smoke as he laughed and pointed at Bounder's discomfort. Aurykk silenced him with a sweep of his foreleg, then faced Bounder. "You are one of our weapons against the Malevir. All griffins—the few of you that remain—are enemies of the basilisk. Its gaze will not harm you, at least for brief periods. You can use those wings to soar like an eagle, you will soon learn that you have the courage of a lion, and those legs—yes, those unusual legs."

Anadraka spoke up. "Tell him, Aurykk—about the nest, I mean, and his hind legs."

The Golden cleared his throat of little cinders and smoke puffs and continued: "Orferans have made their nests and laid their eggs in the Cave of the Ancestors for countless Turns of the World. One day, a lone griffin dam came to our ledge and begged the family for refuge. Orla was her name. She had expected to lay the last of her three eggs in her own nest, but a flock of rocs attacked her, and she flew off in a panic. To escape the giant eagles twice her size, she looked for a hiding place on Sunriseside Mountain. When she found our cave, one of the Reds, who was preparing a nest for her own egg, took pity on the griffin dam and invited Orla to share her nest."

Bounder sat gingerly on his haunches again, with new respect for the weapons attached to his hind legs, and said, "Griffins have an eagle's head and wings, and a lion's body, legs, and tail; but I am different. I have these scaly back legs, for example."

Anadraka sighed. "Bounder, you are—how shall I say it? You are a very new sort of creature."

Aurykk went on: "Your dam crouched and dozed in the nest long after the Red's egg had hatched. The rocs must have lost interest in her; we never heard them again after she settled into the Red's nest. Rocs can be noisy, quite the nuisance, really. One day, while the red hatchling was playing beside her, the griffin dam woke suddenly and flew out of the cave without a sound. We watched her soar up and away into the Coldside Lands."

Aurykk paused lost in thought. He shook his head and continued: "Your egg lay there in the nest for endless World-Turns, without a peep or a wiggle. The family wanted to toss it over the cliff outside, but your nestmate, now growing into a sturdy dragonet, like 'Argo here, insisted on keeping you in the nest—as his toy, he said. And so they did."

Anadraka added, "Then one day you hatched!"

"Yes, you hatched, but instead of emerging as a little wet eagle-lion, your body amazed everyone there, especially your red nestmate. As it lay next to him, your egg had been absorbing dragon essence, which added the strength and appearance of dragonkind to your hind legs and tail. They say you were the liveliest hatchling ever seen. You hopped all around the great cavern and were in danger of disappearing into one of the many tunnels leading away from it, but . . ."

Draako's mouth hung open during this strange tale and little sparks danced around his fangs. "I don't understand. Bounder came to us as a dog, not this marvelous creature. I suspected that he was a shape-shifter of sorts, but—"

Aurykk cut him off. "You met his nestling mate. He was that angry spirit called Ruddykin."

Draako's jaws parted as steam spurted from his nostrils. Bounder leaped to his feet. "Ruddykin? Ruddykin?" Trembling, the griffin swung his head from side to side. His sharp claws tore up the sod beneath him as he hopped from leg to leg. "Just the thought of him . . ." He shivered. "But why a dog?"

Abulafria spoke up. "Please, we meant to protect you and still do. Remember, Ruddykin was my mate, the father of 'Argo. You know how the Malevir wounded him and he died, despite Aurykk's efforts to save him. We did not know that early on, before he died, Ruddykin had disguised you as a dog and sent you to live in Fossarelick—to protect

PART III: OLD FRIENDSHIPS RENEWED   195

you from your own powers, to keep you safe and hidden. You had no memory of the change, only the echo of Ruddykin's spell."

"Spell?" whispered Bounder.

"Yes, that whatever he commanded, you would do—like spy on Eunan and the Moktawls. Until the time came for you to return to your own self, your memory would remain clouded and you would think of yourself as a dog."

Aurykk's snout drew close to Bounder's burnished beak. "The madness that drove his spirit from the cave after the Malevir's attack only made Ruddykin angrier and more eager for revenge against those of us dragons who remained alive. When he lost his powers to the Malevir, he ordered you to take back the Erif stone. He made you his tool against the Valley folk and us."

"Until we met at the river!" blurted Draako. "Once he heard me chant,

Erif erif ot em enola
Only to me is given the Fire
Erif erif ot em enola
When men alone cannot prevail,

he promised his loyalty and that of all the Ancestors when we next would meet to fight the Malevir. And he spoke of the Mystic Scintilla."

A noise from the shadows interrupted Draako. A goat-headed giant peeked from behind the ruined hearth. He startled 'Argo, who snarled and spread his wings. The giant bowed his goat's head and bleated, "Spare me. Your dams know me. I am Fulgid, your friend, long cursed by the Malevir to roam as this monster within my Sunriseside Forest."

Aurykk coughed a cloud of sparks as he called out Fulgid's name. He fluttered his wings, which filled the air with deep vibrations, like waves pounding a seashore, and flashes of green, yellow, and gold lights hid him from view. His dragon body faded, only to reappear as a handsome dragonrider. Wisps of smoke encircled him as he approached the giant.

Fulgid held out his long arms. "My dear friend! Had I known you were such a beautiful dragon when we met . . ."

Dragons love flattery, and Aurykk was no exception. "I can speak to you in this guise without my heavy dragon body distracting you. All of us understand your goat speech because we call you our friend. We welcome you."

Fulgid nodded his thanks and he squatted by the hearth.

"Tell me, Fulgid," said Aurykk, "shall we end your cruel enchantment now, or would you risk staying as you are for just a little longer?"

"Why would I choose to keep this wretched form?"

Aurykk laid his tawny hand on Fulgid's arm. "As a Formorian, you have the strength of a hundred men. When we face our enemy, that strength will be a great help."

Fulgid scratched his billy-goat chin hairs. "My dragon prince, let me serve you all with as much force as I can find in these terrible times. With the hope that one day Luxie and I will find our own old selves again, I agree to stay as I am. What can you promise me?"

"Thank you, Fulgid. When the time is right, the enchantment will end, I promise. Now, about those Moktawls—how shall we renew our friendship with them? They have hunted us for so long. Will they ever change their ways?"

Fulgid answered, "Not too long ago, they saw Draako and the dams flying over them in the forest and heard Azile's story. They understood how the Malevir's lies and dark magic had fooled them. Alluxana and I got to know them, in more difficult ways than I care to remember. We became allies and have agreed to follow your plan as Azile shared it."

Aurykk the rider walked over to the crumbling hearth wall, sat next to Fulgid, and picked up one of the scorched bricks lying at its foot. "Go on."

"Azile and Luxie have gone around the mountain to spy on Nosidam. We feared that the Malevir would go there to enchant the townspeople, perhaps to enslave them as well. He's good at that." Fulgid scowled and spat into the cinders behind him.

"And the Moktawls?" Aurykk said, scraping ashes from the brick

PART III: OLD FRIENDSHIPS RENEWED 197

with a gem-encrusted durk.

"Eunan—you know him? Father of Nnylf and Azile—set out with two others for Fossarelick, and the other Moktawls led by Atty are waiting for us by the road. I stayed here to wait for you, so I had the honor of meeting these fine dams." Fulgid turned to smile at Anadraka and the others, but his goat face only increased his look of melancholy.

Abulafria was sitting a short distance from the site of the bakehouse, where the destructive fire had started. She had not spoken for a while, intent as she was on Aurykk. She watched him clean the brick and restore it to its original shape. "Father, what are you doing with that brick?"

As she finished her question, Aurykk tossed the brick into the tunnel entrance that led from the hearth. The ground shook as it exploded. In the same moment, Fulgid jumped away from the wall and into a nearby tree. He watched the stones and bricks of the wall dance in the air, then rearrange themselves into a new clean hearth enclosure and a thick door to the tunnel, which slammed shut with a bone-shaking thud. Aurykk's dragon magic was like a paintbrush sweeping back and forth. With each wave of his hand, a flurry of stones, bricks, and mortar rearranged themselves until rebuilt walls shot up and the entire great hall of the lodge stood before them.

"We shall gather here again, when the Malevir meets his end and the Protectors regain their home. Do you understand, Fulgid?" he called to the trembling giant, who clung to a large branch.

"Understood," he answered in a small bleat. "Thank you."

Aurykk said, "We dragons must return to the Cave of the Ancestors to secure the treasure. Fulgid, I shall return you to Alluxana." Within moments, amid thunderclaps and swirls of smoke, the Golden regained his dragon form. "Now, I think we should go, don't you?"

The other dragons agreed at once. Bounder began to stretch and flap his eagle wings, then shot up into the air above them. He flew in an upward spiral, surprised by his newfound skills and eager to test his powers.

Fulgid tucked his cap into the waist of his breeches, jumped down from the tree, and leaped onto Aurykk's lowered neck. He barely had time to grab the dragon's neck frill as they all took flight and headed toward the mountain.

Chapter 5

ENCLOSED WITHIN THE CIRCLE OF their cottages and Cahal's great hall, the villagers drew close to Cahalson, who was shaking his fist toward the Sunriseside Forest. He said with a grimace, "All these years spent chasing dragons when we should have been hunting the Malevir. At least Eunan's own wife and children still trusted them."

The crowd gasped. Alana stepped forward and repeated Cahal's accusations. "How do we know that you're really my uncle and not under a terrible enchantment? Or worse, that we're not talking with demons who took over your bodies?" She smirked and crossed her arms over her chest.

"Demons would have no need of such deceptions, Alana. They prefer to make us miserable, not hopeful and united in our purpose," Cahalson answered.

Alana looked at the young man and a knot formed between her eyebrows. She reddened and turned away, staring hard at the ground.

Kirrill approached her and smoothed her long brown hair with a gentle hand. "My daughter, you have every right to doubt us, but we have seen the real danger threatening our valley—the Malevir. We can't survive without the dragons." He smiled at her. "Don't fret about your mirror. Soon it will be in your hands."

Alana's lips trembled, and she wept, burying her wet face in her father's sleeve. "I don't care about the mirror; I have been so afraid," she wailed.

Eunan looked into the faces of his fellow villagers. Then, pointing at Kirrill, he said, "This brave man is the most commonsensical one in our village. If he tells you—"

"If I tell you the dragons will help us, then you can believe it!" Kirrill hugged his daughter and held out his hand to his wife. "Some of our children have been far braver than we grown-ups. A copper dragon has chosen to befriend our son Kurnan. That means something! Azile has ridden a young dragon; her brother Nnylf, too—oh, Eunan, I'm so sorry."

Seerlana stepped forward from under the great hall's eaves. "Why are you so sorry to mention my son Nnylf?" she asked in a trembling voice.

Eunan went to her and whispered the story of Nnylf's capture and his hope that their forest allies would help find and defend him.

Seerlana bit her lower lip and took a deep breath. "May the Ways of the World protect him." Looking past the fields, she said, "Right now we have another challenge. The Copper is coming."

In the distance beyond Fossarelick, Seerlana could see Isabella soaring then diving over the same far meadow. She heard the dragon's questions and was about to speak when Cahalson raised his voice again.

"We all have respected my father and his wish to keep us safe and well. Struck down in his anger, he is now too weak to advise the people of Fossarelick. What would you have us do?"

"Choose a new leader: I say Eunan!"

"I say Kirrill!"

"I want either son of Cahal to lead us!"

"No, Seerlana knows more than any of them!"

Many different voices called for one particular villager or another to lead them, but after much heated talk, everyone fell silent when Eunan whistled between his fingers and turned to the crowd. "We Moktawls and Seerlana agreed to break from tradition. We ask you to accept Cahalson as our leader, while Seerlana, Kirrill, and I shall serve as his advisors with the authority to overrule his decisions if they endanger the folk of Fossarelick. We shall turn to the dragons for help. How say you all?"

PART III: OLD FRIENDSHIPS RENEWED   201

A hush followed Eunan's speech. He tried cornering a few neighbors, talking to them, urging them to accept himself and the others as leaders and dragons as friends. People backed away from him, shook their heads, and bent to pick weeds from the herb garden or clean their tools. Children gazed absently at the clouds overhead. The villagers were looking everywhere but at Eunan.

A deep sigh caught their attention. Alana took her father's hands in her own. "I said I was scared, Father. These doubts of mine won't leave me alone, but if you believe in the power of the dragons, so shall I. Cahalson should lead us, and . . ." She smiled at her uncle. "And I think Seerlana has much wisdom to share with us, too."

A few of the old men nodded at these words, then Sherca rushed to Seerlana's side and hugged her. "This brave cousin of ours protected Kurnan from Cahal's misguided rage. Let's hear her story and learn about the Valley dragons, if only *they* can defend us from the Malevir."

Shaklana and several other village women walked across the garden to stand next to Sherca. They wiped their palms on their skirts and aprons and grasped each other's hands. "Who will join us and our brave Moktawls to defeat the beast?"

The younger men grumbled, but they, too, came forward and agreed to band together with the others.

Eunan looked at his companions and released a deep sigh of relief. After inviting everyone to meet in the great hall later, when the sun was directly overhead, he had Cahalson ask every household to make note of any weapons, farming tools, and food and drink that they could carry with them on the road to Nosidam.

Seerlana promised to tell her story and describe the bond that tied Kurnan to his copper dragon. She urged some of them to stay behind— well hidden—and guard the village, while the rest traveled sunriseside. After the others left her, she walked through the herb garden and looked coldside, watching the flight of the approaching Copper.

"Slowly, dear Isabella. Stall. They need more time to think and plan."

SUSAN BASS MARCUS

*   *   *

Isabella heard Seerlana's thoughts. She flew upward to start a new loop over the meadows, and Kurnan waited for her to speak, at least in his head, because the wind rushing past his ears would have shredded any sound sailing from her huge jaws. He asked, *"What if no one listens to Seerlana and Cahal has them shoot us out of the sky? We can't stay here forever. Maybe we should fly sunriseside to find Azile."*

She answered, *"Kurnan, listen carefully. The villagers need more time to lose their fear. We shall fly to that meadow near the road to Nosidam and settle for a while under the shade of fruit trees in the glade. Can you see them?"*

"Yes, Isabella. I think I see them. I'm hungry—haven't eaten since yesterday."

The Copper laughed and agreed that she would enjoy a few tasty field mice or some plump giant scorpions, if any were running about the grassy fields. She dipped lower and glided into an open space just beyond the grove of trees. Kurnan stayed on her shoulder as she reached toward the top of a pear tree. She tossed the boy several pieces of fruit and he tucked them into his shirt. With a gentle bob, Isabella eased her chest lower until she lay comfortably prone on the ground. Kurnan slid down her flank then leaned back against her and munched on one of the juicy brown pears.

"Kurnan, go find a tree and lean on it instead of me. I'm going to look for some mouse morsels."

The boy groaned and stood again. Looking into the grove of trees, he saw one with a sturdy trunk. The bark was rough, but he was grateful for a place to sit and lean. Once he felt the tree at his back and stretched his legs out before him on the ground, he pulled out another pear. As he bit into its sweet flesh and licked its juices, he closed his eyes and sighed.

Isabella was already circling away from the grove toward the open meadow when he fell asleep. He did not hear the crack of twigs and the crunch of leaves in the grove behind him.

Only the sound of a few embers popping in the hearth of the great hall interrupted the hush that followed Seerlana's description of her life

PART III: OLD FRIENDSHIPS RENEWED

before she came to Fossarelick. She looked around the long room at the faces of her neighbors and family, especially Shaklana, whose tear-streaked face reddened as she sat at the long table clenching her fists.

"When you came here from the Trace," said her cousin, "I was so happy to have some family near me again. Even when that silly Kolvak wandered into Fossarelick, those of us who had relatives up in Coldside welcomed him like a brother." She dried her face with her sleeve. "Now I feel like a fool. What can I believe? You say you hid your true story, that you are a dragonrider, that you taught your children to ride dragons?"

"All of this is true, Shaklana, except that I am indeed your cousin, even if distant. When the Veiled Valley was at peace and dragons lived in their ancestral cave, dragonriders left the forest and settled across the Valley. Many of you are the great-great-grandchildren of riders, but your parents have forgotten their stories. Like Kirrill. His mother's grandmother rode a dazzling dragon famed beyond the Valley for her bravery and kindness, a true Golden."

Kirrill shook his head in wonder as Sherca gasped and squeezed his hand. Alana's mouth dropped open and she stared at her father.

"But the happy times ended when the Malevir came to our valley. Two Protectors were living in the forest lodge by Sunriseside Mountain, pledged to summon the dragons whenever danger threatened the Valley. The Malevir found them after his last attack on the dragons' cave. Before the Protectors could sound the alarm, he bound them in enchantments. They almost became his slaves forever."

Kirrill spoke up: "Happy to say, they escaped! I met them after that, still in their magicked bodies. There's a little woman with four arms called Alluxana, and her husband is Fulgid, but you know him as the Formorian. The Malevir changed him into a goat-headed giant, but he left Fulgid's good heart untouched. I know this to be true: he saved the lives of your husbands and brothers." He went on to describe the Formorian's attack on Kralbong, the ways he protected them from the Malevir, and his help in leaving the enchanted gardens of the forest lodge.

The fire in the hearth was dying, but no one left his seat to feed it. Kirrill's words had some of the villagers shivering with worry and fear. While Seerlana spoke softly with Shaklana, some women hugged their children. A few of the young men looked at their sisters and little brothers and their jaws tightened as they thought about the dangers to come.

Seerlana aimed her next words at everyone. "Did you know that the people of Anonom Trace fled to Nosidam years ago? The Malevir burned their fields and killed their sheep long before he attacked Fossarelick." With a soft smile, she continued, "And that Kolvak, our 'cousin' from the Trace—let me tell you that you *can* believe in his friendship. When we rise up against the beast, you will learn how much more than a little baker and cook he is."

Cahalson had been leaning against the mantel that spanned the hearth. He looked at Kirrill, Sherca, and Alana, who were standing nearby, hugging each other in the morning light coming through the clerestory windows overhead. With a nod to Kirrill, Cahalson walked toward Seerlana and, grinning, said, "Always thought that Kolvak was hiding something, besides some tasty bits of food." His face soon turned more serious. "Shouldn't we find the Trace folk who stayed behind? If needed, we could help them, and they could join us too when we head sunriseside."

Seerlana shrugged her shoulders and shook her head. "I can't think that anyone is left in Anonom Trace. How would they survive if all the farmers and tradespeople left? Even my parents . . ." Her last words hung in the air. With a few nimble steps, she stood facing Shaklana, reached for her hands, and pulled her up.

"You are more than a cousin to me. Since the day I came here from the Trace, your kindness and friendship have given me strength. We both shall need that again as we face the beast."

The nearby sound of a throat clearing startled her. Seerlana jumped, then smiled as she found Eunan standing next to her, his arm around her shoulders. Her eyes met his.

PART III: OLD FRIENDSHIPS RENEWED

"I should be angry with you for hiding your purpose from me," he said.

Seerlana dropped her chin and stared at the floor as he continued, "If you could tell me that those years we lived and worked together have meant something, I . . . I . . ." Eunan's words fell away as he looked intently into her eyes, barely hiding his trembling jaw.

"Dear Eunan, without you and our children, my life would have little meaning."

Eunan said nothing for a moment, then he released a long sigh. One arm shot up over his head and he wiped a few tears with the back of his hand. "Then thank the Ways of the World that you came to us long ago and now have returned home! Stuck in our ways, we Moktawls and our kin ignored the signs and thought only of ways to kill our true friends. Perhaps now we all will listen to you and take heed."

Amid a long round of cheers and clapping, villagers came up to Seerlana for a hug, or to squeeze her hand or whisper their thanks. After a few minutes of this, she held up one hand for quiet and asked to speak again. "My heart is with my family and all the good people of this valley. We face a common danger, but soon you will come to know our dragons and believe in their goodness. Please, go to your homes now to pack all the tools and supplies we'll need for our journey sunriseside and the great struggle for our freedom."

With Eunan by her side, Seerlana left the great hall and walked into the large open space that enclosed the village's withered garden patches. She smiled in surprise as Eunan told her about meeting up with Kurnan and the dragon as Kirrill, Cahalson, and he were approaching Fossarelick.

"Isabella and Kurnan should be joining us as soon as they know they will be accepted. I hope they will convince our neighbors to accept the dragons in our struggle against the Malevir." Seerlana sighed and looked around the common as their neighbors hurried home and into their sheds. "But now, give me some time alone, please, Eunan, so that Isabella can hear my thoughts, and I hers."

Eunan folded her into his arms and rested his head against hers. "I will do my best to persuade our neighbors to respect and trust the dragons, although I must say that it's hard to break old habits of thought! Then I'll be in our cottage, Seerlana, until we all gather here again at midday." He kissed her forehead and walked away toward their home.

The dragonrider remained in the open, facing the far meadows. She paused, listened, then frowned.

Isabella, Isabella, why can I not hear you? Where did you go?

Isabella was busy.

Kurnan was dreaming that the soles of his feet were on fire. Heart thumping against his ribs, he sat up quickly and bumped his head on the tree trunk behind him. Confused by the smoke and orange flares, he realized almost too late that Isabella was chasing a small man with a rounded paunch in circles around the trees. She fired small cannonballs of flame just behind his heels and the poor fellow was screaming, "Stop, stop, I can explain everything!"

Through the smoke and sparks, Kurnan squinted until he realized he knew the man. "Isabella, he's Kolvak, our friend the cook!"

A friend? He was creeping through the grove with a durk in hand!

Isabella stopped her cannonade and sat back on her haunches, nostrils fuming, while Kolvak stood with trembling legs and bent forward, coughing. After taking a deep, jagged breath, he said, "Yes, a friend—and I do understand you, Isabella. By the way, that was no knife." He held up his sack in one hand and a stout branch in the other. "Used this as a walking stick."

You know my name? You understand my thoughts!

"Most certainly, dear lady."

You are perhaps from Fossarelick, born of the riders?

Kolvak smiled. "I'm a Lobli, Fernfallow, O beauteous copper dam. The great giant Rocánonom do I serve, and I am traveling to help battle the Malevir."

PART III: OLD FRIENDSHIPS RENEWED

207

Ah, Rocánonom, once known many World-Turns ago—but you do resemble a man!

"He has me serving the Valley in this guise."

When the smoke had drifted away into the trees and Isabella stood stretching her neck to sniff Kolvak more closely, Kurnan caught sight of two small shadows moving behind another tree nearby. He tiptoed around the other side of the tree.

"Yow!" he cried, and the creatures hiding there leaped back and squealed with surprise. Kolvak excused himself and waddled over to the tree.

"So you've met. Milkthistle, Bitterbud, this is Kurnan, who appears to be a dragonrider from Fossarelick."

Kurnan's smile barely curved his lips, but hearing himself called a rider set his heart thumping again. In the same moment, the two Loblin bowed in respect. "We, too, follow Rocánonom," they said, their high-pitched voices sounding very much like a sweet song to Kurnan.

The boy's thoughts jumbled: *Who is Rocánonom? What will happen when I return with Isabella, Kolvak, and these Loblin? Will Fossarelick attack us?*

Kurnan groaned, but Isabella cut him short with a skyward blast of flame. *"Welcome, Milkthistle and Bitterbud. I must interrupt you. I permit you all to hear me."* She paused, then rumbled, *"The moment has come. Seerlana is calling us. The folk of Fossarelick are ready to meet me and make plans. Who will ride to Fossarelick in my pouch? Who on my hump?"*

Chapter 6

NNYLF WIPED HIS BROW AND marched behind Rocánonom through narrow passages that ran under the streets of Nosidam at the base of Sunriseside Mountain. Rocánonom assured his followers that the townspeople had long forgotten the stale and dusty underground routes. Fallen rocks, stones, and bits of rotting timber from crumbling foundations left a permanent gritty haze in the air. Some sprites coughed or sneezed. Others held rags to their noses or wiped their eyes as they walked. Heeding their distress, Rocánonom hummed a few notes and pointed skyward. Gusts of fresh air filled the passage and a silver shaft of light broke through the murk.

The giant and his sprites brushed dust from their shoulders and caps and resumed their journey. Nnylf pulled on Rocánonom's sleeve and asked him to pause. "Kind giant, you returned strength to these arms and legs and this heart of mine. You nourished me with your forest-wise cakes and sweet juices. You healed my wounds with balms and wisdom. I thank you for all of this."

"Nnylf, we need no thanks," answered Rocánonom. "Happy are we to see you free and ready to fight our enemy."

"That is why I must speak. I have no weapon, nothing to use against him."

"No weapon yet," spoke up Sweetnettle, the little second-in-command, his copper shoes gleaming in the magic light. "When you find

PART III: OLD FRIENDSHIPS RENEWED 209

your dragon Draako, he will be your weapon and you his."

Nnylf scratched his head and said to the little round sprite, "If Draako and I meet again, he might not accept me. The prophecy says he's destined to lead us all against the Malevir. Just listen to this part of the writings I read in the Cave of the Ancestors:

> One and only one will dare
> To banish pain and fear
> And this will be the Draako,
> Son of Lugent, blessed with Sight."

Hearing those words, Rocánonom gazed into the distance. "Draako will find you."

"We both were so young when we met. I'm sure he's forgotten me. How useful could I be?"

Sweetnettle was about to hug Nnylf's leg, but stepped back when Rocánonom took the boy aside and said, "Very useful! Draako will remember you and you will remember how to ride him. For now, with your fighting spirit and my spells, we'll hold off the Malevir. Remember not to look the beast in the eye if he should find us."

With a nod, Nnylf dropped his hands to his side and kept pace with Sweetnettle as the band moved along the passage. Rocánonom walked ahead of them all, crouching as he dodged stalactites and inward-leaning walls along the narrowing path.

Just when his legs were shaking from the effort of keeping up with the giant, Nnylf bumped into the line of sprites. They had halted abruptly before a broad opening in the wall. Rocánonom's silhouette blocked the entryway. His magical silver beam cast a glow that gave his body a flat, sharp outline.

Rocánonom called out to his followers, "We have reached the Loblin shelter, hidden among tunnels that run under the cellars of Nosidam's Council Hall and the town. As they go about their daily business, the people of Nosidam have no idea we work directly below them. Here we must await word about the beast. You are welcome to sit and share your food and drink."

A tight crowd of sprites entered the vaulted chamber with caution. Satisfied that no harm lurked in the shadows, they found cushions and stones for sitting and nodded with pleasure at being in their own space. Hearing the Loblin hum a gentle tune, Nnylf smiled and relaxed. A few moments later, his mouth hung open when little bundles of berries, cakes, and nectar pods floated out of Loblin tool sacks. The sprites sat cross-legged and snatched at passing tidbits. Each sprite offered a morsel to his neighbor.

Sweetnettle pressed a dark brown bun filled with nuts and dried fruit into Nnylf's palm. "Once you eat this," he whispered, "you will feel better." He chewed his own bun slowly and moistened his lips with red nectar. "Many World-Turns ago, the Loblin of Nosidam lived here."

"Here?"

"Some lived in the Trace. Some in Fossarelick. The rest lived here, unnoticed but at peace with the town, doing chores for people like turning milk to butter and cheese. They sang lullabies so babies would sleep. They kept people's hearth embers glowing and filled their fire buckets with fresh water."

"I suppose they baked delicious treats, too." Nnylf licked his bun before taking a small bite. *Better than toast,* he thought. *More like the barley waving under an endless blue sky with a few flowers mixed in.* He licked his lips and, following Sweetnettle's example, ate the bun one small bite at a time. "How could they not love Loblin?"

Sweetnettle blushed dark green. "Umm, sometimes the milk would turn sour. Loblin are fond of pranks, too."

Nnylf laughed and reached for a nectar pod that hung suspended in front of his nose. "Thank you, kind Sweetnettle. I haven't laughed since I left home to sell our barley."

The sprite nodded and chewed a handful of dark berries without answering him.

Nnylf frowned as he thought. *When will I ever go home again?*

PART III: OLD FRIENDSHIPS RENEWED 211

*   *   *

Fossarelick villagers who were leaving behind friends and family fastened their cottage doors. They sent their few remaining goats downhill to roam the barley fields with the oxen. Their sacks and other bundles lay close by their feet. They looked at Seerlana, some with uncertainty in their eyes, others with the twinkle of anticipated adventure.

Seerlana knelt and lifted her face toward the meadows. She opened her mouth to sing, and the rest of the people, swaying to her music, gathered near her in the common. They did not understand her words, but the notes had them thinking about a nap in the sweet grass, the chirrup of crickets, and subtle breezes brushing their cheeks. Their eyes closed and they held each other while humming along.

A fierce but brief gust broke their reverie. When they opened their eyes, the sight before them snatched their breath. Beyond the last houses on the common, just down the path, stood Isabella with Kurnan astride her neck hump. The dragon's mouth opened wide. Kolvak and two sprites crawled out of her jaw pouch and slid to the ground. Her sharp fangs sparkled.

Seerlana's neighbors turned to see her rise and stride toward the dragon. By the time she faced Isabella, Kurnan had leaped to the ground and was taking a small bright object from Milkthistle's hands.

Seerlana smiled at the boy. He returned her smile and walked into the common with the object held tightly against his shirt. As his parents and Alana shook off their bedazzlement and ran to meet him, he held out the mirror—its face shimmered in the bright sun. "Alana, my dragon friend returns this gift to you."

Surprised, Alana coughed and nodded her thanks. Grasping the mirror in one hand, she hugged Kurnan and sputtered, "Thank you, brother. I am happy to hold it again. It will stay here in my pocket. I guess it helped you make friends with that dragon."

"Her name is Isabella. She *is* my friend. She hopes for peace between us and all dragons."

Eunan and Cahalson gulped as Seerlana signaled them to meet the dragon. They lifted their chins and strode toward Isabella and her companions, but when the dragon saw them, her eyes flashed red. She screamed and reared up on her hind legs. The villagers scattered and cowered against their cottages and outbuildings.

At the sound of their shrieks, Cahal staggered out of the great hall and raised his walking stick against the rampant dragon. "You see? I told you that the dragons would bring us misfortune! Be gone, beast, be gone or our Moktawls will slay you for your miserable hide!" After a few more shaky steps, he fell on his face and lay still in the dirt. Kirrill and Cahalson were about to help him when Shaklana waved them away. She and two boys ran to Cahal, picked him up, and carried him into the great hall.

By the end of Cahal's rant, Seerlana had calmed Isabella, who pressed her smoking snout against the rider's armored shoulder. Seerlana beckoned Kirrill, Cahalson, and her husband to approach. "She will never entirely trust a Moktawl, but I have explained to Isabella that you want to be friends, that you have left your Moktawl ways, and that you will join the dragons' fight against the beast. Perhaps you have a gift for Isabella?"

The men looked bewildered. Seerlana nodded toward their kits. When they probed the contents of their sacks, each man felt an unfamiliar article that he hastened to pull out. They brought a gleam to the Copper's now-golden eye. Kirrill held a mesh reed bag at the end of his fingertips. A dozen scorpions squirmed inside. Cahalson wondered at the crystal bowl sitting in his hand; and Eunan marveled at the vibrant ruby that covered his palm. Without a sound, Isabella bent to accept the gifts placed at her feet. Once she had savored the scorpions and stored the jewels in her jaw pouch, she began to hum. The men were transfixed.

Eunan faced his wife and, with widened eyes, said, "Seerlana, I hear her song—or is it her thoughts that have reached my own?"

"Me, too."

"Wonderful Ways of the World!"

PART III: OLD FRIENDSHIPS RENEWED 213

Seerlana sent warm thanks to her dragon friend and said to the men, "Isabella has befriended you, but only Kurnan may ride her, as long as he lives. She will share her thoughts with you as she pleases. From this moment, she trusts you as much as any dragon would trust a human who is not her rider."

Kolvak and the other two sprites wended their way into the circle of villagers. Children quickly surrounded them and bent to touch Milkthistle and Bitterbud, but Kolvak gently pushed them away.

"Not so close and not so fast, children," he warned. "My little brother and sister frighten easily."

"Speak for yourself! We're not that small, Fernfallow." The sprites puffed out their chests and brushed the knees of their breeches.

The children stared at their skin, as green as spring leaves. The sprites stared back and crossed their arms.

"Why do you call them family, Kolvak? Why do they call you Fernfallow? Where have you been? Why do you talk so strangely? Where is Kirrill's donkey?"

"So many questions, little ones, but come sit in the shade with us. I will explain everything."

They sat together in a small circle under the eaves of the great hall. Some of the women and older children joined them and, mouths agape, listened as Kolvak described the founding of their village in the Veiled Valley, the Fossarelick dragonriders, and the little army of sprites long ago fallen to the Malevir as goblin slaves, then rescued by Rocánonom. "Now we are free followers of Rocánonom, happy to join your company."

A gruff voice interrupted him. "Before any more of our children go missing, tell me this. When the beast ensorcelled Nnylf under the live oak, he and his goblin took our boy; we could do nothing to save him. Where did the beast take him?" Eunan had returned to the common. Kolvak's confident speech mystified him, and he asked, "And just where were you and the donkey when the hork and goblin snatched him?"

"He was hiding with me. I'm the donkey," warbled Milkthistle. "And Bitterbud here—"

Bitterbud broke in: "I was that goblin, the Malevir's slave. We took the boy into the goblin burrows, up the Sunriseside Mountain, to the great cave."

"You? You have nothing of the goblin about you!" Eunan blurted. "You're a gentle Lobli. You, too," he said, facing Milkthistle. "And why the Sunriseside Mountain? What cave are you talking about?"

Seerlana stood beside her husband. "They speak of a certain cave of the dragons' ancestors, where Nnylf, Azile, and I met and rode dragons many World-Turns ago." She held both his hands in hers and chose her words with care. "Hidden deep in that cave is the dragons' treasure, and in it lies the Mystic Scintilla, the source of the dragons' fire."

Kolvak stood, and his hand trembled as he pointed to the Sunriseside. "If Aindle—or whichever name he uses—if he destroys the Mystic Scintilla, not only will the dragons lose their fire breath: their power to fight and defeat the beast will wither away. We must keep the dragon treasure out of the beast's claws."

"But Nnylf?" Eunan's patience had evaporated. He had dropped Seerlana's hand and now bent over the little cook. "Have you seen him? Is he alive?"

Seerlana felt her throat tighten. "Kolvak, or Fernfallow, what *do* you know about Nnylf?"

Kolvak's eyes twinkled as he said, "Before we went to the Trace, we met up with another Lobli in the forest, Forestspice, who told us that Rocánonom had freed Nnylf and tended his wounds."

Now a big lump settled in Seerlana's throat. She turned to hug Eunan but stopped at the sight of Kolvak's frown. Clenching his fists, he said, "Forestspice and Mallowseed followed the Malevir to Nosidam. They were going to meet Rocánonom, my brother Loblin, and Nnylf there. What could have happened to them and to the town?"

Chapter 7

ATTY KEPT HIS MEN CLOSE to him. They had not imagined that they would be slogging through thorny shrubs and brambles to leave the lodge lands. Every swipe at the underbrush and low-lying branches jolted Atty's wounded arm. Close behind him, the other Moktawls muttered as spiny nettles tore at their leggings and shirtsleeves. They, too, with their durks and staves, slashed at the thickets that blocked their path to the Nosidam road.

Struggling ahead, Atty took a few uncertain steps, then turned to face his men. "Odd, that," he said, scratching his head.

"Odd, what?" asked one Moktawl, pulling some nettle tufts out of his beard.

"The music . . . don't you hear it?" He paused and looked up through the trees, then pointed overhead. "There!" Above the clouds that dotted the sky, several dragons flew sunriseside in slow figure eights.

"They're circling Nosidam, I'll wager." Atty's gaze followed the dragons until they were out of sight. When he looked back wearily at the path ahead, it was clear of thornbushes. He smiled. "They opened the path for us so we could leave this place."

Another Moktawl grunted, "To think, we've blamed the dragons for all our troubles: the burned fields, the sick and dying goats . . ." He lifted his whiskery chin and strode ahead of his companions. "Time to go after the real evildoer!"

The other men followed until they reached the outer gate, which opened easily when Atty lightly touched its lock. They passed through it and the gate faded away. Ahead of them lay the road. Atty knelt on its grassy verge and said, "I don't much like staying near that enchanted place, but we'll wait here for Azile and the others, as we agreed. Roll out your mats behind those bushes. I'll keep watch while you rest."

No argument came from his companions. The air was still. Atty struggled with his own weariness, as his burning eyes searched the road for the girl and her strange new allies.

Nnylf was about to warn Rocánonom that intruders had entered the Loblin's underground refuge. He could see their shadows growing larger in the candlelight that illuminated the entrance tunnel, and their scuffling echoed from the walls; but Sweetnettle rushed toward the tunnel and shouted, "Our brothers have returned! They are safe!"

As Forestspice and Mallowseed laughed and hugged their fellow sprites, Rocánonom rose to his feet. He stooped under the low ceiling and watched the noisy, cheering crowd. Lowering himself carefully to sit on a broad tree stump in the center of the limestone hollow, he waited until the lively chatter died down. All eyes turned to him. He waved to Nnylf. "Come sit beside me. Our friends bring us news."

Nnylf sat next to the giant and watched the two scouts approach their leader. They bowed their heads. Nnylf smiled at them. "Kind Loblin, you helped care for me. Look, now—I am well and strong again."

Mallowseed and Forestspice looked up again and clapped their hands with pleasure. "Rocánonom, you have healed the boy, and just in time!" said Mallowseed.

"In time?"

"Yes, the whole of Nosidam seethes like an overflowing pot. We overheard the Malevir meet with the Council and tell them lies about Fossarelick. People are scared. They expect an attack, but . . . but . . ."

PART III: OLD FRIENDSHIPS RENEWED   217

The sprite stopped his rapid speech and stood thinking, his mouth agape.

"Mallowseed, go on: 'but'?"

The sprite shook himself and dark green patches of embarrassment spread across his face. "Well, yes, but . . . you tell it, Forestspice. You talked to the nice man first."

His companion stepped forward, and with a sweep of his arm to show the size of his subject, he said, "Someone helped us in Nosidam: Luchaer, the last of the town's Protectors. He saw through Aindle's disguise."

The giant said, "I knew Luchaer long ago and liked him well. Many Turns of the World since I last saw him."

Once they heard Rocánonom speak well of Luchaer, both sprites relaxed and spoke rapidly at once. They described how the Malevir tricked the town's leaders and planned to start a war in the Valley, and how Luchaer wanted to help them. Then they begged Rocánonom for more tasks.

"You have done well enough, and now you must eat. Sweetnettle, what have we to share with our brothers?" said the giant.

Rocánonom's calm mystified Nnylf. Memories of the hork curdled the cakes in his stomach and he felt panic at the thought that he might have to face the beast again.

Sweetnettle trotted to Rocánonom's side with a small bowl half full of berries and a few end slices of nut-dotted brown bread dripping with butter. "Not much left," he whispered to the giant. "Can you sing us some more?" But he offered them the bowl all the same.

Forestspice licked his fingertips while Mallowseed nibbled the last of his share from the bowl and said, "Luchaer might help us bring more food. May we go to him?"

Nnylf sat up straighter and blinked back his tears. "May I go with them? You all fed me, a skeleton dressed in rags. Now you need food. Let me talk to this Luchaer."

Nnylf felt a heavy hand pressing on his shoulder. "My food spells need a tweak," said Rocánonom, "but you owe us no debt. These Loblin want to return to Nosidam without you because if the Malevir catches your scent, he will put aside all else to hunt you down."

Nnylf nodded and slumped a little. Forestspice and Mallowseed slung a few empty sacks over their shoulders and left the cave so quickly that Nnylf missed their exit.

When the two sprites reached the Nosidam Council Hall square, Luchaer was not there. His usual market square seat was empty, too, and they didn't know where he lived. Pressed against the hall's stone wall, they were invisible to townspeople running through the streets and lanes with kitchen knives, gnarled twig brooms, and iron fireplace pokers. A butcher led a mob of storekeepers with a series of orders. "Look to your homes, people. Gather all the weapons you can find. We'll be ready for Fossarelick long before they reach us."

A crowd assembled again in the market square, visible at the far end of the street. Forestspice watched a woman and several small children run to catch up with a burly man carrying a pitchfork. Two young men jogged beside him, each with a long, knurly stick in his hand. Other townspeople came from lanes that fed onto the main street. All of them were hurrying to reach the square.

"While they're not looking this way, I thought I'd come by to have a word with you two."

At the sound of Luchaer's voice, the sprites squealed and leaped up. Forestspice hit his head on something hard. "Ouch! What was that?" he groaned, rubbing his head. He saw a row of iron rings in the wall above him.

"For the donkeys."

"Luchaer! We're happy to see you," sighed Mallowseed. "Our brothers need food. Would you help us find some?"

"More of you, are there? Happy to help. Bread, fruit, and maybe sausages, since that butcher's running through the streets like a chicken chased by an ax!"

"Thank you. You'll come with us to our shelter after you find the food!"

PART III: OLD FRIENDSHIPS RENEWED 219

"What shelter?"

"Where we Loblin hide ourselves from the town."

"Gladly, if I can fit! So, you need food. Wait here. I won't be long."
With his finger, Luchaer patted them on their tiny shoulders and walked
quickly into the shadows along one of the deserted side streets. Soon he
was out of sight. The sprites sighed and, backs to the wall, they sank to
their heels.

Forestspice muttered, "Wait here. They always say, 'Wait here.'"

While they waited, Aindle came back to the marketplace and climbed
onto the tallest barrow. He surveyed the crowd of Nosidam citizens
surrounding him. For a moment, his attention wandered back to the
Council Hall square. He turned to Fergus with a jerk and whispered a
few words in his mangled ear. Standing tall once more, he raised his arms
above his head. His thunderous voice quieted the crowd.

"You all know what we must do. The road from Fossarelick is not
so long, and the Moktawls you fear will be here soon. Form your lines
where the road meets the town and stand firm. I will be there to lead you
in battle."

"What about the children?" one of the women cried out.

"Children? Can they fight? Can they carry heavy loads?"

People looked at each other and shook their heads.

"Then hide them in the donkey shed. They'll be fine."

A few of the children wailed as their mothers took their hands and
pulled them toward the barn on the far side of the square. Another
woman's voice rang out, "That's no way to keep our little ones safe!
Don't you care what happens to them? Who will feed them and keep
them clean and warm?"

Aindle looked through the crowd and found the speaker. A young
mother, who held a baby born six Moon-Passings before, regarded him
with a frown. She stepped back from the force of Aindle's stare; then
neither she nor her baby moved again.

"Our arms are raised now against the enemies of Nosidam. I will lead you forward—but one small task remains to me before we leave. Fergus will show you where to gather and wait to battle Fossarelick. Courage, everyone. I will rejoin you soon. Victory will be ours!"

A cheer went up and the crowd moved away from Aindle. Fergus shepherded them toward the edge of town where the road to the Sunsetside began. Hopping off the barrow, Aindle loped in the opposite direction, toward the Council Hall.

Great gusts were blowing through the deserted streets of Nosidam when Luchaer returned to the market square. Unlocked doors banged in the wind. A few barrows lay overturned on their sides, their contents spilled onto the square's stone pavers. Apples had rolled away from fallen crates that once contained neat pyramids of fruit.

Luchaer opened one of his sacks and thrust as many pieces of fruit into it as he could carry. He scavenged around another barrow, and into a second sack he swept an armful of plump seeded wheat loaves that lay scattered on the ground. He filled his pockets with nuts still in their shells. Slinging the sacks over his shoulder, he hastened away from the square to rejoin the two sprites.

Forestspice and Mallowseed jumped up and waved as Luchaer approached. Each sprite pressed a finger on his lips to signal silence. They led him past a few shacks on one side of town and through a broad meadow.

Luchaer spotted two small animals playing among the meadow grasses, their brown fur gleaming in the sunlight. *Carefree little creatures,* he thought. He continued down a slope into a gulley where the soil, soggy from a stream running through it, stuck to his boots in muddy clumps— yet the old Protector, wheezing from trying to match the sprites' pace, leaned forward and plodded on. *If only I were as nimble as those . . . what are they? Cats? No, maybe woodchucks,* he mused as he struggled through the muck. He waved his hand as if to brush them away from his sight.

The sprites disappeared as they rounded a large boulder ahead.

PART III: OLD FRIENDSHIPS RENEWED   221

Luchaer followed their trail. He looked at the trees and grasses near him and his mouth felt dry as he noticed them begin to fade. Soon he realized he had passed through a sort of invisible curtain; now he was entering a sloping tunnel. Candles stood in small niches along the walls. Twisted tree roots and rotting house poles thrust through the tunnel's ceiling and cast odd shadows in the candlelight. Luchaer suspected that one of the hulking shadows followed many paces behind him, but he shook his head and moved on. *Just the candlelight and this weird place, giving me ideas.*

Ahead of him, Forestspice and Mallowseed had entered a much wider and light-filled space. Scores of other sprites sat on logs, rocks, and cushions, around an enormous man who waved to him and beckoned him forward. He looked familiar—glowing coppery hair, a young face hardened by a powerful jawline, and green eyes that sparkled. His brawny arms opened widely.

To the giant's left sat a very young man, neither sprite nor giant. He'd seen him before, somewhere . . .

"Welcome, Protector Luchaer. You bring food for my friends and news about Nosidam?"

"Yes," answered Luchaer, furrows deepening between his white and woolly eyebrows as he puzzled over the chamber full of sprites. "Yes! I have plenty of both; but the food in these two sacks will never feed all of your company. I am so sorry I did not bring more." He emptied his bulging pockets and nuts tumbled onto the floor in front of the giant.

"Oh, but you did." In that instant, Rocánonom and the sprites began to hum a tune that rose up and down in just a few notes. When the humming echoed from the walls, each sack that Luchaer had placed on the ground in front of the giant began to jiggle and sway. Their seams nearly split apart. Apples, pears, and plums spilled out of one sack by the score. Loaves of warm bread, braided rolls, cooked sausages, and little fruitcakes tumbled out of the other.

Rocánonom's throng sang out in giggles and squeals. Mallowseed and Forestspice brought a hearty portion to Luchaer, Rocánonom, and the young man sitting quietly next to him, then shared the swag with the other sprites.

"Delicious!" Luchaer exclaimed. "I thought these discarded apples and loaves would be spoiled and stale! Not that I didn't hope for better."

"Your good heart has made all the difference, Luchaer. And now that we have soothed our stomachs, you must be asking yourself who we are, why we are here, and, more importantly, how I know you."

The young man nodded at Rocánonom and smiled at Luchaer, who looked around at all the happy sprites, busy with their food and quiet conversations. A buzz of contentment filled the air.

Luchaer asked, "Would you be the giant Rocánonom who disappeared from Anonom Trace so long ago? His sad story made us weep, us Protectors."

Nnylf turned to stare at Rocánonom. "What sad story?"

The giant shrugged his shoulders. "I *am* Rocánonom. Before the Malevir poisoned our valley with his cruel spells and dreadful deeds, I lived in the forests of Anonom Trace. With the help of many Loblin, some the very ones you see here today, we nurtured orchards, vineyards, and flowering meadows. Dragons used to fly between the cave of their ancestors and another one hidden within the Sunsetside Mountains. They would stop in the Trace to rest and hear our news. The dragons, to balance the Ways of the World, had asked us to be Protectors of the Coldside—and it's hard to refuse a dragon! People who lived in our villages never saw us, but their days were good and their nights peaceful as long as we watched over them."

Nnylf interrupted: "No one has lived in Anonom Trace for many, many Moon-Passings."

"No, not for a long, long time," replied Rocánonom. "Because of the Malevir. In his hork guise, he attacked and stunned us as we slept. He bit the Loblin's ears and turned them into loathsome goblins. To weaken me and block my powers, he made a hideous rotting brute

PART III: OLD FRIENDSHIPS RENEWED

of me. After our long forced march to the Sunriseside Mountain, he imprisoned me, helplessly wrapped in heavy chains, my mouth gagged to stifle my spellsongs. He left me to die"—Rocánonom shivered—"and he kept the goblins in deep burrows near the Protectors' lodge that he had stolen. Well, not all of them. He took a few to the surface to work as his servants."

Nnylf whispered, "Kralbong!"

Rocánonom sighed as the sprites uttered a collective groan. "We knew him as Creepervine, the strongest of our family, but also the most mischievous, the one who soured milk in the Trace and painted grapes with mold. How many times did we plead with him to remember our promise? Later, as Kralbong, he fit easily into the Malevir's schemes."

Mallowseed coughed and stepped between Nnylf and Luchaer. "When Alluxana's fire destroyed the lodge, the beast called us out from the burrow prison, but Forestspice did not heed his commands. He led our gang of goblins into the bakehouse tunnel and away from the beast because Aurykk had broken the spell Aindle had placed on him and Bitterbud. We had one thought: to free Rocánonom. Forestspice showed us the way to find him."

"We went so fast. Goblin legs. Much stronger than Loblin legs," added Forestspice.

Rocánonom said, "You see, my loyal friends rescued me: they felt my grief, even while trapped in goblin bodies and suffering the beast's enchantments. They found me and together we freed ourselves from the Malevir.

"Luchaer, you and I met back in the Trace when you were young— like this fellow." He tapped Nnylf's shoulder. "Meet Nnylf, son of Eunan of Fossarelick and the rider Seerlana. Do you know each other?"

Chapter 8

SWEETNETTLE HAD BEEN GUARDING THE tunnel entrance. He thought he heard the sound of scraping pebbles. He crouched and tiptoed along a wall, then peered from behind a thick clump of tree roots.

He gasped when he discovered an intruder, dressed as a dragonrider whose handsome head did not match his disfigured body. A faint greenish-blue cast tinted his skin. *That smell! It's like . . . it's like . . . the Malevir!* Sweetnettle froze as the memory of his miserable goblin life swept over him.

Clumsy in his ill-fitting garb, Aindle stumbled forward and passed Sweetnettle's hiding place. The sprite could see his cold breath dropping like green crystals to the cave floor and his stony gaze aimed at the open chamber ahead. The beast's shambling frame cast crooked shadows in the flickering candlelight. With one snap of his newly clawed fingers, he turned the flames to trailing smoke.

As Aindle crept closer to Rocánonom and his followers, Sweetnettle could feel his own hearts beating. The thump of the one under his right shoulder sent ripples up his neck. His other heart, next to his belly, beat in rhythm with his quickening breath. Both organs nearly leaped out of his skin as Sweetnettle ran out of the shadows toward Aindle and jumped in front of the startled monster.

PART III: OLD FRIENDSHIPS RENEWED 225

"Stop!" he screamed. The air was still. He looked at the beast's shoes, avoiding the deadly gaze of his eyes. "Stop here!"

Claws extended, Aindle's hand swiped at Sweetnettle, but the little sprite dodged the blow and butted his head against the glowering beast's thigh. As he bit into his flesh, the sprite tasted something like sulfur. It burned his tongue and teeth. His mouth was melting. Green ichor dripped across his chin and over his shoulder. One of his hearts no longer pulsed and the world went black.

Rocánonom gathered his followers around him as soon as he heard Sweetnettle's cry. Mallowseed and Forestspice stood immediately behind him. He sent Luchaer and Nnylf to hide in a side tunnel leading back to the shadows of the mountain passages. He said, "We are strong, but the Malevir might overwhelm us. If he does, make your way quickly to the Cave of the Ancestors."

Nnylf protested that the passages went every which way. How to choose the right one?

"You will know: The mountain will guide you at every turn."

Aindle stepped out of the shadows and into the light of the limestone chamber, Sweetnettle's limp body dangling from his claws. With each step, droplets of acid from his wounded leg bubbled on the cavern floor. No one returned his harsh gaze.

"You plan to challenge me again, you gutless giant?" Aindle's bellow echoed off the chamber walls.

Rocánonom said nothing. His eyes focused on the distant tunnel entrance behind the beast.

"Speak, Rocánonom! You know you cannot save the Valley's wyrms and weaklings." He glared and knit his brows. Through swelling lips he shouted, "Answer me—what do you think you can do?"

The giant still gazed into the distance. No sprite raised his or her eyes. Pressed against the interior tunnel wall, Nnylf and Luchaer barely breathed.

Aindle threw Sweetnettle's body to the floor and kicked it to roll by the giant's feet. "There! Use your magic to revive this clod, this speck of dirt."

Forestspice knelt beside his companion's inert body and felt his shoulder, then his belly. "Can't feel his shoulder heart," the sprite whispered. "His belly heart beats, but it is weak." He pulled Sweetnettle behind Rocánonom's legs and began to massage the sprite's side and stomach. Mallowseed had taken a few herbs from his pack, which his brother worked into the stricken sprite's mottled green skin.

The cave floor sizzled as acid continued to drip from Aindle's leg wound. He turned away from Rocánonom for a moment to examine the wound, and as he did, he saw two small furry creatures sauntering toward him. He pulled at his knobby fingers and scowled at them. *Not them! Not now!*

Aindle screeched and backed up to the wall. Forgetting Rocánonom and the others, he covered his nose with one hand and brushed past the little animals in a dash for the tunnel entrance.

The two weasels watched Aindle's retreat and patted paws. Gormley greeted the giant. "Hello, Rocánonom. See what we can do? The Malevir always screams and runs from us. We'll stay on his trail, but first we have some news. The dragons and Fossarelick are finally talking to each other. Have to run. See you later." Turning, they sprinted after Aindle. Gúrmulo chortled, "Hello, Mally-vir. Wait for us!"

Rocánonom quickly turned to his followers and urged them to hurry into the passage where Nnylf and Luchaer were hiding. A few of them carried Sweetnettle's inert body, and once within the shadows of the passage, they laid him at Rocánonom's feet. The giant placed his hand over the Lobli's belly heart and let it rest there for a few moments. Sweetnettle opened his eyes a crack, smiled at the giant, and closed his eyes again with a soft sigh. Rocánonom lifted his hand to cover the sprite's eyes.

Forestspice began to weep in soft little sobs. Rocánonom looked around at every sprite as he said, "Sweetnettle has left us. We shall sing of his brave deeds and love for us all. Use this cloak, my friends, to wrap him. We shall carry him with us."

PART III: OLD FRIENDSHIPS RENEWED   227

Luchaer sighed. He had watched the Malevir's reaction to their unexpected rescuers and told Rocánonom he ought to follow them, to learn the beast's next move. He was anxious to leave. After saying a few kind words about their dead companion, he picked up his sacks and tucked them into his belt.

"Luchaer, soon all of Nosidam will be in ashes. The beast has a boundless need to destroy us, and the people of this town will blame Fossarelick unless you persuade them otherwise. Go up to Nosidam, if you must, but keep yourself safe, and when the right moment comes . . ."

Luchaer winked and hitched up his leggings. He pulled his whittling knife from his pocket pouch and wiggled it in front of his nose.

"With this little friend, I'll be safe," he chuckled, "as long as I stay out of Aindle's sight." He felt a tug on his sleeve.

Nnylf had been watching the old man, and when he saw his knife, he blurted, "I recognize you now!" He looked up into the giant's eyes. "Luchaer and I met in the market when Lustre tricked my sister and me into visiting his lodge."

Luchaer smiled, "The marketplace. Yes, I remember you and your barley. But it's not *his* lodge, young man. That fine place—"

"The Loblin said it burned to the ground."

"Burned?" Luchaer cried out. "That lodge belonged to Alluxana and Fulgid, among the last of the Protectors, like me."

"No one else lived there when we were prisoners, other than that little lady with four arms who ran the bakehouse and a goat-faced giant that the hork hated. The giant roamed all about the place. The lady helped me escape from the hork and Kralbong."

Rocánonom's huge hands tapped their shoulders, and they looked up in surprise. "I can see that you have a lot to talk about, but not now. Luchaer, as you leave, I thank you. The rest of us . . ." He turned to speak to his followers. "We return to the Cave of the Ancestors to find our dragon friends."

*   *   *

Aindle lost his boots, and his talons curled and flexed in the dirt as he chewed over ways to destroy Rocánonom and his followers. He found Fergus at the Council Hall and spewed out his orders: "Fergus, hurry to the city gate. Tell the town leaders to carry oil and torches to the Council Hall basement. There you will find a trap door, near the wood pile. Pour oil into the room below and set it on fire."

"Yes, of course, sir. You know best." Fergus trembled and rings of sweat stained the armpits of his shiny green suit. His white shirt had turned yellow and his knee-high boots drooped toward his ankles. "May I ask why, sir?"

"No! You may not!" the beast screamed. He softened his tone when passersby paused to stare at them. "But since you did ask, I'll enlighten you. A network of tunnels connects the Valley to Nosidam. It begins under the Council Hall. The hordes from Fossarelick have reached it and they will attack soon, to take the town from below. We must stop them! Go, go, go to the people, before it's too late!"

Aindle's shape-changing spell was weakening. He had to leave Nosidam before his basilisk body returned and ruined his plans. The fires and smoke would give him cover.

Fergus ran to the town gates. Nearly out of breath, he repeated Lustre's orders to the men and women leading the crowd. Furious, they sent their fellow townspeople to gather the needed supplies and follow through.

Azile and Alluxana were watching for Aindle from a hiding place on the slope above town. Time passed slowly and their sleepy heads began to nod. Their own coughing woke them up. They stared with open mouths at Nosidam. Fire and billowing smoke rose out of the ground. Great holes gaped and flames burst upward. Houses and shop buildings folded in on themselves and plunged into the widening fiery fissures.

On the far side of town, near merchants' and guild masters' fine houses not yet touched by the conflagration, sat an inn adorned with ironwork and wood. The broad central doors of the inn stood ajar. Alluxana and Azile could see them melting. Dense steam clung to the façade.

They jumped and stifled their screams as a grotesque beaked head appeared in the doorframe. "Ways of the World, protect us! It's the basilisk!" whispered Alluxana to her companion.

"A basi—*what?*" Azile asked.

"The basilisk takes many forms. That one could be the Malevir."

Azile nearly stopped breathing. "No, the Malevir is a hork."

"Was a hork. Was a man. Now, something's gone wrong for him. Look how his clothes are ripped and falling away. Soon, he'll have a rooster body and a deadly beak, the tail of a small dragon, and leathery wings."

Azile covered her mouth and whispered, "He's so big. I can't believe that's the same creature that locked me in the . . . Look! What is he doing?"

Alluxana pulled Azile's sleeve with all four hands. "He's coming this way. Quick, Azile. Back to the forest. We must warn the men!"

Part IV
Starting Over

Fulgid as Formorian and Man©

Chapter 1

Luchaer stood with one hand on his hip and the other, gripping his durk, over his head. "So, people of Nosidam, you followed that deceiver to the edge of your own destruction." Far from the burned-out shell of the Council Hall, only the inn and its gaping doorway stood among the smoking ruins of a once-prosperous market town. He looked around the square. "Lustre was no dragonrider, you fools. He's a cruel and powerful beast, a shape-changing basilisk who tricked you into setting Nosidam ablaze through tunnels that run under every street and house. Do you still believe his lies about Fossarelick?"

Two of the men were bending over Fergus's barely recognizable corpse. The street over one of the blazing tunnels had collapsed and he had fallen into it. Bravely, he had scrabbled his way out again, but died of his injuries.

"Luchaer, we didn't know, we didn't know. Fergus said—"

"Look at Fergus's ear. The bite marks—you can see 'em. He was the beast's slave. Fossarelick was not about to attack. They are coming here, but not for you. They want Lustre."

A young woman shuffled forward, her infant wrapped in a sooty blanket. "Luchaer, he ensorcelled me, like Fergus. Just one look of his: my baby and I felt nothing. Couldn't move."

Another woman, the wife of the apple vendor, came to her side and

PART IV: STARTING OVER 233

wrapped her arms around them, while her husband stepped forward. "I say we gather whatever weapons remain to us and go after the beast."

Cheers went up from the bedraggled crowd, until another voice called out, "With what weapons? The beast has magic and we have only shovels!"

Luchaer cleared his throat.

It's time. They need to know—but how to tell them?

The young mother spoke again. "Luchaer, what is happening to our valley? Why has this Lustre creature hurt us so?"

There it is. Thank you, dear woman.

"This so-called Lustre has long planned to enslave our valley for his own revenge and greed. If I understand him, he hoped to take our land and capture us. The ancient dragons called him the Malevir. They protected the Veiled Valley from him."

The apple vendor pulled at his hair and sat weeping on the ground in a sad heap. "Then we have no future. The dragons are long gone, and we have no defenses against this Malevir and his magic."

More townspeople wandered into the square. Few had died in the fire that swept through the tunnels lying under all their homes and businesses. Most, however, had lost nearly everything they owned and cherished. *They have nothing more to lose except each other,* Luchaer realized, and he spoke up.

"Let me remind you of what you'd rather forget. In the past, Protectors and dragons defended you. Then the Malevir banished or destroyed most of them. The few who still live are coming now to Nosidam, or to this great mountain behind us. They come to fight the beast with their own powers and magic."

A man stepped out of the crowd and asked, "As Fergus is no longer among us, I, Councilor Prendel, represent the town, and I insist that you tell us: what Protectors, Luchaer? And what does an old fogy like you know?" He laughed and looked around. No one else was laughing. He frowned and said, "You're simply repeating old grandmother tales."

A deep voice rang out across the square. "He knows because his family served yours for generations. You have forgotten them."

Luchaer swiveled his head to find the source of those words and saw a misty vision of Rocánonom high above him, many times larger than he had appeared in the cave chamber. The giant floated like a cloud over the hushed mob. Luchaer could see through him to the town's crumbled walls.

"To save the Valley from the Malevir and rebuild your lives of peace and prosperity, you must listen to this wise man. When you were young and heard stories about the dragons of the Veiled Valley, you were learning about your very own families' past, not tales to frighten naughty children. Dragons once protected all those who lived here and shielded them from the likes of the Malevir. The Protectors—yes, like your neighbor Luchaer—descended from brave dragonriders of earlier ages."

Prendel shouted at the apparition, "Why should we trust you any more than the beast who destroyed our town?" People standing near Prendel stepped back, terrified of the giant.

Rocánonom's handsome face filled the broad cloud and he smiled. "I am Rocánonom, friend to all rightful dwellers in this valley and sworn to protect you. The Malevir wanted to kill me, too, and he nearly did."

The cloud was breaking into ragged wisps and Rocánonom faded away. With his departing words, he warned the townspeople, "Dragons are alive and coming to fight the beast. Fossarelick comes with them. Meet them in peace and help save yourselves."

Luchaer and the others stared overhead at clouds that filled the air once dancing with Rocánonom's wavering image.

The apple vendor whispered, "Dragons are coming?"

"Luchaer, what do you know of this Rocánonom?" trembled Prendel.

"A good giant, part of the army gathering to destroy the Malevir. Will you join him, join me, join us?"

The young mother comforted her wailing baby, then asked, "But he said dragons are coming. Don't dragons eat people?"

PART IV: STARTING OVER   235

Luchaer could hear a lot of scuffling and saw people shake their heads, rub the back of their necks, or kick at the scorched debris piled on the street. "No, these dragons would much prefer a juicy scorpion to your sorry bones. Now, listen everyone. Soon the Valley forces will be gathering on the road beyond Nosidam, where it turns sunsetside. We'll meet the folks of Fossarelick there. They have been preparing to fight the Malevir and will lead the way."

The crowd was quiet now. No one spoke. Luchaer hardly could hear them breathe. One woman wheezed and coughed as she wiped sooty flakes from her face and shook out her head scarf. The baby cried again, and a few little children whimpered.

Finally, the councilor brushed ashes from his suit sleeves and said, "Luchaer, look at this hungry little boy. He just wants some bread. This day has brought us a complete menu of feelings: fear for breakfast, fury for lunch, and sorrow for dinner. You say we should feed our hunger with a battle. How can we fight on empty stomachs?"

"If you could eat hearty right now, would you feel more like fighting? I could feed you—I think."

Luchaer staggered back as the full force of the hurly-burly hit him. People grabbed his shirt and hugged him while others lifted him on their shoulders to carry him around the square.

"Yes!" they roared. "Feed us and we'll do it!"

Prendel grunted as he pushed people away from the old Protector. With fists on his hips, he demanded, "Just how are you going to feed us? Everything is in cinders."

His feet once more on the ground, Luchaer dropped his two sacks and ordered everyone to step back. He closed his eyes and took a deep breath. In his head, he heard Rocánonom's song, the one that had filled the Loblin shelter. He hummed it. With every new phrase of the song, his sacks swelled. When the song ended and he opened his eyes, the sacks were overflowing with loaves, dry sausages, cakes, apples, and plums.

"How's this?" he asked, smiling at everyone. He held up his hand to stop the surge of people about to surround him again. "Councilor Prendel, please help me distribute this food. The sacks hold enough for everyone."

Chapter 2

IN THE SETTING SUN, TREES along the roadside cast long shadows. With every few steps, Azile looked back to reassure herself that no one was following them. The bend of the road was only a short distance away. She stopped and clutched Alluxana's sleeve—something was running toward them, something small, dark, and light on its feet.

"Azile, this way," Alluxana yelped, and she pulled the girl into a clump of shrubs. They crouched behind a thick tangle of leaves and waited . . . and waited . . . but they heard nothing. Not a sound.

Azile peered over the thicket. The road was clear. She stood up and signaled Alluxana to follow her. Looking up and down the road and seeing no one, they eyed each other and shrugged.

"Probably a fox or rabbit," Azile said. "I'm so jumpy right now that everything makes me want to hide." She smiled and took one of Alluxana's four hands. "I'm glad to be with you."

"As you should be, young lady," said someone nearby.

Alluxana and Azile jumped back into the thicket. The high and squeaky voice had belonged to neither of them. "And I'm not on the road. Look behind you."

Sitting back on his hind legs, his forepaws pressed together, Gúrmulo frowned at the two of them. "Why are you here? My sister Gormley and I were chasing the Malevir, but he threw a thick fog around us and we lost him. Have you seen the beast? Well? Did he freeze your tongues?"

Alluxana was the first to shake her head and ask, "And when did the weasels of the Valley learn to talk so saucy?"

"Alluxana, I know him. He's the dragons' friend. Gúrmulo, we were watching the beast. He left Nosidam for Sunriseside Mountain."

Alluxana added, "The Malevir must be on his way to the Cave of the Ancestors to find the dragon's hidden lair."

Azile nodded. "Gúrmulo, why are *you* here?"

Gúrmulo dropped to his forepaws and shook his head. "To chase the Malevir—and Gormley and I are the Orferans' messengers."

Alluxana snorted. "I've never heard of you. And when did weasels receive the gift of speech?"

Gúrmulo scowled. "Gormley and I can talk with all friends of dragons. You're their friends, too, aren't you? And we have a plan to defeat the Malevir that—"

Azile cut him off. "Dragons do call us friends. Since you are their messenger, have you heard anything about my brother, Nnylf?"

"Good news: your brother is well. Gormley and I saw him in the giant's shelter below Nosidam just before the fire. He looked strong."

"Oh, thank the Ways of the World! Did you say in the tunnels? But fire destroyed the town—"

Alluxana asked, "And you saw 'a giant'? Was it a goat-faced giant?"

Azile smiled softly at the memory of Fulgid's kindness.

Gúrmulo groomed his whiskers and sighed. "Haven't seen a goat-faced giant. As for Nnylf, with Rocánonom to protect him, I'm sure they all escaped the fire and are on their way to safety. Gormley asked me to tell Fossarelick about the fire and such. She's gone to the mountain to track the Malevir, maybe finish him off."

Alluxana pulled Azile toward the road. With one right arm she waved dismissively at the weasel and said, "Weasels killing a basilisk! Such nonsense! Come, now, Azile. Atty and his men are waiting for us. The

PART IV: STARTING OVER

other folks of Fossarelick should be along soon, too."

Gúrmulo hissed, "She *could* kill it. You'll see! By the way, you look a lot worse than the Alluxana I used to see at the lodge!" Retracing his path toward the bend in the road, he ran ahead of them.

Astounded, Alluxana's mouth dropped open. She squinted and watched the sleek little animal dash ahead on its short legs, light puffs of dirt and sand trailing behind him. She shook her head. *Should I believe him? How does he know me?*

"Come, Azile, we had better catch up with him."

Kirrill, Eunan, and Cahalson walked at a quick pace ahead of their Fossarelick neighbors. Their conversation jumped around like a squirrel at breakfast as each man argued for his plan of attack. Toward the rear, Fernfallow and Bitterbud looked back to the village. The thought that the Malevir could ambush them from anywhere had them trembling.

Milkthistle nudged her brothers. "Calm yourselves." She looked up. "See, Isabella and Kurnan are scouting above us. The monster can't surprise us." She squeezed Bitterbud's shoulders, then looked behind them with her own worried glance. "At least, I think not."

Isabella dipped and hovered over the villagers. Children waved at her and giggled as they skipped along. The road turned up ahead and some of the bigger children raced each other to the bend.

Sherca called to her son, "Kurnan, can you hear me up there?"

Isabella flew in lazy descending circles until she and her rider were close enough to hear Sherca call out, "Stop the children, Kurnan. Tell them to slow down. They will soon be out of sight and we'll be mad with worry."

When Sherca's gaze returned to the road ahead, she groaned and her hand covered her mouth. As the children rounded the turn, several dark figures leaped out of the bushes to encircle them. She thought she could see the children waving their arms in the air as their captors lifted them and carried them away from the road and beyond her view.

Kurnan and his dragon flew to the spot as quickly as lightening hits a steeple, but they, too, disappeared from sight. Sherca thought, *Oh, Ways of the World, protect them! The hork has sent his goblins to eat our babes.* She hurried to Kirrill's side. Interrupting the men's argument, she pointed up the road and described the creatures' attack. Eunan called to the other men and, with Cahalson in the lead, they ran toward the site.

Kirrill drew his durk from his pouch. Cahalson's was also in hand. The three Moktawls, followed by a few boys of Nnylf's age, left the road and darted into the woods that ran alongside it. Thorns and sharp twigs caught at their sleeves and leggings, but they pushed them aside in their haste to reach the abducted children. Only Eunan stopped for a moment and stooped to pull at a nettle that was cutting into his calf. Lowering his head to tug at the barbed pod, he noticed a jumble of boot prints in the dirt at his feet.

Eunan ran to catch up with his companions. He pulled at Cahalson's sleeve and waved them all back in the direction of the tracks. As Kirrill and Cahalson crouched to study the impressions, Eunan whispered, "These are no goblin footprints."

"More likely boots, men's boots. All running around in circles, looks like," sniffed Kirrill. He stood up, eyes glued to the tracks. He muttered, "They go this way, back toward the road." While the others poked at the markings and studied the ground for more clues, Kirrill followed one set that he could separate from the others. He held his durk at the ready.

The trail continued around a copse and along a little dry streambed, then disappeared. Looking over his shoulder, Kirrill realized he had left his companions behind. When he turned to look forward again, where the boot marks ended, a smile slowly creased his broad face. Stowing his durk, he straightened his pack and hurried forward, arms outstretched.

As Aurykk and the other dragons circled above the Valley, the Golden let Fulgid hear his thoughts: *I can see the road from here. Alluxana is coming from Nosidam and she will rejoin the people of Fossarelick. You will guide them*

PART IV: STARTING OVER

all to your lodge. We Orferans will fly ahead to our ancestral cave. The Malevir will attack it soon.

The magnificent dragon stretched his neck and swooped down to a field of wildflowers bordering the road. Fulgid released Aurykk's frill, slipped off the dragon's shoulder and looked around.

Before they had alighted, Fulgid had noticed Fossarelick villagers hastening toward a spot in the road where a large group of men and older boys were clustered together. They were watching him and the Golden with intensity. Isabella—and a rider—dipped to greet them then flew on toward the town.

Farther off in that direction, he had seen two people chasing after a small furry animal whose scampering kicked up clouds of dust that hid their faces. At a good distance behind them, a throng of people was marching at a quick pace away from Nosidam, waving rakes and durks in the air. Fulgid thought he could hear them chanting as they went along.

Handing his dragon friend a pair of mice crushed by their landing, he pointed out, "Aurykk, all sorts of Valley folk will be coming together near here. If they see me, I'm sure some will think I'm the Malevir and will try to kill me."

Aurykk licked his fangs as he swallowed the last little bones. "Tasty, those. No, they won't kill you. Many of those men know you already, and the others should . . ."

He had turned his head slightly and looked down the road. "Ah, there they are, behind Gúrmulo, our friend." He snorted and a few mouse cinders floated up on the breeze. "Anyhow, those men across the way . . . they'd better not come near. So many Turns of the World since I last fought them off. Azile and Alluxana have nearly reached them."

Fulgid had sunk into the thick growth of flowers and was leaning against Aurykk's flank. At those words, he pushed himself upright. "Luxie, my dear! She's coming here?"

"Wait, Fulgid. Azile and Alluxana must explain to everyone that *you* are not the Malevir. Remember, to the Valley people your words sound like a goat's bleat!"

"Those Moktawls won't hurt me. We fought the Malevir together. The other villagers and townspeople worry me."

"Don't worry."

Fulgid crouched low in the flower patch. Only his goat head peeked above a tall mass of orange and yellow petals. His long nose twitched as he watched several children hugging the Moktawls he knew. "Look, there's Kirrill! Oh, come on, Aurykk. He knows me. We'll be fine."

The Golden rose to his full height and stretched his neck. In a flash, his wings expanded and Fulgid felt himself swept toward the road by a blast of wind.

"Kirrill, you say?" bellowed the dragon. "If he weren't such a poor shot, his shower of arrows once would have shredded my wings."

Across the way, Kirrill and the others were nearing the roadside. The Moktawl warrior waved at the Golden. Fulgid had rolled to the edge of the flower field. Just as Azile and Alluxana were approaching the group, Aurykk reared up, his eyes red and his nostrils flared.

Chapter 3

NNYLF WASN'T AT ALL HAPPY about struggling through the mountain tunnels again. Surrounded by clusters of chattering sprites, he could barely keep his eyes on Rocánonom as they climbed away from Nosidam. The giant moved so quickly. Sweat dripped from his forehead at the thought of being alone and trapped once more in these dim passages, lit only by the blue sparks that danced around Rocánonom's head.

He could feel little hands pushing him along, but when he turned to look behind him, he saw only a deep darkness. Hastening to regain Rocánonom's company, he tripped over a pile of stones in his path. Many little hands lifted him from the hard floor, brushed his clothes, and urged him forward.

Rocánonom stopped, and as Nnylf approached him, he saw the giant press his forefinger to his lips. Nnylf heard dozens of little footsteps patter along the walls of the tunnel. The giant took Nnylf's hand and led him into another larger passage that glowed dimly. The sprites crept along the walls behind them. When the whole company had gathered, Rocánonom raised his arms and sang three notes—high, low, high—again and again. Nnylf felt gentle, cool breezes wrap around him and his companions. A filmy curtain of vapors surrounded them all and Rocánonom lowered his arms.

"There are many Veils in our Valley. The one you see around us is the Dimming Veil. No one, not even the Malevir, can see or hear us now. Come closer, my friends. Come hear my plans."

Nnylf's heart beat quickly as the giant spoke of protecting dragons and ancient treasure, of an approaching attack. He felt lost in these passageways that were leading him and the others into the unknown. Without realizing it, he uttered a soft groan.

Rocánonom's voice broke into his thoughts: "My friends, my very brave friends, we soon will reach the Cave of the Ancestors as I promised you."

A buzz of little voices filled the air. Forestspice and Mallowseed came forward with Sweetnettle's wrapped body.

Nnylf cleared his throat and stood next to them. "Before you take us into the dragons' cave, Rocánonom, I would like to know, if you please, why we have to go there."

"The Malevir wants the dragons' treasure and, most of all, the Mystic Scintilla, the source of their powers. He comes here to take it. We shall wait for him, but not without help."

The sprites began to chatter and shout. Mallowseed shifted Sweetnettle's weight in his arms and asked, "Who will help us against the Malevir?"

"You tell me," Rocánonom replied with a soft smile.

"Why, the dragons!" shouted Forestspice.

"They will stand with us," said Rocánonom, his mouth hardened to a stiff line. "First, however, we must find a safe resting place for Sweetnettle's remains. This way."

Nnylf and dozens of Loblin followed the giant up steps carved into the rocky floor that took them higher into the passage. At the top of the stairway, a vast chamber opened up before them. Nnylf gasped.

"This is where the beast bound me to the rock!"

"Where we found you. Look over there, toward that other passage lined in marble studded with gems."

"The Malevir went there. He was looking for something. At the time I did not understand."

"Now you know. Was a goblin with him?" Rocánonom narrowed his eyes and looked into the passage as he listened to Nnylf.

PART IV: STARTING OVER   245

"Oh, yes! He was kind to me—not at all like Kralbong." He shuddered.

"He left his red rag in that passage as a sign. We found it when we rescued you. That passage leads to the dragons' hidden lair."

After assuring himself that no danger lay ahead, Rocánonom whispered a few words and the Dimming Veil lifted, The giant led his company across the main chamber to the marble-lined passage.

They all froze before reaching the opening. Something crouched and blocked their way. At their approach, the creature stood and roared in their direction.

From the mountain's base, Gormley had little trouble leaping through scree as she followed the struggling basilisk. *Wrong,* she thought, *he still has a bit of human in him. Can't call him a basilisk—yet.* She paused behind a pile of rocks and stones and watched the beast's struggles.

Aindle's arms splayed sideways and jerked as he failed to find a handhold among the slippery stones. He clucked as his elbows thickened and his shirtsleeves ripped open. His huge rooster head, with its hard and gleaming beak, twisted backwards. He scanned the groove he had left behind him, cutting deeply into the layers of rocks, stones, and gravel along the slope. He stopped when his gaze landed on Gormley's hiding place.

The weasel saw his yellow eyes widen as he stared with all his strength at her head, but Gormley sauntered in front of her rock pile, sat up on her back legs, and stared back.

You can't freeze us weasels with your eyes, old beast. A squeaky chortle escaped from her pointed snout.

At the sound of her laughter, Aindle squawked. He turned to grapple with the slope, but by now two stubby, scaly wings that thrust from his shoulders had replaced his arms. Useless for climbing. He stretched his neck to pick up a loose stone near his feet. With a snap of his head, he threw the stone at Gormley, but she dodged it. Again and again, Aindle hurled stones at her and missed.

Aindle dipped his beak to lob another missile, and Gormley used the moment to run sideways across the slippery stones. Another hiding place would shield her from the beast's view. She wanted to surprise him. Perhaps she might sneak up behind him.

As she watched her quarry, she could see more changes in the beast. The spell that had tricked the people of Nosidam into believing he was a hero had vanished. Tremors shook the beast and his whole body burst through his tattered clothes that now lay in shreds among the pebbles and gravel. Standing on legs fitting a gigantic bird of prey, Aindle stretched his talons with satisfaction. Each of his heels was studded with gleaming claws that could slice a tree trunk easily with one swipe. He steadied himself as he faced uphill. His legs pushed away from the slope and he leaped through the scree in great bounds.

Gormley left her cover and ran to catch up with him. *Very well, we can call him a basilisk now.* She sniffed at the ruined clothes Aindle had left behind and chewed on a corner of his torn shirtsleeve. Burping a little bubble of acid and gas, she patted her belly. "That wasn't so bad," she said and resumed tracking him.

At dusk, the ancestral cave's main chamber darkened. In that moment Nnylf lost sight of the animal blocking the marble passageway. When Rocánonom drew closer to it, the creature cried out. Everyone—except Rocánonom—shrank back as its strange sound filled the space. Nnylf thought he had heard it somewhere before, but he couldn't be sure.

"Sounds like the barking of a giant dog," whispered Forestspice, after placing Sweetnettle's body gently on the floor. He turned to ask two other sprites to guard the bundle.

"No!" rasped Mallowseed. "That was a shriek mixed with howls. The hork transformed something or someone into a cave serpent."

"No, no, I think it sounds like a young dragon," muttered Nnylf, "like Draako's voice when I first met him so long ago." He took their hands and pulled them forward. "Come on. Remember, I come from a

PART IV: STARTING OVER 247

long line of dragonriders." He gulped, hoping that in the gloom no one could see the sweat on his brow.

Rocánonom's soft steps had brought him to the very center of the chamber. He peered into the shadows. "Definitely a dragon scent," he whispered, "young but foul-smelling. Why is he alone here in the ancestral cave?" With a few quiet waves of his hand and a soft song, he threw orbs of rosy light toward the ceiling. They radiated glowing silky shafts that waved and floated downward to hover in midair.

Nnylf thought that the unfamiliar dragon crouching opposite Rocánonom looked ready to spring at him. Every time he opened his mouth to roar, he belched sulfurous fumes and hiccupped. Shaking his head from side to side and rising up on his hind legs, he glared at the giant, then dropped again to his forelegs and wrapped his tail around his side. One wing covered his head.

"I know about the pain in your burning eyes. In my Protector days, I had a salve that brought relief to not a few dragonets like you."

As he folded his wing back and looked at Rocánonom, the dragon yawned, revealing newly sprouted adult fangs and spark glands. *You'd take more care if only this stinging gas would turn into a proper fiery blast.* He sniffed, then stared at the giant. His eyes widened. *You understood me?*

Rocánonom nodded and smiled.

A Protector, say you? Where from?

"From the Veiled Valley." He paused and asked in a low voice, "May I come closer?" Hearing a friendly grunt, he approached the dragon.

"I am Rocánonom, once Protector of Anonom Trace meadows and glades. The great Silver, Lugent, was my friend. I can count most of the dragons of the Veiled Valley as my friends—but you, Prince, I meet for the first time." He cleared his throat and blinked his eyes to calm the dragonet. "May I give you a gift?"

Sitting back on his haunches, the dragonet stared at the squawking objects Rocánonom pulled from his sack. *Yes. Come even closer.*

"Please tell me your name."

The young dragon spoke out, "I am a dragon of the Veiled Valley. My mother Abulafria named me Drac'Argo. I come from the first Copper, Lustredust, and the first Bronze dam, Eminfoil. Loved I am by my mother and my grandfather Aurykk, who is a Golden. My cousin Draako is son of the great Silver, Lugent." He blinked and drew in a long breath. His hoarse voice dropped to a whisper as the scent of fresh chickens drifted toward his long snout. "I haven't eaten for a . . . for a while."

Rocánonom took several long strides until he stood in front of the young dragon. He lay the chickens on the cave floor and stepped back. The two birds ran in tight circles until, exhausted, they flopped in a heap.

"Good dragon, these chickens would taste so much better if you would scorch them a bit. I know dragons can be excellent cooks."

Drac'Argo nipped the head off one chicken and stomped on the other. "I don't mind raw birds, really." He licked at the chicken's feet, then cocked his head and sighed. "I can't make my mouth turn my belly gas into flames."

Glowing orbs bobbed around them. Their soft light illuminated stalactites that hung from the ceiling of the main chamber. When the giant's followers saw that the young dragon had settled into a peaceful conversation with Rocánonom, they drifted into the chamber.

Nnylf stood not far behind the giant. The two sprites cringed and pressed into the back of Nnylf's knees. When Rocánonom stepped aside and nodded to him, Nnylf forgot to breathe. He heard Rocánonom say to 'Argo, "I would like to teach you to use your spark glands properly, but before I do, please permit me to introduce my friends."

The young man came to Rocánonom's side while the shivering sprites gripped each other. "Tell him please that we are not so tasty," Mallowseed pleaded in a tight, low voice.

Nnylf smiled and spoke to Drac'Argo. "I am called Nnylf, and my own ancestors were the riders of Fossarelick. My mother's named Seerlana."

Although Drac'Argo had placed a possessive foot on the cluster of chickens and was hiccupping fiercely when Nnylf and his companions

PART IV: STARTING OVER   249

stepped into the light, he relaxed at the sound of Seerlana's name. He pushed his gift aside and stomped across the floor.

"Seerlana, you say? She's Aunt Anadraka's rider."

Rocánonom said, "Drac'Argo, please excuse my interruption. I would like to teach you to use your spark glands. Take in a deep breath and hold it."

Drac'Argo halted in mid-sentence, nodded vigorously, and opened his mouth. "Hiiiiiiiiiiiiinh," he squealed as he inhaled for several moments.

"Good, now curl your tongue and place the rough-edged underside over your spark glands."

"Um id."

"Could you point your head away from us toward the cave entrance? Very good. Ready? Slowly release fire gas from your second stomach. No, no, don't look at me. That's the way. When you feel the gas in your throat, rub your tongue on the glands and open your mouth. Slowly, slowly. There you go! Excellent!"

Drac'Argo belched fire into the night until nearly all the bushes and saplings growing near the ledge were burned to crisped veins and pith. Pleased with himself, he danced in circles around the main chamber, stirring up gravel and debris on the floor, while Rocánonom and his companions flattened themselves against the cavern walls.

When the dust settled, Rocánonom came to the exhausted dragon's side and congratulated him. "Well done! And how are your eyes?"

"They feel clear and bright again, good giant! You taught me well." He cleared his cooling throat. "We dragons know how to show our thanks. To celebrate our friendship, I shall roast those chickens and host a feast for all of you."

Nnylf heard a weak cheer rise in the passageway, where many other sprites had remained during this encounter. Rocánonom urged them to join him. Slowly they emerged from the tunnel, a few of them carrying Sweetnettle's remains. When they lay the dead sprite on a large rock, Nnylf cried out: "Not there! The Malevir bolted me to that rock." With a shiver, they all turned to Rocánonom, whose great hand pointed to the pool at the end of the marble passage.

Drac'Argo was engrossed in torching his chickens and marveling at the way they shimmied and split in two as soon as they were cooked through. At the sound of the beast's name, he looked up from his work and shot a blast of smoke to the ceiling.

"The Malevir!" he belched. "Because of him—well, and also the Moktawls—we went into hiding. Aurykk says that the people of the Veiled Valley, even Moktawls, soon will hunt the beast with us—if they don't try to kill us first." He snorted and a rotten smell drifted toward his guests. "Oh, sorry," he apologized and clicked a series of sparks that cleared the air.

With the dragon's permission, two sprites carried Sweetnettle to a spot inside the marble passageway and laid him next to the pool. They smoothed a red coverlet that wrapped his body and gave him a few loving pats.

Eager to share in the dragon's good mood, they gathered in small groups and sat near their host. Preferring berries, nuts, and cakes to meat, they happily munched their own provisions and chatted, while Rocánonom gathered some information between bites of the seared poultry 'Argo had offered him.

"Tasty, Drac'Argo! Thank you for sharing this feast."

'Argo nodded and burped. Rocánonom wasted no time and asked many questions. Eager to answer the giant, 'Argo revealed that his grandfather had left him to guard the passageway while he descended into the Orferans' family lair. "Of course, Bounder is there, too. He can guard the treasure best."

Nnylf nearly choked on his chicken wing at the mention of Bounder's name. Wiping away a few coughed-up bits with the back of his hand, he croaked, "Bounder is—or was—our dog. He ran away from home, from Fossarelick, the day before Azile and I went to Nosidam to sell barley."

"Ho! He didn't run away from you. He ran to us, to follow your mother. She brought the packet to us, you know, the one my aunt gave her. She brought it to the cave where I hatched."

"So Mother took the packet!" Nnylf rubbed his forehead and shook his head.

"Anyway," said Drac'Argo, "he's not really a dog. He hatched here."

"Hatched!" Nnylf blurted. "That's not how puppies come into the world."

"Well, he did hatch here. When was he your dog?"

Nnylf smiled and answered, "That dog found *us*. One evening after we'd finished our supper and I was scrubbing our kettle, Azile heard a loud scratching on our door. Good thing it was loud, too, because Father was snoring, his head upon his arms resting on the table. I picked up our biggest spoon as a weapon and opened the door a crack. The strangest-looking dog was sitting just beyond it and his tail was wagging back and forth, back and forth. He was covered in brown fur and his legs were odd, really short for such a big dog. As he waited for us to invite him inside, he cocked his head at us, again and again, just like a bird.

"Azile ran to him. When she held out her hand and he licked it, she opened the door wide. All that commotion woke Father. With one leap, the dog was on the table. Father jumped up and hit his knee on its edge and he yelled. The dog howled and hid under the table." Nnylf shook his head. "After that, they never did get along, but we loved him, Azile and I. Now you say he's not a dog?" Nnylf ran his fingers through his curly brown hair. "What else would he be?"

Drac'Argo raised himself to stand on his hind legs. In the midst of cleaning his face with the backs of his tongue-wetted forefeet, he froze, then swiveled his head to peer deep into the marble passageway. He turned back to his guests and waved his forefeet at them.

"Go back, all of you, to that other passageway. I hear him coming up from the lair. Don't be afraid. I'll protect you until he has a chance to know who you are."

"Bounder?"

The young dragon shook his head.

Rocánonom smiled at him. "Good Drac'Argo, I'm sure you will protect us, so please permit me to remain with you." Nnylf gathered the sprites and hurried them back into the passage that had brought them to the main chamber.

'Argo shrugged his wings and would have said a few more encouraging words when the ground shook under their feet. Rocánonom widened his stance, while Nnylf, watchful and mindful of his rapidly beating heart, stood under the arched opening into the back passage, all the sprites pressed against its walls far behind him.

When a Golden dragon and not Bounder appeared in the opposite passage entrance, 'Argo danced a jig and blew draughts of flame up to the ceiling. "Look, Grandfather, this fine giant and Protector taught me how to make sparks from belly gas!" With a little practice he had mastered a few puffs of smoke and cinder showers as well.

Aurykk nodded with a low growl and stared at the giant rooted in place before him. He opened his mouth wide. Musical notes sailed into the air, and Nnylf thought they sounded like hundreds of unimaginably beautiful bells. Rapt, he listened until words gradually replaced the melody and he realized that he was hearing the thoughts of this towering and splendid creature. He slapped his forehead, amazed that he never noticed before how easily he had understood Drac'Argo.

The voice in his head said, *A Protector stands before us, one of the worthies I thought long gone. Welcome, friend. Who and what have you brought us?*

Rocánonom had remained quite still. Not even his eyelids blinked. When the Golden's song ended, he bowed his head. "If I had more fitting gifts to offer you, great Aurykk of the Orferans, I would. Nevertheless, you might like these small tokens of my respect." He held out his hand.

Diamonds, rubies, and sapphires—two each—sparkled in his palm. Aurykk moved closer and sniffed the gems without scorching the hand that offered them.

Delectable, good sir. But you have not fully answered me. Who stands there with you?

PART IV: STARTING OVER

When Rocánonom turned, he saw Nnylf walking slowly toward him and the Golden. His hands were open and hung at his sides; he kept his eyes on the front of his toes until he stopped and stood at Rocánonom's side.

"We rescued this young fellow not long ago here in this chamber. The Malevir had chained him to that rock and left him to die. My companions, Loblin, cared for him with their herbs and spells—"

Nnylf interrupted: "No, great Golden, *his* spells produced the healing. You know him as Rocánonom, Protector of Anonom Trace." He bowed his head again. "My name is Nnylf, son of Eunan and Seerlana. I am from Fossarelick."

As they spoke, the dragon stood quite still and regarded them with his amber eyes, a small smile curling the edges of his long snout. When Nnylf mentioned his parentage, a mix of emotions flitted across his features. With a sigh he lowered himself to lie like a sphinx across the floor and said, "Rocánonom, many Turns of the World ago, you served my family well, especially during the years when the Moktawls first hunted us and we flew coldside to escape their arrows. Moktawls like your father, Nnylf."

The young man's face fell and he shook his head, muttering, "So very, very sorry."

"As is your father—at least that's what Azile says."

Hearing his sister's name, Nnylf raised his head, his eyes widened, and his mouth dropped open. He swallowed hard. "Azile is alive? She is free?"

"She is well and has joined with the Moktawls and others from Fossarelick and beyond. Ahead of them lie great danger and physical hardship—they intend to attack the Malevir."

Nnylf collapsed, mindless of the hard cave floor and scattered stalagmites that had accumulated across it long before he had ever visited the cave. Mallowseed and Forestspice rushed from their hiding place to help him stand again. He brushed the lime dust from his clothes, gritted his teeth, then said, "They need my help now. I can't stay here. I must go to them."

"Not without me," thundered a dragonish voice from behind Aurykk.

Ducking his blue-striped silver head under the archway, Draako lumbered out of the marble passageway and turned toward their visitors. "You are Nnylf, whose commands saved me when the Ancestors attacked. You are my rider."

Chapter 4

WHEN THE FOSSARELICK VILLAGERS pulled their children away from the road as the golden dragon reared up on his hind legs, Azile regretted calling for the Orferans so soon. Aurykk spread his wings and extended his neck frill and spikes like an array of swords and shields. Belching sparks and black smoke, he glared at Kirrill, then shook his head and flew away toward Sunriseside Mountain without hurting anyone.

The people gasped, but with some relief Azile watched the furious dragon leave. Sending thoughts of peace and calm in his direction, she rushed toward the people of her village. Stunned by the encounter, they stood mute.

Alluxana, panting from her effort to keep up with Azile, arrived and emptied her pockets while no one was looking at her. Feathers, bits of stale bread rolls, and scraps of cloth fluttered to the ground. She urged the weasel to come closer and held out her apron. With one quick jump, Gúrmulo buried himself in one pocket before any villager saw him.

Kirrill was the first to shake off his stupefaction. He looked around at his brother Moktawls, who remained motionless, mouths hanging open. With a sharp clap to each man's shoulder he set about reviving them all. When he'd finished making his rounds, he was surprised to see Alluxana and Azile standing in front of him. Close behind them stood the goat-faced giant.

"Flabbergasted! That's what I am. Maybe feverish, too. Here you are, just as you promised."

Fulgid leaned close to Azile and whispered in her ear.

"Fulgid would like to know what you did to Aurykk that angered him so."

"Never mind that old story. You might guess Aurykk's not too fond of this Moktawl. He flew over our village and my arrow just missed his wing. He put down Nnylf and Azile near home. We thought he had taken them."

The giant stepped between the women and Kirrill and patted the Moktawl gently on his shoulder. With a nod and a few bleats he asked Azile once more to translate for him.

"All that has changed, thank the Ways of the World." Fulgid bobbed his head in the direction of the Fossarelick villagers. "But they need to hear my story. I'm afraid they will try to rescue you and the others from my terrible monstrousness." Translation at an end, Azile pressed her lips together.

Her mother and other Fossarelick folk slowed their pace as they realized that the abduction Sherca had witnessed had actually been a reunion; but when they saw Fulgid, they raised their makeshift weapons. Azile stood between them and the giant.

Cahalson stepped forward, arms upraised. Kirrill and Eunan, with durks in their fists, quickly flanked the giant. Cahalson eyed every one of his fellow villagers and shouted, "This fierce-looking fellow is not our enemy. Meet Fulgid of the Sunriseside Forest, Protector of the dragons' Cave of the Ancestors. As your leader, I say whoever attacks him attacks us."

Sherca lowered her pitchfork. Scowling, she asked, "Is he the Formorian, the monster said to have torched our fields and stolen our animals?"

With shouts and curses, other villagers echoed her remarks and shook their weapons in the air. Seerlana by now had reached her husband's side. She spoke up, "Your memories are short, my friends. Have you forgotten

PART IV: STARTING OVER   257

all that we told you about the Malevir and his curses, about his spells and the destruction he intends to bring on all of us?"

Cahalson added, "The Malevir turned Fulgid into a giant and gave this lady four arms." He beckoned them to come closer. "Alluxana is Fulgid's wife. Her bravery helped free the Valley's gentle Loblin, like the three you met back in Fossarelick. They long to return to their own bodies and old life just as we do."

As Cahalson spoke, Alluxana held Fulgid's massive hand in two of hers and stood by his side. Her other hands patted the bundle wiggling in her apron pocket. The weasel's coarse whispers reminded her to tell everyone about Nosidam. Her jaw muscles tensed as she looked at the crowd around them.

Seeing her distress, Fernfallow and his kin, kicking up road dust, pushed their way through the crowd. "None of us will have our old lives back unless we learn to trust each other and the dragons," he shouted.

"Kolvak, ha!" called out a man, looking around for approval. "What do you know about it? Silly fool." He aimed a shower of pebbles at Fernfallow's feet.

Fernfallow danced a little jig and turned to answer him, but the villagers had lost interest. They milled about, some arguing with their neighbors, others scowling or taking a closer, if cautious, look at Fulgid. Atty produced a loud whistle between his fingers and teeth, which caught everyone's attention.

"Don't imagine we were having a picnic, us Moktawls, over there." He jerked his head in the direction of the Sunriseside Forest. "Some nasty brutes attacked us while we searched for this Formorian, but he turned out to be our friend. He saved my life, and Azile's, and—"

"And most of your fathers and brothers sent there by Cahal," said Eunan. "Our true friends have hidden themselves from us for more than one generation . . ."

Kirrill added: ". . . and our true enemy aims to destroy them and us."

Bending down, he hugged Alluxana about her shoulders. "What shall we tell them, Alluxana? Now that our families have joined with us and these fine little whatchamacallits—"

"Loblin!" burbled Milkthistle and Bitterbud.

"Loblin, you are! What do we do now?"

Alluxana was looking to the Sunriseside. Her eyes narrowed as she focused on a dark mass approaching from far down the road. She dropped Fulgid's hand and pointed in that direction.

"Do you see it, the billowing gray cloud over the town? Azile and I saw Nosidam burn. We left when the Malevir appeared and made his way toward the mountain." Gúrmulo wiggled in her pocket again.

Azile spoke up: "That's not the whole story. I'm sure that the—"

A few gusts of wind rocked the onlookers when Isabella landed. Kurnan jumped off her neck and, with a brief nod to his parents, ran to Seerlana, his face reddened as much by excitement as by the effort. "Nosidam is no more! The town has burned to rubble and its people have left. They're coming this way."

"Thank you, Kurnan. You and Isabella have to describe everything you have seen," said Seerlana, "before Nosidam's people reach us with their weapons and woes."

Alana crossed her arms tightly over her chest and grimaced. "I think we should prepare ourselves to fight them. The Malevir must have poisoned their hearts against us."

A frantic tune filled the air. Isabella sang while she flew back and forth above them. Azile and Seerlana listened and nodded.

Seerlana was the first to say, "Perhaps not. A Protector is leading them."

As the sky darkened, Luchaer's band of townspeople rounded a bend in the road and called to their leader. They begged him to turn back. Prendel in particular tugged on the Protector's tunic hem and pointed to a crowd of figures on the road beyond them that had materialized in the growing gloom and gathering mists.

PART IV: STARTING OVER

Luchaer halted his steady pace and looked back toward his not-so-willing followers. Many of them lagged behind or drifted from the road. They sat on the verge among tall grasses or searched for cover in the woods nearby. Returning to scan the road before them, Luchaer put down his sack. "No use turning back," he called out to his companions. "Nothing remains for us in Nosidam. If you must, rest your feet and I'll find out what's going on up there," he said, gesturing with his durk to the indeterminate gathering ahead.

Prendel objected and tried to pull him away from the road, but Luchaer gently pushed him away. Picking up his sack and slinging it over his shoulder, he strode on. Only the shaking hand that gripped his durk betrayed his fraying nerves.

The last light of day was fading as Luchaer strained to see whatever lay ahead of him. The Veiled Valley's evening mists thickened. Just before darkness set in, he caught sight of something that set his heart galloping. His eagerness pushed him to quicken his pace as he made out the figure of a woman dressed like a dragonrider, who bolted away from two other people walking beside her. She soon reached him. The shortest person among them was a woman with four arms. The third resembled a younger version of the rider.

Luchaer stopped and dabbed his forehead with his red rag, his heart thumping like a wooden wheel rolling over ruts, and he jabbed his durk into his sack. Strands of the rider's long dark hair fluttered behind her in the night breezes blowing across the Valley. Her strong legs, armored across the thighs and wrapped in brown leggings, were tucked into green knee-high boots. She strode forward and extended both arms to him. Before she could shake his hand, the shorter woman dashed forward and hugged him until he gasped.

"Luchaer! And just wait until you see Fulgid. You won't believe—"

"Fulgid? How do you know him? Who are you?" he paused and tucked his rag into his sack. He took a moment to consider her appearance. Then, squinting a bit as he looked at her, he burst out, "Why of course! You're

Luxie! I should have known that sweet face of yours right away. Those strong little arms distracted me, but, well . . . just look at you now!"

Luchaer frowned as he noticed her bulging pocket move a little. He almost asked about the paw that curled briefly over the pocket's edge, but Gúrmulo's head poked out first. Before he could question the weasel's appearance, Alluxana put a finger to her lips, shook her head, and gently pushed the weasel's head down.

With a nod of silent assent, Luchaer turned to the others and said, "Alluxana, I hope you will tell me more about what happened to you and Fulgid." Before she could answer, Luchaer turned to her companions. "But first, my mother would be ashamed of me if I did not greet your two friends properly." After a slight bow, Luchaer spoke to them. "My name is Luchaer, as Luxie already has said. Her cousin I am and I came to Nosidam from the Trace. My parents were Protectors there, aides to the kindliest of giants, Rocánonom."

Azile's eyes widened with surprise and she smiled. Seerlana grasped his hand to greet him. "I, too, come from the Trace, but you would know my father's face better than mine. The face of *her* grandfather, Lahsrayn." She opened her hand to indicate Azile. "My daughter, Azile."

Luchaer could see that Seerlana's gaze had the color and sparkle of his old friend Lahsrayn's. "I left the Trace long before you were born, but I recognize your father's bold stride and chin. I knew your mother Flanna, too. Where are they now that no one lives in the Trace? I never saw them in Nosidam."

With a cool hand on his wrist, Azile drew Luchaer's attention to herself. She said in a low voice, "My grandparents left Anonom village just before Mother went down to Fossarelick. They told her that riders beyond the Valley were meeting up coldside, and that they hoped to return soon. Something about a dragon, but we have not heard from them since."

As her daughter spoke, Luchaer saw Seerlana's chin quiver. She brushed her moist eyes with her sleeve and sniffed, "That's behind us

PART IV: STARTING OVER

now. We have our own gathering to attend. Luchaer, happily for our plans, you have mustered the people of Nosidam, but I also see that they are losing heart. The thick mists and darkness only make it worse."

"You see their despair only too well. They have lost nearly everything except the knowledge that the Malevir intends to enslave them. Does the spirit of Fossarelick fly higher than that?"

"Higher than grief and despair? Yes. Although our Moktawls once hunted and killed dragons, many Turns of the World have passed, and dragons of the Valley now see that Fossarelick has changed. They believe us worthy to fight the Malevir with them. That evil beast murdered all but six dragons; those survivors are ready to fight him, with us by their side."

A gentle cough and some light tugs on his sleeve from four little hands brought Luchaer's attention back to Alluxana. "Cousin," she said, "your people need sleep, warm food, and shelter from the night."

Before the old Protector could agree with her, an outburst of bleats surprised him from behind. He turned and stumbled back as he faced a muscular giant more than twice his size, whose mournful goat face filled him with thoughts of ruined cities and desolate fields. But when Alluxana reached for one of the giant's massive hands, Luchaer lost all fear of the creature.

"He is saying, 'I know a place they can rest.' This is my husband Fulgid, still under the Malevir's spell but in every other way a Protector like yourself."

Whether from Fossarelick, Nosidam, Anonom Trace, or beyond, the refugees had been drawing closer to Luchaer to hear his conversation with the women and giant. Kirrill was the first to show no fear. He embraced Fulgid, at least up to his belly. Other Moktawls soon joined him, with friendly slaps to the giant's thigh. While the townspeople buzzed among themselves, mindful of the strange creatures in the center of their leader's conversation, one man raised his voice and silenced all the murmurs. "Good people of Nosidam, I am Cahalson of Fossarelick, and I speak for all who come here in the name of our village. This giant Fulgid and the lady Alluxana stand here as our friends. With the strength that abides in those hefty arms of his, Fulgid has saved Fossarelick lives many times over."

Alluxana spoke up after giving all her attention to more of Fulgid's insistent cries. "That's all very nice, Cahalson, and we thank you, but now everyone here needs to rest. My husband would like you to know that you can take shelter in what was once our home, the lodge that we built near here many long Turns of the World ago."

Milkthistle, arm in arm with Fernfallow/Kolvak and Bitterbud, squealed and danced into the center of attention. "But Alluxana, the lodge was burned to the ground."

Nosidam's people gasped at the sight of a dainty sprite in their midst, and they shrank away again. In too short a time, they had seen the Malevir's deceptions, the loss of friends or neighbors' lives, their homes and shops burned, and now fierce Moktawls, a trio of sprites, a four-armed woman, and a goat-faced giant.

Alluxana replied, "Sweet Loblin, have no fear, I did know about the fire. I started it! All you people of Nosidam, I tell you that these kindly Loblin join us as friends, too. They are but three of many who have watched over and helped us for generations. As for the lodge, Fulgid tells me that the great hall stands again."

Prendel pushed forward, and with grizzled and bristled chin jutting toward his leader, he shouted, "You've led us away from the only home we've known to camp in the forest with those who would kill us? Your sack is empty and so is your head!"

Luchaer opened his mouth to reply, but the young mother who survived the fire and fled the city with her neighbors held out her baby for everyone to see. Wrapped in a small red blanket, the infant coughed and cried.

"We are one people now against that lying Malevir. No one but that beast means to kill us. My child and I, Margalana, are not going to spend

PART IV: STARTING OVER

this night in the middle of the road, shivering with hunger and thirst. Since Luchaer's supply of good food flows slowly from that sack of his, I intend to follow the giant who offers us his lodge where we can rest and refresh ourselves."

A buzzing wave of murmurs rose up from villagers and townspeople alike. Alluxana nodded to Cahalson and his men. They followed her and Fulgid into the forest. Azile, Seerlana, and the sprites were close behind them. With a fierce frown directed at her neighbors, Margalana embraced her child and whispered reassurances before she also followed Alluxana into the forest.

Prendel sighed, "You win, Luchaer. They offer us our only chance."

Before setting off for the lodge, Luchaer answered, "Prendel, they offer more than a chance. They promise us a future free from the Malevir."

Prendel shrugged his shoulders. With a few waves of his hand, he beckoned his neighbors to follow the giant.

Ahead of them, Fulgid had cleared tangles of undergrowth from their path, and his white-horned head gleamed through the mists blanketing the dark trees. The collective Valley folk, human or otherwise, followed him in a long line from the road, through the hedges and brush and into the depths of the forest.

Chapter 5

AINDLE FELT SURE THAT HE had escaped the weasel, but there she was, resting fifty leaps away from him. Too far for him to cripple her with a spell. Too far for his stare to stun her; she laughed at him whenever he blasted it at her. The thought of her coming any closer squeezed his head and made him dizzy.

How could such a weak and little beast make him feel that way? From the moment he saw those weasels in a tunnel beneath Nosidam, a familiar dread drove him to run away. He remembered his first Moon-Risings after he hatched. He would hear the basilisk hens hissing from one nesting chamber to the next: *Hatchlings, stay fierce, stay strong, and stay away from weasels. Stay away or die.*

Aindle hopped from one gravel-strewn ledge to the next until he cleared the scree-covered slope. *Surely by now she would be far behind.* He looked up toward the top of the mountain. *The entrance to the dragons' cave shouldn't be far. Only a few more leaps.*

He clacked his beak in anticipation of finding his boy prisoner inside the cave's entrance. *Just dash inside. Nnylf will cower and scream, then reveal everything—but what if the boy refuses to help?* Aindle grunted with pleasure as he mulled over the ways he would torture Nnylf, the spells he would use, the triumph he would feel when he forced the boy to reveal the dragons' treasure.

PART IV: STARTING OVER   265

One clawed foot, then the other scrabbled onto the dragons' ledge. Each step closer to the cave entrance sprayed gravel and dust. Aindle stretched his wings and a loud cackle left his open beak and echoed from the rocky mountainside.

The entrance was in shadow as the sun began to set. A few more steps and the basilisk stood inside the cave's main chamber. Something moved in the cool dark. As he sniffed and peered into the gloom, a sharp and peppery scent met his nostrils. He shuffled toward the boulder where he had chained the boy.

Aindle felt queasy as the scent grew stronger. The boy had smelled like dirt and sweat, not musky. The stake and chains were gone. He raged at the unbroken surface of the stone that had bound Nnylf.

One of his eyes caught the moving shadow again. He pounced at it. The creature scuttled away. He chased it into a side tunnel, where it dashed through a gauntlet of debris; sharp stones and jutting stalagmites narrowed the passage. Moving fast and breaking rock formations as he went, Aindle was still no closer to catching his prey. *Somehow, the boy got loose; somehow, he managed to stay alive here.* Although a knife-edged stalagmite rising from the floor scraped his leg, Aindle pressed on.

As he hurried around a corner, walls along the dim passage began to glow. Aindle paused to sniff other scents that wafted through the air, each new one more appetizing than the last. Light bathing one wall grew brighter and he could see that a fountain hung along its surface, just at the height of his broad chest. Gurgling juices ran from its spout—but as Aindle bent to open his beak for a drink, the stream bounced off the bones of his upper bill and splashed into his eyes. He squawked in frustration and stepped back.

Aindle flapped his wings then lifted his beak and cackled. With his head and long neck tucked under his wing, he began to vibrate until his shaking legs and wings raised a dense cloud of chalky dust from the floor. After the cloud had settled around his feet, the beast straightened up, stepped away from the dust, and patted his old hork's body.

This should work, he thought. *I could eat a donkey!*

He thrust his blue-green head under the fountain's stream and opened wide his purple lips. Dark red berry juice trickled over his fangs and down his stretched throat.

He drank until he groaned a loud belch. Wiping his mouth with the back of one clawed hand, he turned to see a table covered by a dark cloth. A row of dishes and baskets ran its length—hardly visible in the weakening light.

Heedless of shadows growing around him, Aindle grabbed loaves stacked in the closest basket. Sausages hidden in each piece burst with steam and grease as he bit into the fistfuls he had plucked. Each new platter offered a different delight: baked apples, succulent root vegetables dripping in fat-laden spices and berries, cakes oozing honey, and an assortment of cheeses that floated on flakey, golden crusts.

Burping with pleasure, Aindle rubbed his belly and prepared to gobble one remaining delicacy sitting untouched at the end of the table. Resting on a long silver platter was something that looked like a large and juicy meat pudding; it nearly matched the tablecloth on which the platter rested. Aindle reached toward it with both hands. It moved.

The meat pudding sat up. A strong, musky odor hit Aindle's nose, the same odor he had noticed before when he entered the cave. It spoke.

"May I jump down your throat, old Mally-vir?"

Aindle gasped as the meatloaf jumped off the table and landed a few paces from his feet. *This is no tasty morsel. Couldn't be the boy . . . have to stop him. Turn him to stone . . .*

Aindle roared and swiped at the creature, but it did not retreat. He stared, then screeched: *Weasel!* In a panic, he struggled to regain the cave entrance, but his sleeves caught on the jagged limestone columns sticking out of the floor at every turn. Frantic and panting, he tore his way through the rocks until he reached the ledge.

With a shriek, Aindle jumped over the rim, whirling in a cloud of purple-black vapors. His hork's body blurred and a basilisk emerged

PART IV: STARTING OVER   267

from twisting bands of mist while his beaked head strained toward the sky. With a frantic thrust of his almost useless wings, he rose briefly over the mountain peak, but having lost strength from shape-changing, he crashed into the forest below.

Nnylf left the shelter of a stalagmite that had hidden him from Aindle. He followed Gormley as she ambled out to the ledge and asked her, "How can you just sit there after facing the Malevir?"

Gormley scratched her belly fur with a hind leg and said, "He doesn't scare me. And I nearly got him this time. I wish Gúrmulo had been here to see."

Rocánonom joined them. "The Malevir will rest in the forest until he heals. You can be sure that he will come back for the treasure. I think I'll follow him, see what he's up to. Watch for the dragons; they're coming up from their lair."

Gormley moved away from the edge. "Count on me to scare him away again if he comes back. I love the way his eyes bulge whenever he sees me. Tell me, who will guard the treasure if the dragons go after him, too?"

"Bounder—with his griffin ancestors' strength and eagle-eyed vision. He will not fail."

"I'd like to see what he looks like now. Maybe he'd enjoy a visitor." She ran to the pool and slapped at the surface with her paw.

Rocánonom called after her, "He'd enjoy hearing about your brave deeds. Be careful, now." He muttered to himself, "Not that being careful comes easily to a weasel."

Rocánonom left the cave with Forestspice and Mallowseed. They followed a path that curved down the slope from the cave. The other sprites remained in the marble passage and a few of them were busy with Nnylf's dragonrider armor. With quick strokes, tuckings, and pullings, they sewed and arranged sturdy leather pieces across his chest, back, and legs. Nnylf felt the weight of thick boots girding his feet as sprites laced them up tightly with soft metal thongs.

"There go you, sir!" chirped a round, girlish sprite. Her little double chin jiggled as her eyes crinkled happily. "You're the image of a grand dragonrider."

"And armed well, too," piped up another sprite as he thrust the handle of a gleaming lance into Nnylf's hand. The sprites stepped back a bit to look at their handiwork. Nnylf squirmed as he tugged at the armor covering his tunic.

"Just a little more room here, please, under the arms?"

"No, it will stretch when you fly with your dragon," said the sprite. Her eyes widened as waves in the deep pool swelled upward. One after the other, four dragons broke through the water's surface and flapped their broad wings to dry. The tumult scattered sprites nearby, who clutched their tool sacks and leather scraps. They ran back along the tunnel toward the main chamber.

Moments later, another smaller dragon crawled over the pool's edge. Like a dog, the dragonet's soaked body shimmied, starting with his tail and ending with his snout until he had waggled away all the water that annoyed him. He belched a plume of dark smoke. "Just testing," he sniffed and waddled toward the main chamber.

Nnylf shrank into the cave wall behind him and shivered, despite the armor covering him all around, as the marble's chill met the small of his back. He smiled as silver-blue Draako snorted and bobbed his head in greeting.

"Now that the Malevir lies far below the ledge, we think he will be looking for you and Azile at the Protectors' lodge. My mother and the others wait for us in the main chamber. They're leaving to find their riders, then fly to the lodge. Are you ready to ride me?"

Nnylf gulped and felt sweat trickle across his ribs. Wriggling under his body armor, he grasped the hem of his damp tunic to wipe his brow, but stopped as a sprite thrust his own red rag into Nnylf's hand.

"This works better," he whispered to the young rider. "You'll feel its power."

PART IV: STARTING OVER

Nnylf leaned down to thank him, then dabbed his forehead and neck. He took in a deep breath and felt strength surge through his arms and chest. With a bow, he nodded to Draako. "I am ready to ride, Dragon Prince of the Orferans. Where do we go?"

Draako answered, "Isabella and Kurnan came to tell us that the Valley people are at the lodge. Once there, we shall do something about that Malevir." Draako folded his legs and sank to his belly. "First, slip your lance into a pocket lying across the armor that covers your back."

With both hands, Nnylf reached behind his shoulders and was surprised to find a rugged sleeve attached to the thick leather that protected his back and neck. With difficulty, he threaded his lance into the pocket.

"Again. Pull it out and put it back."

Nnylf struggled to remove the lance and replace it in the pocket. As he practiced, Draako reminded him about basic dragonriding skills: "Remember that I keep my body straight when I fly. To maneuver in flight, I depend on my wings and the degree to which I extend my neck. Also, my tail works as rudder, and I use my hind legs for drag."

Nnylf was concentrating on stowing and drawing out his lance. When he finally managed the operation with grace and conviction, he realized that the dragon was waiting for him to respond.

"Sorry? This lance business . . ."

"I was talking about dragonflight and asked if you understood."

"Oh . . . um, yes, of course!" Nnylf shrugged his shoulders and rubbed the back of his neck.

"Good! Come up now." A faint plume of gray smoke escaped from Draako's nostrils and he narrowed his golden eyes. "Look for the rope that Rocánonom has fixed around my neck and frill. Use it to hoist yourself to my upper back. Use that first big spine to brace your own back."

Nnylf found the end of a thick rope, rough and prickly against his palm, and tugged at it gingerly with both hands. Holding on and leaning back, he pulled himself up the dragon's flank until he stood next to the ridge of his immense backbone. With unsteady steps and burning, reddened palms, he reached a fluted neck frill and a hump that covered the top of Draako's scale-protected spine, and he swung one leg to straddle it. He settled his bottom onto the soft bump of fat sheathing the spine and waited for instructions.

"Very good, Nnylf. Now, hold the rope firmly and grip that bump with your legs. We're going out to the ledge."

Chapter 6

GORMLEY ENVIED HER OTTER FRIENDS; they had so much fun in the water. She was a good swimmer but felt clumsy when her lovely brown fur hung damp along her slender body. And a wet tail, what a bother! She yawned widely and drew in large gulps of air. Her sharp little teeth sparkled in the dim light of the cave.

Jumping in with all four feet, Gormley landed with a splash and slowly sank into the pool. She drifted downward and marveled at the emeralds and sapphires embedded in the pool's curved wall. Another body, on its own downward plunge, passed her and blocked her view of the gems. Suddenly, the water twirled her long, slender body several times and tossed her onto a rock-strewn platform. As she coughed and wiped droplets from her eyes, she saw the pool rise away from her and hang just overhead at the top of the wall.

Spewing out mouthfuls of water, she crawled away from the platform, down a few broad steps toward a halo of radiant amber light that rose from a mound at the entrance to another dim passage. She could see the silhouette of someone or something crossing and circling the mound. Her front claws dislodged a small pile of stones and she slipped. Landing on her sodden tail, she let loose a loud squeak.

The creature on the mound stopped moving. A dark shadow spread itself over the top of the mound as if it meant to contain the beams of light that otherwise poured from it. Gormley blinked as the outline of two dusky wings hovered over the creature. They folded, then fluttered open again. The creature hung above the mound for a moment, then flew at her and would have torn her to shreds with his talons had the weasel not called out.

"Stop, Bounder! Don't hurt me, Gormley, your friend from the Cave of Refuge."

The griffin pulled back his hooked claws just before they would have caught the soft flesh of Gormley's belly. He stumbled backward and landed, sitting on his long tail. The weasel licked her paws and circled around Bounder with short, careful steps. Behind him, she could see a towering pile of gold coins, platters, goblets, and even a sword with a gem-studded gold hilt. A scattering of jewels in every hue sparkled like stars on the surface of a pond; but they paled next to the rays of light that pulsed into the air straight up from the mound, their source hidden somewhere deep under the treasure.

Hoarse and panting, Bounder barked, "You're looking at the pulse of our Mystic Scintilla's power, under all the pretty trinkets and gems. I defend it."

"I won't touch it. You rascal, hiding as a wretched, stubborn stray spellbound by Ruddykin's spirit. When did your life as a griffin begin?" asked Gormley. She settled back on her haunches and folded one forepaw over the other.

Bounder began to pace back and forth between her and the treasure mound. Every time he returned to Gormley, the griffin complained about his unwilling service to his nestmate, Ruddykin, the flight from the Cave of Refuge to the Protectors' lodge, and his strange sleep in Draako's pouch during the flight.

The griffin's pacing dislodged stones from the chamber's floor and kicked up sand and gravel in his path. Gormley brushed grit from her fur and, edging away from Bounder, bumped into a damp bundle propped against a pile of smooth stones. Her forepaws clutched at the air and she fell onto the bundle. A thin cloth covering one part of it fell aside.

PART IV: STARTING OVER   273

Gormley squeaked as she lay nose to nose with the intact little green speckled face of a dead sprite. If his eyes had not been closed, he would have looked very much alive. Afraid to touch the sprite with her sharp claws, the weasel nudged his chest with her nose, but he did not stir.

"He must have floated down here with you," Bounder growled. "What did you do to him?"

Gormley bristled and yelped, "Not a thing. The Malevir's poison killed him. The Loblin meant to bury him in one of the passages but left him by the pool, and he rolled into the water with me, I suppose."

"Killed by the beast? Has Aindle's cruelty no limits? Let's wrap him up again. We'll treat him proper."

In one leap, Bounder was standing next to Gormley and the dead sprite. With care, the weasel wrapped Sweetnettle's head again with the cloth and tucked in its loose ends. The griffin picked up the bundle with his talons and lifted it from the floor as he flapped his wings. In a few strokes, he flew to the side of the mound and placed the sprite inside its rim and directly over a pulsing beam of golden light.

Bounder growled, "The Malevir's foul forces have maimed or destroyed so much that is good in our Valley. Now he harms loyal Loblin who live to help the Valley's folk. Here, we'll hold his little body steady. Close your eyes."

Bounder yowled and a high-pitched hum filled the air. The light beam's energy rocked the little bundle while they held it in place. With her eyes closed, Gormley felt the air around her warm up, the pebbly floor shake, and an odor of dust and cooked stinging nettle fill her nostrils. After what felt like a very long and tiring time, Gormley's bones softened and she thought she just might faint.

At that moment, Bounder shouted out, "Step back, far back, and let me carry him to the platform."

Gormley stumbled backwards and opened her bright black eyes. She saw her russet-brown fur coated in fine golden dust. She cleaned her long, sensitive whiskers and turned to look at the bundle.

It moved. Bounder and the weasel heard a small cough, then a string of gasps and wheezes. Gormley tore the bundle's wrapping from Sweetnettle's face and jumped back as the sprite's bright green eyes blinked rapidly.

"Um, would you mind taking off this wrapping?"

Shifting back onto her forepaws, Gormley sniffed Sweetnettle's face and sneezed.

"Wonder at the Ways of the World! You are very much alive again, little Lobli."

Bounder looked up through the pool above them with a scowl. "He never *was* dead. The Malevir's power to make him look so fooled us all." The griffin lifted another edge of the wrappings and pulled hard. Sweetnettle rolled across the platform as the cloth unwound, then sat up and attempted to dust off his shirt and leggings with limp hands.

After straightening his twisted twine belt and the tool sack, he rose to his wobbly knees and, shakily bracing himself on his thighs, he managed to stand and take a deep breath.

"I looked lifeless but I heard everything," the sprite blurted. He sneezed and whispered, "I am a bit hungry . . ."

Gormley bobbed her head and sniffed along the rocky wall to her left. With a sudden leap, she sped after a small animal darting into the shadows. Soon she returned with a lifeless mouse in her mouth.

Sweetnettle stared down at the offering Gormley laid at his feet and shook his head. "Thanks, but no. In my sack, please."

Gormley rummaged inside his pouch and found some hard cakes and dried fruit, which she carried to the sprite.

Between eager bites, Sweetnettle remarked, "I thank you for your powers and kindness. I thank my brothers and sisters, too, for their love and care. I must hurry now to help them. Where is Rocánonom?" He sneezed again.

With heavy, dust-raising strides, Bounder had been pacing between treasure mound and platform during Sweetnettle's short speech. He

PART IV: STARTING OVER

paused to snarl, "The Malevir fell into the forest on the mountain's far side. I suppose Rocánonom followed him there, he and some other Loblin."

"How do I leave this place to follow him?"

Gormley circled the sprite in figure eights. Trying to push him away from the platform, she cried out, "The Malevir's strength will return. Stay awhile with us until you are stronger."

"I've had enough rest," Sweetnettle giggled. "Thanks to the Mystic Scintilla, I am ready. Now tell me: how do I leave?"

"Can you swim?" the griffin muttered.

The sprite nodded and Bounder showed him where to stand. In a few moments, the pool of water suspended overhead began to deepen until it hung an arm's length from the floor.

"Brave little Lobli, may the power of the Mystic Scintilla stay with you. Dive into that." The griffin pointed with his wing to a vortex swirling within the broad cylinder of dark green water. "The whirlpool will carry you up to the marble passageway. As you leave the pool, take the tunnel to the main chamber. You'll see the cave's opening and the forest below."

Bounder stepped back toward the treasure mound while Gormley put her front paws on the sprite's knees and extended her neck toward his face. Sweetnettle bent his head and Gormley licked his nose before backing away to join Bounder. With a wave of his green-speckled hand, Sweetnettle leaped into the whirlpool and the green gloom swallowed him.

On a steep path that led downhill from the dragons' cave, the giant and his sprites stepped softly, threading through scattered forest debris. Without cracking a twig or kicking a pebble, they reached a stand of chokeberry bushes and crouched behind them. The giant sank to his knees. At his side, Mallowseed and Forestspice did the same. They watched Aindle through a tangle of green leaves and berry clusters.

Pulling out a few handfuls of herbs and dried mushrooms from his pocket, Rocánonom clenched his fists and pounded one against the other, signaling. Mallowseed took a deep breath and pulled a small clay pot and short blunt rod out of his tool sack. He set to mashing the herbs until they formed a paste. The three companions dipped their fingers into the mixture and licked up the bits until just a few spoonsful remained in the bowl. The giant nodded and returned to watching Aindle.

The beast's back pressed against acid-scorched shrubs and thick, broken tree limbs. He stretched his neck to examine his wounded wings and leg. Small patches of new scales were already closing many of the gashes gaping through his hide. Looking up at the mountain, his eyes narrowed, and he groaned as if a stew of rage and exasperation boiled in his belly. When the Malevir opened his beak to bellow his fury, Mallowseed could see his right shoulder twitching.

Rocking forward, the beast managed to sit up and squat on shaky legs. Then, with one thrust of his talons, he stood amid the ruined vegetation. Aindle closed his eyes and released a string of clucks that he softly repeated as he rocked back and forth. Acid no longer dripped from his leg, and a sheath of bilious green feathers spread across the scales of his healing wings.

Mallowseed held his breath, horrified, as another beak popped out of Aindle's shoulder. The beast stretched his legs and newly feathered wings and he turned to regard his second head, now facing him like a mirror image. Two sets of enormous yellow eyes stared at each other. Each sat above its own wide and fearsome beak, edged like a sharp blade and dripping acid ichor.

Backing away from each other and opening to the sky, the maws of the two-headed beast released horrendous cries, like a thousand crows cawing in chorus with a thousand screaming gulls. "An aiglonax," Forestspice gasped before Rocánonom could stifle him, and Aindle's two heads swiveled in their direction. The giant insisted that the two sprites flee toward the cave. Before they could argue with him, Rocánonom pushed past the bushes and stood on the edge of the devastated clearing to face Aindle.

PART IV: STARTING OVER 277

Mallowseed and Forestspice ran. Confused by the tears coursing down their pale green cheeks, they lost the trail and stumbled up the mountainside through thick brambles and shrubs. Forestspice's hand blindly tested the air before him, then dropped as he came to a halt.

Close behind him, Mallowseed bumped against his back, then whispered, "The beast surely will finish him." A small sob shook his chest.

Forestspice squeezed his companion's hand and reassured him: "We'll call Bounder. He can help." He sighed and looked around for the trail.

"Wait for me!" said a voice ahead of them.

The sprites dabbed at their clouded eyes to see who had spoken. Together they whispered, "Sweetnettle!" and sank to the ground. Surrounded by mounds of leaves, Forestspice and Mallowseed looked up at their brother sprite in disbelief.

Forestspice declared, "Dear ghost, have you come to destroy the Malevir?"

"I'm no ghost," Sweetnettle assured them. "The Malevir's poison almost broke my belly heart, but Bounder the griffin healed me with the Mystic Scintilla's light."

"You've seen the Mystic Scintilla?" asked Mallowseed. Giving Sweetnettle a fierce hug, he whispered, "Bounder must leave it to help us protect Rocánonom from the Malevir."

"The Malevir has him?"

Mallowseed asked him to follow and crept downhill off the trail.

The three sprites pushed through the undergrowth until they were a few strides from the bushes that had hidden them and Rocánonom earlier. Mallowseed put a finger to his lips and pulled the small clay pot from his sack. A bit of the rue and mushroom mixture clung to its side. Sweetnettle dipped his finger in the mash and licked up a mouthful. The three of them huddled close to a bush.

Gently parting a few branches, they held their breath and watched two giant creatures face each other in the clearing. They could see the aiglonax quite clearly. He rose from the ruined vegetation to hover over his prey, then landed close to a rigid Rocánonom. Although the aiglonax screeched and spit at him, the rugged giant said nothing and offered no resistance.

Sweetnettle was the first to whisper, "Look! He's not moving. The Malevir has ensorcelled him again."

"I don't think so," answered Forestspice in the same low tone. With a slight smile, he pointed to his herb-stained clay pot, then waggled his head. "The rue's protecting him. So, we'll leave Bounder to his duties and go to that old shelter we used to use, the one with the root fountain. We'll rest there, then find Luchaer and the Valley folk. Follow me—the tunnel's uphill just a bit."

At that moment, a shadow covered them and the monster swooped over their heads. Three of his feathers grazed their heads as they ducked. Stilled by fear, they felt their collective six hearts thrash about for a few moments. They did not move. Probably satisfied that his feathers had immobilized them, Aindle whipped upwards into the clouds before spiraling down to land at Rocánonom's feet.

Mallowseed breathed deeply, wiggled his fingers, then slurred a few words to his companions: *The rue works!*

They nodded and smiled weakly at him. Hard to focus. After another woozy glance through the shrubbery branches, Mallowseed looked uphill again. "Hurry, before the beast . . ." He stumbled. "Before the beast returns." The three sprites staggered up the path.

Chapter 7

ISABELLA OFTEN THOUGHT OF HER mother, Serpinafria. In her grief, she struggled against memories of the copper-gold dam defending herself from Moktawls who had ambushed her, but that painful image hung on.

She remembered how, on that last terrible day, Serpinafria had been teaching her about using her tail to hurl boulders from the Coldside Mountains. The aged dam left her and went to rest in a flower-filled meadow near Anonom Trace. With a happy sigh, she had folded her weary wings, gold flecks glinting in the sunlight. Her head was drooping sleepily between her outstretched forelegs, while her flanks rose and fell slowly. First one eye had closed and then the other. Isabella could hear her mother's rumbling snores.

The attack had been sudden and deadly. A band of men from Fossarelick—Moktawls, they called themselves—had surrounded her while she slept deeply. One of them pierced her heart with a thick spear while another quickly stabbed the dragon's spark gland. Before the fatal wound killed her, Serpinafria screamed and her cry rang across the Valley.

As she lay dying among crushed flowers matted on the ground near her still body, one man had approached her with his durk. He said to another one, "Your spear it was that struck her heart, so her hide is yours." He tugged his moustache and pointed toward the dragon's flank.

The scales of his blue tunic gleamed as he knelt beside her and began to mark where his companion would strip the gold-striped copper skin from her side. His large silver amulet hung around his dirt-streaked neck.

"Much thanks, Atty," replied the man. "It's time I had my own dragon-skin tunic." He grinned.

Isabella had heard her mother's cry and the men's voices. In a flash, she reached the meadow. Although still a juvenile, her spark and fume glands worked well. With a blast from both, she spewed her breath over the Moktawls.

Startled, the men gaped at her, then at their limbs as their movements slowed. Their weapons fell from their hands and they collapsed to the ground. Blistering steam had scalded their faces and hands and they were weeping with pain. Isabella readied herself to destroy them by snorting several times through her spark gland.

Before she could reduce them all to ashes, her father Aurykk arrived and cast his shadow over her. He called her away from her mother's corpse. As they hovered over the horrific scene, Isabella could see tears running from her father's fiery red eyes—but she knew that a Golden rarely kills his enemy, and these Moktawls would not die this day.

"They attacked Mother," she argued. "They killed their friend. They were going to skin her! I want to burn them alive!"

"No, my dam deserves better. We shall take her body to the mountains and bury her there. In time, these men will regret their attack and will need us again. Come help me give your mother the burial she deserves."

With that, the Golden and the young Copper flew to the Coldside with Serpinafria's body held between them. They laid her body on a flat rocky shelf near the peak of the mountain. One by one, they piled boulders on top of her remains. Aurykk and Isabella paused when the cairn covered his dam and came to a point above the peak.

"Now all who come here will see her resting place and will remember her sad end. May she be the last dragon to die by a Moktawl blade!"

Isabella felt a shudder run from her snout to her neck.

PART IV: STARTING OVER

"Wake up, my friend," Kurnan shouted. "Your dreams loosened my grip."

All those sad memories had distracted the Copper, and she'd forgotten that Kurnan was sitting astride her saddle hump. She struggled to push away the anger her memories had stirred. When she heard Kurnan say, "I would like to know more about your mother's kindness and beauty," she blinked with surprise.

Strange words from the son of a Moktawl! Isabella pouted as she sent her thoughts to her rider.

"Maybe." Kurnan pressed his lips together and patted the Copper's sinewy neck. "Your friendship has changed me, and I thank you for that. The boy who hid from shadows now rides a beautiful and wise dragon. Together we are helping our Valley defeat the beast—the very one whose mischief made Moktawls of Fossarelick men."

A gust of wind from the far side of the mountain buffeted them. Kurnan wrapped his arms partway around Isabella's neck and urged her to fly higher, past the peak, with a view to the forest below.

"When I saw the aiglonax beat that giant and carry him off to the Cave of the Ancestors, I wanted to follow them and have you blanket them with your fumes. We could have plucked the giant from the monster's beaks, I'm sure of it."

Yes, my fumes might have slowed the creature. He would have felt as though he were moving through thick mud. For a short time, he would have been quite weak, and it is true, his acid would not have harmed me, but I am no match for his strength and powers. I have a different strategy: I can cause boulders to fly. Remember that— but look! Three of the giant's Loblin are on that uphill trail. We have to stop them before the Malevir sees them.

Kurnan held on as Isabella dived toward the mountainside. Reversing herself with a whip of her tail and short wingthrusts backward, she hung above Sweetnettle and his companions. The three sprites covered their heads and ducked into the underbrush. Isabella blew a few whiffs of her fumes in their direction and the sprites' movements slowed to sluggish.

Little ones, an aiglonax has captured your leader. We've come to warn you.

Sweetnettle slowly pushed his head through a tangle of leaves and branches. "We know, but he ate rue," he mumbled through swollen lips. "The paste . . . saved us from the beast. . . . Now . . . be off," he added with a weary wave, "and . . . leave . . . us to our . . . mission." He pulled his head into the bush.

Kurnan shouted to them, "We share your mission, my dragon friend and I."

Isabella and her rider waited a while for their response. Eventually, Forestspice—his eyes half opened—showed his head. "Then we have the same enemy. The aiglonax . . . Malevir . . . Aindle. All the same. Rocánonom—*hiccup*—has tricked the beast." Looking up at the dragon and her rider, he repeated Sweetnettle's plea: "Be off, we beg you . . . the aiglonax will see us."

"Where are you going?"

All three sprites crept out from under the bushes on their hands and knees and returned to stand unsteadily on the trail. "To one of our shelters near the Protectors' lodge," Forestspice answered.

"May the Ways of the World protect you," Kurnan answered.

"Likewise," burbled the sprites as the Copper and her rider flew into the clouds overhead.

On their way to the lodge with its promise of shelter and food, Alluxana worried that she had made a mistake. "They won't have anywhere to sleep or bathe," she whispered to Fulgid as they walked through the forest. Dragging her feet, she turned to look at Luchaer and the long line of Valley folk following close behind.

With a snort, Fulgid shook his massive goat head and bleated that much had changed since she had last seen the place. "The Golden made the difference. You'll see."

"What difference? The fire I set burned it all, save the hearth," said Alluxana.

PART IV: STARTING OVER 283

Fulgid snorted again. "After you left me there, two dragon dams found me. We talked for a while, then we heard the wing beat of other dragons, so I hid. A splendid golden dragon and a silver-blue dragonet landed nearby. I came out from hiding, my rider hat in hand, and the Golden transformed himself into the very man who had knocked on our door long ago, before Aindle stole the lodge. He rebuilt the main hall, everything the same except for the tower, and he closed the tunnel opening that leads to goblin burrows. We left the lodge after that and he delivered me to you along the road."

The news heartened Alluxana. Picking up her pace, she reached the wall surrounding the lodge grounds before sunset. The gates were gone. She walked into the garden with Fulgid. Next came Luchaer, then the apple vendor Mëlo and his wife, the Councilor Prendel, and Margalana, carrying her baby girl in a makeshift rucksack. Close behind them were Seerlana and Sherca's families, their friends and fellow villagers from Fossarelick, and the three loyal sprites, Kolvak/Fernfallow (still disguised as the Moktawls' cook and baker), Milkthistle, and Bitterbud.

Reaching the lodge, Alluxana felt a surge of happiness at the sight of its familiar facade, built in straight courses of stone over which ivy climbed toward solid eaves. The slate-covered roof angled sharply upward to a high peak, interrupted only by two dormer windows that blinked like eyes facing the fading light of day.

The main hall was large, but not large enough for the crowd of Valley folk trying to enter. When no room was left, the last to arrive sat in small groups on the grass and benches of the garden.

"This won't do," said Alluxana. "They'll need some sort of shelter." She searched through supplies stacked on shelves flanking the hearth. "No, not blankets. Wait, wait—what's this?" She pulled down heavy folds of fabric, which she dropped onto the long trestle table standing before the hearth. While she was smoothing the material, a curious child pulled on it and tipped her water cup onto the cloth. Clucking her tongue, Alluxana shook off the droplets beading on its surface and smiled when she realized the cloth had not absorbed the water. She called to Luchaer, "This *will* do. Help me cut it up into pieces for tenting."

Alluxana had Fulgid hoist her onto the table so everyone could hear her. "Most of us will need to sleep in the clearing tonight. We'll store our belongings under the tents we make from this cloth until we can build more space here. You there, Kolvak, give us a hand."

The cook/sprite looked at his hand and squinted. "Alluxana, I can't give you my hand. How about my *durk*?"

Her laughter bounced off the high ceiling, and soon many of the others relaxed and joined in. Kolvak, Atty, and Sherca cut tenting while Luchaer shouted above the raised voices and laughter. "We have much to do here. Thank you, everyone."

Counting on the giant's great strength and knowledge to help with rebuilding the lodge and its outbuildings, Luchaer turned to Fulgid. Together they would organize the villagers into teams that would search for wood, stones, lime, and tools the next day. Azile would help everyone understand Fulgid's bleats.

Luchaer shouldered a ladder and led Mëlo, his wife, and a few of the older children into the orchard to tend the trees and pluck any available fruit. Sure that soon the dragons would arrive and defend them, he returned to the main hall, where a large cauldron was heating on a steady fire and the aroma of cooking grain, forest vegetables, and peppercorns wafted past his nose. Sitting by the hearth, he watched Alluxana and her new friends lean their heads together. The fire's crackle and the stew's bubbling masked their talk.

For the remainder of the evening, everyone worked hard to tidy the lodge and make the tents in the clearing comfortable. They ate nourishing food and bathed their children with water hauled from the pond. At day's end, most of the Valley folk crawled into tents to fall asleep almost instantly between thick, soft layers of bedding.

A few people still lingered in the main hall. They had gathered around its long trestle table. Wearied and anxious, Cahalson sat with Eunan,

PART IV: STARTING OVER   285

Seerlana, Alluxana, and Luchaer. All of them warmed their hands around cups of herbal tea. Three sprites sipped apple juice from tiny flasks as they sat cross-legged on the table. Fulgid stood behind Alluxana and rested his enormous hand on her shoulder. Luchaer's sack bulged open and a platter's worth of honey biscuits spilled out. Breaking a biscuit in thirds, the sprites gobbled every crumb.

Yawning, Cahalson spoke first. "All these preparations have made our people and"—he nodded to the sprites, then to Fulgid—"our new friends comfortable and given them rest." He stood up, jostling the bench, and the sprites grabbed the table's edge to steady themselves.

"But we're fooling ourselves," he continued, "and we're wasting our strength building more space. The Malevir will come here to find Azile. We will be helpless to fight him without the dragons. Weren't they supposed to join up with us here? Where are they, Seerlana? How can we face the Malevir without them, eh?" Cahalson circled the table until he stood next to Fulgid.

Alluxana turned to face him. "Cahalson of Fossarelick, strange it is to hear a Moktawl yearn for the arrival of dragons!" She smiled. After a long pause while she looked into his narrowed eyes, she spoke again. "You're right. Seerlana has heard nothing from Isabella or the other Orferans. Perhaps one of these Loblin knows a safer place to hide until they do come?" She pointed to Kolvak, who paled and shook his head.

Milkthistle gave him a shove, and after some hesitation, Kolvak stood up on a bench and cleared his throat. "Some of you might not know about the tunnels that begin just under the ruined bakehouse."

Kirrill shouted, "Of course we do! We met Nnylf coming out of one close to the orchard; but he was soaked and foul-smelling from his slog through it."

"That short tunnel is the worst of them. There are more tunnels that cut through the mountain—to many secret places." He stared at his boots.

Milkthistle cleared her throat loudly and all eyes turned toward her. "I remember the one that led to Rocánonom's dark prison. Where our friend broke spells and returned our true bodies to us. We have to follow that tunnel to find a safer place."

Seerlana looked around the table and said, "I share Cahalson's worries. It's true that no dragon thoughts have reached me since we arrived in the lodge, and I fear that the Malevir's mischief has kept them from us. Our plan must change, Luchaer. We don't want the Malevir to attack us in the lodge. Show us where to go, Loblin."

Kolvak swallowed the last bite of his biscuit, brushed some crumbs off his tunic, and swung his legs over the side of the bench. Walking toward the door, he invited his companions to follow him outside.

"These charred logs are all that remain of the bakehouse," Alluxana whispered. "And the tunnel leading from it stinks from filth and slime. I can't recall an entrance to dry tunnels."

Milkthistle tugged on her sleeve. "No, not here. Come, past the orchard. The entrance hides in the Great Oak."

Eunan slapped his forehead. "If only I'd known that before the Malevir made off with Nnylf!"

Seerlana patted his shoulder, but the grim set of her mouth betrayed her concern. Holding her husband's hand, she walked quickly through the orchard, followed by the others, until they entered the clearing and approached the one thick and sprawling tree at its far edge. Milkthistle vanished behind the tree and the others, not wishing to wake anyone asleep in tents scattered across the clearing, followed her on tiptoes.

On the far side of the tree, away from the campfires and tents, they found Milkthistle. Holding one finger to her lips, she beckoned them to follow her and she slipped through the tree's tough bark, heavy with moist, green moss. The people who had trailed behind her stood motionless in confusion.

Bitterbud stepped between them and the tree. "Here inside, we'll walk two hundred of your paces to reach a cool, dry place underground. There below we have cupboards and tables where we'll store our bedding and supplies. We'll be safe there when the Malevir comes to the lodge."

PART IV: STARTING OVER 287

Alluxana and Fulgid nodded and thanked the sprite. Kolvak and Bitterbud stepped up and lay their hands on the tree trunk, which shuddered for a few moments before peeling back to make an opening as large as Fulgid. He entered first, followed by Alluxana, then, with some hesitation, Seerlana, Eunan, Atty, and the other Moktawl men. As the opening closed behind them, the group followed a ramp that turned and twisted until everyone reached the beginning of a new path.

A dancing wave of faint light led the way until they reached an iron door, where Milkthistle was waiting for them. Kolvak opened it with a few mumbled words and a snap of his short fingers, and beyond the door stretched a longer passageway. It opened into a broad raised area, which they reached by climbing a few wide stairs. High earthen walls pierced by the ends of tree roots surrounded the platform. The air smelled fresh and clean. The sandy floor was dry.

Luchaer laid his sack on the top step and sat next to it. "I don't understand how this place could be so light, but it's the perfect hiding place. We'll all fit in here, even with furniture and our belongings. But does the place have water?"

Kolvak pointed to a niche in the far wall. "Look over there. You'll find another door that leads to more tunnels, and next to it a small fountain of fresh water."

Luchaer followed the little cook's pointing finger and found a stone basin filled with clean water flowing from the end of a hollow root that jutted from the wall. Beneath the basin, a hole in the floor as big as Luchaer's hand received the basin's overflow from a spout.

"Well, then, as long as we have water, we can hide here for quite a while. What do you think, Alluxana?"

Luchaer fell silent as rough banging on the iron door to his right startled them all. Before anyone could stop him, Kolvak dashed to the door and flipped it open with one wiggling finger. Three little sprites tumbled into the space and rolled forward until they stopped and sprang to their feet.

"Mallowseed! Forestspice!" Milkthistle and Bitterbud ran to embrace their brothers, but they gasped and stepped back as they recognized the third intruder.

Kolvak hugged him and said, "Now, Sweetnettle, hug your brother Fernfallow. You have a lot of explaining to do . . . and so do I."

Chapter 8

AINDLE'S NECKS DIPPED BRIEFLY AS he dangled Rocánonom's rigid body from both beaks. His wings beat the air and thrust his enormous bulk upward so forcefully that he reached the ledge outside the Cave of the Ancestors in a heartbeat. After landing just outside the arched entrance, Aindle tossed the giant onto its threshold.

"Get up," he growled. "Lead me to their hoard."

Rocánonom did not move. His head lay sideways facing away from the cave and his eyes fixed on a distant spot in the Valley below them. His blank face enraged the monster. Aindle picked him up again and threw him inside.

As the giant lay on the sandy floor, Aindle circled him and spewed a sickly green mist over him. He screamed, "Get up. You *will* show me the way to their treasure." Back and forth, he whipped his growing tail, tipped by a new needle-thin barb.

Putrid droplets ran down Rocánonom's head and pooled on the ground. With slow, jerky movements, as if his body were made of wood, the giant threw his arms and legs about until he stood upright, took a few stiff steps, and lurched ahead. When he stopped, Aindle slammed one of his beaks between the giant's shoulder blades and Rocánonom stumbled on. Aindle pushed him through the main hall into the marble-lined passage.

Aindle looked around the gleaming space and thought: *Miserable boy, tricked me. No treasure. Where could he be . . . the lodge? Yes, the lodge!* The beast snorted and hissed at the slouching giant: "Think you fooled me? I know this place. They left nothing in this tunnel. Go on or you'll shrivel again like a rotten apple!"

Deaf to his threats, Rocánonom continued his slow walk through the passage until he stopped at the edge of a pool filled with water sloshing over its rim. He gazed past the gently swirling water.

"I've looked here before. It's just a pool."

Rocánonom did not answer him but continued to look ahead. Aindle pushed him aside and the giant stumbled backward until he hit his head on the flowstone wall and slid to the floor.

Aindle's heads scraped against the room's low ceiling as he tried to fly above the pool and he squawked in pain. Pacing around the water's edge, he stretched his necks to gaze into the pool's depths. Seeing a shadow below the swirls of water, he crouched low on his enormous scaly legs. *Something's down there.*

He cannonballed into the pool. The surface water folded over him as he fell through a suddenly shallow puddle. When he landed on a hard clay and stone floor, his heads hit scattered, jagged rocks. Wobbling back and forth, he collapsed and lay dazed on the floor.

Two creatures were watching Aindle. He could barely see them huddled near a mound. A weasel ran to his side and murmured, "Look, Bounder, the Mally-vir has dropped in for tea. Let's offer him some hospitality."

A griffin joined the weasel. His feathered ears stood straight up and his lion's body tensed. Propelled by his strong dragon legs, he leaped to the weasel's side and clacked his own razor-sharp beak. Raising one set of talons, he drew long scratches into the soft flesh along Aindle's necks. The aiglonax's four eyes popped open and he stiffened. Smothered cries tried to escape Aindle's beaks, but Bounder's power to immobilize his natural enemy trapped them in his throats.

"Good evening and welcome to our little hideaway," the weasel chirped. She leaped onto Aindle's chest and clicked her sharp little teeth. "Do you have time to stay awhile? Before the griffin's poison wears off? You and I, Gormley, have so much to talk about!"

Bounder reared up and opened his broad wings as he stood behind Gormley. The aiglonax growled deep in his throats and stared into Bounder's eyes.

The griffin laughed. "No use, Aindle. Your stare has no effect on me." He kicked Aindle's swollen leg and the monster stiffened again.

"Our guest has very bad manners, my friend. Not one word of thanks. Maybe he needs help." Gormley patted one of the aiglonax's beaks and Aindle loosened a low rumble from deep in his throat. "Listen to that! Wonder what's inside there making that ugly noise."

Aindle felt his eyes bulge in terror: he remembered his mother's warning.

"I don't think he's ready to join us." Gormley edged toward his right beak. "If I could just open this beak and pour in a bit of tea, just poke my head down his throat and . . . why do you tremble, beastie? I am just a little weasel. Now, let's see what's in there."

"Not yet, little friend," Bounder replied. "He has two heads and you're just one weasel. Leave it for later."

Gormley sniffed at Aindle's rigid beaks, but Bounder pushed her off the aiglonax's chest. Without another word, the griffin's wide jaws gripped Aindle's legs and whirled him around the chamber. He heaved him up into the pool, which had grown deeper and floated a short distance over their heads. The pool's vortex sucked him upward and tossed him back into the marble-lined passageway above.

By the time Aindle lay splayed on the floor in front of Rocánonom, still unmoving and slumped against the wall, Bounder's paralyzing poison was wearing off. The aiglonax scrambled to his feet and staggered back to the cave opening. With a few feeble flaps, he opened his wings and flew off the ledge, only to fall just as quickly into the scree far below.

Hopping in a frenzy through the loose stones, he roared his fury as he licked at an injured wing. Tucking it into his side, he leaped and jumped downhill.

Still chuckling at the terror she saw in Aindle's eyes when he thought she would pry open his jaws, Gormley pulled herself out of the pool, shook the water from her fur, and sniffed the cave floor. Her nose skimmed the ground as she followed Aindle's foul scent. Around the edge of the pool, she smelled dragon, sprite, then the strong scent of someone else—Rocánonom!

Spotting the giant's motionless figure in the shadows, she scurried to his side and ran up his legs and across his belly to sniff his face. Satisfied that he was breathing and otherwise unharmed, Gormley left him and went to the cave entrance. She looked over the ledge and followed the Malevir's trail downhill. Happy that Bounder had shown his power to protect the treasure, she turned her thoughts to finding Gúrmulo, now that the beast had sprouted a second head.

After Gormley left the Cave of the Ancestors, Rocánonom opened his eyes. A sly smile parted his lips and he pushed away from the wall.

Part V

Reinforcements

The Malevir as an Aiglonax©

Chapter 1

THEY WERE FLYING TOWARD COLDSIDE. The dams' questions darted back and forth between them: *Why Anonom Trace? We should be headed for the lodge. The Valley folk need us.* At last they heard Aurykk's voice and sighed with relief: he reassured them they were not lost. Resolved to finish the task he described, the dragons soared above the Valley mists toward rolling green hills.

Beyond the hills rose the coldside limits of mountain ridges that met near the Trace. Below their heights, a growing cloud mass draped the slopes and slid toward the lowland and a vast bog, where the ruins of the Anonom settlement and its neglected orchards sat veiled in mist.

Like boiling water in a giant cauldron, the cloud mass churned and whipped about. Aurykk signaled his companions to cut through it and land on the warmside face of the hill, where cliffs along the mountain wall jutted skyward and gave them some protection. Aurykk, Drac'Argo, and the dams thrust their legs into slippery, wet grasses, folded their wings, and formed a small circle with their heads facing the center. Slightly swaying as wet gusts pelted them, they lowered their bellies and lay together, sphinxlike and silent.

Nnylf heard Aurykk order Draako to remain aloft and climb higher. The young dragon nodded and struggled to fly upward. Nnylf clung to his neck fringe and, grateful for his leather leggings, he gripped Draako's

PART V: REINFORCEMENTS   295

spiny neck with his knees. Looking down at the roiling clouds turning blue-black, he thought, *Where are we going? Don't we need to stay with the others?*

No answer from Draako. Nnylf leaned forward to grip his friend tightly. The wind buffeted them as if driven to tear Nnylf from his dragon and toss him into the Valley below. A crackle of lightning caught his attention, and he looked up to see fiery spheres course along the mountain ridges, then wheel about and shoot up into the darkening sky. Thunder rumbled as the orbs climbed high overhead and crashed into the Valley with explosive force.

Sharply banking to his right, Draako flew away from the storm. After a few spins and rolls, he flew in a downward spiral toward the ruins of Anonom. In his head, Nnylf heard the dragon's faint instructions: *We have only a few moments. Leave me. Run to the castle ruins. Find shelter inside the wall with a green copper door. I will come for you after the storm.*

Draako landed with a thump and shook off his rider. As he slid to the spongy ground, Nnylf shrank from a ball of fire exploding nearby. He shouted through the howling wind, "I don't know this place, Draako. Don't leave me. I'll die here."

Sulfurous fumes mixed with the odor of dead and decaying trees filled his nose. He heard Draako again: *Run now, before the storm picks you up like a leaf in the wind. You have more strength than you know.*

Draako's snout found Nnylf's backside and pushed him in the direction of Anonom's crumbling halls and skeletal cottages. The dragon needed only one great thrust of his wings to lift away from the terrified youth, but his words remained in Nnylf's head:

More than you know—more than you know.

Rain seemed to be rising from the earth as the force of the storm grew and whirled around Nnylf. Dizzy, he gripped a rotting tree trunk. When the mists parted for a few moments, he saw a broad wall a few long strides beyond him. Supporting the towering structure, rough gray stones ran in even courses interrupted only by a low copper door, green and weathered with age. Pushing against the wind, Nnylf strained to reach it. As his hand pressed against its worn surface, Nnylf felt the door open slowly inwards and he stepped inside.

With a whisper of dust and cobwebs, the door closed behind him and shut out the storm.

Nnylf caught his breath and blinked in disbelief. He no longer heard the rain and wind. He expected to be surrounded by absolute darkness. Instead, a sort of twilight filled the quiet narrow space, as if from a window that opened to early evening. Nnylf looked around the gloom that enveloped him but saw no openings to the outside world, not even an outline of the door he had entered.

He took a step forward and flinched: a wide staircase emerged from the shadows in front of him. The strange light grew and flowed like water down the stairs. He followed the light. *Draako, help me!*

Draako's wings strained to rise above the storm pounding Anonom's once-thriving village. Fierce crosswinds battered him and rain pelted his head, but Aurykk's voice pierced through the tempest and he followed it. Through the mist, he saw a cascade of boulders rolling down the mountains on either side of his family.

The earth shuddered. He heard a tearing roar as the two mountain heads pulled away from each other. Through a flurry of glistening wet stones and fumes, Draako shrank from the sight of a spinning ball of flame hovering over his family. None of the Orferans moved.

Aurykk called to him. *Hide! I can reason with it.*

Draako considered disobeying his uncle, but he heard Aurykk's urgent call: *Hide. Now!*

Looking for cover, Draako flew to a jagged cliff above the clouds. As the rock wall continued to shake, a chunk of the cliff, larger than the great hall of Fossarelick, broke away and crashed down the mountainside. Sliding in a stream of rocks and pebbles, the piece skidded and stopped only a few dragon-lengths away from his family. The hollow left by the

PART V: REINFORCEMENTS

small avalanche gave Draako enough room to conceal himself in the rock face.

Over the cleft riven by continual small earthquakes and storm blasts, the flaming sphere became a mass of red vapors that began to twist in the air. It lunged and flung hissing balls of lightning at the dragons. Above their heads, it wrung rain-laden clouds like wet rags and torrents of water flooded them.

Aurykk stirred. He backed away from the circle, looking at the apparition. With outspread wings, he called to it. *Ruddykin, hear me: the Malevir controls your spirit, but I can release you.*

Draako watched as the roiling red vapors took the shape of the red dragon that had challenged him by the river—Ruddykin, who had promised him loyal support against the Malevir. He heard the spirit roar, *Speak not of the Malevir. My quarrel is with you, Aurykk . . .* He paused, and long tremors shook his wraithlike body. *I cannot forgive you for leaving Lugent, Tinta, and me to die. My Abulafria—lost to me forever. You have stolen my life.*

Before the Golden could argue, Ruddykin's ghost wrapped itself around his long neck. Aurykk held steady and fixed on a distant point, as if the ghost were merely a scarf. The vapors thickened and Draako knew that the Red was strangling his uncle. None of the other dragons moved, not even 'Argo. A trance held them.

Draako dived from his hiding place, and when he reached Ruddykin, he fluttered his wings against the Red's back. They passed through the spirit dragon as if he were a cloud, but Draako could sense that the distracted Red had relaxed his hold. Aurykk took in a deep and noisy breath.

Sodden, Draako strained to stay in the air. With all the force that he had used by the river, he bellowed,

> *"Erif erif ot em enola*
> *Only to me is given the Fire*
> *Erif erif ot em enola*

When men alone cannot prevail,

By the river, you agreed that we need the strength of many to fight the Malevir. Ruddykin, you promised you would follow me, Draako, the Rightful Reader, against our enemies. Do you intend to honor your word?"

The storm abated. Like a soaked shirt that dries in the hot sun, Ruddykin's misty spirit body shrank into the outline of a mature dragon. Gliding slowly into the center of the dragon circle, he scraped his front fangs against his lower lip and dipped his head in respect.

Fire, fire to you alone—I quench my own. His ruby-colored eyes met Draako's. *But this elder betrayed us all. He left us when he should have battled the Malevir.*

"Ruddykin, you know that a Golden cannot render the basilisk helpless without allies."

But we were dead, all of us. What—

"Not all of us," rang out a stern voice from the circle. "Your dam Abulafria sits here, next to your dragonet, Drac'Argo. We live, although you tried to kill us with fire and flood."

Ruddykin whipped his head in the direction of the voice. The glare of his fiery eyes softened to an amber glow as he sank into his wobbling forelegs. Covering his head with his wings, he cried, *You escaped! I didn't know, I didn't know.*

Abulafria edged closer to him and continued, "After you raged against those of us who survived the Malevir's attacks, we regained our strength and purpose in the Cave of Refuge after many Turns of the World. Look, you have a son."

'Argo shook his head and snorted, "See, Father, my wings are streaked with red, much like yours!"

Lowering a wing, Ruddykin gawked at the dragonet. *But you were just an egg . . . I never . . . I mean to say . . .* He sat up, speechless, and looked around the circle until his gaze met the Golden's warm amber eyes.

All the dragons stood and sniffed the spirit. Aurykk's throat vibrated

PART V: REINFORCEMENTS

as he began to chant a musical spell. The dams bobbed their heads as they hummed along with him. Draako's jaw dropped open as he watched the Red's hazy body become sharp and solid.

He turned to his uncle. "How can this happen? The Malevir killed Ruddykin."

Aurykk answered, "No, not killed. The beast enchanted him, Tinta, and other Orferans long absent from our lair."

As they spoke, Ruddykin licked his wings and happy curls of white smoke wreathed his head. Abulafria and 'Argo bumped their heads into his side and he returned the loving gesture.

Anadraka watched them, then looked at Draako and sighed, "Would that your own father could share such happiness." She sat back on her haunches and switched her tail. With a fiery snort, she turned her head. Her long, pointed ears picked up a new sound far to the Coldside. "Do you hear it? Like distant thunder? Is it another storm?"

Aurykk and Ruddykin sniffed each other's snouts and shook their heads. The Golden answered, "Our yewr will grow in strength soon. Do not be afraid. The approaching thunder is not a storm, but a sign of hope for us all."

While the elder dragon was speaking, Ruddykin backed away from his dam and son and jumped into the air to hover over them. "Aurykk, my heart once more embraces you. I wish all of you strength and courage in these hard times to come. My dam, my son—be brave, for the day we shall be together will come again. Nevertheless, my duty as First Red is to guard the Mystic Scintilla with my life, and I must return to our ancestral home."

Draako said, "Much has changed since we last met. You'll see that Bounder is the griffin you used to know. Aurykk released him from your bond. He protects the mound of the Treasure."

The Red puffed wreaths of white smoke and laughed. "Much I owe you, young Rightful Reader. Bounder is my brother and happy will be our meeting. May you all fare well and wish me the same." Ruddykin beat his wings hard against the dying winds and, without a backward glance, flew sunriseside toward the mountain overlooking Nosidam. The other dragons turned coldside to face the growing thunder and regrouped in their circle.

Chapter 2

WITH EACH CAUTIOUS FOOTSTEP, NNYLF felt the stair treads bounce and sag. He slid one hand along a gritty wall to steady himself. When he reached the bottom of the stairway, he stopped. Pressing one hand to his chest, he felt his rapidly beating heart. It pounded in his ears. An arm's length in front of him stretched a dark curtain. When Nnylf touched it with a shaking finger, it crumbled and a coat of fine black dust covered the floor in front of him. Beyond lay a broad chamber.

The light that had guided him down the stairway began to fade. Nnylf held his breath. Deepening shadows in each corner of the chamber were moving. They glided toward him until he felt enveloped by a growing chill that penetrated his armor and seeped into his bones. Unable to step backward, he closed his eyes and wrapped his arms across his chest. He heard loud, persistent scratching. He opened one eye to a slit and looked around but saw nothing. He began to panic. *Draako sent me here to die!* His shaking hands lost their grip around his arms.

In the gloom, Nnylf could barely see his icy feet. The shadows had encircled his ankles and were creeping up his numbing legs. He slapped and brushed at the slithering darkness and thought: *When the shadows reach my heart, they will kill me!* He felt them crawl over his knees and up his thighs.

"Stop!" he mouthed, then cleared his throat. "Stop, whatever you are! Draako, my dragon, sent me here."

At those words, the scratching sound faded. A tall figure approached him from one corner of the room. It wore a long, ash-gray cape wrapped around a thin body. One corner of the cape hid all but a half-closed eye.

"Who is this Draako dragon you dare to name?" A man's voice echoed in the high-ceilinged room. Nnylf saw more of the room's features now, for the strange light that had illuminated the stairway returned to spread throughout the chamber.

The chilling shadows tightened around Nnylf's legs and he felt faint. The man drew closer and leaned forward to look into his face as Nnylf whispered, "Draako, son of Anadraka and Lugent, Silver prince of the Orferans clan."

The man let the cape drop from his face, and Nnylf felt that something about the eyes and the bold chin looked familiar. "A son of Lugent, the Silver? And who are you to know this dragon? Speak up!"

Nnylf could scarcely reply; his dry tongue felt like a heavy river rock. With great effort, he opened his mouth and could only mumble, "Nnylf of Fossarelick, son of Seerlana and Eunan." Ashamed of his fear and confusion, he covered his face. His palms felt wet from unwanted tears that spilled over his lower eyelids.

Aware of the man's silence, Nnylf lowered his hands. The man's head was still very near his own. His thick gray hair framed a lean and lined face, but his muscular body was that of a younger man. Although dusty and worn in spots, his armor and other garments suggested that he might have been a rider himself. He had exchanged his scowl for a soft smile.

"Seerlana's son?" he asked in a low voice. "What proof can you offer me that you know Seerlana?"

Raising his chin, Nnylf looked directly into the man's green eyes and said, "She is my mother, who taught me all I know about the dragons of the Veiled Valley. What proof do you need?"

PART V: REINFORCEMENTS

"Where was she born?"

"Anonom Village."

"Why did she leave?"

"Her parents sent her away to my home, Fossarelick."

"And is she a Moktawl? If she lives in Fossa—"

"How dare you call her that? She is a dragonrider, and the dam Anadraka is her friend."

"One more question: does your mother bear a special mark?"

A scar covered the inside of Seerlana's right forearm, from wrist to elbow. Nnylf remembered the first time he saw it. His mother had rolled up her sleeves to scrub out the porridge pot and he had asked her why her skin was red and wrinkled. He always took care around cooking oil after hearing that story.

"A terrible oil burn she suffered as a child scarred her right arm."

At those words, another figure emerged from an opposite corner, an older woman who glided toward him before stopping next to the man. Her heavy gray dress matched the color of her thick hair, woven into braids that crowned her head. Her large brown eyes and thick dark eyebrows gave her a younger appearance than her pale, splotched skin would suggest.

Nnylf stared at the woman. The shape of her face, especially the smile that creased her cheeks, reminded him of his mother.

She raised one slender hand to her chest and spoke: "I am Flanna, and this man is my husband, Lahsrayn." She looked at Nnylf's feet. "Stand back, you shades. Forgive us, young man, for frightening you so." Her other hand swept from one side to the other. "Shades, return to your resting places. He is no enemy."

Nnylf felt his shoulders relax and he breathed more easily. "No, not your enemy at all, but I don't know who you are."

Lahsrayn's eyelids fluttered and he said, "Seerlana is our daughter."

As the icy shadows slipped from Nnylf's legs and retreated toward the back wall, they pooled at the base of large stone ossuaries. Thick slabs covering each box lifted and the shadows slithered inside. Nnylf felt a wave of warmth surge up his legs, yet he could not move. The shock of meeting his mother's parents had stunned and confused him into speechlessness.

"Tell us, please," continued the woman. "What news can you share with us? Does your mother live? Do you have a sister or brother? Why are the dragons gathering in the Coldside?"

As she spoke, Lahsrayn released the edges of his cape. It fell open as he reached out to embrace his grandson. "Flanna, can't you see that he had no idea we were alive? Is that true, Nnylf of Fossarelick?" He grasped Nnylf's shoulders with strong hands and squeezed gently.

Nnylf noticed that Lahsrayn smelled like a meadow in morning. He also saw that his grandfather's loose blue shirt, torn or threadbare in spots, nevertheless matched the tunic that Atty had worn to hunt dragons—but this silky one bore no dragon scales. Around Lahsrayn's neck hung the same amulet Atty carried, a silver disk with the profile of a dragon head pressed into the metal. He stared at the runes that surrounded the dragon's image:

One and only one will dare to banish pain and fear

Underneath the saying, he saw his grandfather's name spelled out. When he flipped the disk, he read the name of the legendary Silver, Argenfort.

"Mother did tell Azile and me about you when she shared her secrets and taught us about the Orferans, but she never told us your names. Azile is my sister." He stared at the floor. "The Valley folk are gathering to fight the very Malevir that smashed Anonom Village and burned your fields. I hear that my mother is among them."

Flanna's hand covered her mouth and she turned her head away for a moment. She wiped her eyes with one sleeve and looked at Nnylf once more. "Which dragons have come coldside? Why are they not with the Protectors and Loblin?"

"I don't know why they have flown to the mountains. Aurykk must have some plan."

Lahsrayn spoke again. Pacing in the now-bright chamber, he opened his arms to the side. "Aurykk. I know him—the nephew of my dragon, Argenfort. Perhaps he wants us to join them."

Remembering his dragon's last words to him before they parted—*Run now, before the storm picks you up like a leaf in the wind. You have more strength than you know*—Nnylf cautioned his grandparents, "Draako told me to wait here until he came for me."

Flanna smiled and nodded to her husband. "Then we shall wait, too, and to pass the time, Lahsrayn and I will tell you how we came to this sad and desolate place."

The elderly rider invited his wife and Nnylf to follow him to a corner of the room far from the bone boxes. Three wooden armchairs padded with cushions surrounded a solid oak table on which sat an array of dishes and cups. A silver candelabrum holding three thick candles sat in the center of the table and warmed the corner.

Nnylf stared at the fine furnishings and wondered, *I never imagined grandparents like them. Draako must have known about this magical place!* He could feel sweat dampening his tunic again. Flanna was taking her seat at the table, and she invited Nnylf and Lahsrayn to join her. Still stunned by this unexpected reunion, Nnylf sat wordless until a door in the wall appeared behind Lahsrayn. It opened and four sprites, half Nnylf's height, jostled each other through the doorway. Their heads bent under the weight of serving dishes and spoons. Giggling among themselves, they bowed as they offered portions from each platter to Flanna and her dinner companions.

Flanna selected some morsels for her gaping grandson. She filled his plate with honeyed oatcakes studded with almonds, smoked trout, slices of hard cheese, and dark barley-oat bread. Into a small bowl, one curly-haired sprite poured a chunky stew of green vegetables and grain simmered in a honey vinegar sauce, while another sprite, a bit taller than the others, raised his slender arms to pour cider into Nnylf's cup.

"Please eat," Flanna urged him. "We are celebrating our hope for better times. Besides, you must be quite hungry!"

Nnylf shook his head as if he had just awakened. His grimy hands felt sticky and looked like he had been digging in a mud hole. Before he could ask for something to clean them, another sprite wearing a leafy cap and sporting a little braided beard offered him a basin of warm water and a rough stone to rub away the dirt. One more sprite in leather leggings and a brown vest woven from meadow grasses offered a red cloth for drying his fingers. Thanking his servers as they left the room through the mysterious door, Nnylf turned to Flanna with a questioning look.

"Of course. You would not know. Those little fellows are Loblin who stayed with us when the Malevir captured our Protector, Rocánonom. They fed us and helped us keep this sad place livable for many World-Turns. But do eat while we tell you our tale." Flanna leaned back in her chair and sipped her cup of cider before speaking.

> Our family lived in Anonom Village for generations. Here we riders and the Protectors—Daygg, Evlyn, and the giant Rocánonom—protected the villagers from all hostile intruders, until the Malevir's attacks on the Veiled Valley began. Your mother grew up in this place, as you know, but as our crops withered and our animals slowly perished, we could not let her stay. When so many others left here, we sent her away. Then we retreated upcountry.

> We believed that we would find safety in the lands just beyond the mountains. These little Loblin and we planned to hide there in a network of burrows until our dragons destroyed the Malevir.

> Your mother, a rider like us, flew warmside with Anadraka. Beyond the sight of the Fossarelick

PART V: REINFORCEMENTS

villagers, she and the dragon parted. As Seerlana walked along the paths toward Fossarelick, Anadraka flew high overhead, and this is what she told us:

> When our daughter arrived at the hilltop village, she discovered that her cousin Shaklana, with whom she was staying, and many of the other inhabitants had turned against the dragons. After she met Eunan and married him, some of the men— including your father—began to hunt our dragon friends. Their arrows nearly wounded my own ride, Calliopfera, but she escaped somehow. Since then, I have been in hiding and have not heard her voice."

"My father and the other Moktawls no longer hunt dragons. Their quarry is the Malevir," added the boy.

"As you say, Nnylf of Fossarelick. Even so, the Malevir's strength and magic grew because of Moktawls' attacks. Listen to my sad tale:

> With fewer dragons to protect the Valley, the beast misled our Protectors. All but one abandoned the Trace. Rocánonom remained with us for a while, but one night he heard a clamor in the fields and left us to see the cause. He never returned, and these Loblin you see here warned us to stay hidden."

Nnylf interrupted again: "Loblin found Rocánonom and released him from a death spell; then they found me and undid the enchantment that bound me. I returned with them to the Cave of the Ancestors and reunited with Draako, which has led to our meeting here, I suppose."

Flanna shook her head and wiped a few tears from her cheek with the back of one hand. "So Rocánonom lives. Your words hold the promise that one day we might see each other again. But let me go on:

> Because of the Malevir's lies, the Valley people mistrusted each other. It is amazing that they managed to survive in Fossarelick and Nosidam. We knew something was very wrong when signs of a great calamity appeared.
>
> Late one day, as the sun was setting, we were foraging for herbs in the meadows. Suddenly we felt the earth shake at our feet and a huge wind nearly toppled us. To the Coldside we could see the mountains split. A vast churning cloud was massing over the gap. We were astonished to see the skeletal figures of unfamiliar dragons emerge from the clouds. We looked right through their bodies as they passed and their rage and panic overhead had us trembling.
>
> One of them, the ghost of a Red who called himself Ruddykin, did not join the others who plunged into the cleft of the mountains. He flew toward us bellowing a fearsome message: "Your dragons are no more. The Malevir has killed us all. Abandon the Valley."

"My mother, Azile, and I escaped from Ruddykin at the cave!"
Flanna frowned and shook her head. "She put you in such danger?"
"She didn't know. The attack was a surprise."
"Still . . . quite unwise. Yet here you are to tell the tale. Nevertheless, we cannot hope that those dragon spirits think of us as friends. Even now, we dare not go beyond the protection of these walls. As they flew

PART V: REINFORCEMENTS   309

overhead, we felt torn between our loyalty to the dragon folk and our need for safety." Flanna beckoned the bearded sprite holding a basket filled with thick slices of brown bread. "Here, Nnylf, take more bread. I shall continue my story:

> Unsure of their intentions, we hurried to hide deep within our burrow until they had passed beyond us. We remained hidden for a night and a day. When the sun set again, we and our Loblin set out for Anonom Village, or what was left of it.
>
> We discovered the ruins in which you now sit. This great hall and the small chambers beyond it are all that remain of the settlement's center. Somehow, Rocánonom had wrapped it in enchantments that allowed Lahsrayn, our Loblin, and me to remain here, undetected . . . on one condition.
>
> The shadows that bound you when first we met are the spirits of riders whom the Malevir sent to a world outside time, along with their dragons. The Loblin said Rocánonom insisted we protect their remains inside those bone boxes until we join him in a battle against the Malevir—but when that will happen, we don't know."

"Under the beast's spell, Rocánonom could hardly protect them," said Nnylf. "The Malevir destroyed Lugent, too. Why did he not kill Grandfather or you? Of course, I am grateful that you live, I assure you."

Flanna and Lahsrayn looked at each other quickly. The elder rose from his chair. He paced along the walls and stopped next to the line of ossuaries. "Before our Protector left us, he prepared a stew of barley, wild onions, mushrooms, and herbs, including rue. That herb protected us from the Malevir's spells. It protects us now. You've just eaten some yourself. It loses its power after a day, so we cook more of it every morning. Planted by dragons many World-Turns ago to protect their riders, rue still grows in our forests and along the rims of dragon cave ledges."

Nnylf licked his lips and dabbed them with his red cloth. His eyes looked up the faintly glowing stairway as he said, "Did you hear a noise up there?"

Lahsrayn crossed the room and waved his hand in front of its arched doorway. After he passed over the threshold, the space filled with the black curtain Nnylf had seen earlier. "Quiet, now," Lahsrayn hissed from the other side. "Flanna, prepare to leave by the other way out if I do not return." He bounded up the stairs. Two sprites appeared at the rear door with bundles in their arms, while two others held out capes for Flanna and Nnylf.

A blast of wind blew the curtain into the room. It whipped about, and they all could see searing flashes of light shoot into the tower above. As Flanna and Nnylf turned away and hurried to the rear door, the curtain crumbled again.

Lahsrayn dashed into the room, calling out, "Lids, open. I summon you, ancient riders. Your time has come! Flanna, Nnylf . . . little friends, this way, hurry, up the stairs to freedom!"

Chapter 3

"THAT WILL BE THE LAST time I fail," Aindle thought as each head stretched to preen his feathers and pick at his talons. He kicked away the thick underbrush that lay in tangles around his feet and began his wobbly descent toward the Protectors' lodge.

Determined to reach the column of smoke he saw in the distance, he unfolded his wings to examine his wounds. Seeing that they had healed, Aindle flapped them and flew away from the slope. Soaring high for a better view, he rose over the forest, then dipped and glided just above the treetops. His gaze turned toward the lands surrounding the lodge.

"Smoke from the chimney means . . ." squawked one head.

"Valley folk! Nnylf and Azile!" screeched the other.

Skimming the tree canopy, he landed on the skeletal remains of a lightning-damaged fir, its thick, scorched trunk still standing like a sentinel halfway up the slope. As it swayed under his weight, Aindle tightened his grip.

The aiglonax rested there a short while, then leaped up and flew directly toward the smoke. Screeching and squawking, he could think of nothing but mayhem and the creatures he would capture or destroy.

That same morning, Veiled Valley folk were preparing for the day, tugging at their bedding and shaking out the mice and beetles that had snuggled with them during the night. Alana and several other younger people from Fossarelick were among the last to leave the clearing on their way to breakfast in the lodge. Alana felt her mouth water at the thought of the delicious stews and broth they had been eating. Her stomach no longer growled, and she felt an odd urge to run, jump, and play that rarely happened in Fossarelick.

In clusters of three or four, Alana's friends and family walked through the orchard toward the lodge. They greeted Mëlo and his wife, who were carrying apples picked in the company of the young mother Margalana, her baby wrapped snugly in a shawl and tied to her back. Alana felt warm happiness spread through her body as she watched the sky brighten over the Sunriseside Mountains—but her joy turned to confusion when she caught sight of a dark shadow approaching from the horizon. It swooped in and out of low, rosy clouds rising with the dawn. Its outspread wings could have spanned her family's cottage.

Alana pointed to the dark figure and said, "Father, what is that? Could Kurnan be on his way?"

Kirrill shrugged his shoulders and turned to Luchaer strolling beside him. "Do you see one of our dragons, Luchaer, or maybe my son and his Copper?"

Luchaer squinted as he looked at the distant figure silhouetted by the rising sun. One hand shaded his eyes while the other gripped his sack. "Don't know . . . it's hard to tell. Looks awfully big." Then his eyes opened wide and he blurted, "May the Ways of the World protect us! That's an aiglonax!"

He saw that everyone who had been walking with him now stood like startled rabbits and gaped at the beast. Luchaer shouted, "Quick, to the lodge," but only Alana heard him. She moved quickly as Luchaer directed her to shake the frozen villagers and stick them with her hairpin. Apples tumbled out of their aprons and arms as the villagers raced to the safety of the great hall. Luchaer threw the door's three heavy bolts as soon as the last dawdling toddler passed over the threshold. With

PART V: REINFORCEMENTS   313

his back against the door's thick panels, he surveyed everyone who had crowded into the otherwise ample space.

"That's the Malevir in his most monstrous, truest form," Luchaer announced. "Those two heads spew venomous vapor that can stop your heartbeat, permanently. His feathers paralyze anyone or anything they touch. His eyes drain away your will to move or think."

With a glance at the hearth, Alluxana whispered to him, "Fulgid has something to show you." The goat-faced giant was pounding a silver disk on the hearth wall. Each push disturbed a few stones surrounding it, yet the disk remained fixed to its setting. Fulgid's goat hairs lay matted against his head and he bleated in frustration.

"He wants to open the tunnel entrance," Alluxana explained, "but it won't budge. I hate to say this, but we might be trapped here."

Alana looked away from the efforts at the hearth when a loud thump of the lodge door caught her attention. "Who's there?" she cried out.

Those standing near the door could hear Bitterbud's faint reply from the other side: "Sweetnettle and Forestspice are with me in the garden. We're going to the clearing to spy on the Malevir."

Milkthistle huddled by the door next to the girl and said, "Don't do that, brothers! Come inside," as Alana urged them, "Little ones, that beast will kill you for sport!"

"His poison cannot harm us; we've drunk plenty of rue broth. Milkthistle, you must stay inside to help our friends," Bitterbud answered and jogged away from the lodge with his brothers.

Alana climbed up the rough stone wall above the door to a platform at the base of one of the high dormer windows. Through the panes, she could see beyond the garden and meadow close to the lodge. The aiglonax had reached the clearing. Alana felt her stomach lurch at the sight of his monstrous body and heads. She cringed at the sight of the brown vapor that the beast's mouths spewed. It settled over the clearing and obscured her view of the sprites, who were scattering to distract Aindle from the lodge and its occupants.

Gripping a nearby crossbeam to steady herself, Alana called down to the upturned faces below her. "The Malevir landed in the clearing. Our Loblin don't interest him." She shivered. "He's looking at the lodge."

At that instant, Aindle's beaks opened wide. His screech shook every tree in the orchard and fruit covered the ground in a thick green and red layer. Aindle stepped up to the first row of trees and sprayed his acid across their trunks. The trees withered within moments.

The aiglonax cackled and raised his heads to destroy the rest of the orchard, but he froze when a sound pierced the air—the scream of an enraged dragon. Isabella swooped over the clearing, pulling a long cloud of boulders and rocks behind her tail.

Kurnan sat on her hump. He hunched over her frill and pressed his knees against her thick neck muscles. Dizzy from the dragon's twists and turns, he closed his eyes. Isabella's command cut through the fog in his head: *Grip my frill! Keep your legs tucked close to my body. I am going to vex this beast and keep him from harming our friends.*

As Isabella flew just out of Aindle's reach, the aiglonax struggled to fly at her, but the mass of rocks that followed her battered the beast. Heavy stones formed a rising mound around his legs until only his writhing heads remained free, which the Copper teased as she circled him. Satisfied that the rocks had trapped Aindle, she released fumes from her smoke glands. Aindle's necks stopped twisting, but his yellow eyes glared at her as she darted back and forth.

Rocks and boulders continued to fall upon the beast as Isabella carried out her plan to bury him, but one of them grazed Kurnan's shoulder. Startled, he lost his grip. Before Isabella was aware that he was hanging undefended, the boy slipped down her flank and dangled from her shoulder spines. Slowly, his sweating hands weakened. The trees and smoke and the monster whirled around him.

Deafened by fury, Isabella did not hear Kurnan's anguished thoughts, and she passed the beast to lay another volley of rocks. Aindle's beak opened just a little—enough to hiss out a small cloud of venom that brushed Kurnan's face.

PART V: REINFORCEMENTS   315

The boy cried out and fell. Before Aindle could lunge at him, the dragon plucked Kurnan out of the air. She carried his limp body to the highest thick branch of the live oak, still standing tall in the clearing, and gently laid him across it. Before returning to the aiglonax's cairn, Isabella called to her rider. When he did not answer or move, her wail rang across the clearing. The aiglonax hooted and crowed his pleasure until a pair of massive boulders buried his heads; then the air became very, very still.

The refugees from Valley settlements heard the dragon's keening and they turned to Alana for news. She had watched nearly every step of the battle between Isabella and Aindle and had been reporting the struggle to everyone in the lodge. But in the moment that Kurnan fell off Isabella, Alana lost her footing and slipped off the platform.

She fell sideways and would have smashed onto the hard stone floor had Fulgid not reached out to catch her. With the girl safe in his huge arms, he carried her to the long table by the hearth. Kirrill and Sherca ran to comfort her but hesitated when they heard hammering on the door.

Luchaer heard Bitterbud's voice and let in the sprites. They staggered forward and collapsed by the hearth.

Seeing the three Loblin breathless and exhausted, Seerlana called to Azile, "Come. We will bring them something warm to restore their strength. They've been breathing those foul aiglonax fumes." Mother and daughter filled three tiny cups with stewed vegetables cooking in the cauldron and offered them to their little friends.

Sweetnettle was the first to sit up, but his stubby fingers covered his leaf-green lips and he shook his head. Forestspice sighed and took a cup from Azile, but did not raise it to his mouth. Bitterbud still lay on his belly, his head buried in his curled arm.

Alana jumped off the table and pushed through the people surrounding the trio. Facing Sweetnettle, she said, "Why do you show such fear, Sweetnettle, you who have survived the Malevir's poisons? Tell us why the dragon wails. It's so quiet out there except for her cries."

Azile stood by her side. "Yes, dear friend, what has happened in the clearing and orchard?"

Greenish-blue tears like drops of pond water slowly ran down Sweetnettle's round cheeks. Soon Forestspice and Bitterbud joined him and their sobs echoed from the surrounding stone walls. People turned to each other and shook their heads. Kirrill grimaced and wrung his hands. Squatting next to the three sprites, he whispered, "Tell us. You were there. What has happened to our Kurnan?"

Sweetnettle dabbed his cheeks with his red cloth and said, "A mound of boulders traps the beast—for now. The Copper hurled rocks at him . . ." He gulped. "You must hurry to the other shelter. Aindle will free himself. He will attack again."

In the midst of the people's murmuring and questions, Sherca stood tall again and shouted at the sprites, "What has happened to Kurnan? We'll not move until you tell us."

Forestspice stood up, brushed ashes and wood chips from his legging, and faced Kirrill. "The beast's fumes smothered the boy. He collapsed. Isabella carried him to the oak tree."

With a sharp cry, Sherca fell into Kirrill's arms and hid her face in the folds of his tunic. Alana held her mother's hand and wept without a sound.

Kirrill held them closely. He stared at Forestspice as if his words had made no sense. After a long silence, he groaned and his voice cracked as he spoke, "Take us to him. Is it safe now?"

"He's out of reach. The dragon will care for him. We have enough time to carry our supplies to the tree while the beast lies buried. Go to the clearing. Enter the oak. By the time we are deep in the mountain, the Malevir's powers will have returned."

Sucking bits of fresh cave rat from his fangs, Bounder felt every scale on his crest bristle in alarm when a fiery red body dropped through the lair pool's swirling waters. He had been resting on the lip of the treasure

PART V: REINFORCEMENTS 317

mound, and when his unexpected visitor landed on the stone floor, the griffin felt panic course through his body.

Bounder coughed out a few small bones caught in his throat and steadied himself to leap at the intruder's neck. No one could bully him now. Who dared to threaten the Mystic Scintilla?

The enormous creature stood up to face him and its head tapped the roof of the cave chamber. Bounder nearly rolled backwards in surprise as he looked up at its large scarlet head.

"Ruddykin? You, in the flesh? But you are . . . were . . ."

"Dead?" the Red replied.

Bounder nodded. He thought he heard laughter bubbling up the dragon's throat.

"Ruddykin I am, indeed, and very much alive!"

The griffin fluffed his ear crests and raised himself to stand on his own hind legs, his tail curled like a spring to prop him upright. Waving both forelegs, he pleaded, "Don't be angry with me, Ruddykin. I can explain everything that has happened since we met at the river by the Sunsetside Mountains."

"Angry? No, you're my brother. I learned that you were your old griffin self when the Orferans brought me back to life at the Meeting of Mountains. Aurykk had the power to end the Malevir's enchantment. The Orferans had formed a dragon circle up there and their magic grew stronger."

"Your body is whole, brother, but how did Aurykk mend your broken spirit?"

"My grief and anger vanished when I understood that my family was safe, and that Aurykk had done all he could to keep us all from harm. As for the dog spell, it protected you from the Malevir."

"And I, with some help, kept the beast from the Mystic Scintilla."

"How?"

"He was here. I attacked him with my claws. He stopped moving, of course. The weasel Gormley was here, too; she has some kind of power over him. You should have seen the fear in his eyes when she sat on his chest. Well, to get him away from the treasure I threw him up and out of here. He never saw it."

"Well done. Now you should join Aurykk's kin and their riders to fight the Malevir."

"No, I can't leave the treasure unprotected."

"*I* shall protect it. Although my taste for gems draws me to it, I shall defend it. I will cover it with my wings."

The Red sauntered to his nest brother's side and nuzzled Bounder's ears with his snout. Curls of dark smoke wafted from his nostrils. "Even now the dragons of the Veiled Valley, both living and cursed, gather to challenge the Malevir. How will the aiglonax resist all our combined powers, especially if you add your own?"

Bounder tapped his talons against the stone floor. "You mean I could use these to help the Valley folk? My claws did stop the beast once; they could do so again."

"Your claws, your agile wings, and your powerful lion's body will tire the beast. Then the dragons will finish him. Go now. Give back the love your dragon family gave you since the time your egg first lay in the nest we shared."

"How can I refuse you?" Bounder tilted his head sideways and looked into the dragon's eyes. "But until we crush the Malevir, you won't have much to do. While you wait for the dragons' return, what will you eat? Rats, beetles, bats, and snakes won't satisfy a dragon like you."

"The Mystic Scintilla has a way of easing hunger, and a few gems will fill my stomach. You ate more than rats and bats, didn't you, while you guarded the Treasure?"

Bounder stretched his long, thick neck and patted the dragon's shoulder with his beak. "Yes, Brother. I ate a gem or two . . . or three." He blinked and changed the subject. "How strong I feel knowing that dragons might undo the Malevir's enchantments. I've seen Aurykk's powers."

PART V: REINFORCEMENTS

"He can't undo all of the Malevir's spells, although Aurykk safeguarded the Orferans and revived one of us thought lost forever, speaking of myself . . ." Ruddykin sighed, then shook off his sadness. "So, ready yourself. Eat a bit more of your cave's bounty, then fly off to the lodge. I passed Valley people as I flew over the place. They have set up some sort of shelter but have no defense against the beast when he attacks—and he will."

"They will have one when I arrive!" Bounder fluttered his wings and puffed up his chest. "The Malevir has more than a little dog to face now!"

Chapter 4

"BURIED THE BEAST'S HEADS TOO late, she did," Gormley muttered to herself as she watched Isabella. Hiding in the orchard, she turned her eyes to the mass of rocks that covered Aindle. "Dishonorable, despicable dustbin of a creature. I ran under your shadow and saw you strike that boy, you cowardly owl pellet!"

Gormley hurried her little weasel body between the skeletal trees while the sound of Isabella's keening shook creaking and broken branches overhead. A few quick dashes through the garden and she reached the lodge just as its immense door creaked open. She leaped behind some flowering bushes and held her breath.

The Valley refugees, arms filled with supplies, rushed out the door and Gormley scampered up the wall to watch them leave. An old man and sprites led their companions in a wide detour around the clearing, until they reached the live oak. Gormley thought she might catch up to them, but she tripped over her paws when she heard a stern voice saying, "And just where have you been?"

Gormley swiveled to face her brother. "Gúrmulo, I could ask the same of you!" Her needle-sharp teeth snapped at his ear. "You left me to face the beast all by myself, but I must say I did a good job of it—scared the wind out of him I did!" She frowned. "And just what have you been doing all this time?"

PART V: REINFORCEMENTS   321

Gúrmulo licked his paw and smoothed his ear. After giving her a quick glance, he began to dig a hole in the flowerbed bordering the lodge. "Waiting for dragons," he answered. "Saw Isabella when everyone was on the road between Fossarelick and Nosidam. She wouldn't listen to me when I told her about the Orferans' coming. Alluxana, the Forest Protector, carried me here in her apron. There's Alluxana, climbing up the tree with that giant."

Gormley followed his pointing paw. She saw a woman with four arms and a goat-headed giant climbing toward the stout oak branch that supported Kurnan. Isabella hovered just above them. The people who had been following the old man to the oak tree disappeared behind it. The old man ran a hand through his thatch of white hair and looked up, into the oak's limbs. The dragon dam beat her wings overhead, blinking at him, but she made no threats. His gaze then took in the whole clearing, until it fell on the rocks piled atop Aindle. He stood rigid with fear.

"I'll be back before you can dig the length of your body and tail," Gormley squeaked and made a swift run for the tree. She reached the far side of the tree just as the man passed through the door. When the door closed, its outline faded.

Gormley groaned and ran back to her brother. The black tip of his tail wiggled inside the opening of the hole he had started to dig. "Where are you going?" she asked.

He huffed, "If I make this hole deep enough it'll take us to tunnels that connect to that tree, but also to others that go up the mountain. We can run to the Cave of the Ancestors. We'll persuade Bounder to help us fight the Malevir. You know our gift for—"

"Oh, no, it's not the right time for that! You saw the Valley folk leave, for a safer place underground near the tree's roots, I think. We need to get there, too, and warn the people that Aindle will track them once he wiggles out of Isabella's trap. Move over; I'll help you dig."

Aindle worked at freeing himself. He wriggled in the spaces left by a few boulders that had slid away from his legs. His talons scratched and clawed at the dirt beneath his feet. Heavy rocks pressed against his heads and shoulders, but he scraped until he had carved an ever-deepening bowl. Only a thin layer of stones and soil separated him from the roof of a tunnel. He willed his acid glands to drip and burn until the dirt and rocks shuddered. He slid downward, into the dark.

Alluxana and Fulgid sat perched in the oak tree. The woman poked an elbow into Fulgid's ribs. "Listen, Isabella stopped wailing!"

"What is she looking at?" The giant swiveled his head to look at the object of the dragon's intense stare. "Ways of the World save us—the pile of rocks has collapsed!" He could see the striped boulders and dark stones sinking into the earth as if the aiglonax they had once covered had evaporated. "We should have gone with the others."

"But they are counting on us to help Isabella and Kurnan. His family would never have gone to the tunnels if we hadn't stayed behind—like true Protectors, let me remind you."

Isabella flew past the two Protectors. She grunted and raised a clawed foreleg to speak. Smoke curled up from her nostrils and her amber eyes had turned crimson.

"I don't like the color of her eyes, Luxie," Fulgid whispered. "She might be feeling a little hungry now that she's taken a rest from yowling."

"Quiet, my dear. She is saying something to me. I can almost hear her. Let's do as she says. Ah, yes! That's it. She has asked us to care for Kurnan after she carries him to the lodge."

"Why? Didn't the beast kill him?"

"She doesn't say, but the aiglonax has her attention." Alluxana paused and listened to a voice that escaped the giant's goat ears. "She says she is going to find help. Good! Fulgid, my dear, help me. I may have four arms, but climbing down from this tree is a lot harder than climbing up."

Fulgid held out one huge hand and they made their way down the trunk. As soon as his feet touched the ground, the giant gathered Alluxana in his arms and ran back to the lodge. Casting a faint shadow over them,

PART V: REINFORCEMENTS

Isabella bore Kurnan draped over her forelegs as she flew toward the lodge. Fulgid set Alluxana on the front step and pushed open the heavy door. The smell of still-simmering barley and rue broth greeted them as they entered the main hall. In their haste, none of the Valley folk had doused the hearth fire. A reptilian rumble outside the door reminded them that Isabella had brought her rider, and Fulgid hurried to take the boy from her.

With a piercing screech, Isabella wheeled around to face the coldside course of the mountains. She dipped her head and plumes of smoke and fire billowed from her open jaws. They scorched the tumulus of rocks that had once enclosed Aindle. Her wings beat the air and she leaped into the sky. Within moments, Fulgid lost sight of her. He stepped back from the door and Alluxana closed it tightly.

Gently, the giant laid Kurnan on the broad table, atop cushions that Alluxana had gathered. The boy's skin felt cool but had not stiffened. Alluxana held her damp finger near his nose but felt no breath. When she lifted Kurnan's eyelids, however, she could see that his bright and solid eyes stared ahead, unmoving. Fulgid raised the boy's head and pushed his lower lip open with a gentle finger while Alluxana tilted a spoonful of broth drop by drop onto his tongue.

"Careful. Now, close his mouth. Massage his throat. That's the way. Ease him down again." Alluxana covered the boy with a patchwork quilt and over his eyes placed a flattened rag damp from a soak in willow bark tea. "Let him lie there, then; we'll check his eyes every so often."

Fulgid nodded, gave Kurnan a soft pat on his forehead, and lumbered to the door and windows, saying, "Just to be sure they are closed tight." He banged the metal shutters that covered the windows and secured their latches and all the door bolts.

Below the foundations of the lodge, the earth began to shake.

Chapter 5

SWEETNETTLE LICKED HIS LIPS AS he sipped from his cup. The fountain gurgled. Fresh water flowed from its hollow tree root pipe and filled the basin. He watched Fernfallow dip his gourd and fill two buckets that he carried to a large trough in the middle of the room. Luchaer rushed to help him pour them. Water sloshed from one end of the long trough to the other.

Luchaer announced, "There you are, everyone! Plenty of water for bathing. Fill your washbowls. If you need water for drinking, go straight to the fountain. Must keep the supply clean, y'know."

What is Fernfallow up to? Sweetnettle thought as he noticed him rummaging in his sack.

The cook's brown, bushy eyebrows furrowed, then a smile smoothed his face as he pulled out a wooden flute. "Luchaer," he whispered to the woodcarver standing close by him. "I'd like you to open up that sack of yours. I see that our company would like to eat something besides the broth we've been sharing."

"Yes, but . . . but the sack has been nearly empty for days."

"Ah—when I play this flute of mine and you hum that little tune of Rocánonom's, the sack might refill. Shall we try?"

Sitting with his back against the trough, Luchaer shrugged and tugged at his sack until its opening rested across his belly. Across from

PART V: REINFORCEMENTS   325

him, Kolvak sat cross-legged on the dry, sandy floor and coaxed sweet, familiar notes from his instrument. Luchaer hummed along.

Councilor Prendel pushed past the onlookers gathered around the musical duo. Clucking in disapproval as he had on the road many days earlier, he poked at Luchaer's shoulder and said, "We won't survive here on your magicked food. It's fairy fodder. We eat it, rest a bit, then we're hungry again."

Margalana's green eyes flashed as she stepped forward and thrust her heart-shaped face close to Prendel's nose. "Wrong you are again, Councilor. Your fat paunch misses the grand meals you had in your Nosidam palace. Luchaer's sack fed all of us very well. Not one belly here is tickling its body's backbone." She took his arm and dragged him away from Kolvak and the old Protector, who carried on in spite of Prendel's protests.

Prendel wrenched his arm from her grip and stomped across the wide chamber to stand near its outer door, his hands tucked into his armpits. He glared as Luchaer's sack bulged and pressed into the Protector's stomach. Loaves of heavy dark bread, cooked sausages, barley cakes, apples, and plums tumbled over its edges and spilled down Luchaer's legs. No one noticed Prendel anymore. They clustered around their leader and held out hands and baskets for portions of food.

Sweetnettle rose from the cushion he shared with Milkthistle and smiled at his happy companions, then caught a glimpse of Prendel sulking by the doorway. Circling the chamber, he carried a chunk of bread wrapped around a juicy browned sausage. He guessed that one bite of that delicious tidbit would brighten the councilor's glum face. Unnoticed and standing silently next to Prendel, Sweetnettle watched him lick his lips at the sight of juicy meat—and scowl.

Luchaer's chuckles filled the room as he handed out servings with plenty for those who asked for extra helpings. Sweetnettle sensed Prendel's angry thoughts and he heard him mutter, "My neighbors love that old bear more than they ever cared for me, just because he has that magicked sack. I should show them who is really looking out for them. I should inspect those tunnels out there. My stomach is growling, but I don't care. Got to show them."

Hoping to bring him back to the happy group, Sweetnettle followed Prendel. The councilor had slid a latch and pushed against the door that opened without a sound into a tunnel. He entered it and closed the door.

Sweetnettle was just behind him. *Something's wrong here,* he thought. *This should lead back to the tree, but . . .*

Prendel took a step forward and stumbled. A deep gloom lay ahead of him now. He looked back, but darkness hid the tunnel's features from him. He slid one hand along the nearest wall and made his way with careful steps.

Sweetnettle felt his own hearts thumping behind his shoulder and his belly, but he stayed with the councilor, whose feet explored the floor with taps and scraping. A loud grating noise startled them both. Prendel shrank against the wall.

"Who's there?" he squeaked into the dark.

No one answered, but the noise grew louder. Something else was moving through the tunnel.

Sweetnettle could feel cold sweat run down his neck as Prendel turned and patted along the wall back to the chamber and his fellow refugees. The sprite saw him step forward, swinging his arms to feel out the space. He wavered and fell into a pit in the tunnel floor. Sweetnettle rushed to help him but shrank against the rough wall as the stench of rotting meat filled the tunnel.

Something heavier and thicker than the darkness around them loomed above the pit. Sweetnettle crawled closer to the edge of the pit and saw that Prendel had rolled to his side and pulled his knees against his chest.

When he looked up, an immense shadow, black as a cold hearth at midnight, leaned into the pit. Stinking vapors made Sweetnettle gag and he dropped the sausage he'd been gripping. He stifled his coughs with

PART V: REINFORCEMENTS

both hands and squeezed his eyes shut. Hearing Prendel's soft groans, he looked into the pit again. Prendel's body was shaking and his feet curled in tight spasms.

A thunderous squawk forced Sweetnettle to look up. Sparks were flying about the tunnel. With his durk in hand, the sprite stabbed at the shadowy monster. He felt his hand burn as a gluey fluid oozed over it. Ignoring the pain, he lay on his belly at the edge of the pit and offered his other hand to Prendel.

"Quick, hold on. I can help you, Prendel," he called out.

Prendel had stopped shaking, but Sweetnettle could no longer see him very well. The sprite felt as if he were shrinking. The sparks faded and he fell away, into a nightmare.

He dreamed that an enormous bird with two heads was holding Prendel between two beaks and he could see their sharp edges cutting into the councilor's arms and legs. They soared over the orchard, over the lodge, and he knew that Prendel's arms ached and his legs were turning numb. Higher—the beast flew higher until it hovered over a treeless patch on the mountainside. More of the sickening vapor settled over his face, then the dream went black and he saw no more.

In the tunnel, Sweetnettle lay unconscious, cradled in Rocánonom's arms. All those who had found refuge in the underground chamber crowded into the open doorway and stared gaping and wide-eyed at the strange new giant who had rescued them. Ice crystals glinted in thick fog that filled the passageway. Hoarfrost covered its walls.

Luchaer stepped into the tunnel and blinked until his eyes became accustomed to the sparkling snowflakes that haloed Rocánonom. He dabbed at the poisonous film on Sweetnettle's face, wrapped his little body in a crimson blanket, and carried him back into the chamber, to a broad pile of quilts Fernfallow had arranged in a warm corner. The sprites gathered around Sweetnettle and sang peculiar words to a quiet little tune Fernfallow played on his flute.

Rocánonom dipped his head under the lintel and opened his mouth to speak, but only a belly-borne groan left his lips. His giant hands dropped to his thighs as he shook his head from side to side. Sighing, he wiped tears from his ruddy cheeks with the back of his hand, and in a low, hoarse cry, he said, "Our Sweetnettle—fallen again—he only wanted to help that man by stabbing the Malevir's leg. If my little friends had not 'dropped' in, the beast would have destroyed him utterly."

Bitterbud left the circle of sprites surrounding Sweetnettle and invited the giant into the chamber. The crowd gasped.

Luchaer raised his voice and called out to his followers: "Do not fear him! This brave giant will protect us. Stories of his strength and kindness are known across the Veiled Valley. Eunan and Seerlana, this is the giant who rescued your son Nnylf." The woodcarver turned to face Rocánonom. "Now, what 'little friends' saved Sweetnettle, sir? Have more Loblin found us?"

From behind the giant's robust legs, the two weasels Luchaer had seen in the Nosidam tunnel trotted toward the crowd. Although most onlookers hastily stepped away from them, Bitterbud and Forestspice brought them small bowls filled with crisp sausage slices. Gúrmulo stood in the shadows and nibbled his portion as his sister frowned at him and held up her front paws. "Thank you for the meat, but nothing for me now," she said with a wave of her paws, while Gúrmulo gobbled his sister's portion.

"Don't be afraid of me. Some people scare me just as much." She hung her tongue out the side of her mouth, but no one laughed. She sat back, her tail wrapped around her, and said in a squeaky voice, "Well, people of Fossarelick and Nosidam, my friend Rocánonom here is helping you understand what I'm saying."

Rocánonom nodded and folded his arms.

"My brother and I serve the Veiled Valley and its dragons. Yes, you heard me—the still-living dragons, coming to help us. I hope you've decided to be friends with them again. None of us alone can hope to defeat the Malevir."

PART V: REINFORCEMENTS   329

Kirrill spoke up. "We have seen the dragons and know their good intent. Our son . . ." A sob caught in his throat. "Our Kurnan and a dragon dam have proven that."

Gormley shared a quick glance with her brother, who shook his head and pressed his empty paw to his mouth. "Our sympathies, sir." She sneezed and a murmur of blessings arose from her audience. "Here's our story. When we left our mother's nest, Gúrmulo and I lived in Anonom Trace, a place protected by this very Rocánonom and his Loblin. One day, Seerlana, your neighbor and a rider born and trained by the finest, most honorable of all riders, left the Trace for Fossarelick, and we followed her—on Rocánonom's orders. We watched over her as she settled there and made a family with Eunan. Two Loblin went with us, in disguise.

"Under the cover of night, Fernfallow and Milkthistle settled into life in the village. They set the butter; they coaxed the barley to grow; they soothed the babies, Azile and Nnylf, in their cradles. By day, the villagers knew them as Kolvak and Kirrill's donkey.

"When the Malevir attacked the Trace, he enchanted Rocánonom before the giant could defend himself. The beast forced him into a dungeon deep in the Sunriseside Mountain. Sweetnettle and other Loblin had stayed by the giant's side. After enchanting Rocánonom, the beast attacked them as well and bit the ear of every single one. They endured a terrible transformation, turning into goblins, the beast's slaves.

"Meanwhile, we made our burrow in Fossarelick and guarded Seerlana and Eunan's cottage from the Malevir. Gúrmulo and I have a power he fears. He sees us, screeches, and runs away. He never attacked Fossarelick, but we haven't been able to stop him from hunting two of its young people."

Gormley searched through the crowd and found Azile. "Where is your brother?"

Azile lifted a damp rag that covered Sweetnettle's brow. She dipped the rag in a basin and wrung it out. After smoothing it on the sprite's forehead, she raised her eyes. "The Malevir captured Nnylf and cast a deadly spell over him. Kolvak told me that Rocánonom and his Loblin rescued him and broke the spell, but I don't know where he is now," she said, tears trickling down her cheeks.

Rocánonom cleared his throat. "When last I saw him, in a chamber of the ancestral cave, he and the young dragon Draako were planning to fly with Aurykk's yewr."

Seerlana squeezed Azile's arm and spoke before her daughter could open her mouth again. "We thank you, Rocánonom, for such good news—that Nnylf is well and that Draako accepted him."

Gormley scampered onto Seerlana's shoulder and said, "Draako will be leading the Orferans now that he is the Rightful Reader. Ruddykin, that fiery Red, promised the dragon spirits' loyalty. Gúrmulo and I saw him promise."

Some people groaned at the mention of dragon spirits. Cahalson muttered that it was hard enough to work with dragons again, let alone dragon ghosts. Gormley licked her paw and rubbed behind one ear.

"Don't worry about those spirits. When the dragons come here, you'll be so happy to see them. Now, let's have a look at this Lobli . . ."

Gormley's claws scratched along the sandy floor as she circled Sweetnettle's cushions. She jumped up to sniff his nose and pressed her right ear on the cover warming his belly. "This heart's not dead, yet!" she chirped and went to another cushion, where she lay on her side and began to lick her paws. Cleaning her face, she whistled to her brother.

Skittering out of the shadows, Gúrmulo halted by his sister's side and nuzzled her for a moment, then sat back on his haunches and groomed his white belly fur. When he was satisfied with his work, he looked around the room and squeaked at the sight of Rocánonom's face.

The giant's lips pressed tightly together and tears filled his eyes as he knelt at Sweetnettle's side. After rubbing his hands together slowly, he peeled away Sweetnettle's coverings. Placing one palm on the sprite's belly, he left it there for what Gúrmulo felt were several World-Turns.

Rocánonom must have sensed something good, for when he stood again a smile had softened his face. "Something about this little warrior

PART V: REINFORCEMENTS 331

. . . his belly heart, as Gormley said, beats the way it should. His shoulder heart is faint . . . they never work as well as the belly heart . . . but it, too, grows stronger. Keep him warm and give him more rue broth. It protected him before and should heal him again." He paused and looked around the room. "All of you, do eat big bowls of the broth to strengthen yourselves against the Malevir's next attack."

Seerlana was crouching at Sweetnettle's feet. As Rocánonom spoke, she stood and looked up into his eyes. "How did you find us? Will you share your plan with us? I've heard nothing from my dragons, although you say our son is with Draako. Until I do hear Anadraka's voice, until they come here, how shall we fight off the Malevir? The beast must think that the dragons' friends hide here and that he will force us, his captives, to show him their treasure's hiding place."

Tucking the coverlet around Sweetnettle, the giant answered Seerlana with a warm smile. "The dragons *will* come and we *will* stop the beast. You ask how I found you. I've come from the Cave of the Ancestors, where Aurykk told me you all were here. I reached the clearing nearby and saw a collapsed rock pile and the dragon Isabella flying off toward the Coldside. Then I understood what had happened—since the Malevir somehow had slipped away from her, she had left to find help. I ran to the rock pile and followed the beast through a hole he had left behind. When I entered the tunnel near your hiding place, the Malevir had just raised one head to strike Sweetnettle while holding Prendel's legs in his other beak. When I chanted the proper spell, an ice fog entered the passageway and began to slow the beast's movements. From some other place—I could not see where—the weasels ran over the Malevir's feet. You heard his screech at the sight of them. The beast fled before the fog could freeze him.

"You see, I have elemental powers—like making a fog that freezes everything—wherever I wish, given the chance! Before the Malevir returns, I shall summon a fog over the clearing and orchard while all of you secure yourselves in the lodge. I will fortify the lodge with spells to fend off the beast. We shall wait for the dragons, and when they come, we will help them destroy the Malevir."

Chapter 6

WEAKENED BY HIS EFFORTS IN the tunnel and by the ice fog, Aindle took most of the night to reshape his body into a hork, best for the next step of his plan. In the morning he sat picking scabs from his blue-green arms. His stomach growled. Two field mice ran out from bushes that his acid touch had scorched. He snatched them with one hand and crushed their lungs. With his head leaning back, he held the rodents over his open mouth, squeezed their life juices down his throat, stuffed them between his black lips, and swallowed them whole.

Aindle groaned and belched loudly. Still hungry, he slapped at the bushes and stomped around their roots. Frightening a snake that had been stalking the mice, he caught it as it slithered away and tossed it into his mouth. Licking his lips, he belched once more and turned to look at his human prey.

Prendel lay motionless on his side. The hork squatted next to him and gripped the councilor's head in one hand. With his other hand, Aindle pulled Prendel's ear and stretched it taut. Grunting, he chomped on it. Drops of sticky moss-green slobber sank into the seeping wound. Sitting back on his heels, Aindle raised one claw to flick away spittle clinging to his chin and settled in to watch the man's belly begin to rise and fall. Satisfied, Aindle stood up again and paced around him.

One of Prendel's legs jerked forward, then the other leg bent beneath him and cramped. The once-swaggering councilor opened his eyes and gasped with pain. His screams echoed from the mountainside as he writhed and twisted on the ground.

"I can end the pain, Councilor. Just say, 'Yes, my Mage.' Right now. A nod will do."

Prendel looked in the direction of the voice above him and fainted.

Aindle shook him by the shoulders. "Wake up, you clod. You'll do as I say." Prendel looked at him cross-eyed and nearly fainted again, but Aindle picked him up and steadied him against the trunk of a stunted tree. His acid slobber singed a hole in Prendel's shirt. "You do understand me? Let me hear it." He mouthed the words.

"Yes, my . . . my . . . Ma—age," Prendel answered in a daze. Aindle grunted again and stepped back a pace. Prendel's legs relaxed and he took in a great gulp of air. "Yes, my Mage, I . . . I understand you."

"A test, then. Find us something to eat."

Prendel pushed away from the tree trunk. Confused, he searched the ground at his feet and toed a dung beetle burrow.

"No," the hork screeched. "Beetles won't do. Go uphill."

Nodding quickly, Prendel struggled through tangled bushes and nettles until he came to a narrow path. He staggered up and down the slope until he found a den hidden behind a fallen tree. On his knees, he peered into it and felt around inside. His hand closed on something small and furry. Grabbing it, he pulled out a young rabbit that squealed and wriggled to free itself; but Prendel held on, despite gashes the rabbit's teeth made in his arm and hand. He shuffled back to the hork and held out his quarry.

Aindle snatched it from Prendel's hand and gobbled all but the rabbit's head, which he tossed to Prendel. The man ate it without hesitation, then wiped his lips with the back of his bleeding hand. He stood in front of the ogre and rocked back and forth on the balls of his feet.

"What would you have me do now, my Mage?"

Aindle's yellow eyes glowed with pleasure. He circled his new servant and pointed to a gravel-covered ledge above them. "I shall spend the day

PART V: REINFORCEMENTS 335

up there. When night comes, I will return to this place, but you will not be here. You will go down to the clearing and . . ." He paused. "Come here. I'll show you just where to go."

Prendel walked with him to the edge of a nearby crag. From there he could see the forests below and lands surrounding the lodge. Aindle pressed one gnarled hand on the top of Prendel's head and bent down to whisper instructions into his mangled ear. The councilor stared straight ahead without blinking as the hork spoke. Then he muttered, "Yes, my Mage," and began to pick his way down the mountainside.

Luchaer helped Milkthistle organize the villagers' belongings. He followed her as she led them from their wrecked underground shelter through a puddle-filled tunnel toward the live oak tree's charmed door. She stopped when an unfamiliar wall blocked her path. *More Malevir mischief,* Luchaer thought.

Milkthistle held out her tiny hands to Rocánonom and Fernfallow. The giant knelt between the sprites and opened his broad hands like trays. Palm to palm, Milkthistle laid her tiny hand on his, as did Fernfallow. They faced the wall and began to hum.

Luchaer realized that Azile and Seerlana were standing stock-still ahead of him, as if trying to catch words spoken on the wind. He held Sweetnettle in his arms and felt an annoying twitch ripple under his cheek. Anxious sweat dampened his tunic. He watched Rocánonom with impatience and wondered just what that giant was doing.

Eunan, Atty, Cahalson, and the other Fossarelick men were gripping their durks and clubs. Luchaer overheard Cahalson whispering to Margalana, "The beast has sealed the tunnel. We'll have to turn around." Atty shook his head and hissed a sharp "Shhh" to quiet him. With a kiss to the baby's forehead, Margalana covered her with a delicate shawl Fernfallow had found for her in his sack. All of them felt their hearts beat rapidly.

Just when Luchaer thought that the sprites' meditation was passing as slowly as a long, dark winter, the wall in front of them began to pulse as if lit by innumerable glowworms. It wavered then opened to the clearing under a sparkling dome of night sky—too sparkling for a safe passage to the lodge.

Everyone wanted to push forward and leave the fetid tunnel, but Rocánonom strode ahead of them into the clearing and signaled them to stop. He raised his arms and stretched his fingers. Ball lightening flew from his palms toward the sky and across the ground. As he called on his bond with the elements, a dense cloud of cold mist settled over the clearing and orchard and floated just above the giant's head. He turned to his companions and waved them forward.

With sprites leading them, the Valley folk crossed the clearing. Driven by fear and excitement, some of the younger villagers dashed toward the lodge and left their families behind. Alana urged her own breathless parents to hurry, but their need to reunite with Kurnan had renewed their strength. A few sprites skipped along beside whoever struggled with baskets or sacks and helped lighten their burden with their song. The last stragglers, Mëlo and his wife, were stumbling under the load of a basket filled with apples that they carried between them. Rocánonom and Luchaer followed them and Luchaer blinked in disbelief—firelight from inside the high windows cast a warm light on the fog that was settling over the garden.

Milkthistle was the first to cross the lodge threshold. She dashed through the doorway and leaped onto the table.

Alluxana yelped in surprise and Fulgid jumped up, hitting his elbows on the hearthstones behind him. Rubbing them vigorously, he stomped back to the table sputtering a string of bleats, which Alluxana quickly translated.

"He asks you to be more considerate when you drop in for a chat. As you can see, the boy still lives—barely. We have been caring for him, as Isabella requested," she breathed in a low voice, then turned to the pots in the hearth. A smell sweet as baked apples yet sour as sorrel wafted through the room.

The weasels had scurried inside along with Milkthistle. Gormley climbed up Alluxana's skirt and jumped into her apron pocket. After poking her head out and craning her long neck toward the hearth, she asked, "What's that green mess in the small pot?"

"That's *schaff* I've brewed for Kurnan's fever. He doesn't move, the poor thing, but he's very much alive," the woman mumbled. "Why are you here and not in the tunnel?"

"Everyone's coming back to the lodge. Can't you hear them? Aindle attacked again. He hurt Sweetnettle. They're bringing him here. Good thing that Rocánonom showed up. His ice fog is shielding us from the Malevir who snatched Prendel. Probably ate him for dinner."

Alluxana shook her head. "Poor Prendel." She laid another cushion on the table for Sweetnettle and lifted Gormley out of her pocket. "Shoo," she said. "The boy's family is coming. I have to be ready for them."

Kirrill, his wife, and their daughter reached the doorway. They paused for only a moment before staggering across the room, their arms reaching out to Kurnan. Sherca stroked the boy's face and felt his cheeks with the back of her hand. "He is feverish," she said hoarsely.

Kirrill gripped one of Alluxana's shoulders. He shook her slightly as he pleaded, "Help him, can't you? I know you have magic in you."

Alluxana lifted her free hands to remove Kirrill's, one finger at a time, and her soft gaze calmed the Moktawl. "I've no magic, Kirrill, just good sense and recipes." She stood on a bench alongside the table and beckoned Luchaer, who was carrying Sweetnettle's body. People stepped aside to let him pass. "Luchaer, lay that Lobli here on the cushion. That's the way. Gentle now." She clicked her tongue and shook her head. "This table has become a place for the wounded instead of the hungry."

As more Valley folk entered the lodge, their voices filled the large hall with cheers and shouts of relief. When they saw Kurnan surrounded by his family and the four-armed woman, they fell silent.

Alluxana spoke again, "The broth you have eaten by this hearth has served you well. I see that the aiglonax's poison has hurt no one except these two."

Fulgid bowed as Rocánonom entered and bolted the door shut

behind him. Standing next to Rocánonom, Fulgid fidgeted and whispered, "Excuse me. Can you understand my bleats?""

"Yes, and please don't apologize. I hear your true voice."

"Good! Tell me—we have given the boy much rue broth and cooled his fever with *schaff* compresses. Now, what shall we do for the Lobli?"

"The same, but his two hearts help him heal more quickly—the boy has only one."

Fulgid nodded and he watched the other giant approach Kurnan's grieving family at the table.

"Alluxana and Fulgid have cared for your brave son, and they attend my courageous little captain, too. We must thank them for their kindness. Your son feels the love you have for him, although you cannot see it, and that love warms his one heart. Even my magic cannot speed his healing; that depends on powers greater than mine."

Kirrill's broad shoulders slumped as tears dripped off the end of his broad nose. Sherca and Alana tucked the coverlet around Kurnan and refreshed his compresses.

Luchaer followed Rocánonom as he circled the room to speak with families and friends clustered in small groups. His voice was low but firm as he advised them on ways to protect themselves when the Malevir returned to the clearing. He answered questions and focused on the people's concerns. Only Luchaer noticed that Gormley and Gúrmulo had slipped into the giant's pouch.

Assured that everyone understood the situation, Rocánonom returned to the hearth and wiped soot from the silver disk embedded in the stone wall. He tapped the disk three times, paused, and tapped again.

From somewhere behind the hearth, a rumbling, grinding sound grew louder until a knob popped out of the wall. Rocánonom wrapped his hand around it and pulled. Hinges appeared, then the outline of a door, which swung open. A blast of damp, moldy air shook the cooking pots and nearly extinguished the fire. Muttering a few words, Rocánonom produced a blue-green ball of ice, which he tossed through the doorway.

PART V: REINFORCEMENTS   339

The sour smells disappeared, replaced by the aroma of baking bread mingled with the perfume of roses and lilies. The good smells wafted throughout the great hall and settled over all those encamped there. The depths of the tunnel glowed faintly, and the stones framing its opening in the hearth wall pulsed with light.

Rocánonom said, "We'll use this as our escape tunnel. It goes to the Cave of the Ancestors, but none of you may use it unless Alluxana, Fulgid, or I lead you." With one finger, the giant traced the opening's outline and a shimmering mesh curtain divided the tunnel from the hearth. He turned to face all the Valley folk gathered in the hall. "Nothing can enter this space through that curtain. And nothing should—do you understand?"

The new sweet smells soothed the crowd of villagers, who cheerfully nodded their heads and waved to Rocánonom in agreement.

Luchaer, more alert to imminent danger than the others, asked, "Why are you leaving us? What can I do to help?"

"Fulgid, Alluxana, and I will inspect the grounds of the lodge. Even as the Malevir hides from us, he prepares another attack—a worse one, since we defy him. While we three are away, do all you can to keep everyone calm and busy with tasks. Do not leave the lodge—and remember, you are a Protector."

"I will do all I can, but the Loblin . . ."

"They will help and obey you when you need them. You showed your courage before, Luchaer. You will show it again."

Luchaer sighed, then pulled in his stomach and puffed his chest. "You can count on me," he answered with a quiver in his voice.

Rocánonom's lips tightened as he signaled to Alluxana and Fulgid. They met him at the door and together they entered the garden just as the sun's rays were brightening the thick mist overhead. Gormley poked her head out from under the pouch's flap. Luchaer heard her giggle, "Here we go!" before she slipped inside the pouch again.

Luchaer returned to the table by the hearth. He could see that the compresses had reduced Kurnan's fever—his skin was cool and soft—but his eyes stared at the ceiling and his fingers curled tightly into his palms.

Sweetnettle's eyes remained shut, but a smile had crept into his face, and Luchaer could see that the sprite was enjoying a good dream. He tucked the coverlet around the little fellow's body and turned to stir some embers in the hearth.

A cough startled him and he jumped. A second, louder cough drew his eyes to the curtain covering the tunnel entrance.

Luchaer could see through it. On the other side stood Prendel.

"Prendel, is it really you?"

"Yes."

Luchaer's mouth felt dry and he had trouble breathing. "Is it you or your ghost?" he croaked. "We thought the Malevir ate you for supper!"

"No. Not to his taste. Let me in. I . . . I am hungry."

"I can't let you in, Prendel. The curtain . . . but how did you find the tunnel? Rocánonom said—"

"I can guess what he said. The Malevir showed me the way."

"He set you free? But your arms and legs . . . he must have torn them apart."

"No."

"Why are you here?"

"I bring good news! The beast left the Valley. He gave up. You all can leave the lodge."

While Prendel spoke, Luchaer studied his face and gestures. The councilor's hands jerked up and down like a puppet's, his voice played one note, and he stared at the old Protector without blinking. When Prendel cranked his head toward groups of people and sprites scattered throughout the great hall, Luchaer saw that several small wounds had torn his ear. Pus oozed from one of the cuts.

"The curtain will allow no one to pass, Prendel. You must leave the way you entered."

"Pull aside the curtain, honored Protector."

PART V: REINFORCEMENTS

"The word 'honored' never once left your lips when we lived in Nosidam."

"My mistake. I have learned. Pull the curtain—now."

Luchaer felt himself drawn toward the curtain. A vein over his left eyebrow began to throb. He stepped carefully along the edge of the hearth until he stood face to face with the town councilor. His hand rose and one finger extended toward the ghostly figure behind the curtain. A sharp pain traveled up his arm to his shoulder and the tip of his finger turned orange. He jumped back, nearly stepping into the hot embers glowing around the hearth fire. His forehead ached.

Mëlo and a few other Valley people had been watching the conversation. Chewing on an apple core, Mëlo pulled Luchaer away from the hearth with his free hand and whispered, "I never liked that Prendel, but if he says that the Malevir has left, then we should find Rocánonom and the other Protectors and tell them the news." He dropped the apple without noticing it had left his hand.

Luchaer reached inside his shirt to rub skin that prickled in the middle of his chest. He had forgotten about his amulet, the one he had worn for many, many World-Turns, the one that Rocánonom had given to him and other Protectors when they were young. As he touched it, the ache behind his eyes disappeared and his breathing evened out.

When he looked back at the figure behind the curtain, Prendel was standing quite still, staring at Mëlo. The councilor's gaze then turned to other people standing near the apple farmer. In what sounded like one voice, they shouted: "Yes, we must find Rocánonom and tell him the news!"

Everyone in the room except Luchaer and the sprites began to move toward the door. Luchaer rushed to stop them and the sprites hurried to his side, but with slow, steady steps, Eunan, Atty, and the other Moktawls pushed them aside. They struggled with latches that sealed the door. They threw their shoulders against its thick wood panels and dug their durks into its grooves.

The door stayed firmly closed in its frame.

342   SUSAN BASS MARCUS

While most of the men around the door were trying different ways to force it open, Luchaer realized that the women had not seen Prendel. He urged them to follow him back to the table where Sweetnettle and Kurnan lay.

"We cannot leave these two unprotected. Drink this." He and the sprites thrust cups of rue broth into their hands. Slowly each woman and girl sipped the soup. As they drank, the sprites hummed a sad-sounding tune. The pounding and hammering at the door nearly deafened Luchaer; but when he looked at the women again, he could see that the rue broth had strengthened them. He looked for Prendel behind the curtain and saw that he no longer stood in the darkening tunnel.

Luchaer peered into the corners of the broad hearth and all around the great hall, but Prendel had disappeared. When he met Seerlana's gaze, she held her own durk above her head, winked at him, and elbowed her way through the men attacking the door.

"Men, I can help you," she cried out, "but you need more power if we are to escape. Drink the broth that our sprite friends have prepared for us and the door will bend to our combined strength."

A few of the men grumbled, but all of them except Mëlo returned to the hearth and gulped down a few small bowls of the rue broth. Luchaer and Seerlana looked at each other, then surveyed their work. After the last man to finish his soup had wiped his mouth with the back of his hand, every one of them ran his fingers through his hair—if he had hair—rubbed his eyes, and gaped at Seerlana.

Eunan spoke first. "Seerlana, Luchaer, what happened to that man in the tunnel? I don't understand; I was just talking with Atty, over there by the cupboard, and . . . I can't remember walking over here by the hearth."

Before the old Protector could answer, cackling laughter above them drew their eyes up to the high window that looked out past the orchard. Mëlo had opened its thick shutters and was standing on a narrow platform just inside the window. They could hear him shouting, "The clearing is calm and beautiful. I have to rescue any apples left in the orchard. And

PART V: REINFORCEMENTS

I see Prendel. He's out there, picking apples, too. And music—I hear a pipe playing."

"Stop, Mëlo. Come down," cried his wife. "I need your help here. Prendel's tricking you."

The others also urged him to turn back, but he did not hear them. They saw him throw one leg over the windowsill, sit there a moment, then turn and hang from the sill until he dropped to the ground with a thud.

No one spoke. They barely breathed. Everyone expected to hear the Malevir's piercing screech and the terrible sound of Mëlo caught in the monster's maw, but only the sound of wind moving through the trees reached their ears.

The shutters banged. A few sprites clambered up the stone wall to close them, but as they reached for the rope pulls dangling in the breeze, they saw threads of fuscous vapor winding through the apple trees toward the lodge. Some of the vapor entered the window before Milkthistle and Bitterbud could pull in the shutters. The sprites slammed them shut and scrambled down to the floor, but the grayish-brown mist had already spread through the great hall and people began to cough. Children ran to their mothers and buried their heads against their skirts, while the sprites urged everyone to lay rags dipped in rue broth over their faces.

Atty and Cahalson waved away the sprite's rags and sank to their knees. They held their heads and moaned with pain. Eunan vomited into the steaming hearth, while Seerlana and Azile, sapped of all strength, slumped against a wall. Kirrill and his family stumbled to the door. Sherca pulled at it, gasping for fresh air. "What is happening?" she cried.

"The Malevir used Prendel to trick us. His vapor meant to kill us," said Luchaer. "The rue broth saved you. Lie down now. Rocánonom will return soon." Then he added softly, "I hope." Feeling weakness spread through his legs, he sank to the floor.

The sprites carried cushions to the sick, stroked their heads, and hummed gently until everyone else fell asleep.

Chapter 7

THE MOUNTAIN PEAKS CAST LONG afternoon shadows over the plateau where Aurykk and his family formed a circle. Below them, a gathering of dragons—some more transparent than others—paced around Draako. Nnylf crouched at his dragon's side under a protective wing. Lahsrayn and Flanna stood close to Draako's other side and faced their former companion dragons, the broad-chested Silver, Argenfort, and his blue dam, Calliopfera.

Argenfort stood on his hind legs and pulled back his shoulders, which made his scales and spikes stand up. He looked like a glittering ice sculpture. His mate had folded her legs under her chest and rump like a cat and was watching the two elder riders with half-closed red eyes.

Nnylf, that Silver is my grandfather. His statue, the one I saw in Aurykk's chambers, in no way matches the great might of this dragon.

Draako thrust his tongue into his cheek pouch and spat out two fat, writhing snakes, which Lahsrayn seized and offered to Argenfort. The Silver dropped his forelegs to the ground and stretched his bristling neck toward Lahsrayn's hand.

"Please accept my humble gift, great sire of heroes, peacemaker, and Protector of the Veiled Valley, once my dearest friend," Lahsrayn pleaded.

"Also handsome, most powerful, and wise," Nnylf whispered loudly.

PART V: REINFORCEMENTS

Be still. Remember whose wing is protecting you, young man. Draako sniffed and pulled him closer.

Argenfort snorted a cloud of gray soot. "Humble it is! After all our suffering, you bring me tidbits?"

Calliopfera coughed. "Just to add spice, dear one. Flanna's gift of these delectable pearls and their many words of praise show great respect. Here, taste this one." Her eyes had softened to a dull orange and she rolled a luminous pearl, as big as an apple, over the grass. Argenfort sniffed it, then lapped it up and licked his lips.

Grasping one snake caught under his leg, he offered it to Calliopfera with a flourish. "I would like to offer this tiny tidbit to you, dear one, to savor after that feast of pearls."

Her long tongue wrapped around the desperate wiggler and she swallowed it with closed eyes and a contented burp. "Thank you. I must say, your toes and claws are looking thicker, yes, far less gauzy. Your scales and spikes are splendid, too. Really they are. I have not seen you so solid in ages. You gleam."

"Thanks to Aurykk," Argenfort replied with a nod up the hill. He turned back to Lahsrayn. "Without our nephew's help, we would still be floating in that prison of howling winds beyond the mountain heads—all of us, trapped in an endless storm, until my grandson, Draako, and his family rescued us."

Draako lifted his wing and pushed Nnylf forward. "Honored Grandfather, in this happy moment, may I present my dragonrider, Nnylf of Fossarelick? Lahsrayn and Flanna are *his* grandparents. I think you have met before."

Nnylf's knees knocked together and his teeth chattered as he remembered his last meeting with the dragon ancestors.

Argenfort looked at him closely. His red eyes had faded to a friendly yellow. "We met before?" asked the dragon. "Where?"

"In our home cave," Draako answered for Nnylf.

Argenfort frowned. "The cave . . . our home . . . it's so hard to recall that time. It is like a disagreeable dream; the Malevir forced us to attack our own. We could not do it. Do you remember, dear one—two children and a woman rider who challenged us?" He looked at Calliopfera, who shook her head. "Perhaps not . . . all that is hazy now."

Turning to Draako, he said, "I am sorry, but I cannot recall meeting your rider." Argenfort banished the thought with a wave of his forefoot. "We weren't ourselves then, merely a mass of angry, shrunken spirits, wounded and enchanted by the Malevir. We will talk no more of that."

"You did meet a woman rider—Seerlana, our daughter and Anadraka's friend. Her son stands before you," Flanna offered.

As Argenfort's eyes traveled from Nnylf's booted feet to his tousled brown hair, the Silver released a few wisps of gently spiraling smoke. "Draako, you chose your rider well. His family is loyal to our line. Calliopfera and I approve. Now that is settled. How are my followers doing?"

The other dragons had materialized very well and were strolling next to wavering shadows of people who looked to be on quite good terms with them. Nnylf took a deep breath and rubbed his upper arms to stop his shivering. He watched as a few of the figures floating a hand's breadth above the ground began to grow more distinct. Some of them sank slowly beside their mount and brushed the toes of their boots through the grass, before setting down firmly on the ground. Nnylf could hear delicate laughter ripple through the cold air.

Before their hasty departure from Anonom Village, Lahsrayn and Flanna had opened the bone boxes lining the walls of their shelter. Nnylf had watched swirling mists rise from the boxes and hover over him. He felt icy rivulets run down his neck and a cold mist seep through his armor. Once Lahsrayn had unbolted the door to the outside, Nnylf followed him to reunite with his dragon. The mists thickened into strands that wound through the night air. They caught a strong wind current and snaked their way coldside. Nnylf remembered hearing faint groans and cries as he and Draako flew beside the streaming spirits.

PART V: REINFORCEMENTS 347

Now, as the ghostly riders regained the bodies they once possessed, Nnylf realized that they, like their dragons, displayed brilliant colors. Their armor gleamed red, bronze, blue, copper, or even black or white. He marveled at a silver- and blue-striped pair downhill from him, and a dainty female Red that looked to be about the same age as Drac'Argo, as well as a metallic green dam whose nose was nuzzling her now-robust woman rider, dressed in moss-colored armor very much like the gear that his mother once wore.

The ground under his feet shook for a moment and Nnylf ignored it. *Only the leaps and thumps of restless dragons,* he thought. *If only my mother . . .*

Recalling the dangers Seerlana faced, Nnylf called out to Draako, "Why are we celebrating? What are we happy about? The Malevir surely is attacking my family and others while we just stand here—unlike those ancient riders dancing in this dusky gloom."

Rather than scold Nnylf in front of his elders, Draako extended his wing and drew him next to his flank. His thoughts flooded Nnylf's own. *Patience. Look up there. For every ghostly rider and dragon spirit that breaks free of the Malevir's spells, one of my family lies closer to exhaustion; and, yet, we need every one of them. Say no more. Climb the hillside and see the reason for our delay.*

With a rude grunt, Nnylf crawled out from under Draako's wing. Without looking at his elders or their mounts, he wrapped his cape tightly around him and stomped away. Muttering "sorry, sorry" as he bumped into massive dragon legs or stepped on dragon tails along the twisting path, he began to climb up the slope. He looked with disapproval at the carefree creatures downhill from him whenever he felt tremors under his feet, which he was sure were caused by their celebrations. By the time he reached a berm surrounding the broad cliff ledge, however, the rumbling had quieted. He pulled himself over the top.

Nnylf stopped. He scarcely breathed, so great was the shock of what he saw. Anadraka and Abulafria lay next to each other, their necks intertwined and their legs splayed away from their bodies. Aurykk was sitting back on his haunches, his head drooping between his front legs.

Drac'Argo had rolled to his side and only an occasional thump of his tail against the hard ground reassured Nnylf that the young dragon was still alive.

Nnylf skirted around the two dams, whose only sign of life was a string of burbling snorts. He drew near the massive Golden rocking back and forth on his tail, but he stayed beyond the reach of his claws.

"Brave Leader of the Valley's Protectors . . ."

Aurykk growled and lifted his head. His eyes had faded to gray. His tongue lolled over his lower fangs and tiny cinders lay across his snout. "Young rider," he gasped, "the Ways of the World are with us." His head drooped again and sooty coughs darkened the rocky ground under his feet. He mumbled a few more words as he studied Nnylf's face.

Nnylf leaned closer to Aurykk and heard, "When the Malevir's enchantment of our ancestors began to lose its power, your grandparents released their riders' spirits from their stone tombs." The dragon paused to take a deep breath and continued shakily, "We grow in number as fruit on springtime trees. You are here to lead them?"

"Most wise dragon elder, I know nothing of leading great dragons and their riders happily dancing on the slopes below us. While they tuck their spirits into their old bodies like shirttails into breeches, I am sure they'd rather have you Orferans advise and lead them than an untried boy."

Aurykk stared at him. Rings of pale smoke circled his head. "Me— advise and lead them? For now, you and Draako will do it. He is the Rightful Reader."

"Draako and I? Alone? But if all of us return to the Veiled Valley together, we can rescue our people from the Malevir. Our strength will defeat him—for all time."

"Not yet. No dragon but Draako stands ready. Anadraka and Abulafria have collapsed and Drac'Argo lies like a newly-hatched eggling."

"You sent Draako away to save his strength?"

"Yes, and I'd hoped the Ways of the World would send Isabella to us,

PART V: REINFORCEMENTS

too." The Golden slumped to the ground, his forelegs stretched out in front of him. "But she has not come. We need more time before battling the Malevir." He sat silent for a few moments, took a deep breath, then spoke again. Nnylf could hardly hear him as he said, "Those riders below—they still move as if in a dream, you see. They will falter without a strong leader, and my own strength fails me."

Nnylf opened his mouth to argue, but when he saw the Orferan's weakness, he shook his head and sighed. "I understand, Wise One. When we next go to battle, we must not fail. I will leave you to rest. Draako and I will practice lance work and flying attacks while we wait for your command." He bowed. "Thank you for all you have done. May your rest renew your powers."

Aurykk's nostrils flared and sweet-smelling smoke, like pine kindling in the hearth, wafted from them and wrapped around Nnylf's shoulders. "Young riders itch for action. Tell those below that soon we shall be with them, with the help of the Ways."

Nnylf waved and threw one leg over the berm. The shadows lengthened as he clambered backwards down the steep slope. Once he came to the gentle hillside, Nnylf wove his way through the large flokk of dragons in search of Draako. So much of the day had passed since he had left his own dragon.

He saw Draako's head bobbing around the metallic green female and her rider. Only a few sounds passed between them. Nnylf barely caught their meaning, but the young dragon looked happy. When Nnylf finally stood in front of Draako's snout, he saw that the scales covering his mount's head sparkled. They had all turned silver.

Nnylf had no time to ask Draako about his changing color nor tell him about Aurykk, for he heard a commotion near Argenfort. The elder Silver was chasing a small, furry animal and Nnylf could hear him shout, "You'll do until I find something bigger to eat." The animal's shrill replies sounded familiar. Nnylf hurried to the scene, but before his feet could bring him closer to the uproar, he felt them fly out from under him.

The hillside was shaking again. Nnylf's palms took the brunt of his fall. They stung and his arms ached. Most of the ghost riders had taken to the air on the backs of their dragons. He looked around for Draako and felt relieved that his friend's shadow hid him from Argenfort, who had lost track of his prey while the other dragons fluttered clumsily in the air above them.

Nnylf heard the land groan as a jagged cleft ripped the Sunriseside Mountain range from its opposite. Rocks and boulders careened down the slopes and over the crags as temblors rolled across the land. Above the new gap, Nnylf saw a long, slender cloud rise and float away to the Coldside. Squinting into the distance, he managed to catch it changing shape before disappearing.

Was that a long, spine-studded tail that switched back and forth? Nnylf thought. *No, how could it be? Maybe the wind blowing the cloud apart?* He shook his head. *Now, where did that weasel go?*

Nnylf searched the grasses and shadows of shrubs without spotting the little creature. A rustle among some dried leaves caught his ear. Hearing a familiar chirp, he saw a weasel's head poke above a clump of wilting wildflowers. It skittered across the grass and jumped onto Nnylf's shoulder. Licking his cheek with its little tongue, it raised itself on its hind legs and held onto his ear with one little paw.

"You must be Nnylf. I bring news. Everyone should hear it."

"Gúrmulo? You've lost weight."

"Gúrmulo? Ridiculous—obviously I am his sister, Gormley, friend to the Orferans and Rocánonom's messenger."

Argenfort snorted with disgust. Calliopfera trotted to his side and extended both forefeet. "Dear one, these scorpions will better soothe your hunger." She dropped a mass of writhing red scorpions that milled on the ground in front of them. "The earth's rumblings coughed them up. A gift, I'd say, wouldn't you?"

The great Silver opened his jaws and bent to lick up a few of the spidery creatures with an eye for their tasty tails. "But I've never eaten a weasel. You know I love to try new foods," he whined.

PART V: REINFORCEMENTS   351

The Blue shook her head and said, "Myself, I prefer snakes, although I wouldn't refuse the gift of a tender lamb, but go on, enjoy those little morsels. Weasels do not suit us." Argenfort sighed and trapped the rest of the scorpions in a flash of red flames.

"I like them toasted." He turned his gaze toward Nnylf. "What shall we do with this weasel?"

Nnylf held out his hands and pleaded, "Mighty Argenfort, don't eat Gormley, or you'll have gobbled one of our truest friends. She brings us news from the Valley. Would you ask your flokk and their riders to join us? I think the quakes have stopped."

The throng of dragons and riders drifted back to the hillside and formed a large circle around their leader and Nnylf. The little weasel clung to Nnylf's head and buried her nose in his brown curls.

"Courage, Gormley. Draako and I will protect you. Share your news, please."

Gormley looked around, cleared her throat with a few squeaks, and began her story.

Nnylf's eyes widened as she described the Malevir's attacks on the Valley's people in the tunnels, the orchard, and the lodge. Calliopfera groaned as the weasel related Kurnan and Isabella's brave attack on the beast.

"Serpinafria would have been proud of my niece," she sniffed. Billows of faintly pink smoke rose in the air around them.

Nnylf wiped his eyes. "My little friend, Kurnan," he said to himself.

Gormley coughed, then continued as the air cleared. "Isabella flew off just before I left the lodge. Have you seen her?"

No one answered.

Gormley scratched behind her ear with a back claw. "I suppose if she were coming this way, you'd have seen her."

Silence.

"The giant Rocánonom knew you'd be up this way. Before running to find you here, I followed him and two other Protectors. They had left everyone safely in the lodge and went looking for the Malevir. Gúrmulo attached himself to one of them, in a way."

"What way?" Lahsrayn asked.

"We hid in Rocánonom's pouch." She quickly added, "The Protectors didn't see us. They didn't know I left to find you."

"Thank you for bringing us news, but you should be more careful," Nnylf whispered into her fur. Her body still pressed against his cheek and shoulder.

"Of course," she purred, then to everyone she blurted, "Oh, also, the Malevir will attack the lodge again, soon. Where are my friends Aurykk, Anadraka, and Abulafria? And little 'Argo?"

When Gormley saw Draako look uphill toward the mountain cliff, she leaped off Nnylf's shoulder and dashed up the slope. Nnylf called to her and begged her to stay below, but she ran even faster. They lost sight of her just as another series of tremors began.

Clutching Flanna's hand, Lahsrayn strode to the center of the circle and called all the riders. "Please come closer to me, dear friends, cousins, and ancient warriors. The World Herself trembles from the wrongs we have suffered. We have no more time to celebrate our newfound strength and companions. Let us talk about our attack on the beast while we rest and eat."

As the daylight waned, riders gathered kindling to feed their dried moss fires. Dragons and riders huddled near the warmth of their scattered campfires and ate the last of their dry sausages and rusks. Darkness of deepening night enveloped them as they thrilled each other with tales of past threats to the Veiled Valley and the ways they overcame them.

One of the ancient riders, a tall, gaunt man, raised a bony finger and pointed toward the Sunsetside Mountains. "Do you remember Lasringthan, the Bronze?"

Flanna muttered, almost to herself, "I remember her rider, that boastful girl." She sniffed and folded her arms across her armor-clad chest. "All the same, our valley would have had no land to farm had she and Lasringthan not tricked every Uprooter, those invaders from the Warmside, into the chasm that swallowed them forever. How it closed over those beasts before they could escape"—she shook her head—"I still marvel at it."

Flanna began to cough and gasp as a spray of gravel and dust filled the air. Abulafria's wing beats were whipping up debris on the ground as she settled in behind Argenfort and Calliopfera, and she said, "I remember my mother's blazing rout of gremlins that infested the cave in the Sunriseside Mountains. She roasted them well that day. Isabella and I had barely shed our wyrmling skin. Aurykk was foraging beyond the mountains and we were alone by the entrance when we heard hideous cackling."

"My own mother told me that story. I didn't know it was true," whispered the woman dressed in moss-colored armor.

"We couldn't see them, but the sounds drew nearer—and nearer. Just as Isabella felt an icy touch on her foreleg, Mother flew into the cave, brushed us against the wall with one wing, and scorched the floor with her strongest fire breath. Only then could we see their twisted and gruesome forms, long claws, knobby knees, hairless tails . . . it was horrible."

Lahsrayn spoke up, "Welcome, Abulafria, and thank you for your story about brave Serpinafria. We all have our moments of courage and our gifts. Now that we are together, we shall combine them to fight the Malevir. Where are the other Orferans?"

Out of the gloom, a hoarse but resolute voice answered him. "We are nearly ready, Lahsrayn, for the Ways of the World are generous." Aurykk hovered over the gathering, with Gormley astride his head and hanging backwards onto his frill. "On the plateau above us, Anadraka is feeding her strength with wild rue and other herbs. She will join us soon. Drac'Argo is testing his wings just over there." He pointed with one claw toward the ruins of Anonom village.

"Nephew, son of Lustredust and sole Golden of our Valley,

welcome," Argenfort sang out. "Make a place for him, Llamswell. You, Nosrepa, stand aside."

A spotted Bronze and a young Copper stepped away from each other to make room for the Golden alighting between them. Although his hind legs trembled slightly, Aurykk stood tall among his followers. With a sure voice, he talked to those gathered around him. Argenfort and Calliopfera nodded as he looked into the wide valley below them and pointed toward the lodge with one claw. "We shall bring the Valley folk to Sunriseside Mountain where they will be safe from the Malevir. Then we shall challenge the beast."

While the elder dragons and their riders put their heads together to make plans, Gormley hopped off Aurykk's head. She circled around the leaders and tapped them on their legs. No one paid attention to her shrill squeaks until a rush of leathery wings nearly slapped Argenfort's head. Nosrepa, the young Copper, shrieked, "Another Copper! Another Copper!"

They all stared as Isabella dipped her head and Gormley grabbed her whiskers. With one flip, the weasel landed on Isabella's neck hump, while the Copper settled into an open space on the hillside and roared, "Hear me, Orferans, Valley dragon clans, and riders. The Malevir has laid siege to the lodge!"

Chapter 8

HIDDEN IN THE LONG SHADOWS of afternoon behind a scorched tree trunk, Gúrmulo watched Rocánonom face the aiglonax. The giant thrust one of his arms high above his head while the other pointed toward the earth at his feet. Bolts of lightning shot from the earth and the sky and met near the monster's heads, but Aindle dodged them. With a shrill cry, he crouched and leaped above the giant. Out of his gaping beaks, he hurled cold, blue flames.

Rocánonom shielded himself from them with a spell. Wrapped in a cloud of pulsing light, he pushed his palms in front of his chest and sang out a chant. The fog overhead thickened into a roof of ice. Separating the beast from his prey, it covered the clearing, the orchard, and the lodge. A floe of crystalline walls then whipped around the area and enclosed it. Aindle shrieked in anger and battered the frozen defenses with his talons and beaks.

Gúrmulo scurried through the unnatural dusk until he reached the giant's side and jumped again into his pouch. Rocánonom dipped his hand inside but quickly pulled it out when Gúrmulo's sharp little teeth nipped it. "Leave me be. You'll soon be glad I'm so close to you."

"Where is your sister, little one?"

"Where do you think?"

"She's run to the Trace?"

When Rocánonom heard no answer, he sighed and asked, "What does she think she will find up there?"

Once more, the weasel refused to answer. He returned to the warmth of Rocánonom's pouch, but peeked over the edge when he heard Fulgid and Alluxana approach. The goat-headed giant was staggering toward Rocánonom with someone draped across his arms.

Gúrmulo heard the frozen canopy overhead groan as the Malevir beat at the thick ice. He ducked inside the pouch again just as Alluxana was saying, "When Aindle flew over the clearing, we thought the worst, giant. Thank the Ways of the World you stopped him."

"Yes, Alluxana, but my spells won't last long."

Fulgid pleaded, "You'll chant another spell then, won't you?"

"My friends, spells will not defeat the Malevir. We must put an end to him another way." He paused and brushed back strands of hair that covered the limp person's eyes. "Who is this? Where did you find him?"

"Oh, this poor fellow. Mëlo, the apple vendor. Should have been in the lodge. Looks like the beast's venom killed him. His face is so, so . . . shrunken. Why did he leave the lodge? Luchaer promised . . ." Alluxana's four hands covered her mouth and cheeks as she strained to see the lodge through the murk.

Gúrmulo clung to the pouch's lining as Rocánonom strode through the orchard's wizened trees. The weasel sniffed at the stink of acid-burned fruit and he pulled himself up again to see where they were going. An oddly twisted branch caught the red-haired giant's attention. Rocánonom knelt beside it, then leaped to his feet and pulled Alluxana and Fulgid away.

"It's Prendel. The beast's acid cooked him through and through, worse than Mëlo. Let's move." Breathless when they reached the lodge, they hurried inside and saw that all the humans lay asleep on the floor. Sprites were running back and forth from the sleepers to the hearth as they tended the flames and threw more wood on the fire.

"What happened here?" bleated Fulgid as he laid Mëlo's body on a

PART V: REINFORCEMENTS   357

rug near the slumbering apple seller's wife. "She'll have a bitter awakening, this poor lady," he sighed.

"Airing it out," panted Bitterbud, skidding to a halt by Fulgid's knees. "Poison vapors. Seeped through an open window." He ran back to the hearth and brought them cups of soup.

"This broth saved us, but Kurnan and Sweetnettle—they're not so well." He shook his head and pulled Alluxana's sleeve to bring her close to the table. "Look, so much coughing and little gasps now."

Alluxana placed her cup on the table, reached for a jar on a low shelf near the dry sink, and fished out a small ball of pressed green leaves, bark, and seeds. She warmed the ball between her palms and divided it between two scraps of cloth. Drawing the corners together to make two packets, she knotted a long cord around each one and hung them around Kurnan and Sweetnettle's necks. She then tucked coverlets around the boy and the sprite and rinsed her own hands in a basin before pouring the washwater into a pot that hung over the cook-fire.

"Can't waste a drop of that concoction. Milfoil, comfrey, catsfoot, and a few other healing herbs I know that work well against cough and fever. I'm hanging them close to the fire so heat will release the herbs' oils and vapors. When the people wake up, the herbs will restore them. Now these two, we'll have to put them somewhere else, somewhere quiet. Help me carry them."

Fulgid lifted the sprite and looked to Alluxana for directions. She pointed to a corner of the great hall that they had not noticed before. A section of the far wall had somehow bulged outward in the shape of a wide half circle. It rose to twice Fulgid's height and a glistening white ceiling covered it. Two stone benches lined the curved space, and on one of them, he laid Sweetnettle. Soon after that, Fulgid settled Kurnan along the length of the other bench. Both of the invalids breathed evenly.

Rocánonom tossed up gently glowing balls that hung in the air over each bench, before holding Fulgid's arm and weaving through the sleeping villagers toward Alluxana, who stood gazing at the curtained passage at the side of the hearth. Calling her, he broke into her reverie. She cleared her throat, patted her sweaty brow with a scarlet cloth, and ambled to his side.

Huddled together in the center of the great hall, the giants and the little four-armed woman called softly to the sprites, who skipped across the room toward their Protectors, then pressed close to their sides.

"Do you have your red rags, my little friends?" asked Rocánonom. "We shall need them soon."

They nodded and opened their pouches to show they were well supplied.

A shrill cry tore the night air. Fulgid ran to the door. As he stood looking out, searching the gloom for a sign, he sighed, "Gúrmulo, if you keep weaving in and out of my legs like that, I'll trip." Slamming the door and sealing its latches, he bleated, "Nothing has broken the ice canopy, but I've never heard the aiglonax scream like that. Something else is out there, I think, and the Malevir is not happy." He slammed the door and bolted it.

The icy sheet reflected pale starlight and that was enough. Aindle found a crack and pounced on it again. His talons caught an edge and he pulled with both feet. The crack would not give; its edges were sliding closer together. Soon the opening would freeze shut. Aindle pulled harder. Flapping in a fury, he did not hear another set of wings approaching from behind.

Bounder flew at him, sending Aindle's massive body skidding across the ice. The aiglonax's shrieks mingled with the griffin's cries as Bounder leaped onto the beast's back and attacked it with his sharp beak. The aiglonax flipped to face him and fixed his four eyes on Bounder's two, but the griffin was immune to the paralyzing effect of his stare. The colossal creatures twisted around each other and rolled over the ice. Bounder tore the beast's belly with his claws. At once, Aindle froze, his wings open wide and legs splayed.

Bounder gripped the aiglonax tightly until he was certain Aindle

PART V: REINFORCEMENTS

could not move. Releasing his hold, he hopped back for a clear look at his work. Aindle would remain immobile for a while—one swipe of a griffin's claws was enough to still any basilisk or aiglonax—but the force of the griffin's poison would weaken before dawn. Summoning his immense strength, Bounder seized Aindle's necks in his two front feet, squeezing his talons to steady his grip, and flew toward the Coldside Mountains.

Struggling against the buffeting of a strong coldside wind, he changed direction and veered sunsetside. Below him, he could see the deserted village of Fossarelick, the burned fields surrounding it, and the mountains beyond. He passed through the river valley that cut behind the Sunsetside Mountains and pumped his wings with all his might until he reached a high plateau far beyond the Veiled Valley. After dropping Aindle there, he covered him with rocks and boulders he found strewn about. Satisfied that the rock pile and the wounds he'd inflicted would hold Aindle for a stretch of time, Bounder left the plateau and floated down to the bank of the river below.

As he dipped his beak into the strong current and tossed his head back to swallow large gulps of cool water, he nearly choked when a gravelly voice asked, "You're an awfully strange sort of dragon."

Bounder looked around, but he found no source for the words that tumbled in the air like stones rolling in a swiftly flowing creek. He shook his head and dipped down for another sip. When his beak touched the water, a webbed paw tapped it and he heard, "Are you another one of those fierce Uprooters? I don't like Uprooters."

The griffin jumped away from the riverbank and sat back on his tail. A furry creature, bigger than a weasel, pulled itself onto the shore, shrugged off the water streaming from his fur, and sat in front of him. Instead of answering the animal, Bounder tilted his head sideways and stared at him for a few moments. When the griffin coughed, the startled creature dived into the river.

Bounder called out to him, "Come back. I am no Uprooter. You know me! You're the otter who lives here!"

A furry brown head rested on the riverbank and wiggled his black nose pad. "Indeed I am, but I have never seen you before."

"Do you recall a fierce, ghostly red dragon and a young Silver-Blue? Remember how you dragged me out of the water with a dragons' stone in my mouth? The dragonet took me back to the Cave of Refuge and—"

"Can't be—I rescued a dog."

"That was *me*. I was that dog caught in a spell."

The otter scurried up the bank and settled again on his haunches in front of Bounder. "You, a griffin—*you* are Bounder? Much stronger now, I'd say. Saw you pass over the river with a frightful bundle in your claws. Let me guess. Was it an aiglonax from the Coldside desert you took to the cliff?"

When Bounder nodded, the otter added, "Good. That clifftop you chose is enchanted. I don't know how you broke through its protections, but the beast won't leave it easily."

"Who or what enchanted it?"

"A powerful Silver that hasn't been seen in the Valley for a very long time." The otter tapped his tail, then tucked it under his hind legs. Smoothing his long whiskers, he asked, "How may I help you now?"

Bounder thought for a moment and said, "Help me? You saved my life. How could I ask for more?"

"Ask."

After looking sunriseside, Bounder turned to the otter. "I must return to the Protectors' lodge, but Aindle will work himself free from the rocks and leave the cliff top when my claw poison wears off. What should I do? How can I go?"

"You *should* go. I know a very good messenger who will tell you when the beast flies again," the otter winked. "I'll take care of it. Leave this place and return to the Valley, to the people who need you now." With those words, he stood up, stretched his short legs, and slid back into the water.

"A messenger?" whispered Bounder. He waved his foot as ripples

PART V: REINFORCEMENTS   361

spread out across the water.

With his powerful wings, Bounder thrust himself into the clouds, flew over the cairn covering Aindle's inert body, then headed sunriseside.

The rough winds that tore at his wings earlier that day hastened Bounder's flight back to the lodge. As before, a dome of ice still covered the lodge grounds. Flying low, he spotted a light glowing under the ice not too far from the place he had struggled with Aindle. After landing where the ring of light glowed most intensely, he rapped rhythmically against the frozen surface until he heard responding taps from below.

The center of the circle began to pulse deep red where one of Rocánonom's torch globes was working its way to the surface. It melted a small opening in the ice, then popped through it and shot into the sky above Bounder. Startled, the griffin fell onto his tail, but soon righted himself and leaned over the hole.

Far below, he could see a giant waving at him. He was shouting, "I am Rocánonom, a Protector. We're all safe here for the moment. Where is the Malevir? And the dragons?"

A weasel poked its head over the edge of Rocánonom's pouch and squeaked, "And have you seen my sister?"

Remembering Gormley's bravery around the dragons' treasure, Bounder shook his head and let spill a long story: the Malevir's attempt on the Mystic Scintilla, Ruddykin and the Treasure, Gormley's chase after the aiglonax, and his own flight as he tracked the beast. Warning them that the beast would remain frozen up in the Coldside only a short while longer, he urged Rocánonom to prepare for another attack. He knew only that the dragons had flown to the Coldside.

Gúrmulo sighed. Rocánonom patted his little triangular head to comfort him. The weasel licked the giant's knuckles and pulled himself out of the pouch. Unnoticed, he scampered inside to the hearth.

Turning to Alluxana and Fulgid, Rocánonom spoke with new urgency in a low voice. "We must wake the people. We must find a way to defend ourselves from the Malevir while we wait for . . ." He paused. "For magic stronger than our own."

Fulgid scratched tufts of spikey fur behind one ear and asked, "What do you mean? Is help coming?"

Rocánonom pointed to a shadowy figure standing next to Gúrmulo. "There's the messenger." Gormley had appeared beside her brother.

Bounder left the steaming surface of the ice dome and wove through columns of vapor rising into the sky. The Valley's inhabitants soon would awaken and follow the Protectors' instructions. The lodge's walls and its tower were climbing and courses of stone thickened the outer walls as they grew broader and higher, pushing through the melting ice.

Bounder hovered over the tower and watched its roof harden as each pass of Rocánonom's fiery orbs added another layer of thick iron to its roof—and just in time. A storm was gathering coldside. Dense, churning clouds blocked his view of the Meeting of the Mountains. As they loomed and covered the horizon, the clouds darkened and took the shape of enormous beasts. The griffin shook his head: was that thunder he heard, or a tangle of shouts and cries?

He flew higher still, through rough currents of icy wind that blew him from side to side. Through his half-closed lids, he looked coldside and saw a creature gliding toward him. It looked like a huge brown bird whose broad wings beat with mighty thrusts. As it approached with great speed, he noticed its feathered horse ears and fearsome talons on its legs. Bounder rose higher still, yet the creature passed above him. He could see that its body and legs were like a lion's. It held back and did not attack him.

The creature's large brown eyes locked onto his own. Bounder felt a stillness growing inside, and without understanding why, he floated down to earth in a slow spiral. The creature followed him and landed nearby in the puddle-filled clearing. Feeling no fear of this stranger, Bounder hopped to face it, his head tilted to one side.

"The otter sent me," it squawked with a rumble in its throat.

Bounder took a few steps to regard its muscular shape with two strong wings much like his own. "The otter?"

"The otter that lives by the river over there," it said, pointing with its wingtip beyond the Sunsetside.

"Ah, that otter," he whispered. "You are my messenger."

The strange bird hopped across the clearing and back again to face him. "What are you?" she asked.

"The dragons tell me I am a griffin, but also one of them because of my nestmate."

"You do look like me, a bit, but that tail and those legs—not the legs of a true griffin, like me."

"You are a griffin? Perhaps I . . . but, no, that could not be," he mused.

She hopped closer to Bounder. "I'm Orla of the Coldside griffins. Long ago, savage rocs chased me sunriseside to a cave, where a family of dragons gave me shelter and protection. I was in pain, about to lay my last egg. One of the dragons, a red dam, invited me to share her nest. Sure that my egg sat warm and safe within the nest, I left to distract my tormentors. They chased me to the Coldside where I hid for a few nights. Afraid and hurt, I flew on and met otters, weasels, and Loblin that cared for my wounds. Do you know that family of dragons?"

He nodded.

"My egg . . . did it hatch?"

Silent, Bounder sat on his haunches. He raised one wing and spread a few black primary feathers toward his chest. "You are looking at it," he croaked.

The female griffin crouched into a tight ball. With closed eyes, she bowed her head and her beak opened to release a long sigh. When she looked into Bounder's eyes once more, she warned, "Soon you will need the power of ten dragon cousins. The aiglonax has awakened. Before long, he will feel strong enough to attack again."

The sky had cleared and, directly overhead, the sun dazzled Bounder as he looked coldside to the mountains and squinted. Many quiet moments passed as he watched for a sign of his enemy through narrowed eyes. Shaking his head, he murmured, "Alone, I can delay the beast for a short while. After that . . ."

"You won't be alone," she answered.

When Bounder looked puzzled, she went on, "You are the last of my hatchlings and the only one to survive the rocs. When the Malevir returns here, *two* griffins will challenge him." She hopped to face him and rubbed the tip of his beak with her own. "My chick."

After one more hop, she vaulted into the air and Bounder followed her. They flew over the orchard and landed on the armored roof of the lodge tower. "We shall roost here and wait for the beast."

Part VI
The Dragons Return

Aurykk the Golden Dragon©

Chapter 1

THE BEAST STIRRED IN HIS plateau-high trap. Withdrawn deep inside himself, Aindle held his breath and pushed against a heavy boulder. Every movement sent searing pain along his wings and necks. When he tried to change shape, he felt dizzy and acid rose in his throats, especially when he chanted the lizard spell. If it had worked, he might have crawled between the rocks that enclosed him.

The griffin's poison began to weaken and he found he could move a little. He ducked his heads and pushed harder with his back against the boulder. It slid sideways and one of his heads passed through the space, no longer blocked. He opened his beak and drew in the cold, clean air. One more thrust and several other boulders tumbled away. Both of his heads and his shoulders were free of the rocks. His talons scrambled up small stones that lined the shallow pit in which he had been imprisoned, and he stood on its edge.

No longer feeling the pains that tortured him as he lay trapped, Aindle shook his wings until their feathers and scales fell into place. Within a short time, he could stretch them high and wide. Looking toward the Warmside, he could see that the Veiled Valley lay far away. He would need to feed or he would lack the strength to return there, to destroy the griffin, and, at last, seize the Scintilla.

Below him, running along a riverbank, he spotted an otter. He hurtled himself down toward a promising meal. A wave of rocks and scree slid

PART VI: THE DRAGONS RETURN   367

down the cliff as he descended and the noise startled the animal. It dived into the swift current and disappeared below the surface.

Aindle landed on a small island in the middle of the river and turned his heads in all directions. The animal would need to breathe soon. He would catch it when it came up for air. Crouching, he watched the water that flowed around him. His belly felt pinched. A trail of bubbles passed him. Sure that they came from his prey, he plunged one foot into the water. Flexing his talons, he felt something soft and grabbed it. One squeeze would kill it.

Whatever he caught was quite strong. It pulled his leg into the river. His body followed. Aindle could barely keep his heads above the water's surface as the current swept him downstream. Gasping, he tried to lift his wings above the surface, but they dragged under the water's weight. The current rolled him around, and when one of his heads slipped under the surface, something wrapped around his neck. It felt like a rope drawing tighter with every passing moment.

Sure he was going to drown, Aindle called on his remaining strength while uttering a short spell. Fortified for the moment, his legs thrust against the hard riverbed and he leaped high above the water. He beat his soggy wings and smashed onto a grassy slope above the bank. Exhausted, he lay quite still.

A curious tortoise, as large as Aindle's foot, crawled near his beak. It had picked up a strange scent and poked its head around Aindle's strangled neck, its own neck stretched far out of a brightly colored shell. Like many of its kind, it could not hear the aiglonax, who was spraying venom into the air, and it crept closer, collapsing as Aindle's poison suffocated it. The beast swallowed the tortoise whole with his one still-vital beak.

The aiglonax snipped at his own garroted neck, mottled green and black above the weed that choked it. He finished the weed's work by biting off his other withering head. Some of his ichor oozed from the wound. Soon a thick crust formed along the cut and sealed it.

Three buff-colored vultures caught Aindle's eye. They were sitting on a branch that stretched over his remaining head. They leaned forward to watch him and hopped to the ground, hissing and quarreling over the severed head that had rolled toward them. As they pecked at each other, Aindle opened his wide beak and swept them into his gullet. He belched and some dark flight feathers shot out of his beak. Caught by a breeze, they floated over the river's surface until, snagged in the current, they drifted downstream.

Cackling, Aindle stood on still-shaky legs. He staggered through tall grasses and flowering weeds that covered a meadow. After a few more tasty bites like that, perhaps he would be ready to fly.

Chapter 2

DRAGON CLANS CROWDED THE ORFERANS' home cave. Scattered among the many limestone columns, they listened to Aurykk explain his plan. The long flight had tired him, but he lifted his golden head and his scales gleamed in the glow of bobbing orbs that floated along the slick cave walls.

Standing opposite him, a very grumpy Ruddykin growled his displeasure. "Honored Orferan, we can't fight like the griffin Bounder. He can overwhelm Aindle and never suffer from his touch or poisonous vapors. We could surround the beast and attack, but with one blast of his sickening vapors, we'd all be flat and dead on the ground."

Aurykk puffed tendrils of dark smoke as he considered Ruddykin's concerns. "Ruddykin, like every one of us who has particular strengths, you have the means to do your job—defend yourself and our Treasure. When we dragons choose to work together, we are an overwhelming force. Remain here as the Mystic Scintilla's guardian while we others use that force to overwhelm the Malevir." He turned to the only full Silver present. "Now, I ask Argenfort to share the Mystic Scintilla's story with our young ones."

With a thump of his lustrous thick tail, Argenfort took his place next to the Golden and his gaze took in every dragon and rider surrounding him. "Aurykk has gathered us to plan our attack on the Malevir. Ruddykin frets, since the Malevir has searched for the Mystic Scintilla in the galleries below. Thanks to the Ways, he did not find it, but the danger grows."

"Please forgive me, Great Silver Warrior," Nnylf said as he stepped up to face the ancient dragon, "but I do not understand the importance of the Mystic Scintilla, except that it is the source of your fire breath."

"That it is, but without it, you and Draako could not share thoughts. No dragon would carry a rider. No dragon could summon the earth, waters, or sky to cast a spell. No dragon would think of anything but eating and sleeping. We would be mindless giant lizards again." Argenfort paused to lift his head as high as the cave ceiling would allow. His words echoed around the chamber. "Deep within the treasure hoard lies a sealed box, gold on all sides except for a clear and hard lens in the lid, once a powerful dragon's eye. The box contains an egg, which sends strong light pulses through that lens. Ruddykin has seen them."

The Red, impatient to return to his duties, puffed until a light gray haze wrapped around his jaws, but he nodded.

"The Scintilla's energy comes from the First Turns, when the World formed and lizards both large and small lived in the lands. They had no fire breath, no strengths other than their teeth, claws, and muscles. One of their dams had unusual scales that gleamed a mix of metals and hues—or so goes the story. She laid an egg and brought it to this cave, a much smaller space at the time; its walls always sweated from the damp. This stream crossing the floor here used to be broader.

"Spots of blue and silver covered the egg's shell, and as it lay in the dam's nest, dancing lights flickered inside it, but the egg did not hatch. The dam could feel the heartbeat of a little dragon, but the wyrmling never cracked its shell. Generations of dragons cared for the egg by tucking it into a nest and making one of the family its guardian. From that time long ago—and none of us knows why—dragons not only gained the gift of fire breath, but each of us also has had a special power or set of powers."

Aurykk added, "The first Golden of the Orferans who became the egg's guardian fashioned the Scintilla's box. Wrapped in a light red

PART VI: THE DRAGONS RETURN   371

cloth to protect it from the damp, it lay hidden in the treasure hoard for hundreds of generations. Protectors and Loblin always carry pieces of that cloth, which have healing powers if used with incantations. While living in this cave, Orferans have used their unique powers to protect the Veiled Valley and the Scintilla.

"Until the Malevir attacked. Several times. He nearly destroyed us. If the Malevir steals the Mystic Scintilla, he will shatter it and destroy its light. As Argenfort said, we will become senseless lizards as in the time of the First Turns."

While Argenfort and Aurykk were speaking to the gathering, Nnylf looked around the chamber and, with a shiver, recalled all the dangers and kindnesses he had known here. As his eye fell on the entrance to the tunnels that led back to the lodge, he squinted into the darkness. Tapping Draako on the leg, Nnylf gestured toward the tunnel.

"Draako, please cast one of the orbs over there. I saw something move."

The far tunnel? Let's look into it.

While the other dragons were listening to Aurykk, who had settled into describing the Malevir's enchantments and mischief, Draako slipped away unnoticed toward the tunnel entrance. Nnylf jogged to the opening and hid behind a large stalagmite. He saw elongated shadows moving along the tunnel walls and thought, *Could that be the hork? Should we warn the others?*

Nnylf blinked and tried to clear his head. Was he hearing a dragon laugh? What was so funny? He came around the stalagmite and dashed to the side of the tunnel opening. The orb dropped a short distance and the shadows shortened.

Draako, it's too short for a hork. I'll look closer.

Before he could take another step, Nnylf felt two warm arms embrace him and a familiar voice say, "Oh, Nnylf! We are so happy to see you alive and protected by your dragon friend!"

"Azile . . . and Mother! Alana! How did you all escape the beast? How did you find us here?"

Seerlana embraced both of her children and, annoyed with the tears that escaped her eyes, she sniffed and wiped her cheeks dry with her sleeve. She pointed to the weasels that were resting on low marble ripples near the wall. "Gormley and Gúrmulo led the way. The giant sent us to find our dragons. The others are still hiding in the lodge. Rocánonom opened the hearth tunnel for us." She went on, "You remember Alana? Kurnan's sister?"

Seeing that Nnylf gave Alana a short little wave and nodded at the mention of Kurnan, Seerlana continued, "Isabella chose Kurnan as her friend and rider, but the aiglonax wounded him badly and we don't know if he will heal. I hope that Isabella will accept Alana in his stead."

Nnylf, I will speak to Isabella about Kurnan. And Aurykk and Argenfort must hear about the riders'—and the weasels'—arrival. Draako pulled his head out of the narrow tunnel and returned to the gathering of dragons.

"I am sad to hear about Kurnan. He will heal, I'm sure, but follow me now. I have something to show you." Nnylf squeezed Seerlana's hand and pulled her into the chamber. He held out his other hand to Alana. "I think you will like this surprise, Alana."

Alana's wide eyes surveyed the throng of dragons filling the chamber. Nnylf could feel her hand trembling as he held it firmly in his own. "Don't be afraid. They won't hurt you. And, listen, Isabella might even accept you as her rider. When you meet her, she might be gruff, but a gift will soften her up. Do you have anything shiny to offer her?"

"Perhaps," Alana answered as she patted her deep skirt pocket. "So many dragons. So big," she whispered to herself.

"Yes, it's a flokk of them, from the Valley and beyond. Mostly Orferans. Other clans, too."

"Are you sure they are friendly? They don't look so friendly." With dragging feet, she followed her companions into the broad space facing the cave's entrance. As the dragons and riders dispersed to make room for the newcomers, Lahsrayn and Flanna stepped out of the towering shadows thrown by their dragons and stood facing Seerlana.

PART VI: THE DRAGONS RETURN   373

"Daughter," they said, the word catching in their throats.

Shocked, Seerlana and Azile's legs shook as Nnylf drew them closer to his grandparents. After many hugs, each tighter than the last, the elder riders invited Seerlana and Azile to rest on the remains of a gigantic boulder. Azile crawled to the top; Nnylf dropped Alana's hand and ran to his sister.

"Azile, don't touch that!"

"Why, Nnylf? I'm fine. Getting stronger all the time," she giggled.

"That rock, it's . . . the Malevir chained me to it. I nearly died there."

Azile drew back her hands as if the rock were on fire and stared at it. "He tried to kill you?"

"He wanted me to reveal the treasure's hiding place. You and I and Mother know it's here, but no more than that." He then whispered in her ear, "But I did find the prophecy that gave me courage. Look over the entrance. Do you see it, the broken tablet? When joined to its other part, it reads:

> In nests of rainbow brightness
> Shall the wyrmlings come to light,
> Sheltered from the Malevir,
> The ruler of the night.
> One and only one will dare to banish pain and fear
> And this will be the Draako, heir of Lugent, blessed with Sight."

Approaching them with a weasel on each shoulder, Aurykk interrupted the reunion. "Argenfort, your father was a seer. He carved that prophecy. Now, Draako's day has come and he shall share the lead with you. Four others will follow the Silvers into the Valley, partnered with Rider Lahsrayn and Rider Nnylf. The Malevir has returned, according to our small friends here, and you will form the first attack yewr."

"What's a yewr?" gulped Azile.

Seerlana answered in a whisper, "A small group of dragons, flying together."

Aurykk continued, "Sort out your powers and plan the ways you will use them to confuse the Malevir. The weasels and I must hurry down through the tunnels to guide the Valley folk, who will be coming here, too. Rocánonom is moving everyone out of the lodge."

With those words, the weasels jumped to the ground. A light mist enveloped the Golden. His scales shimmered. Within moments, they whirled away from his body in a vortex of dazzling lights. Aurykk stepped out of the whirlwind as a man, dressed in amber armor. He wore a light leather tunic and breeches with a short lance slung over his shoulder, and he waved to the gathering and dashed into the far tunnel from which Seerlana and her companions had emerged. Gormley and Gúrmulo were at his side.

No one moved for a few moments, so stunning was the transformation. The sound of shuffling dragon feet startled Seerlana. She looked back toward the cave entrance and smiled. Holding out her arms, she ran toward Anadraka, who bowed her head as Seerlana sprang up to her shoulder and settled onto the Silver-Blue's hump.

Abulafria and Azile had a more cautious encounter. Unsure that the dam would accept her, Azile let only gentle thoughts run through her head. She rummaged in her pouch and offered the blue dam a single round sapphire as large as her thumb.

"Rocánonom sends his greeting and wishes for your well-being," she murmured.

"Azile," said the dragon, "no need to offer me a gift. Your mother's kindness and good heart have strengthened our friendship, and you share those loving qualities. Would you honor me as my rider?" Abulafria settled into the floor, tucked her legs under herself, and curled her tail along her flank. "Use my tail as a bridge and climb up to my hump."

Stunned, Azile could only stare into the dragon's honey-colored eyes.

"Come, now. I won't hurt you," Abulafria called to her and thumped her tail.

PART VI: THE DRAGONS RETURN

Azile jumped, but spotting the tip of Abulafria's tail by her feet, she raised a foot to climb onto it, gripping one of the spikes that ran along the tail's ridge to balance herself. She had few good memories of that frightening ride on Draako years ago. They had fled from this very cave back to Fossarelick lands. The dragon's cool hide soothed her hands.

"Take another step . . . good . . . and then another . . . you're almost there. Watch that spike; your memories of Draako distract you. You should know you calmed him even when Nnylf's cries added to the confusion of your escape. Without your brave words, that dragonet would never have opened his wings and leaped from the ledge in time to save you and himself."

Azile climbed onto Abulafria's haunches and worked her way along the dragon's backbone until she reached the radiant frill that curved around her neck. She settled onto the broad hump just behind the frill and gripped folds of skin as the dragon rose slowly to her full height.

Azile, you are sharing my thoughts now as we did a while ago when you were in the forest and saw us flying above you. I will guide you as we practice flying.

"I'm ready."

Abulafria ambled to the ledge outside the cave and, urging Azile to grip with her knees, soared up and around. Azile opened her eyes and a loud "Whoo-eeeee!" escaped her lips.

Standing in the middle of the broad chamber, Alana marveled at the variety of dragons assembled there. A high voice startled her and she stumbled over a low rimstone ridge bordering the stream.

"Are you looking for someone?"

Finding her balance again, Alana looked into the beautiful, large green eyes of a young Copper. The color of spring lettuce circled her endlessly black pupil slits. Cold sweat made Alana's palms slick and she wiped them dry on her chemise sleeves. Hoping to banish the fright that clouded her thoughts, she answered quickly, "Yes, for Isabella, my brother Kurnan's friend. She's a Copper. Are you Isabella?"

The young dragon's laughter sounded like water running in a brook. "No, my name is Nosrepa. Your Copper is there, by the entrance to the cave." Nosrepa sighed. "She is so sad. I can hear her heart shake and groan. If she rejects you, come back to me and we'll chat some more."

"Thank you, Nosrepa," Azile said as she walked toward the entrance. She stopped a body's length from Isabella. Dozing, the Copper lay curled on her side against the rock wall. Pulling a mirror from her pouch and offering it to the Copper, Alana whispered, "Beautiful Isabella, awake and let me help heal your heart. I am Kurnan's sister, Alana. If you let me ride with you, we shall weary and wound the Malevir to his death."

The Copper opened one eye and glared at the girl until she saw the mirror in Alana's hand. A silvery tear rolled down her snout. One swipe of her long, forked tongue licked the tear from her nostril; but she said nothing. Pale smoke wafted from her parted jaws.

Alana lifted the mirror so that it was even with Isabella's open eye and waited. The dragon blinked a few times, then flicked her tongue at the mirror. Alana's throat tightened as the dragon's thoughts filled her head.

Dear girl, my grief has darkened my heart. Thank you for returning Kurnan's gift. If you are not afraid to ride me, I am not afraid to trust you—but tell me of my boy. Have they buried him near the great tree?

"Buried? No, no! Kurnan lives, but barely," Alana replied. "And I am not afraid of you. He loves you so. If we are to see my brother riding you again, we must work together to help destroy the Malevir."

Come, then, be my friend and we shall avenge good Kurnan. Up you go, Alana. Let me show you the gift of flight.

As the World and the sun played their late-day game of tag, the shadows grew longer and the dragons, weary from long flying practice, settled once more into the cave's main chamber. Argenfort sat back on his haunches. He signaled with a jet of flames that scorched a nearby stalactite that he was ready to speak to all assembled.

PART VI: THE DRAGONS RETURN

"Two of us Silvers and the four Blues or Silver-Blues will mesh our powers against the Malevir. At nightfall, we shall fly into the Veiled Valley, encircle the lodge lands, and strike the beast with our combined strengths. We'll use our fire breath and add the Silvers' paralyzing gases, the Numbing Blast, the Blues' electric charges, and their Power of Water. Then you dams—hmmm, I think you have one other hidden ability?"

"Calliopfera has been keeping a secret!" cried Flanna.

"No, dear rider; your heart will jump in your chest when you learn about it. I'll keep it secret for a while longer."

The remaining dragons grumbled about the plan. A few growled that Aurykk had forgotten that their special strengths—acid phlegm, fire bombs, frost clouds, and sleep gas—would be just as devastating to the Malevir. Each one called out to offer his or her own power. Tinta shouldered aside a small green dragon and bellowed, "You also forgot that we Reds are the fiercest fighters among the yewrs. Put us at the head of your little group and we'll assure the death of that wretch." A veil of pea porridge–colored smoke partly hid her features, but her glaring red eyes pierced the fumes.

Before she could blink, Argenfort was standing in front of her. He pressed his snout into her own. "Your bravery is only outdone by your rashness," he growled between his fangs. "Aurykk is the peacemaker, the planner, and has the final word. He asks that Ruddykin and 'Argo stay to guard the Treasure and that you and the others wait for a sign before you fly into battle. You will know the sign when it comes, and only then will you join the struggle. Is. That. Understood?"

Tinta bowed her head and a blast of steam escaped her nostrils. When she looked up again, her eyes had softened to a dark green. "Yes, I understand. If Ruddykin stays behind, then I also can wait to serve." Tinta backed away from the Silver and retreated behind a massive limestone column. Argenfort puffed a few white wisps then turned away.

"Isabella, how well does Alana ride?" Argenfort's soft voice invited the Copper to approach.

"Remarkably well, great Silver. She and her brave brother share the gift."

"Good. Remember this: when you fly into the Valley, keep yourself at a distance from the aiglonax, far from his poisons. His acid will not harm you, but Alana has no defense. Protect her at all costs."

"But we are not in the first cohort. You said two Silvers and four Blues—"

"You will be our scouts," said Argenfort.

"But Alana, she's so new at this—"

Isabella, we are ready, thought Alana.

"*I am not so sure . . . but we do have the mirror,*" answered Isabella's thoughts.

The mirror?

"*Kurnan's gift—your gift—it will help us if the Malevir attacks.*"

The Copper smiled, and when Alana nodded in agreement, Argenfort understood that they had accepted the order. He raised a wing. "Hear me now, everyone. Brave Isabella and Rider Alana leave now as night begins to cover us. They will look for the Malevir's hiding place and then we shall join them for the attack. May the Ways of the World give you courage and might. We await your signal."

Alana looked back into the cave only once before she felt her dragon thrust into the air and soar up into the night sky. Isabella flew with such speed that Alana's long brown hair streamed behind her in the wind. She squeezed the Copper's frill and hunkered down as they rose high over the Valley.

Chapter 3

The weasels had the habit of running ahead, then stopping abruptly and turning back to see if Aurykk was following. Swift as a dragon in human guise might be, nevertheless his pace rarely matched that of the weasels. Their rapid journey through the tunnels ended in the lodge garden at the mouth of the burrow they had dug earlier. Clawing away at the hole, Gormley and Gúrmulo pushed clods of earth aside. Aurykk helped them widen it and pulled himself up and out of the opening.

"Nice work, sister mine," muttered Gúrmulo as he chewed on the remains of a chipmunk.

"I could have used more help, but no, you had to have a snack," she huffed. "Come, Aurykk, we have more important matters than filling our bellies."

Gúrmulo chased after them, whining that weasels are always hungry, that Gormley was unnatural, and that Aurykk would understand, but he quieted down as they approached the lodge. Through the open door, they saw the Valley folk gathered around Rocánonom near the hearth.

The giant was advising Kolvak and a few other sprites about their trek up to the Cave of the Ancestors. At their feet sat bundles of dried foodstuffs and other necessities for the humans. "Dragons might still be there. If so, they will not harm you. Prepare the main gallery for all these good people." He studied Kolvak for a few moments. "My friend, your Loblin family, so long separated from you, is also up in the cave. When you arrive you should look like the Lobli they once knew. Come closer."

Rocánonom's broad hand reached toward the little cook and pressed him to his side. He placed a red rag in the little man's hands. Then he sang four lines:

"This loyal Lobli left his clan
The Malevir he wished to fight
Ways of the World O hear my call
Return to us our noble sprite."

Every light in the lodge went out. The front door and the high shutters closed with a thud. The hearth fire turned to smoke. A few of the children whimpered, but a small voice called out from the absolute darkness:

"Don't worry. I'm fine."

Rocánonom's warm baritone reassured his companions: "Fernfallow, right you are. Now twirl on your toes and show them your true self."

Fernfallow giggled when tiny blue and green sparks tickled his nose then floated overhead to lighten the gloom. From the hall's corners, more sparks glimmered, joining the first few to form a flickering ribbon that wrapped around the little cook until no one could see more than a glimpse of his twirling figure. The ribbon grew in length and twisted like a whirlwind around him. Those watching in amazement could hear him say, "Help me, everybody. Blink your eyes."

Everyone blinked. The lodge shutters flew open again. Sweet air filled the great hall. The floor sparkled as moonbeams caught flakes of crystal buried in its stones. All the Valley folk who had gathered around the potbellied cook gasped. They no longer saw a little man who for so long had offered them savory soups and barley breads. Instead, standing in the middle of the room, a sprite skipped about in his copper shoes,

PART VI: THE DRAGONS RETURN 381

shouting, "I'm Fernfallow again—Fernfallow!"

Cheers filled the air as the other sprites ran to hug him and welcome his familiar face—but they froze when they heard a loud crash at the front door.

A tall rider strode into the hall. Two familiar weasels scampered at his sides. He quickly raised his hand and all the shutters and the door sealed shut again. The hearth fire surged and floating orbs illuminated the vast space.

"Who are you?" blurted Cahalson. The other Moktawls stood next to their young leader and reached for their durks.

Fulgid pushed the men aside and blocked Cahalson, who scowled into the goat-faced giant's face and shouted, "Out of my way. This stranger could be another form of the beast!"

Fernfallow slapped the Moktawl's leg and shouted, "No, no. this fine—um—fellow was our friend, even before the Malevir stole the lodge from Fulgid and Alluxana. Listen to him with open hearts."

The stranger added, "The weasels and I have come here to take you to a safer place, before the Malevir's next attack. Seerlana, Azile, Nnylf, and Alana are there. I left them as they were preparing their dragons for battle against the Malevir."

Fernfallow winked at Rocánonom. "The dragons *are* at the cave, my friend!"

The giant smiled at Fernfallow. "Yes, Fernfallow. Now, please introduce this man, no stranger to Alluxana and Fulgid but unknown to the rest."

A smile lit Fernfallow's dappled green face. "Everyone, please meet the Valley's most powerful—um—dragonrider." He removed his cap and made a deep bow. "A long-awaited pleasure to see you again, Aurykk," he announced and turned to whisper a few words to Rocánonom: "His arrival fills me with the hope that soon we shall shorten the Malevir's time in this World."

Rocánonom mussed Fernfallow's tangled curls and said, "Good

thoughts to keep in both your hearts."

Gormley ran up Rocánonom's leg and perched on his shoulder while Gúrmulo sniffed around the pots once more bubbling on the hearth fire. The handsome giant stroked his little friend's curved back and said to Aurykk, "I was preparing the Loblin. They will go to the dragons' cave with supplies—and Sweetnettle. Are you ready, Bitterbud and Forestspice?"

"Yes. This time, the stream will not frighten us, eh, Bitterbud?"

"Oh so true, Forestspice! No more goblin skin. No more water burns."

The giant continued, "An occasional bath would do you no harm! Listen now: after you reach the cave, prepare it for Alluxana, Fulgid, and everyone else gathered here. You all will find comfort in the Cave of the Ancestors, but I shall remain here."

The sprites patted their filled pouches and entered the hearth's tunnel opening. Fernfallow led the way and Bitterbud followed close behind, his narrow shoulders shaking with unpleasant memories of the passages ahead of them. Milkthistle and Forestspice carried Sweetnettle resting on a litter.

The other Valley folk watched the sprites leave and Luchaer sighed. "What now?"

Rocánonom answered, "We shall eat this hearty forest stew and fill our bellies with sweet barley cakes. Then you will pick up your bundles and follow Aurykk into that same tunnel."

Kirrill and Sherca helped the giant pass around bowls and platters until everyone had plenty to eat. When broth was low in the cauldron and only a few crumbs remained on the platters, Rocánonom had the Valley folk shoulder their belongings and told Aurykk that they were ready to leave.

The empty lodge hall echoed as Rocánonom sealed the door and locked the silver knob in place. In a few moments, the knob faded altogether. Trailed by the weasels, he bounded lightly up the tower's spiral staircase until he reached the top landing. As his fiery orbs continued their circuits outside the tower, the giant could feel its curved wall shiver with each new layer of stone that reinforced it. Behind Gúrmulo and Gormley, the staircase crumbled and turned to dust.

A ring of small slits pierced the tower just under the roofline. Through them, Rocánonom could look out in all directions. When he heard the sound of scratching on roof tiles overhead, he peered out a slit facing the Coldside, then whispered, "If the Malevir were overhead, by now we'd be bathed in his vapors. Something else is roosting above us. Gormley and Gúrmulo, slip through this opening, please, and have a look up there. Don't dawdle. Come back here as soon as you see what or who it is."

The weasels touched noses, licked each other's ears, then clambered through opposite slits and scrambled up to the roof. The scratching stopped, but the weasels did not return.

Rocánonom pressed his ear to one slit and heard nothing but the wind whistling by. A huge gust surprised him and sent him sprawling on the floor. When he looked up, a large brown creature was flying around the ring of slits. The giant looked outside again. He saw a griffin pass, rise above the tower, and disappear. The scratching resumed.

Gúrmulo slipped back into the tower room through a slit opposite the giant and said, "My sister has just met up with an old friend."

"An old friend?" Rocánonom smiled. "A weasel that flies?"

Gúrmulo squeaked, "No, not a flying weasel. A flying griffin. Two of them." He sniffed the floor. "Say Rocánonom, you have a chipmunk in your pocket, perhaps? I'm hungry."

"Has Bounder returned?"

"Bounder and his mother." He sniffed and licked the bottom stones of the wall until he reached the edge where the stairway used to be. Only a few steps remained attached to the floor.

"Ah, his mother. I wondered about her. Say, Gormley ought to come back. I told her—"

"Here I am!" Gormley squeaked, jumping through a slit into the room. Instead of reporting to the giant, she led Gúrmulo down three steps and through a hole in the wall. In a short time, they reappeared. Each weasel held a limp mouse in its jaws. They set to eating with enthusiasm.

"How quickly the field mice found this new tower," Rocánonom muttered. He turned again to look through each wall slit and paused at the one facing the Coldside. "I see a dark cloud approaching from just over the mountains."

"That would be the aiglonax. Bounder and his mother were expecting him." Gormley paused to clean her snout and neck with a damp paw. "Bounder captured the beast and trapped him, but his spell weakened. So, yes, they wait for him now."

"They won't have long to wait," grumbled Gúrmulo.

"Come to me, you two. I must keep you safe. Stay close. I shall wrap us in a spell, but first—I know you don't like it—eat this rue pellet."

Rocánonom thrust a small brown pellet into each weasel's open jaws, ate some himself, and then summoned his orbs from their work outside. The orbs shattered into tiny crystal flakes, passed through the slits, and bathed the tower room in a soft glow.

"Defend us!" the giant cried out.

The flakes whirled around Rocánonom and the weasels so quickly that they formed a shimmering curtain of light. As the curtain rose, Rocánonom was happy to see a large dark globe sitting in the middle of the floor. He and the weasels slipped into it and waited in safety for the Malevir.

Chapter 4

AINDLE'S SLASHED NECK ACHED AND his budding new head itched. Thoughts that bubbled in one head confused plans shaping in his other, healthy skull. *Wings are dry. Ready to hunt. Where's the mountain? Must find the Scintilla. Use Prendel.* He snorted. *No. Useless clod.* One head examined the other. *Why so small? Grow, little head.*

His beak slapped the crown of his smaller head and he felt pain surge through his sturdier neck. Both beaks opened in a loud scream and he leaped away from a cliff overlooking the river. *Just cross the Valley. The clearing. That big tree. They're hiding.*

With the uneven weight of his heads, the aiglonax flew off-balance sunriseside and surveyed the Valley as he passed high above it. Thick, dark clouds covered all of Anonom Trace and spread over the mountain pass. He could see flashes of lightning that shot through the clouds, but nothing more. Toward the Warmside, Fossarelick and its surroundings looked deserted. Woody forest plants were invading the fields and Aindle could see their green shoots poking through barley straw.

Those fields will be mine.

Higher still, he banked sunriseside and scanned the remains of Nosidam. Scorched timbers and stones littered the town's streets. A jumble of barrows, carts, and broken furniture filled the market square. Nothing remained of its fine houses but an outline of burned postholes.

He screeched and turned toward the Warmside.

Aindle wanted to see the lodge, even if burned to the ground. *I'll find that ice dome, melt it somehow, then take back the whole place.* He searched the terrain between Nosidam and the lodge lands. He saw forest but little else as clouds rolled down the mountainsides and into the Veiled Valley. *Gostered mist—I cannot see . . .* He drifted lower still, closer to the site of the old lodge. *Where's the ice? And the giant and the griffin?* He hovered over the clearing. *There it is! The old wall—and the tower's standing again! Must get to the tower.*

Aindle's necks strained ahead as he dived toward the lodge. Despite the massing fog that reduced the lodge's features to faint outlines, he swooped across the flattened orchard, leaped through the drooping vegetable garden, and smashed the lodge's broad door with a thrust of his talons. Peering inside, he saw only a dim, dust-filled hall and, opposite the door, the cold, dark hearth, once his own access to the mountain tunnels. A silver disk no longer gleamed on the hearth's smooth wall.

Never mind. I am too big for that tunnel now, and my hork's body would be useless.

No sign of humans or sprites met Aindle's four eyes. The tower's spiral staircase was missing, just as it was after the fire, but the curved walls looked new. Both his beaks clacked as he screeched, "I know you hide from me. You cannot escape."

No answer. He backed out of the lodge and hopped across the garden, his wings folded tightly against his body. Coming to the remains of the bakehouse, he dipped his larger head toward its fragmented stone floor. *The goblins used this tunnel.*

He kicked away some broad, flat stones blocking the tunnel entrance. A few more thrusts widened the opening. Sinking to his knees, he poked his smaller head into the dark passageway and drew in deep draughts of rot and mold. As those eyes adjusted to the gloom, he looked for something that the Valley folk might have left behind. His other set of eyes, in the stronger head, watched the hole. His task so absorbed him

PART VI: THE DRAGONS RETURN   387

that neither head sensed owl-like silent wings rushing toward him.

In an instant, two griffins were on Aindle's back. Their talons left
deep grooves along his scales. The aiglonax slumped as their poison
coursed through his body. He lay motionless, one head hanging through
the bakehouse floor and his body prone on its broken stones.

Rocánonom heard Bounder and Orla attack, then fly away from the
fallen aiglonax. They circled the lodge grounds before coming to perch
once more on the tower's roof. The giant called out from inside the black
globe, "Bounder, and my Lady Orla, lest the Malevir discover us here,
go away—please." Gormley and Gúrmulo repeated his plea and huddled
inside the giant's pouch.

A howling scream shook the tower. Rocánonom covered his eyes and
called upon the element of light to help him see beyond the dark globe.
A terrible vision materialized: Aindle had recovered from the griffins'
attack and hovered over them. The beast's heads now matched in size
and menace. With outspread wings that trapped the griffins on the roof,
the aiglonax hissed, "Your poison loses ever more of its hold every time
you strike me."

Rocánonom shivered as the beast opened both beaks wide and
screamed again. The giant could see green ichor dripping from their
jagged edges as Aindle prepared to lunge at the griffins' heads; but the
beast pulled back when a different piercing cry sent shudders through
the tower.

Rocánonom stepped through the protective shell of the orb and
looked through a slit in the tower wall. Bounder and his mother were
dodging jets of flame and cinders, which were scorching Aindle's tail
scales, while the beast surged upward and twisted toward the clearing.

Isabella and her rider pursued Aindle, the Copper blasting him with
scalding steam. As she swooped over him, a mass of boulders that trailed
behind her tail pummeled his heads. The aiglonax plummeted into the
clearing and lay unmoving, except for a twitch in his left leg. But as Isabella's

shadow fell over his body, he kicked his other leg and shook out a wing.

Alana shouted, "The rocks and steam didn't work—the Malevir's heads are rising!"

"*Use the mirror.*"

Aindle stood again. Swaying slightly, he threw one head back and crowed, "My acid will maim and melt your helpless rider." In one forceful jump, he was in the air and flew at the dragon. His burning spittle overshot Alana. Isabella's billows of steam breath blinded him once more. When he opened his eyes, he was looking into the glaring reflection of his own deadly gaze. He hovered briefly before crashing to the ground in a writhing mass of feathers and scales.

"He saw the mirror."

Yes, the mirror. One look at himself and the beast nearly died.

"Let's hope his weakness lasts, until the others . . ."

Ah, the others . . . I shall send Argenfort my report.

Isabella flew to the live oak, alighted on the sturdiest top branch, and sent her news back to the dragons in the Cave of the Ancestors.

Alana lowered her head to rest on the Copper's frill and closed her mind to all but the comfort of where she clung at that moment. She began to dream, oddly, of Nnylf. He lounged on a cloud that floated above her. Before she could understand what the dream-Nnylf was saying, another voice interrupted:

The beast sickens still. See how he twists and coughs up his food.

Alana rubbed her face and blinked. "He might be too weak to fly."

Not for long. Close your eyes. I shall keep watch.

Bounder and his mother sat once more on the lodge tower parapet. He called down to Rocánonom: "Isabella has chased the beast and he fell out of the sky. He only lifts his head now to spew old food and venom."

"Can you see the rider?"

Without another word, the griffin flew over the clearing, nodded to Isabella, and circled back to the roof. "A tall girl with brown hair rides the Copper's hump. Fossarelick folk. She's holding a mirror."

PART VI: THE DRAGONS RETURN 389

"Mirror? Must be Kurnan's mirror! Only his sister would have that weapon! Good, now the Malevir will lie helpless a little longer. Any sign of the others?"

Rocánonom heard heavy thumps on the roof as Orla beat her wings and soared high above the lodge. "My chick," she called down to Bounder, "I see bright and glimmering shapes flying here from the Sunriseside. They will bring the help you need, so I'll return home to tell the others. Be strong. Don't forget to preen your feathers." She flew off before Bounder could ask her to stay.

Bounder bobbed his head in farewell, then answered the giant, "Others? Not sure, but I think I see Orferans approaching."

"We shall stay hidden in here, for now. Go to Isabella. The Orferans and she have some tricks to play on the beast." Bounder nodded and flew to the clearing.

Aindle shook his heads until his sight cleared. Flexing his legs and stretching his wings, he filled the clearing. He looked at the topmost sturdy limb of the live oak and saw Isabella glare at him as she lifted up and away from the tree. Her rider held the mirror toward the sun and it reflected a bright sunbeam into Aindle's eyes. For a short time, the aiglonax's vision filled with patches of glowing amber and emerald. He stumbled across the grounds and ducked when he felt Bounder swoop over him.

Aindle opened both his beaks wide and two heavy, mold-green clouds of paralyzing gas ringed him. "I can't see you, griffin, but soon you'll regret your attacks," his two rasping maws roared. He shook his heads again. When his eyes cleared, he could see Bounder darting through clouds overhead.

The screech of another griffin came from the lodge. A third one answered behind him. Bounder called from overhead, but when Aindle prepared to chase him, he heard more griffin calls from different directions. Baffled, he staggered toward each call until his heads whirled and his necks twisted around each other. His legs did the same and he fell forward.

Fire bolts blasted him as he lay in a tangle. He winced every time a searing dart grazed his scales. When he loosened one neck from the other and stood again to face his attackers, his beaks fell open in surprise. A team of blue dragons and riders coursed above and around him. To confuse the aiglonax, each dragon had imitated Bounder's cry. Now the Blues were showering the beast with lightning bolts.

Aindle spread his wings and flapped them with such speed that dust, dried leaves, and twigs whirled around him. The whirlwind wreathed the monster in vapors of acid droplets, which reversed the dragons' electrical charges. Repulsed, the bolts hit each dragon squarely in the chest. Aindle blasted his paralyzing breath at them as they tumbled in quickening spirals into the clearing. Before they fainted, the dragons covered their riders with a wing to protect them from the poison.

Flanna, Azile, and Seerlana huddled under their dragons' wings and called out to Draako and Argenfort, who were coasting over the forest. Hearing Flanna's cry, Argenfort rose above the tree line and prepared to attack with a fierce, shrill call. Draako and Nnylf flew up to stop him.

Staring into Argenfort's eyes, as scarlet as Rocánonom's rags, their message rang clear: *Don't go after the beast. It's a trap. Don't you see what is coming?*

A surging mass of bright colors swelled on the horizon and rolled quickly toward them. Waves of shining bronze, copper, red, and green soared and dipped as it approached. A gleaming Silver rose and fell ahead of it, and as the gap between them shrank, Argenfort could see wings propelling bodies all across the sky—dozens of dragons, all the dragons ever known to the Valley.

Draako heard Seerlana calling for help again: *Argenfort, Draako, our dragons have fallen! The aiglonax will destroy us!*

Lie still, all of you. The Malevir is in for a surprise.

PART VI: THE DRAGONS RETURN

Seerlana called out, *Draako, I hear you and your voice is strong. What is happening?*

The dragons return—all of them!

Chapter 5

THE MOKTAWL MEN HAD BUILT a fire just inside the entrance to the Cave of the Ancestors. As the sun's light waned and thickening clouds began to fill the early evening sky, Atty shivered and rubbed his hands over the flames. He watched Cahalson slap his durk in his palm as he paced around the broad ledge outside.

"Come back by the fire. You will tire yourself stomping around out there. Kolvak . . . er, I mean Fernfallow has cleaned all the fish in this basket and I'll be cooking them soon."

Cahalson grimaced and waved away Atty's words. "I'm not hungry. Those clouds are veiling the Valley again and I can't see if any Blues or Silvers are flying."

Aurykk, radiant in his rider's armor, walked past the open cook fire and gripped Cahalson's shoulders. "You and your men must eat and share in the dishes that the Loblin have prepared. Isabella has sent word to the dragons with us"—he pointed to the Coppers, Reds, and Greens gathered near the stream running through the widespread stalagmites—"that the Malevir has brought down the Blues, and she has not seen or heard from Argenfort or Draako."

"We can do no good here," blurted Kirrill. "My daughter rides Isabella, you know. Of course, the Copper honors her, but the privilege of her friendship does nothing to calm my fear; the Malevir will hurt

PART VI: THE DRAGONS RETURN 393

Alana as he did our Kurnan." Kirrill's big hands covered his face as he cried, "My children, my children."

Cahalson came inside and squatted next to Kirrill. Patting his knee, he said, "Brother, Isabella's wisdom will protect Alana. We both know she will find a way to outwit the Malevir."

Crouching beside the other men gathered around the fire, Aurykk added, "I know those dragons well. They have more than one way to fight the beast. You will have a part to play soon."

"Maybe so, but I feel like a coward, hiding here with the children and little Loblin," grumbled Atty.

"Me, too." "Right you are." "We ought to be there," muttered his companions.

Aurykk stood up, walked around, and looked hard at every man. An aura of Golden power surrounded him. His gaze met each man's eye and left all of them speechless, drained of strength—Atty holding a soggy fish, Kirrill's tear-dampened beard dripping onto his tunic, and Cahalson on his knees.

"The survival of the Valley's people depends on their safety here in the cave. A few watchful dragons, devoted Loblin, wise Alluxana, and Luchaer have protected the Valley for longer than you have lived. Stay by the hearth. Do not be afraid when you see what happens when I meet with the dragons."

None of the Moktawls moved. Nor did the other Valley people. Seated around long tables running along the center of a marble passageway, humans and sprites dropped their spoons and sat quietly, their heads turned toward the flokk of dragons. Aurykk strode to the stream and stood as a man among the dragons, who formed a circle around the resplendent rider. He summoned a light mist that thickened, covered him, and fanned out until it reached the cave's ceiling. From a thousand different points, lights shimmered within the mist until it lifted and whirled away from the body at its heart—the body of Aurykk the golden-scaled dragon.

Before any of the Valley folk could grasp the rider's magical transformation, a sudden and awful roar came from the ledge. Everyone turned and stared at the magnificent, gleaming Silver that had landed there, pawing the stones and dirt. He called for Aurykk. "Cousin," he bellowed, "we come from the Coldside, to vanquish the beast."

Aurykk stood amazed for only a few moments, then he quickly nodded to his dragon friends and family. The Moktawls ran in a panic to the walls of the cave as all but a few dragons thundered past and leaped from the ledge to fly at the Silver's side.

Cahalson looked at his fellow Moktawls and said, "I think it's time we returned to the lodge."

Eunan agreed, "Yes, we have some unfinished business there."

Flying by his side, Aurykk's thoughts questioned the silver dragon intruder:

How did you survive?

I did not.

I do not understand. You are here, now. Despite the Malevir.

The Malevir's whirlwind carried me coldside and tossed me into the depths of the Meeting of Mountains, where he thought I would die.

Aurykk answered, *While I searched everywhere for you, even beyond the Coldside, the Malevir's powers grew. To challenge the beast, our flokk gathered at the Meeting of Mountains. When we used all our powers to break the Malevir's spells, we felt the ground jump. What happened?*

The spell did break. The mountains opened and released me. Now, I want us to destroy the power that cast that spell.

But, first, look at your wyrmling over there beyond the forest.

*My wyrmling? You said **my** wyrmling?*

Your son, Draako.

The dragons' long shadows dappled fir-shrouded slopes far below. While the cousins questioned each other, Fulgid hugged Aurykk's spines. He remembered nearly slipping off this Golden not long before. His grip tightened and he felt his long legs squeeze Aurykk's hump as the dragons parted in a defensive split and angled away from center. Fulgid's stomach lurched with fear and he buried his head under the Golden's frill.

When the dragon's path felt steady once more, the giant raised his head and grunted in surprise. Two other Silvers were flying in small loops just ahead. Aurykk and Lugent rushed at them but the silver dragons zigzagged upward and rolled back to meet their attackers. One of them broke out of his roll to hover, his neck stretching toward them. He dipped his head several times and Fulgid recognized that sign—it meant "no harm intended."

Fulgid's goat ears twitched as dragon voices echoed around him. He felt Aurykk's shoulders flexing in long, slow beats as his wings carried him closer to the Silvers. Thankful he could understand unspoken dragon speech, Fulgid listened to their thoughts:

Only one other Silver called the Veiled Valley his nesting place, but the Malevir killed him.

Nearly killed him.

Nearly *killed? But . . .*

But not dead.

Lugent!

Argenfort flew in joyful circles around his son, then rushed up past the clouds. As the riders and their dragons watched him and Lahsrayn rise, Draako called out,

Grandfather, leave the moon and come back to us! Lahsrayn cannot breathe!

The elder Silver descended in a flash: *I could have reached the moon, so great was my happiness. Dear Lugent, Bearer of Light, come meet your own son.*

Argenfort and the other dragons hovered close to each other as the elder invited Nnylf to recite the prophecy:

> In nests of rainbow brightness
> Shall the wyrmlings come to light,

Sheltered from the Malevir,
The ruler of the night.
One and only one will dare to banish pain and fear
And this will be the Draako, heir of
Lugent, blessed with Sight.

With gentle strokes along Draako's crest, Nnylf continued aloud: "If your own dragonet Draako had not dared to call upon your name when the Malevir made so many maddened dragon spirits attack the Orferans, none of us would be here today."

My father, Lugent. My honor, sir. I have no special Sight, but I have heard *a cry for help.* Draako felt his throat tighten as his feelings twisted and muddled in his head. *Your mother, magnificent Calliopfera, lies below and wounded with my mother Anadraka. Abulafria, also.*

Lugent replied, *After the Malevir pays us for our pains, you, Argenfort, and I will find a peaceful place to talk and learn about each other and about the Sight—but later. The dams need us now. Look: help is coming."*

A cohort of furious dragons had fanned out from the mountain. As the sun began to set and clouds covered the moon, Draako saw only their looming silhouettes. "The ancestors," he murmured. "Eager and not afraid of the beast."

The four dragons roared again in unison as the cohort quickly closed the gap between themselves and their leaders. They banked sunsetside and together flew in a V down to the lodge.

Over the clearing, Aindle raged as Isabella carried Alana high above his noxious fumes. Below, Bounder circled and harassed him by diving while lobbing rocks at his heads. The griffin's wings quickly carried him away from the aiglonax after every feint.

Aindle's heads bobbed as he dodged the rocks. One tore through a wing. He cried out. He splattered a gob of ichor across the tear and it soon healed. Aindle's eyes followed Bounder's path across the clearing, as the

PART VI: THE DRAGONS RETURN

griffin flew back to the lodge and perched once more on the tower's roof.

Fury filled his heads. He crouched and followed Bounder. Hovering over the tower, Aindle strained to reach him. Before he could blast the griffin with a deadly spell, two silver dragons appeared in front of him. Aindle gawped in surprise and felt panic as their crimson eyes locked onto his. Countless dragons and riders gathered just behind them, then wheeled around the tower.

Lugent blew a cone of cold over Aindle, who then hung suspended facing the Silvers. Only his eyes moved. The aiglonax's basilisk stare did nothing to the silver dragons. He snarled but they held him helpless in their gaze.

Aindle's eyes widened and glazed over. He gagged and coughed up bits of tortoiseshell and riverweed. Helpless to resist the Silvers' power, he could not stop his beaks from yawning apart.

An explosion below caught Aindle's ear. Something had broken through the tower roof and was calling to him. Lugent relaxed his hold on Aindle, but only enough to let him turn one head to the side. Aindle rolled his eyes. Rocánonom was standing on the roof's remaining stones and timbers. On his shoulders perched Gormley and Gúrmulo, their snouts rubbing the giant's cheeks. At the sight of his little tormentors, Aindle felt his chest tighten and icicles stab him from within.

Lugent's cone of cold trapped him in the air just above Rocánonom. He squealed but otherwise floated immobile over the tower. He could not move his wings to flee. Fear blinded him. He was panting and his jaws ached as they opened wider. In a flash, Gormley flipped her tail, leaped from Rocánonom's shoulder, and fell into one of Aindle's open beaks. Gúrmulo jumped into the other one.

Aindle felt them scratching his throats. His shrieks cut the air, and the few trees remaining in the orchard shook until they toppled in a cloud of dust. He tried to cough but gagged. Spasms racked his body until he felt himself loop through the air and fall onto the orchard debris. Then he saw no more.

398   SUSAN BASS MARCUS

*   *   *

Dragons flew above the Malevir's agonizing body and watched as his wings and legs shriveled. His body lay askew in the dirt. His belly and back withered until only his distended necks and heads remained. His eyes bulged, then burst at the very moment his necks split open along their length. Two wet and weary weasels rolled onto the ground next to Aindle's remains.

Argenfort hovered over his son and Draako. In one voice, the three silver dragons called to Rocánonom:

You planned well, Protector Rocánonom.

Rocánonom answered, "Thank you. Gormley tried more than once, but . . ."

This time, the beast could not escape, said Draako.

Yes, good friends, you see how the weasels destroyed him, just as the legend foretold. Now, loosen your hold on Bounder and let us honor the brave little ones.

Released from the cone of cold, Bounder floated down to the tower's broken roof. Rocánonom climbed on his back and rode the griffin into the devastated orchard grounds. The giant used his red cloths to wipe the aiglonax's ooze from the weasels' coats. Then he gathered Gormley and Gúrmulo in his arms and walked through rising dust and broken tree limbs until he reached a path to the lodge. He strode through the hanging broken door to the long table by the hearth, where he laid his little friends on cushions that once had given comfort to Sweetnettle and Kurnan.

Nnylf coughed as his dragon circled above the lodge grounds. Aurykk and Lugent fanned the air with their wings, driving away the aiglonax's poisonous fumes. Landing wherever they could close to the fallen Blues, Nnylf slipped off Draako's lowered neck and ran to Anadraka's body, stretched out along the ground. He could see her eye blink. Lugent reached his dam just as curls of cream-colored smoke spiraled up from her nostrils. Nnylf could hear her grunt softly as her mate raised her wing.

PART VI: THE DRAGONS RETURN 399

Seerlana crawled out and rubbed her eyes in the dazzling moonlight. When she saw Nnylf, she stumbled toward him and hugged him close under a night sky clear of clouds, then she grabbed his arm and pulled him toward the lodge. "Come, son. We need rue broth for ourselves and our friends. Some should be simmering in the lodge. Oh, look. Here come Azile and Flanna!"

Isabella and Alana, however, had the same idea and had reached the lodge before Seerlana. They found Rocánonom there steadying a huge cauldron of steaming broth on the threshold stones. In no time, Isabella lapped half of the cauldron's contents into her jaw pouch. Alana leaped onto her hump and they flew off in the direction of the sickened Blues.

Nnylf and all his family but for Eunan entered the lodge just as Rocánonom was spooning doses of broth into the weasels' drooping jaws. "Mind the hot cauldron," he said without looking up. "And watch that Copper." Nnylf turned to see Isabella and Alana flying low to the ground over Anadraka, Abulafria, and Calliopfera.

Flanna wrung her hands. "Oh, Calliopfera, don't die now," she cried. "Our time together has been too short. Oh, look! What *is* that Copper doing to her?"

"Dousing the dragons with rue, Grandmother," Nnylf answered, savoring her title as he said it. "See how the broth helps? But what are the other dragons doing?"

"I see them," Azile called out. She had climbed up the tower steps, now restored with new stones. "From these new windows, I can see Aurykk and a yewr of dragons. They have folded their wings and formed a circle, their heads toward the fallen Blues. They are swaying a bit now. They have sunk to their bellies, but I do not think they are hurt. Aurykk is chanting something, but it's too faint to hear."

"I saw them do that up the Coldside, by the Meeting of Mountains," Nnylf said to himself. He scratched his head and strolled toward the doorway.

Frowning, Seerlana gripped his arm and asked, "You were coldside?"

Before Nnylf could answer, Flanna sniffed, "With me and your father, of course."

Nnylf grinned and straddled the threshold. He pointed to the clearing. "Look now, Grandmother's dam is shaking her head! Anadraka is kneeling and Abulafria is licking her forelegs."

They watched the dams' recovery in silence. When Aurykk's circle disbanded, Nnylf whooped, "At last! They are on their feet." He grimaced. "Oh, I didn't think . . ."

"What?"

"How hungry they must be."

"Hungry? Well, then, we'll bring them some . . ."

"Some gems. Dragons like gems," said a gravelly voice.

"Who are you?" Azile coughed in surprise at the elderly stranger who sauntered through the doorway and looked around the hall.

"Most of them like gems. Well," he said, clapping his hands. "Here I am! Aurykk dropped me nearby, but I felt sleepy and lay down for a while."

The man's quavering voice reminded Nnylf of a goat's bleat.

"Came here. Seemed like the right thing to do. Say, the lodge looks so . . . so . . . clean!" He ambled closer to the hearth.

Nnylf and Azile looked at Rocánonom and they caught a smile brightening the giant's face.

The man went on: "And me, I can't get used to my old short legs. Miss my horns, too, but it's so easy to scratch my nose now and . . . say, I think you understand what I'm saying."

Azile ran to the white-haired man and kissed his whiskered cheek. "Dear Fulgid, how good it is to see you again. Of course I can understand you." She looked around for agreement.

Nnylf added, "Yes, Fulgid, now your life as a goat-headed giant has ended. You are your old self again."

"Wasn't my style, really, especially the 'baaaa-ah' part." Fulgid chuckled. "I must say I do miss my giant tricks—like leaping between

PART VI: THE DRAGONS RETURN 401

tree branches and flinging nasty goblins about. Loved when I freed Azile from the tower, and when I gave Atty and Kirrill a big scare!"

His laughter boomed in the vast hall. Rocánonom put a finger over his own lips to silence him, but the merriment had a good effect on Gormley. Rolling onto her belly, she choked and spit out her last spoonful of broth, which splattered over Fulgid's tunic and vest.

"Sorry," she croaked and looked to her side. "Gúrmulo, you silly, wake up!" Pointing her little black snout at Rocánonom, she said, "He always tries to sneak an extra nap. Very bad form." She leaned toward her brother and licked one ear. "Gúrmulo, GÚR-MU-LO, *wake up!*"

The other weasel groaned and turned on his side. "Just a little while longer. Having such a good dream. Malevir exploded."

"That was no dream, my fine fellow," said Fulgid. "His last few parts are lying out there in the clearing. Some of the dragons are seeing to them, I think." Fulgid looked out the door and squinted. "Oh, my addled eyes. Is that the dragon Tinta? And who just fell off her hump—Luxie? Sorry. Have to run, so to speak."

Fulgid nearly toppled the cauldron as he crossed the threshold and hurried as fast as his quavering legs could take him across the clearing. He reached a plump, gray-haired woman dusting off her skirt and setting her cap straight on her head. A red dragon stood not far from them.

"Well, there you are! I'd nearly forgotten what you looked like, Fulgid, so used I was to looking at that goat head of yours."

"Luxie, my love! And just two arms, now. Too bad."

"Too bad? Why, you . . ."

"You baked a lot of pies and cakes with four arms."

"Never mind, sweet," Alluxana answered with a warm and broad smile and a wave to Tinta. "I'll be happy to bake for you now that we're home again." She wrapped Fulgid in a long hug and took his arm as they walked toward the lodge.

They passed Tinta, who had joined two other Reds gathering apples and piling them in the garden. Launching long tongues of flame across the rows of apple tree stumps, the Reds reduced them, leaves, branches, and all, to a thick carpet of white ash. Tinta and her kind scooped and mixed ashes with dirt, then prepared the ground for new growth. Returning to the pile of apples, they found that many apple seeds had sprouted from the cores. The dragons gazed at the two Protectors.

"Yes, Tinta, I hear you. We'll help you plant the sprouts." Fulgid and Alluxana sorted through the seeds and sprouts and returned to the orchard grounds. They moved along shallow trenches lying across the orchard and patted the sprouts in place.

Alluxana called out, "We'll be back soon to help you finish the job. With some rain and warm sunlight, an orchard will grow here again."

The Reds bowed and returned to their tasks.

Draako stood between his parents. Lugent licked his son's crest. "My son! A true Silver, who survived because of my cousin Aurykk, that clever shape-shifter. Like any Orferan, he lives to banish evil, but he'd rather bargain with his enemies than hurt them."

Anadraka nodded and stretched her wings. "His wisdom rescued us more than once." She glared at Aindle's remains. "Draako, help us here. Use your fire breath to cleanse this place of the Malevir's foul parts." She stepped back and Lugent followed her.

"My fire breath? I'm not sure . . ." Draako shook his head, but he soon remembered how his flames had warmed Bounder the dog, nearly drowned in the river beyond the Sunsetside so long ago. He raised his forked tongue and pressed its rough lower side on his spark glands. Slowly releasing fire gas from his second stomach, he felt it fill his throat. At that moment, he rubbed his tongue on the glands. Flames burst from his mouth and covered Aindle's bits and pieces.

When nothing remained but gray ashes that smelled like a fetid swamp, Draako sifted them through his claws. A strong night breeze blew the ashes in swirls. One little whirling cloud lifted away from the ground and floated over their heads, then disappeared into the night. In its place lay a shining object, the size of a small child's hand. It glinted in the moonlight.

Draako called out, "Father, I've found something in the Malevir's ashes."

Lugent ambled back to the scene of the Malevir's fall to earth. He had enjoyed the nourishing gems Nnylf had offered him. Anadraka had just caught a snake, searching for its own evening meal. She swallowed it quickly and joined her mate. "What did you find?"

Draako's claw threaded through a hole in the object and he held it up to the moonlight. "It's a disk."

"Like Atty's, like Grandfather Lahsrayn's," added Nnylf.

Lugent brought his eye closer and licked his fangs. "Why in the Malevir's remains? Rightful Reader, tell us the meaning of those marks."

Draako dangled the disk close to his eye. "On this side it says, 'One and only one will dare to banish pain and fear.' Why, that . . . no, it cannot be! Wait, wait—underneath, carved neatly I see . . . it looks like a name, 'Ainbe . . . Alin . . .' it's not clear."

"Let me see." Lugent looked at the object and his breath stopped. His shoulders were shaking as he cried, "The name is 'Aindle'—the beast wore a rider's amulet and marked it with his true name. Does the other side bear a name, too?"

Draako flipped the disk and turned it so that moonlight brightened the marks. "Written here I see one word, Father."

"What word?"

"Lustredust," Draako mumbled.

"Lustre . . . ?"

"Lustre . . . dust."

Lugent's roars shook the live oak. The other dragons hurried to join them. Lugent had Draako show the amulet to Aurykk, who read it and groaned, "The faithless rider of Argenfort's brother left these ashes. He rode Lustredust," said the Golden.

"The Malevir, a rider? Uncle, I do not understand," said Draako.

Aurykk sat back on his haunches. The other dragons did the same. The Golden turned to his nephew: "My father was the only Golden in the Veiled Valley until I hatched, and his rider was a handsome and clever man of many talents who called himself Lustre. Now we know he was Aindle, the shape-shifter. Aindle, the aiglonax. He's the one who tricked my father into helping him steal Valley riches for himself. He gave my father gems for his hoard, and he lay a trap for my mother, the dam Eminfoil, who discovered his misdeeds. Aindle killed her as she slept."

Argenfort said, "We Orferan ancestors learned of Aindle's deeds and banished him, thinking him a corrupted and faithless rider. But Lustredust died of grief and Aindle disappeared."

Aurykk growled, "Now we know. He came back many World-Turns later to take his revenge on the Orferans."

Draako paced around the small piles of ashes still scattered through the clearing. He returned to face his uncle. "The Mystic Scintilla . . . if he had stolen it, no dragon could have stopped him from taking the Valley and its people. But why did he want the lodge?"

"The dragon Lustredust had a great friendship with the first Protectors that built the lodge and farmed its lands. As Lustredust's rider, Aindle met them, envied them, and wanted the place for himself," said Lugent. "His plan to take the Scintilla and capture the Valley with the lodge as his stronghold did not reckon on Rocánonom and his Loblin— or the weasels! We have to thank them as much as our riders and the ancestors."

Nnylf asked to see the amulet. He said, "That beast first spoke to Azile and me in Nosidam and started to introduced himself as 'Aindle,' but soon after that he asked us to call him 'Lustre.'" Nnylf rubbed the amulet's inscription. "Grandfather Lahsrayn, the same saying is written on your amulet."

"The same—but I never betrayed Argenfort. Flanna and I stood with the last of the riders privileged to befriend our dragons in the time

PART VI: THE DRAGONS RETURN   405

before Aindle's last attacks. The Loblin of Anonom hid us and cared for us until the day we would banish the beast forever. They knew who he really was."

"Speaking of Loblin," a small voice broke into the discussion. "Where are they and the rest of the Valley folk?"

Alana and Isabella had left the pond and its refreshing cool water when the commotion caused by Draako's discovery rippled across the surface of the pond. They pushed their way through the restless flokk. Alana brushed her wind-blown hair from her eyes and spoke up. "When will we see them and our families again? Eunan, Cahalson, and my father must be raging by now."

Aurykk nosed Isabella. "My brave daughter. You used your powers well. Tinta tells me that Alana's father and the other Moktawls are making their way down the mountain. Some of the Loblin have chosen to stay in our ancestral cave. Others are taking the road to Anonom Village to find their brothers. The rest are coming out of the live oak as I speak."

"I heard them as they made their way through the tunnels," the Copper chortled. "Tinta said that the Loblin helped Alluxana care for Kurnan. The boy does not speak and cannot lift his head, but he is awake. We should see him and his parents soon."

At the far side of the clearing, Rocánonom's sprites had released the oak tree door. Riding on Milkthistle's back, a sleepy-eyed Sweetnettle clung to her shoulders and rested his chin on her cap. Sherca carried the front end of a litter bearing Kurnan. Kirrill hefted the other end and Fernfallow followed with a basket of dried herbs. Mëlo's widow and Margalana took turns carrying the baby ahead of a parade of villagers from Nosidam and Fossarelick. At the end of the procession, Luchaer closed the tree's opening, made sure its outline faded, and jogged to catch up with his companions. He entered the circle of riders, who were discussing the Malevir's amulet.

"My friends—" Luchaer bowed to the riders. "Excellent dragons—" Another bow that took in the Orferans. "Dear Loblin—" One last bow as he flung his arms away from his sides. "Yes, you, Forestspice and Bitterbud, who have suffered so much and been so brave. Thank you."

Pointing to the Valley folk, he said, "How I wish to embrace you all and talk of how we shall rebuild our battered and dishonored Veiled Valley. My dragon friends, you are making your own plans, I imagine, and I hope they include renewed friendship with us. May the Ways of the World guide us all as in the time of the Ancestors." With one last bow, he turned to catch up with the other Valley folk hurrying toward the lodge.

While a few dragons and riders were busily cleaning up the grounds of the lodge and talking about Aindle's betrayals, Aurykk approached the lodge unobserved. Relaxing on the garden path, he repeated a spell several times until he had finished restoring the entire lodge and its outbuildings before the Valley folk crowded inside. Satisfied with his work, he called to Alluxana, "Many thanks, dear friend. You've kept your promise and I've kept mine." He soared up and flew toward the Sunriseside Mountain.

Alluxana walked through the doorway of the bakehouse and found it filled with grain, flour, eggs, clean water from a new well just outside, and a searing-hot oven. She smiled at Fulgid, who sat on a stool and folded his hands lightly over his belly. He sighed as he watched her take a bowl and mix sourdough starter with warm honeyed water.

"Fresh bread, Luxie. It's been a while, eh?"

"Too long. Look, Fulgid. The weasels are scurrying around Rocánonom's feet. Soon, we will have a big feast and they will be the guests of honor. What shall we eat?"

"No more rue broth, please."

Alluxana laughed. "A bountiful vegetable stew, warm breads, and cider?"

"A good start. Here, let me help." Fulgid slid off the stool and came to her side. One arm draped across her back and shoulders as he kissed her on the cheek and sighed, "Vegetable stew—with some onion?"

Alluxana blushed and nodded. Both of them looked out the door

PART VI: THE DRAGONS RETURN 407

toward the main lodge at the sound of shouts and laughter.

Gormley and Gúrmulo were scrambling around the garden in pursuit of a ground squirrel. Their prey dived into the weasels' old burrow and they followed it.

Milling about, the Valley folk waited for their little heroes to return, but when they did not, Rocánonom invited his companions to rest in the comfort of the main hall. Everyone had gathered there except Eunan and his family.

On the humps of Draako, Anadraka, and Abulafria, they flew sunsetside until the hilltop of Fossarelick came into view. The dragons descended in slow spirals until their great talons touched the edge of Eunan's barley field.

"Many thanks, dragon friends, for saving our lives," said Eunan.

"Eunan, grandson of great riders, welcome back to the flokk. Your heart was never truly with the Moktawls."

"Draako!" Eunan extended a shaking hand to pat the young Silver's nose.

"Our thoughts will meet easily from now on—but I must return to Rocánonom. He and I have much to discuss."

Anadraka added, "As do we. Shall we go?"

The young dragon nodded to Eunan and Seerlana's family, then leaped into the air.

The dragons looped about in the sky, dived straight down, then pulled out to fly directly over the fields in the direction of the lodge. Azile and Nnylf watched them as they disappeared into the distance, then turned to join their parents, who had climbed up the hill to their cottage.

As the sun rose higher than the mountain home of the dragon ancestors, Nnylf could hear his parents and Azile clattering the cookware and searching shelves for something to make a meal.

Nnylf pulled Aindle's amulet from his pouch. Checking to make sure no one saw him, he lifted a stone from the base of the wall behind the firewood. Wrapping the amulet in a piece of his red rag, he buried the disk in the wall and replaced the stone. After swiping his hands on his tunic, Nnylf went inside the cottage and smiled at the sight of his sister and mother bickering over which pot to use.

Sounds of their shared meal sailed through the late afternoon air—shouts and shushings, spoons scraping crockery bowls for a last, warm bite, laughter and sighs. The family eagerly washed up and fell into their beds.

Night winds picked up. Broken barley stalks swayed and rustled in Eunan's fields. Close to dawn, one of the stones in the wall behind the firewood loosened and slipped. As if poked by an invisible finger, the wrapped amulet fell out of the wall into loose dirt behind the bottom layer of firewood. Shaking until the cloth wrapping fell away, the amulet pulsed with a crimson glow and buried itself in the dirt.

Glossary

Terms and Characters in *MALEVIR: Dragons Return*

Abulafria and Isabella	Dragon dams and sisters; Aurykk's daughters
	Blue and Copper dragons, respectively
Aiglonax	Monstrous two-headed, winged basilisk; shape-shifter
Alana and Kurnan	Children of Kirrill and Sherca
Alluxana	Forest Protector and four-armed woman; wife of Fulgid
Anadraka	Blue dragon dam, mother of Draako and mate of Lugent
Anonom	Ruined town on northwest edge of Veiled Valley; sits within the valley region called Anonom Trace
Aurykk	Elder Golden dragon
Azile	Girl from Fossarelick in her early teens; descendent of dragonriders
Bounder	Dog/enhanced griffin; mother is classic griffin, Orla
Cahal	Fossarelick Elder; Cahalson and Kirrill are his sons
Coldside	North
Dam	Adult female dragon
Draako	Young Blue-to-Silver Dragon
Drac'Argo	Young Copper-Red Dragon
Eunan	Moktawl and father of Nnylf and Azile
Flokk	Large gathering of dragon clans

Formorian	Goat-headed giant
Fossarelick	Village in the heart of the Veiled Valley
Fulgid	Forest Protector enchanted as a Formorian
Goblins	Squat, distorted, green, and smelly monsters
Gormley	Female brown weasel
Griffin	Magical creature with lion's body and eagle's wings, forelegs, and head
Gúrmulo	Male brown weasel and Gormley's sibling
Hork	Humanlike monster, about eight feet tall and similar to an ogre
Lobli	Veiled Valley sprite, about eighteen inches high (plural: Loblin)
Lugent	Legendary Silver dragon; Draako's father
Malevir	Destructive power: as an aiglonax, hork, basilisk, or dragonrider
Moktawls	Dragon-hunting men from Fossarelick
Nosidam	Prosperous town on eastern edge of Veiled Valley
Nnylf	Boy from Fossarelick in his late teens; descendent of dragonriders
Rocánonom	Giant from Anonom Trace; benevolent leader of the Loblin; receives his power from the four elements: earth, air, fire, and water
Seerlana	Mother of Nnylf and Azile; wife of Eunan; dragonrider
Sprite	Small, supernatural being, like an elf; a Lobli in the *Malevir* stories
Sunriseside	East

GLOSSARY

Sunsetside	West
Warmside	South
Yewr	Small group of dragons

Acknowledgments

Many thanks to Flynn and Eliza Marcus for their inspiration; Mollee Marcus for her social media expertise; my editor, Sarah Kolb-Williams; and Stephen D. Marcus for his loving, generous support and beta-reading.

Author Biography

A native Chicagoan, Susan Bass Marcus found inspiration early in her life at her local branch library and later she became a storyteller as well as a professional puppeteer. Those skills and a storehouse of tales enhanced her subsequent career in museum education. Her innovative style of work using legends and accounts of Near Eastern archaeology enlivened her museum's programs in an interactive dig site gallery. Along the way, her passion for dragon myths and legends fueled her first novel set in a world of her own invention, and it is the first in a planned trilogy, *Malevir*. Marcus is also writing a collection of surreal and futuristic short stories with the working title of *Death-Defying Acts*.

CPSIA information can be obtained
at www.ICGtesting.com
Printed in the USA
BVHW031834191220
595817BV00001B/60